SWORD OF THE
BRIGHT LADY

SWORD OF THE
BRIGHT LADY

WORLD OF PRIME BOOK ONE

M.C. PLANCK

an imprint of Prometheus Books
Amherst, NY

Published 2014 by Pyr®, an imprint of Prometheus Books

Cover illustration © Gene Mollica
Cover design by Nicole Sommer-Lecht

Inquiries should be addressed to

Pyr
59 John Glenn Drive
Amherst, New York 14228
VOICE: 716–691–0133
FAX: 716–691–0137
WWW.PYRSF.COM

18 17 16 15 14   5 4 3 2 1

Library of Congress Cataloging-in-Publication Data

Planck, M. C., author.
    Sword of the bright lady / M.C. Planck.
        pages cm — (World of prime; Book One)
    ISBN 978-1-61614-988-8 (paperback) — ISBN 978-1-61614-989-5 (ebook)
    1. Fantasy fiction. 2. Magic—Fiction. I. Title.

PR9616.4.P56S96 2014
823'.92—dc23

                                                                    2014012143

Printed in the United States of America

For Mom, who never stopped hoping I would create.

CONTENTS

8   CONTENTS

1.

WOODEN STICKS AND IRON MEN

He woke in front of a comfortable fire crackling in a stone hearth, in a narrow and uncomfortable bed, and not alone. Sleeping, the girl looked no more than sixteen. Black hair, and he knew it was not his wife. With relief he saw she was still dressed.

But he was naked except for underwear, and that was quite awkward. A dream, of course; any minute now would come the part where he was late for a math test.

Startlingly realistic for a dream, with the pungent smell of woodsmoke and dirt, and, yes, body odor. The girl needed a bath. Not terribly pretty, and no one he recognized. That struck him as quite unsatisfying for a dream. Indeed, the entire room had an unbearably rustic feel, a primitive cabin with the cluttered look of constant occupation. One wall was stone; the others rough-hewn wood, like the bench in front of the fire. Odd bits of a household lay about, and something about them disturbed him. In the firelight it was hard to tell, but though he saw clothes and wicker baskets, firewood and stoneware, something was missing.

Telephones. TVs. A stereo. A light, or even a lamp. These were the things that were absent. He could see nothing in the room that lived on electricity.

A remarkably subtle observation for a dream, he thought. He rubbed his face where the rough blanket had made it itch and waited for the dream to do something.

Then he remembered. He had been cold and lost. He remembered an impossible night sky reflecting off a blanket of untouched snow. He also remembered putting the dogs in the truck, driving out to the hot, dry riverbed for a walk. But the memories didn't connect. There was no bridge between them.

With some unease, he noted that the dream hadn't gone anywhere. The girl stirred in her sleep, the fire crackled, but nothing changed.

All in all, he didn't like this dream. Time to wake up.

He'd had nightmares before, the terror of sleep paralysis and the sensation of losing control. Voice was the one thing you kept; you could still scream, though it was always a struggle, and the sound would awaken you. He drew in a breath, and barely had time to wonder how easy it was before the bellowing shout flew out of him, unrestrained.

The girl shrieked and fell out of bed, and he almost went with her, tangled up in blankets and confusion. Why were his ears ringing? He should have produced no more than a choking cry and then the sensation of falling forward into wakefulness.

Instead, the girl on the floor burst into tears and the door across the room flew open, revealing an old white-haired man in a nightgown, fear and anger on his disheveled face.

Christopher was as surprised as any of them. He lay there trying to understand why he wasn't waking up.

"Helga," the old man said, and his face began to clear, a smile settling into the creases like it belonged there. "*Stanser skriking, du er skremmende gutten.*"

The girl sat up, sniffling. Looking at Christopher seemed to calm her. He knew he was nothing threatening to see, half naked and clutching the blankets to himself, trying to shake the sleep from his head.

Except there was no sleep there. In the welling of a strange and terrible fear, he reached out and slapped the coarse wooden paneling with the back of his hand. Hard, so hard the pain made him wince, and a spot of blood appeared where the skin had split. Instinctively he put his hand to his mouth, and the metallic tang of blood spread truth through him like a poison.

The old man offered the girl a hand, and she climbed to her feet. They exchanged words in their incomprehensible language.

She went to the fireplace, lifting an upturned wicker basket and setting it aside to let flickering light flood the room. Christopher's brain registered that she was wearing a nightshirt as she pulled a tattered dress over it; that she was older than she first appeared, perhaps eighteen; that she turned now to preparing breakfast with a clanking of pots and pans. His brain processed this automatically while the old man came to the bed, adjusted the blankets and made soothing noises. Christopher took it all in but could not make sense of it, could not progress past the brute fact that lay before him.

He was not dreaming.

"*Kan du forstå meg?*" asked the old man, gentle and concerned.

"Where am I?" Christopher demanded. "How long have I been here?" With no answer forthcoming, Christopher put his hand to his chin and found a hint of stubble. A day's worth, at most.

The recognition that he had been in his own bed twenty-four hours ago did not turn out to be comforting. How could he have gone from sand to snow without memory?

"Where are my pants?" he asked, searching for something concrete from his past, his semi-nakedness now terrifying.

The old man guessed his concern, and a laughing comment to the girl sent her to the rack that stood near the fireplace. From it she extracted his jeans and T-shirt. She gave them to him, failing to hide her curiosity over the copper rivets in the denim pockets.

Turning back to her fireplace was all the privacy she was going to give him. Under the blankets he slid into the clothes, grateful for the armor, however thin. Dressed, he felt like a man again.

"Do you speak English?" he demanded.

"*Tålmodighet, min herre,*" the old man said with a grin. "*Piken arbeider så fort som hun kan.*"

That was clearly a "no," although a friendly one. With another smile, the old man ducked back into his room, returning dressed in a dingy white robe belted with rope. The girl handed the man a steaming cup, and he sat on one end of the bench near the fireplace, sipping his drink. The girl offered Christopher a cup, too.

The sheer normalcy of it all required Christopher to accept the cup. The girl poured herself one and returned to overseeing a pot hung over the fire. The tea was tart and musty, a flavor he had never encountered before. The hot drink made him realize how hungry he was, and he stared at the pot. The girl noticed and blushed. She filled a wooden bowl and handed it to him.

He shoveled food into his mouth with a crude wooden spoon, downing three mouthfuls before he stopped to see what he was eating. Boiled oatmeal, flavored with peas. Unbidden, an ancient nursery rhyme sprang to mind.

> *Peas porridge hot,*
> *peas porridge cold,*
> *peas porridge in the pot*
> *nine days old.*

Monks and fireplaces, stoneware and serving girls, a flickering torch on the fireplace mantel. It looked like medieval Europe. Except medieval Europe didn't exist anymore. Even the smallest villages of the old Eastern Bloc countries had electricity now.

Or did they? Maybe he was in some remote Siberian village. Or a Scandinavian hippie commune. A plane crash, amnesia, wandering around in the dark. That was an explanation, or at least a possibility.

"My name is Christopher Sinclair," he told them, wiping the last of the porridge out of the bowl with his fingers.

"*Pater* Svengusta," replied the old man with a bow of his head, an obvious introduction. "*Og dette er vår kjær* Helga," he added, pointing at the girl.

"Nice to meet you," Christopher said, although all things considered, it wasn't. "The porridge was very good," he told Helga, although it wasn't either. Lumpy, soggy, and without even a grain of sugar. Still, he smiled when he gave her back the bowl, and her face started to glow.

He thought about the kind of girl that would get into bed with him without even knowing his name but blushed when he complimented her porridge. Maybe it was a French commune.

"Thank you very much for the food and shelter," he said, looking around for his shoes. "But I really ought to be going now."

Helga was already busy with dishes, but Svengusta watched him with keen interest. Christopher found his sneakers next to the fireplace. They weren't completely dry yet. He put them on anyway.

"Where is my wife?" he asked, fingers fumbling with the lacings. If he had been on a plane, Maggie would have been on it with him. What if she were still out there? He had to go and look for her, now. The urgency rose like a fountain, drawing him to the door where he struggled with the wooden bar that held it closed.

Svengusta followed, concern on his face. The old man jabbered in his foreign tongue. Christopher brushed him aside, driven by panic. When the bar finally fell away, he pushed out into the snow and gulped down the open air of freedom.

The air of freedom was cold. Freezing cold, turning his breath to thick fog in the hard light. He ignored it and stumbled on. The snow was shallow, three or four inches, but the cold leached through his wet shoes like lightning.

After twenty feet, his arms wrapped tight, shaking in the chill, he could go no farther. A village lay around him, silent and dismal— peasant huts, hardly better than log cabins, with thatched roofs. Not a single antenna, power line, or satellite dish to be seen. He was closer to the middle of nowhere than he had ever imagined possible.

The old man stood in the doorway, bemused and sad. One wave of the hand, but in a universal language it said, *Come inside, you'll catch your death of cold.* The bitter truth stung at Christopher, blurring his sight. If Maggie had not already found shelter, it was too late. He had almost died in the night; no one would have survived until morning.

He shouted at the doorway, rebuking the gentle concern. "Were there others? Did you find the crash site? Did you check?"

Of course Svengusta could not understand the words. But he understood the message, it seemed. Sadly he shook his head, spread his hands in emptiness and defeat.

Christopher shivered, paralyzed by despair and anger. His heart pounded with the need to run, to search, to find, but his head could not see past failure. The cold would kill him in a few hours, and he did not even know which direction to start in. Fresh snow covered the ground, obscuring everything.

There was only the hope that Maggie had not been with him on the plane. He would have never walked away from her, under any circumstance. Even if he couldn't remember the crash, he knew that.

Not that he remembered being on a plane. And he couldn't imagine walking away from an aviation disaster without a scratch.

What if he had escaped kidnappers and wandered to safety in this obscure town? Maybe he should be lying low, getting a feel for the lay of land. Drugged, kidnapped, escaped. It made more sense than a plane wreck.

None of it made any damn sense at all.

Reluctantly, angrily, he slogged back into the little wooden room and slumped by the fire. Helga gave him another cup of tea, her lips trembling with his contagious grief.

Svengusta did not let him sit for long. Throwing the last log into the fire, the old man pointed at a hallway next to the fireplace.

"*Er en god unggutt og henter noen mere for en gammel mann og en pike, vil De?*" he asked with wink.

The universal price of enjoying a fire: fetching more wood. At least it was something useful he could do. The door at the end of the short passageway was not barred, so he shuffled through it, expecting a storage closet. Instead he found a chapel.

Wooden pews were scattered throughout a large stone hall, the walls thinly dressed with tapestries where they were not broken by narrow windows. At the far end were double doors, and at the near end a huge, unused fireplace and a half-cord of stacked wood.

The windows were too narrow for a man to crawl through, with thick but ill-fitting shutters. The double doors were made from solid planks and bound with iron fittings. It was as fine a reconstruction of a medieval church as he had ever seen, until he looked up to see where all the light was coming from.

A plain wooden chandelier held a dozen gas flames sprouting from little stone cups, wholly out of character for a Dark Age atmosphere.

The open gas flames struck him as an incredible fire hazard. The walls were stone, but the roof was timber, and there was raw wood everywhere. The tapestries were gray and dusty, not fresh and restored. The rough-hewn benches looked suitably handmade, mostly stacked against the walls instead of laid out in display. If this was a museum, it was a very badly run one.

Above the mantel of the fireplace was a wooden frieze, a bas-relief carving. A hard-faced man stared back at him from the wood, a handsome woman standing behind him, etched in astounding detail. He tapped the frieze to make sure it was real wood, not a plastic molding.

The wooden man did not respond, of course, facing outward with serene determination. He stood between the woman and any possible danger, any imaginable threat. His features were solidly European, with a trimmed beard and mustache, but his stance was Oriental, with a katana held in a classic two-hand grip.

The sword had the correct curve, the round *suba* hand-guard, the distinctively wrapped hilt. Christopher could even see the *hamon*—the characteristic wavy pattern from the hand-folding process along the blade. But the man was wearing unmistakably Occidental armor: steel plates molded like clothing instead of the knotted cords and bamboo of samurai armor.

On the left, a tapestry displayed four men in a defensive semicircle around the same woman. The costumes and the people were solidly medieval Europe. The woman had a halo and was the center of attention. She looked regal, like a queen, or even revered, like some kind of Catholic Marian icon. She was unarmed, but each of the men around her bore a different weapon. One of them was the katana, wielded by the same man in the wooden carving. The others bore a staff, a sickle and a mace, and wore varying kinds of armor, all variations on Western plate or chain.

The tapestry on the right had only the swordsman and the lady. They stood in a delicate embrace, but their status as lovers was unequivocal. So much for Catholicism.

Spurred by the cold, he picked out an armload of wood to replenish the stock in the kitchen. Being productive made him feel better, and the firewood was comfortingly familiar. Not very well cut, however. Most of it still needed splitting.

When he got back to the kitchen, he made chopping motions with his hands. Svengusta produced an ax from the closet at the foot of the bed. Suitably armed, Christopher went back into the chapel to earn his keep.

The ax was ancient, the haft hand-carved and untreated. But the edge was sharp, and it occurred to him that it would make a formidable weapon. Not really his style, however. His university had had a PE requirement, and on a whim he had fulfilled it with kendo, the art of the Japanese sword. The whim had grown into a passion, a love of the pure simplicity, the comradeship of men and women who studied a useless art for the effect it had on their own inner selves. The kata were dances, half stylized and half practical, a silk painting of death and destruction.

Swinging the ax at inert logs was not the same, although it was exercise. As warmth and blood flowed through his limbs, he began to come alive again. Wherever he was, he was safe for now. If it was a plane crash, then sooner or later someone would come looking for him. If he'd escaped from kidnappers, then the later they found him, the better, and besides, he had an ax.

His mind drifting, the next swing missed the log and almost took off his leg. Maybe the unwieldy ax wasn't such a good idea.

But then he saw a branch, three feet long and gently curved. Plucking it out of the woodpile, he handled it experimentally. A little trimming, and it would make a fine bokken, which was what he used in most of his training and practice anyway. Besides, hadn't Musashi, the greatest duelist in all history, won half his duels with a wooden sword?

Scraping at the stick with the ax blade, he whittled away the hours until Helga called him in to lunch.

Again the food was plain: more porridge, with a yellowish bread that was spongy and slightly stale. But the ambiance was friendly, the old man keeping up a steady stream of wisecracks that had the girl giggling and blushing. Despite the language barrier, he included Christopher in the conversation, holding up both ends by himself and apparently doing a fine job of it.

After lunch, Svengusta prepared to go out, indicating with large hand motions that Christopher should stay inside. Christopher was happy enough to comply, since he was working on the laying-low theory and his impromptu weapon. The bokken was as polished as he could make it; now it needed practice.

In the empty, cold hall of the chapel, he found it easy to escape into the kata. Doing the traditional forms took his mind to familiar, comfortable places.

Pausing to catch his breath, he was interrupted by the double doors creaking open and two visitors slipping inside. The disarray of the room had led him to believe the chapel was not used, and he was as surprised to see them as they obviously were to see him.

They were both young, perhaps eighteen. The girl was pretty, the boy was handsome, and though their clothes were poor and plain medieval peasant costumes, the outfits gave the distinct impression of being their "Sunday best."

He belatedly realized they weren't dressed for church, but for each other.

They were polite and respectful, the girl curtsying and the boy bowing his head. Christopher decided he was the interloper here and was about to leave them to their privacy when a third person swaggered through the double doors.

He was not dressed like a peasant. He was richly cloaked in garish colors and fur trim, thirtyish, slightly overweight, and utterly full of himself. Christopher hated him instantly.

The man was as subtle as a foghorn. In one glance he dismissed both Christopher and the boy, and began to address the girl in unctuous tones.

Christopher knew he should walk away, knew he did not understand the subtleties of this affair or even the culture in which it occurred, but the raw emotion of the drama locked him in.

The boy objected; the girl hushed him, and though it was obvious that the girl loathed the richly garbed man, she seemed to be agreeing with him. Maybe he had some authority over her? But from the way he was looking at her, he couldn't possibly be her father. There was too much naked desire for that.

She pleaded with the boy, passion quavering under her hushed tones. Christopher understood that part as plain as day: *If you love me, leave now. Don't make a scene.* The boy's face twisted in anger and pain, while the man smirked.

Suddenly the boy broke and ran, the double doors banging behind him, a swirl of cold snow whisking in his wake. The man laughed and took the girl by the arm. When she shuddered, Christopher snapped.

"No." Though he spoke English, the intent could not fail to be understood.

The man looked at him, his face aflame, and snarled. Christopher shook his head in denial and pointed to the double doors.

The interloper huffed, but he started to go. He stepped toward the doors, pulling the girl with him. She resisted passively, unwilling to fight but unable to surrender.

"No," Christopher said again.

Immediately the man spun and advanced on him in a fury, barking like a savage dog. The girl stood rooted, visibly terrified, and Christopher felt a cold queasiness growing in his belly.

The man was wearing a sword, a long, straight piece of metal that was both elegant and utterly practical. This was no hippie commune, no museum reenactment. The anger that poured out was not an act.

Christopher was trapped. Behind him was a rustic cottage and a serving girl. Behind that the quiet village, snowy miles from any kind of authority or civilization or reasonableness.

Or hospital.

Christopher did not want to provoke violence. He wanted to flee. But he had nowhere to go, so he stood, paralyzed by impossibility.

The man took his silence as opposition. His barking reached a crescendo, filling the stone chapel with sound and fury. Christopher tried not to be threatening, but the pressure of the man's advance made him shift his stance and his hold on the bokken.

Sudden silence, as the man stopped talking and glared with mortal offense. Christopher was under no illusions. Twenty years of smacking people with bamboo sticks, of katas and cutting bundles of paper, did not make him a real swordsman. He had never killed anyone. He had never even tried to hurt someone. This man walked like a professional, the sword hanging from his hip as naturally as the cloak on his back. One mistake, and Christopher would not be allowed to restart the fight, recover from his error, learn from the experience. If the man went for his sword, Christopher would have to—

The man went for his sword.

He was impressively smooth, if not particularly fast. He had the blade almost out of the sheath before Christopher's bokken cracked down on his skull. Christopher knew he had held back some; still, it was a solid blow, and the man should have gone down, cried out, or at least been stunned. Instead, he snarled and stabbed at Christopher with his sword.

Christopher's training saved him and he instinctively parried. After all, hitting people in the head in bamboo-armed sparring matches had never stopped them from attacking him before, why should he expect it to now? His body carried on, even while his mind grappled with the stunning ineffectiveness of his first strike.

He snapped his bokken up into the man's face, smashing the nose. A blow that should have blinded, staggered, distracted, at least gushed blood, only elicited a growl. The man lunged, stabbed again as Christopher stepped back but not far enough. The thick steel blade caressed his left side, opening a six-inch-long gash that spat a fan of red into the air.

But Christopher's bokken was already in motion, wheeling around his head in a great arc, smashing down on the right side of the man's jaw. He did not hold back this time—there was nothing left to hold him, as he passed completely into the moment of the fight, surrendering to the reflex of training. He distinctly heard bone snap and the pitter-patter of drops of blood on the hardwood floor.

The man fell like a stone, Christopher crumpling after him. The double doors creaked, the chapel empty now save for the two bodies.

He came back to real time, and ordinary mind. He held his bleeding flesh together and tried not to panic. The brutal pain helped; the mere thought of moving was petrifying. He tried to cry out, but he could not draw the breath for it. A stomach wound, the worst kind. If he survived the hemorrhage, infection would almost certainly get him. Hopefully the girl had gone for help, although he wasn't sure what kind of help these people could offer. He needed doctors and emergency surgery, not hippies and herbal tea. He needed an American Embassy. He needed his wife.

He did not want to die among strangers.

Time passed, immeasurably. His mind could not focus on anything but the steady pump of blood. One fact finally penetrated: his opponent was still breathing. He was not dead. Christopher idly wondered if that was a good thing or a bad thing.

The doors burst open, and Svengusta and Helga rushed into the room. The old man knelt to Christopher, examined the wound with professional authority. He reached out to trace the bloody gash with one gentle finger while chanting.

The line of fire went out, the pain suddenly just a memory. Christopher looked down in wonder at his whole flesh. Only the drying blood said it had ever been otherwise.

Svengusta was already kneeling over the other man. He examined him briefly, then stood and began removing his own wool cloak.

"*Løp*," he said to Christopher. "Knockford. *Løp!*"

Christopher did not need to speak the language to understand. Knockford was obviously somewhere, anywhere other than here. And "Run!" was utterly self-evident.

But the same lack of direction that had paralyzed him all morning nullified him. He stood up but did not know which way to turn. Helga was struggling into her own cloak as Svengusta struggled out of his, and when it was free, the old man threw it into Christopher's arms.

The impetus released him. He hurried after Helga, out of the doors into the village, down the road, carrying the cloak uselessly in his hands. After two hundred yards he fell to his knees, gasping for air.

Helga tugged at him, also spent, but fear drove her like a whip. He climbed to his feet and into the cloak. Even though it was too small, hanging barely below his waist, the warmth it gave was the difference between life and death. Helga hugged her own thread-bare cloak tight around her shoulders, and they hustled on. She kept looking over her shoulder in terror until he made her quit. They did not have the energy to waste. Already he was dizzy and nauseous.

He began to notice the cold as the adrenaline in his system faded. Though his body burned with latent energy, a deep psychic weariness threatened to overwhelm him every time the wind reached under his cloak and through the rent in his T-shirt to prod him with icy fingers. He had been seriously wounded, more injured than he had ever been before in his life. It had not been a scratch that could be dismissed with conjuring tricks or ignored by the power of suggestion. But the wound was completely gone, his belly not even sore.

Eventually it occurred to him that his opponent might also be healed. In a panic he looked around for a place to hide, but the snow was unbroken on the roadside and would give away their trail. Nor could he last through the night without shelter. And in his confusion he had left his wooden stick behind.

His only option was to follow Helga, who determinedly marched along a wagon-rut cut through the snow. As the sun slipped to the horizon he began to hope that the cover of darkness would protect them. But nightfall brought its own fears—and the return of memory.

At first it was only the glitter of the country sky unobscured by city lights. But as the sun faded, the stars kept coming, until the wrongness of the night sky blazed out at him, a black velvet canopy crowded with diamonds. He could not find Orion's trusty belt; he could not even imagine constellations in that sparkling ocean.

His pretenses collapsed under the weight of twinkling stars. No one could kidnap the constellations; no plane could fly him to any part of the globe that would look like this. He remembered the confusion now, one moment desert heat and the next winter's cold. He had called for his dogs, but the jingle of their collars was gone. He had looked back for the way he had come, only to find his tracks began abruptly in the snow as if he had stepped through an invisible doorway. A doorway that was already closed when he'd rushed back, leaving him freezing and alone in a silent forest. With nothing for company but the trees and the impossible, innumerable stars.

He stopped, gaping at the sky, reading the pitiless message spelled out in brilliant points in the night: *lost*, beyond all hope and understanding, beyond all ordinary meaning of the word. Everything he had built, everything he had struggled for and fought for and won, was gone, stolen away in an instant.

And with it went the only treasure that really mattered: Maggie. He would never see her again. Robbed of purpose, he stood rooted by despair.

Helga pulled him into motion, leading him forward like a dumb beast.

2.

INTERVIEW WITH A PRIEST

They came to a town sprawled in the middle of a gentle valley, a small river running in front of it. Most of the buildings faded into the darkness; a large church dominated from the center of the town, with many-colored shining windows.

As they crossed over the simple stone bridge, he began to outpace the girl. He could no longer feel his feet; his tennis shoes were inadequate for the weather. The modernity of the light called to him, with its promise of shelter. Absurdly he began to hope they would have a telephone. Three large stone steps led to double doors, twice as large and impressive as those of the tiny chapel he had fled. They had no handles, so he grasped a huge bronze ring in the shape of a wreath of wheat and let it clang against the doorplate.

A blast of warm air: to his left, Helga had opened a small doorway framed in one of the large doors. He had to hunch over to follow her through the short, narrow space. Inside, he found a huge hall with light blazing from chandeliers and half a dozen crackling fireplaces.

A handful of tables were scattered about the room, mostly empty. At the closest a young man in a cassock frowned at them over a stack of black slates in wooden frames. The man standing next to the clerk was dressed as a soldier, in a chain-mail tunic with a long, straight sword at his hip. He stared at Christopher intently. Christopher stared back, heartbroken by the absence of a radio or a handgun, and shamed that he had let himself expect them.

Helga had shut the door, and now she hustled over to the two men, shaking and babbling. The clerk rose to his feet, concern on his face and in his reassuring touch. Helga calmed a bit and gasped out the rest of her story. Christopher could tell when she got to the part about the fight from the curious affect that flitted across the soldier's face. But then it was gone, replaced by the mien of the professional military man.

The agitated clerk sat Helga down in his chair and said something to the soldier, who dismissed him with a brief nod. Then the clerk ran off, disappearing through one of the many doors emptying into the hall. Helga sat and sniffled; Christopher stood, swaying from exhaustion. He wanted to move closer to a fireplace, but the pressure of the soldier's gaze pinioned him in place.

Soon the clerk returned, accompanied by a small crowd. A short, stout, middle-aged woman seemed in charge: she glared at Christopher and spoke to him. When he shook his head mutely, she muttered something in a different language, elegant and tonal, and waved her hand. While Christopher tried to decide if he should wave back, she studied him, and then reached a decision. The crowd surged around her, listening to her verdict, and then the soldier came forward to claim him.

Helga came also, and because of her, Christopher followed the soldier deeper into the church, through wood-paneled hallways lit by gas lamps, to a small, windowless office. Inside, a pair of armchairs faced a comfortable fire. One of the chairs contained a priest in crisp white robes trimmed in gold. At first Christopher thought he was young, because of his clean-shaven face. Every other man Christopher had seen here wore a beard; even the young soldier had a permanent rascally five-day growth. But the priest sat like an old man under a heavy burden.

Still, when he turned to Helga, he greeted her with a smile. The girl trembled in obvious celebrity-worship while she related her story, guided by a few gentle prompts. At the end of her tale, she squeezed Christopher's hand reassuringly and then abandoned him. By reflex he turned to follow her out, but the soldier was leaning against the wall, his arms folded in denial.

Christopher turned around again, and the priest waved for him to sit. The chair was padded in old leather, worn thin. Christopher leaned forward to soak in the heat, the crackling logs familiar and safe.

A pot of tea sat on a side-table. The priest poured two mugs and offered him one. Gratefully Christopher took it, wrapping his hands around the smooth stone cup.

"Thank you," he said.

The priest said something, probably polite. Christopher shook his head.

"I'm sorry," Christopher said, "I don't speak your language."

The priest eyed him critically, bowed his head, and began a prayer. Again he spoke in a different language, beautiful and exotic, the same one the woman downstairs had used.

Christopher could not remember the last time a prayer had any effect on him. This one did. The air felt heavy and close, and the pressure of an unseen gaze lay on him, the sensation so vivid that he looked around the room. It was empty, save for the three men.

After his prayers the priest looked up at Christopher and said, in perfect English, "I am Krellyan, Saint of the Bright Lady, and I enjoin you to answer my questions truthfully and fully. Are you a spy?"

Having just accepted he would never see home again, the sound of his own language was disorienting. It gave rise to hope, and with hope came fear. The mixture was indistinguishable from anger.

"No, I'm not a spy. I can't speak the language. Why would you think I'm a spy if I can't even speak the damn language?"

"It is not helpful to speculate on my motives," Krellyan replied calmly. "Please, just answer the questions. Is your intent here hostile?"

"No," Christopher said, misery washing the hard edge out of his voice. "I don't even know where *here* is. My only intent is to not be here. I want to go home. Call the damn Embassy, already." A tremor shook his body.

"What Embassy?"

"The American Embassy. I'm an American." Christopher felt an odd compulsion to provide a complete explanation. "From Arizona." The priest showed no recognition, but Christopher controlled his exasperation. Arizona was a fairly obscure place, after all. "It's right next to California." Everybody in the world knew where California was.

"Where is California?" Krellyan asked with the perfect imitation of innocence.

The exasperation won, and his temper snapped. "Stop fooling around!"

From behind came a jingle of metal; Krellyan raised a forestalling hand and spoke in their foreign tongue. Christopher was reminded that an armed man watched him. The fire no longer seemed quite so cheery.

Krellyan turned back to Christopher with a subtle frown. "Calm yourself. I am not fooling around, as you say. I do not know of any county, realm, or land by those names."

Christopher pounced with killing logic. "Then how in the hell can you speak English?"

"Is that what you call this tongue?" Krellyan answered. "I do not recognize that name, either." When Christopher stared at him, Krellyan continued. "Surely you understand this is merely a spell, and that I do not actually know your language."

"No," Christopher said heavily, "I do not understand."

"You are far from home, then," Krellyan said with genuine compassion. "Helga says they found you unconscious on their doorstep, like a heap of abandoned rags. Do you know how you arrived in this state?"

Christopher shrugged helplessly.

"Tell me what you do know."

"Nothing. I went for a walk, and then I was here. One minute I was at home, and then I wasn't, and I have no idea how or why." Christopher gripped the stone cup fiercely, but it was not an anchor.

Krellyan sighed. "You did not enter any mysterious doorways? Or pass through unfamiliar arches or portals?"

"No, I didn't. I just walked. In the open. There wasn't any warning at all. Well," he had to admit his guilt, "I wasn't paying attention. One minute there was sand, and the next there was snow. But I didn't see or feel anything. When I tried to go back, there wasn't anywhere to go back to."

"I accept your innocence." Krellyan smiled. "I have never passed through a gate myself, so I doubt I would recognize one either."

"You haven't?" Christopher cried. A terrible fear overwhelmed his bafflement over talk of portals and doorways. "Then how can you send me home?"

"I do not recognize your dress, your speech, or your names. I have no idea where to send you back to, even if I could."

Steadied by the priest's calm rationality, driven by a curiously stronger than normal urge to tell the whole truth, Christopher's fear spilled out before his conscious mind could silence it. "I don't think it's on this planet."

In the plain wooden room, with its rustic beams and paneling, its stacked firewood and wrought-iron pokers, its creaking floorboards of knotted pine, the concept was absurd.

Krellyan raised his eyebrows. "You claim to be from another plane? Which one?"

Christopher struggled not to let confusion set in. Which one? What the hell did that mean? How many were there, anyway? But wait—if there were more than one, then space travel must be routine. There was hope!

"It's called, um, I mean, we call it Earth." Christopher was rewarded with a flash of recognition. Krellyan knew that name, despite his frown.

"I do not believe you are from the elemental plane of Earth. You are clearly human and not in any guise, at least as far as I can detect."

"Earth is full of humans," Christopher argued back. "That's where we come from! Send me there!"

"No. The plane of Earth is extremely hostile to human life and populated only by elementals."

"You mean there's a place you call Earth that isn't Earth? I mean, isn't my world?" That sounded like they didn't know how to get to Earth. His Earth, that is. The fear began creeping back.

Krellyan had his own concerns, though. "You mean to claim you are from the ancestral home of mankind?"

"Yes, I do. And so are you." Christopher knew enough about biology to know that convergent evolution was a fantasy. And these people were plainly human. "You—or your ancestors—had to have come from Earth at some point. Judging by your technology, I would guess the last millennium or so. By the way, we've made a lot of progress since then." On the other hand, Earth didn't have interstellar space travel, or universal translators, so maybe bragging was premature. "Send me there."

Emotions struggled on Krellyan's naturally placid face. "I cannot. That plane has never been found, despite centuries of searching. Most consider it legend or possibly no longer extant."

Christopher's hands trembled on the stone cup, splashing what was left of the tea. "But I just came from there."

"To be perfectly honest, I do not believe you. Peace." Krellyan raised his hand to forestall Christopher's outburst. "I know you tell the truth as you know it. I do not know what magic can fool both my spells and your mind, but the alternative is absurdly improbable. It seems far more likely that you are a pawn being used by my enemies, although I cannot guess to what end."

"I'm not a pawn. I'm not your enemy—that I know of," he finished lamely. Maybe he had been brainwashed, like the nonsense you saw in movies. Maybe he would hear a code word and turn into a zombie-like assassin.

He'd never believed in that crap, but then, he hadn't believed in magic spells either. He wasn't sure he did even now.

"Do you have a lot of enemies?" Christopher asked, to break the silence. The guy seemed thoroughly nice. But then, that probably wasn't a bar against having enemies on any planet.

"More than enough for my purposes," Krellyan said ruefully. "But our problem right now is your enemy. Ser Hobilar charges you with assault."

Christopher shrugged. "Then I charge him with attempted rape."

"Rape? Is that what you thought? I am certain Ser Hobilar does not deserve such a charge. Did you see him offer any violence to the girl?"

"Well, no," Christopher admitted. "But she did not want to go with him. And—"

Krellyan cut him off. "Agreed: she has no love for Hobilar. But his rank entitles him to certain privileges. One of which is protection from assault, except at the hands of a noble."

"He drew on me! What was I supposed to do, stand there and let him kill me?"

"That might have been easier to fix," Krellyan said. Anticipating Christopher's fountain of outrage, he continued. "Had the knight wrongfully slain you, he could have been charged for your revival."

Christopher blinked.

"Are you saying," Christopher said as slowly and clearly as he could, "that if he had killed me, you could have . . . *revived* me?" He could not contain his incredulity. "Brought me back from the *dead*?"

Krellyan looked alarmed. "Yes, of course that is what I am saying. I find your amazement to be utterly incomprehensible. Are you not aware that priests outside your own lands possess equivalent powers?"

"Um, priests in my, uh, lands, don't possess any powers. None. All they can do is talk and con people out of their money."

The two men stared at each other in mutual incomprehension.

Krellyan let out a breath. "This we must first establish, or I fear our conversation will be utterly in vain. You have no ranked priests?"

"Actually, I don't understand that either. I thought you meant noble birth, but that doesn't seem to make any sense when we're talking about priests."

"You," Krellyan said slowly, a mirror of Christopher's incredulousness, "don't know what ranks are?"

"No. I obviously don't have any idea what you mean by it."

"You do not know what *tael* is?" he asked with rising intensity.

"Tail?" Christopher tried to match the sound. "I don't think I've ever heard that term before."

Startled, Krellyan rattled off words, watching Christopher's face with growing concern. "Iron. Gold. Hats and beer. All of these ordinary nouns are translated by the spell for you, but *tael* has no translation. And you are compelled to truth, so you cannot be lying. Indeed, who would ever think to lie such an absurdity, such a tremendous folly? You do not know what *tael* is. How can this be?"

Christopher was a bit nettled by Krellyan's astonishment. "Maybe we don't have any where I come from."

Krellyan gaped at him. "Impossible. And yet . . . if the plane of Man is without *tael*, then it would explain why it remains hidden. Almost I believe you—but it is impossible."

"You still haven't told me what it is."

"*Tael* is the source of rank, and rank binds powers to one's command. Powers such as this translation spell or whatever rogue conjuration sent you here." He paused for a correction. "In the case of divine magic, we prefer to assert that we are bound to the god, who works through us. Admittedly, the results are indistinguishable."

That sounded relevant to a man in Christopher's position. "So, if I had a bunch of this stuff, could I find my own way home?" Krellyan began to shake his head, but Christopher pressed on. "Where does *tael* come from?"

"Ultimately? The source of all *tael*? Some say the gods, others say the gods were made from *tael*. But I suspect you mean, where does one obtain enough *tael* to gain a rank," Krellyan said with an iron smile.

"Yes, I suppose I do."

"From the dead brains of sentient creatures." Krellyan looked at him carefully.

Christopher was sorry he'd asked.

"My chief source of *tael* comes from the deaths of my people. Do you find this disturbing?"

"It depends," Christopher said warily, "on how they died."

Krellyan smiled, some private expectation confirmed. "Of course it does. In my lands, they are natural deaths. But let us return to the issue at hand. Do you now understand your crime? You possess no rank, yet you attacked a ranked individual. You have no powers, but you challenged one who does."

"And I kicked his ass," Christopher said. "I suppose that makes it worse." He almost asked what powers the vile Hobilar might command but remembering the ineffectiveness of his first two blows seemed answer enough.

"Yes, actually," Krellyan agreed. "No doubt wounded pride will drive Ser Hobilar to press his case. Had he given you a sound thrashing, probably nothing more would have come of the matter."

"But the girl would have—"

"You did the girl no favors. Now her paramour is shamed that he too is not a law breaker, Hobilar is furious and even more relentless, and her father is placed in a delicate position in town."

Christopher cringed. "I guess I owe her an apology."

Krellyan smiled wanly. "Don't bother. I am certain she does not see it as I do. Her juvenile assessment of the issue is likely more in accordance with yours."

This world wasn't so different from his, after all.

"It is obvious that you were unaware of our laws. That is no defense, yet perhaps I can induce Hobilar to mercy. After that, I have little to offer you. Without the key to your home—wherever it is— you cannot return. We can give you a little charity while you learn our language and customs. Then you must forge a new life and make your own living. If you have no trade skills, there is always room in the fields."

"But—"

"There can be no buts. Whatever accident brought you here is beyond my power to repair. Yours is not the only tragedy I cannot undo, nor is it the worst."

The invisible burden Christopher had seen when he first walked into the room returned now to the priest's shoulders. Any further argument Christopher could hope to make was buried under that weight.

"Thank you," he said, because it was the right thing to do, even though he didn't feel particularly thankful.

Krellyan seemed to agree. "It is little enough. But it is what we have to give. Karl will show you to a room for the night; in the morning, I will deal with Hobilar and you will return to Burseberry village, under the care of Pater Svengusta. When you do learn to speak, I advise you to not discuss your fantastic origins. You must set aside your past; talk of other planes will only make you a stranger in your new home."

Krellyan started to say something else, but it came out in their foreign tongue. Seeing Christopher's confusion, he stopped talking and spread his hands in apology.

The interview was over. Christopher stood, awkward and uncertain, until the young soldier beckoned with one hand. Christopher followed Karl through the halls to a different room. Smaller and unheated, it contained little more than a narrow bed and an end table. At least the blankets were clean, if not plentiful.

A few minutes later Helga joined him in the room, bearing a tray of dishes. Chicken soup, apparently, with onions and some mushy vegetable he could not identify, and a side of the yellow bread. It struck him as rather plain, but Helga devoured it. The quality ceased to matter after the first bite: he was famished, and all that mattered was quantity. When he reached for the last slice of bread, he realized he had not been counting. He did not know if he had already eaten his half. But Helga shyly passed, and he wolfed it down.

Then she began to undress, shedding cloak, boots, and dress into a pile in the corner of the room. Christopher crawled to the farthest side of the bed and pressed himself up against the wall, unprepared for this kind of behavior in a church. But when she put out the light and joined him on the bed, all she was interested in was her share of the blanket.

He lay in the dark, unable to stop himself from wishing the priest's words to be untrue. Those who were swept away by the tsunami or buried by the earthquake wished it to be untrue, too, and just as futilely. At least he still had his life.

But without his wife it did not seem so valuable of a commodity. It had taken him most of it to find her the first time. They had met late in life yet still early enough to hope for children, grandchildren, even golden anniversaries. Meeting her had been like waking from a stale dream, discovering purpose and meaning in the mundane boredom of existence. *I will come home*, he promised her. *There was a way to get here. There will be a way to get back. I will not stop searching until I find you again.*

The words echoed emptily in the cavern of his grief, until sleep came like mercy.

3.

VISIONS

The walk home did not seem as long. They dressed him in cast-offs, gray and brown tunic and leggings with many patches, and fed him a good breakfast—porridge, of course, but livened with sorely appreciated chunks of bacon. Thus fortified, the cold was held at bay. In the morning light the land looked ordinary and Christmas-card pretty.

Helga was radiant and happy, prattling away despite his mute incomprehension. When they reached the chapel she chattered at Svengusta, who laughed at her remarks and made sympathetic eyes at him. Christopher suspected she had been told to talk to him a lot, the quicker to teach him the language.

The old man finally retreated, leaving Christopher to Helga's care. He found some peace in splitting a cord of firewood stacked outside the back wall of the chapel. Once that was done he had to go and ask Helga for another chore. The work made him feel better; it also nourished a terrible worry. What kind of living could he make in a medieval society? He was too old to work in the fields; such backbreaking labor would kill him quickly. He was literate, but he had not seen any paper, even in the church, and in any case he wasn't literate in their language. His profession was mechanical engineering, and he was damn good at it, but he was not a blacksmith. The ax he had been using might represent the height of their manufacturing abilities, and its simplicity defeated him.

When Helga sent him off to fill buckets with snow for their water barrel, he began to wish he had paid more attention in his civil engineering classes. But those were long ago, and he doubted a civil engineer could accomplish anything without metric tons of concrete. Underground sewage systems were probably too large of a step forward. On the other hand, they had all those gas lights, so they must be able to make pipes.

Bending over a clean snowdrift a dozen yards from the chapel, at the edge of the forest, he was wondering why they burned gas for light but not for heat, when he went sprawling face-first into the snow.

Someone had kicked him, hard, and was now laughing. Christopher surged to his feet, furious. His anger congealed into sickening fear when he saw his attacker. An armored knight, clad in steel from head to toe, stood half-hidden behind a large kite-shaped shield. From underneath the helmet Hobilar's eyes blazed with cruelty. His sword tip waved lazily in front of Christopher's face, dismissive and threatening in the same motion.

Hobilar spoke. All Christopher heard was the brutality of the school-yard bully.

"Helga!" Christopher shouted for help, his voice slipping out of his control and into panic. Hobilar grinned in amusement, and privately Christopher agreed with him. What help would a peasant girl be against this monster?

Anger at his own foolishness broke his paralysis. He threw his bucket at Hobilar's head.

The knight blocked it with an easy motion of his shield, but Christopher was already running. Hobilar and his sword were between Christopher and the chapel, so he fled into the forest, cutting at sharp angles around the trees and ducking under low branches. Hobilar followed madly, lagging behind only due to the weight of his armor.

When Hobilar slipped to one knee, Christopher took his best option. He reversed and ran straight for the chapel door. Helga, white-faced and sobbing, held it open for him. He flew past her, struggling to stop before he face-planted into the fireplace, turning just in time to see her throw the door closed and drop the bar.

With no time to spare: Hobilar slammed into the door with all his armored weight, shaking the entire wall. The wooden bar was not meant to withstand such abuse; the wall bracket splintered. Christopher threw himself against the door to hold it closed before Hobilar recovered.

Now they struggled with the door between them, Hobilar's fury matched by Christopher's terror.

"Get Svengusta!" Christopher shouted at the girl. She fled out through the hallway to the main room.

Hobilar, enraged, continued to push, shouting insults. Christopher had the advantage. He could brace a leg against the bed frame. Eventually Hobilar stepped back from the doorway. The silence was more terrifying because Christopher could do nothing against it. Had Hobilar remembered the front door? If so, Christopher's best option was to wait here, then flee out the back when Hobilar came in the front.

Fighting was out of the question. Hobilar's helmet guarded his one weak spot. Christopher was no Musashi.

The door rattled, and splinters flew into Christopher's face. Hobilar had come back with the ax from the woodpile. Christopher held as long as he could, but the door rapidly disintegrated under the assault. He had no choice; he staggered back, suddenly aware of his short breath and flagging legs, retreating to the main hall.

He heard Hobilar finish with the door and step through it without haste. Christopher found his bokken, gripped it in sweating palms. The priest's words had been so reasonable that Christopher had forgotten what kind of world he was in. Now he was caught unready, too tired to run, too weak to fight.

Hobilar came into the room. Indoors, his armored figure was unreal, the quality of a nightmare. His cruel, panting chuckles broke the spell, and all Christopher had left was the fear.

Christopher raised his stick to the guard position. Hobilar's sword lashed out, and the wood cracked and splintered. Stumbling backwards, Christopher fell, staring upwards in hypnotic helplessness.

Behind him the cold wind blew in through open doors, and Svengusta sailed past, waving his arms and shouting. Hobilar tried to brush the old man off. Svengusta gestured commandingly at the frieze hanging over the fireplace. Hobilar snarled, but it seemed he feared the wooden god. Reluctantly the knight retreated past Christopher, through the double doors, and down the stairs. There he stopped, sheathed his sword, and unlimbered his shield, digging its pointed bottom into the ground. Resting his hands on the shield, leaning against it, he smiled at Christopher.

No translation spell was necessary to understand his message: *I can wait.*

⌒⌒⌒

Once again Christopher sat in the little kitchen, drinking hot tea. Svengusta was no longer happy, alternating between scowling at the blankets hung over his ruined door and frowning at Christopher's silence. The old man had tried to draw him out with conversation. Christopher could not see the point of it. He did not speak the language; he did not understand the rules. He did not belong here, and Hobilar would soon resolve that problem. Christopher was only waiting for him to overcome his superstitious fear and finish the killing. When an armored man walked into the kitchen from the main hall, Christopher didn't even look up.

But it was the soldier rather than the knight. Karl frowned at Christopher, frowned at Svengusta, and spoke over his shoulder. Another man followed him into the room—old, white-haired, white-bearded, and dressed in sharp white robes. He greeted Svengusta like a dear friend, but he glared at Christopher like a washer-woman contemplating an unfortunate stain.

Svengusta and Helga went out, leaving Christopher alone with Karl and the new priest. The formality was discomforting.

The priest chanted in the beautiful language, touching his tongue and ears in the same ritual Krellyan had used. When he was done, he spoke to Christopher in English.

"I am Cardinal Faren, the top legal counselor for the Church, and unfortunately the bearer of bad news. As it may have become apparent to you, Ser Hobilar cannot be dissuaded. Though I have convinced him to stop trying to kill you for the moment, he demands a trial."

"Can I win?" Christopher asked.

"No," Faren said. "The facts and the law are clear."

"So I'm to die?" Christopher could not prevent his bitterness from spilling over.

"So we must change the facts," Faren said.

Now Christopher stopped, made himself consciously set aside his emotions.

"I'm listening."

Faren tipped his head, a tiny sign of approval. "One obvious solution to this dilemma is to change your status. If you are ranked, then your assault upon another ranked individual does not carry an automatic and inflexible death sentence."

Suddenly this conversation seemed to be going in a direction Christopher liked.

"But rank is not cheaply come by. Saint Krellyan's pockets are not so deep as to elevate everyone who needs it, or even deserves it, out of mere charity."

The priest seemed to be waiting for something.

"I would be willing to earn my keep, if that is a possibility," Christopher offered. What could they possibly want him to do that was worse than farm work?

"I was expecting as much. Still, I hesitate. What I offer you is fraught with danger. Every year our young men are called to war. With them we send a pair of healers. We have considered you for this position, for two reasons: First, we have taken the liberty of divining your suitability for the priesthood, and you qualify. Secondly, your skill in arms indicates you are not wholly unfamiliar with the battlefield, and thus perhaps you will fare better there than one of our young priestesses, whose innocence is matched only by their naïveté."

They wanted to draft him, and who could blame them? He had no family here to mourn his fall on the battlefield. What did this society owe him, anyway? Hadn't they fed and protected him? Well, not terribly well, actually. He could do with more bacon and fewer rapists.

Then something clicked in his head. If *tael* came from people, and wars killed people, then wouldn't a feudal army count *tael* as part of its loot?

"Does war tend to lead to the collection of large amounts of *tael*?"

"Yes, it does," Faren said. "But this is unlikely to be of value to you. Battlefield promotions, while the stuff of every boy's fantasy, are in fact quite rare. Politics and privilege govern the distribution of booty, as a man of your age must already be aware."

"Let me ask you another question," Christopher said. "Do your armies build siege weapons?"

"Occasionally, I suppose." Faren seemed slightly mystified.

A mechanical engineer could surely make living out of that. It would make him valuable; more importantly, it would keep him off the front lines.

"I'll take it," Christopher said.

Faren raised his hands, slowing Christopher's impetuous charge. "There is more to consider. To be drafted is to serve for three years, but to become a healer is to dedicate your life to the Bright Lady. It is not lightly entered into."

"You said I qualify, right? Or wait, is there a catch? Do I have to give up sex, or stop eating pork, or—" A terrible thought occurred to him. "—cut something off?"

"Nothing as simple as that," Faren said, grinning for a moment before remembering his severity. "You must agree to serve the Bright

Lady's cause. Pursuant to that, of course, is to accept the authority of our Church and its leaders. And naturally, behavior consistent with the Good, which your affiliation suggests will not be unduly restrictive."

Although the magic translated the words, it did not provide meanings. Affiliation with who, or what, and how did the priest know he had one if he didn't know about it? What was the role of the Church in this society? Was it a force for progress and civil liberty, or a bastion of conservative repression? What was its position on, say, farm machinery?

"We could go into this for hours," Christopher said, "so I'm just going to take your word for it. Tell me that I don't have to do anything immoral, or give up my wife, or stop trying to go home, or engage in any perverse self-mutilation, and I'm onboard."

Faren obviously wanted to object, but the pressure of the circumstances swept him forward. "Agreed," he said. "I swear to you that you need not surrender your morals, your wife, your home, or any body parts. In exchange, you must agree with the Lady's credo. To put it so briefly that it causes me physical pain, it is this: Justice for all, even those who have died and those who do not yet live."

That sounded like a pretty reasonable creed.

"Deal," Christopher said.

Faren sighed. "I am sure I must be committing some kind of crime. You know nothing of our Church, you lack the years of training normally demanded of a novitiate, and you know nothing of our realm. Yet I am pressing you into not only war but priesthood, solely because sending a stranger to likely death is easier than sending one of our own."

"Priests get paid, right?" Christopher asked.

"Yes," Faren said with a snort, "you will receive a stipend. It will not make you wealthy, but nor will you starve."

Money meant escape from the peasant class. Every man had his price, and right now, Christopher's was bacon in his porridge.

"Where do I sign?"

Faren pulled a small vial from under his robes, attached to a silver chain around his neck. He opened it and poured out a tiny purple ball, about the size of an M&M.

Christopher stared at it, entranced, although he could not have possibly explained why.

"Consume this, go into the chapel, and pray. You must open yourself to the Bright Lady. Clear your mind and let her speak to you. Ah, how can I teach you this in an afternoon? This is folly!" Faren turned away in frustration.

"I've meditated before," Christopher said. Zazen was part of the ritual of kendo. "I think I can handle it. Is there anything specific I should chant?"

Faren glowered at him from under his bushy white eyebrows. "You are full of surprises. Yes, there is a phrase, though you need not chant it. Simply recite, 'I pledge myself a willing vessel to the Name of Ostara, Bright Lady of Heaven.' Then pray, or meditate, as you put it, until she responds. If after a full day she has not responded, then she will not accept you. I do not expect this to be the case."

Christopher decided to act before he lost his nerve. He picked up the ball, and before Faren could invent further problems, popped it into his mouth.

It dissolved instantly, with no taste or sensation whatsoever. It was as if he had eaten a ball of air. It seemed a bit of a letdown after all the hype.

"Thank you for your generosity," Christopher said awkwardly, trying to cover his disappointment.

The courtesy seemed to sour Faren. "Considering we have coerced you into risking your life, I think the balance is even."

They left him alone in the chapel, with a fire in the massive, dusty fireplace, so he sat down on the floor in front of the wooden frieze of the god and goddess and cleared his mind. Meditation was not his favorite activity. He preferred the action trance of kata. Still, he owed it to them to make an honest effort. Then it occurred to him that his total lack of expectation was unwise. He had been exposed to lots of crazy stuff, so maybe he really was going to be contacted by an other-worldly spirit.

But a god? He didn't think so. Clarke's third law: any sufficiently advanced technology is indistinguishable from magic. However all this stuff worked, it was just technology, even if he couldn't see it. He had faith in that.

"Om" had never worked for him. Instead, he thought of the winter wind drifting along the snowy streets of his childhood Pennsylvania. He thought of that one magical night, a full moon on fresh snow, mid-night as bright as day, the world still silent and sleeping. He walked along the sidewalk, making the only tracks in sight, snow whispering under his rubber boots the only sound.

Time slipped away.

He was hallucinating.

The snow he walked on was now inside a room that grew brighter and larger. The pale moonlight gave way to color, pouring from great stained glass windows. The altar stretched away from him, down a long white carpet. Statues of gold and silver emerged along the walls, objects of art and beauty. Someone was waiting for him.

Slowly he walked forward to the raised altar, where a beautiful woman dressed in white greeted him with a warm smile. He recognized her from the frieze and the tapestries, although he would have known who she was without them; her identity could not be mistaken. She was suffused with a pearly radiance, bright and pure. He knelt, not because he knew he was supposed to but because something in him wanted to.

"You cannot be compelled to this choice," she said in musical tones. She gazed upon him earnestly. "Do you truly wish to pledge to my service?"

Christopher was swept away by awe. She was everything good and right he could think of. Being in the presence of so much moral purity did not make him feel inadequate but only encouraged him to try harder. There was no blame here, only shared desire for the greater good.

He really, really wanted to join the team. He wanted to be on her side. At the same time, her words echoed in his mind. He instinctively knew he could not be compelled to this, even by her. He must choose.

While he struggled to control his emotions and order his thoughts, he noticed, in that unsurprising way of dreams, a man sitting on the edge of the altar, idly playing with a katana.

It was the swordsman from the frieze.

"You are in need of a favor," the swordsman said, "or rather, may soon be. I, too, may possibly require a favor in the not too distant future."

The image of Ostara stood smiling, waiting patiently, like a computer animation waiting for someone to hit the "next" key.

"Who are you," Christopher said to the swordsman, "and what are you doing in my hallucination?"

The swordsman rose to his feet, sheathing the katana in a single fluid move, and bowed.

"I am Marcius, Marshall of Heaven, Consort of Ostara, and an aspect of the Bright Lady."

The titles seemed to indicate a lot of rank. "What could you possibly want from me?"

"First let us talk of what I can offer you. My portfolio would seem topical: Strength, War, Luck, and . . . Travel."

Those were all words that applied to Christopher's situation. Especially the last one.

"I'm listening."

"Luck we already have, in that you are here. Your Strength must be your own. But I would have you serve me in War. In return, I will serve you in Travel. Pledge to my service, and I will offer you my pledge of service: when you have paved a road a thousand miles to your home and are short but one small pebble to bridge the gap, then you will call on me and I will not fail you."

It sounded like a hard deal. Then again, Christopher was in no position to bargain. Marcius was offering him a chance to go home, despite what the priest had said about the way being unknown. The god wanted something in return. Then again, everybody did.

"I accept," Christopher said.

"I accept," repeated Marcius. "But not without gifts." The god spoke the same prayer that Faren had, touching Christopher's lips and ears.

The dream began to fade away, everything emptying into white.

"But what am I supposed to do?" Christopher asked desperately.

The voice of Ostara spoke again, from a distance. "To thine own self be true."

And then he woke, manifestly alone in front of the dead fire, although the sense of presence, of recently departed company, was overwhelming.

What was he to make of this? Were there really gods? They didn't seem omniscient, or omnipotent. In fact, they were making deals. Did this mean they were demons? Did that imply there was actually a real God out there somewhere?

Becoming a priest before studying any theology might have been a bit rash.

The windows were dark; the hour was late. He staggered to his feet and went into the kitchen, where Helga slept with a blanket over her head. She had left the light on for him. Intrigued, he walked over to the mantel to stare at the little gas flame.

It wasn't attached to anything. Where did the gas come from? He couldn't hear any sound, and when he picked up the little stone cup that housed the flames, he couldn't feel any heat. But most disconcerting, when he pointed the cup at the wall, the flames didn't bend up, they went straight out, horizontal to the ground.

The flame wasn't real: it was a hologram. He put his hand in it. The flames stopped at his fingers, and he felt nothing. He covered the cup, and the light went out.

He removed his hand and let the light return. What in the hell? They didn't even have an iron stove, but they had holographic lighting. And worse, it was *stupid* holographic lighting. Why simulate a torch flame? Even fluorescent tubes were less annoying. Why not simulate a steady glow like an incandescent bulb, or even better, pure sunlight?

As far as he could tell, the cup was simply hand-carved stone. He could not find an opening to replace the batteries. Fumbling for the nonexistent catch, his dismay surged at the inexplicableness of it all. Magic healing, but swords to fight with; light from a stone, but no telecommunications; the ability to speak the language of Earth, but no way to travel there; gods who made deals with him, but his life in the hands of a thug.

"What a crock," he muttered, perhaps louder than intended. From the side room Svengusta stirred and poked out his head.

"A big day tomorrow," the old man said. "Best prepared for by sleeping, I would think."

"Of course. Sorry. Didn't mean to wake . . ."

It occurred to him that he had understood the old man. The sounds coming from his own mouth sounded strange after the fact, though they felt natural enough on the way out.

Svengusta was remarkably unsurprised and responded in the beautiful prayer-language. "It appears you have graciously accepted our burden. Thank you, and well met, Brother."

"Our burden?" Christopher began but stopped again when he realized he had responded in the same priestly language.

Svengusta waved aside his confusion and returned to the common tongue.

"Time enough in the morning. I've cleared a bunk for you in here."

Apparently priests weren't supposed to sleep with the help. Christopher followed the old man into the tiny, cluttered room, where two double bunk beds served mostly as shelf space. The mattress was as solid as wood, the hay tick packed down from years of neglect, but Christopher did not feel inclined to complain. He had been given too much already, and the debt of kindness was fast outgrowing his ability to repay.

Morning caught him by surprise, in the space between new and familiar. He could not remember where or who he was, until Svengusta stuck his head in the room.

"Helga's kept your porridge warm for you, Brother."

"Thank her for me," Christopher said.

Svengusta's weathered eyebrow quirked. "You can thank her yourself, easy enough. But not from that bed."

Christopher climbed off the bunk, feeling grungy. It had been days since he'd had a shower, and there was little hope of one on the horizon. The facilities here were crude; the chapel had an outhouse, and even the big church in town had relied on chamber pots.

"Good morning, Pater." Helga handed him a bowl of porridge, smiling shyly.

"Call me Christopher," he said without thinking.

"Fair enough," Svengusta said. "We need not stand on ceremony out here in the fields, as it were. It's no Kingsrock with its 'by your leave, lords' and 'begging my pardon, ladies.'"

Helga giggled, overcoming her momentary confusion, and turned back to her chores.

Christopher realized that while he might know how to talk, he still didn't know what to say. He ate his porridge in silence, considering what would be a safe way to ask questions about last night's vision.

Before he finished either task, he heard the double doors in the main hall open, and the tramp of feet. Karl came into the kitchen, carrying a bundle of cloth.

"You're not still on your knees, so I assume it worked." Without waiting for an answer, he tossed the bundle to Christopher. "Get dressed. The trial starts in half an hour."

"So soon?" Svengusta said.

"Best to deal with hungry wolves quickly. Every day Hobilar spends here is a danger to your villagers. In town at least the Vicar can keep an eye on him."

"It's not an eye he needs, but a leash," Svengusta said. "Here in settled lands, every jackass that buys a rank acts like he's the hero of the ages."

Karl's lips formed a flat, thin line, the closest to a smile Christopher could imagine on that hard face. "You banter that word lightly, given present company."

"Pshaw," the old man said. "Brother Christopher here has done more to earn his rank than any novitiate, simply by hewing to his affiliation for so long."

"If being good in the face of evil were sufficient for a battlefield promotion, we should all be lords by now."

"So we should." Svengusta threw the young soldier a look charged with meaning. "So we should."

"No matter." Karl changed the subject before Christopher could ask what they had been talking about. "Your chapel will serve as a courthouse. Afterwards the Pater will transfer to Knockford, for his training."

"How soon?" Helga asked, her dismay obvious.

Karl was unpitying. "Say your good-byes now. He's been drafted."

Helga gasped, and Svengusta turned a shade paler.

"A bit long in the tooth for that, isn't he?" the old man said.

"As you noted, rank must be earned. By your leave, Paters." The soldier tipped his head and marched away to join the noise still ongoing in the chapel hall.

Christopher picked at the bundle Karl had given him, until he recognized it as a priestly robe, unadorned but reasonably white. When he looked up to compare it with Svengusta's robe, he saw the old man watching Helga and turned to see what she was doing.

Helga was at the fireplace overseeing a pot, her back to them, but it was obvious that she was crying.

"Helga," Svengusta said, "he is a priest and skilled with weapons. Do not weep yet."

Christopher finally found a question to ask. "Why is being drafted worse than being stalked by Hobilar?"

Svengusta looked at him with sorrow. "Each winter, all the boys who are sixteen are sent to the draft for three years of service. Only half of them return."

"Half?" Christopher choked. "Half of . . . all of them?"

"Yes," Svengusta said. "All are called, even the townsmen, even the scions of the nobles. Of course, those rich enough to buy ranks are much more likely to survive, but even they pay their share of dying."

"But can't they be . . . revived?"

Svengusta looked at him mildly. "And who would pay? What a staggering cost that would be, even if anyone could afford it. And in many cases, with the bodies lost on distant battlefields, it is not even an option."

How could a society survive such a continuing holocaust? Who did all the farming? How did women find men to marry?

Helga's flirtations suddenly became understandable.

"It is not thus in your land?" Svengusta asked gently.

"No. Not even close. Such a casualty rate is . . . unthinkable."
Fifty percent of every generation! Christopher's mind reeled under the
weight of such terrible numbers.

"Then you are indeed tragically separated from your home." The
old man sighed. "Still, the ones who return are the good ones. They
are the strong, the blessed, the brave. They take wives and mistresses,
and the realm thrives. They learn trades and crafts, and forget about
the horrors of war until it is time to send their own sons into the
thresher. Then they drink, and hope."

Faren had tried to warn him, but Christopher had ignored the
Cardinal. He had been so focused on going home that he blanked out
the dangers.

And in any case, the alternative seemed to be a one hundred
percent chance of fatality.

"I should change," Christopher said, and he went into the bunk-
room to put on his new clothes.

4.

A TRYING EXPERIENCE

Svengusta's chapel had been transformed. Cardinal Faren had a high seat in front of the fireplace, though Christopher could see it was just a stool on two pews, and his impressive bench was merely double-stacked pews covered in drapes. But he could only see this because he came in from the kitchen hallway. Viewed from the perspective of the sparse audience, it was imposing. The room was half-full of peasants, concentrated close to the double doors.

Christopher sat at one pew, feeling Halloween-ish in plain white robes and tennis shoes. Hobilar, still wearing armor and sword, lounged on a pew on the other side of the room with a bottle in his hand. The only apparent sign of courtesy was his bare head. Probably he just couldn't drink through the helmet.

"With your permission, Ser," Faren said, and when Hobilar indulgently nodded, he began a prayer while Hobilar took a drink from his bottle.

Christopher felt the same unseen pressure that he had experienced in the church. If it affected Hobilar, the man did not reveal it.

"Now, Ser Hobilar, what seems to be the trouble?"

"You've got a rat in your church, and it belongs to me." Hobilar's voice was not slurred; the bottle was just for show. Sadly, Christopher's impression of Hobilar was not improved by understanding the knight's words.

"A remarkable assertion," Faren said. "But please, for the sake of formality, outlay your actual charges."

Hobilar leaned forward. "Felonious assault upon a member of the gentry." He enunciated the phrase carefully, as if he had been coached to it, before lapsing into ordinary speech. "The thrall hit me with a weapon." He jabbed in Christopher's direction, spilling wine from the bottle. "You know the penalty. We all know the penalty."

"Is this true?" Faren asked Christopher. "Did you strike Ser Hobilar?"

Again, Christopher found himself unable to lie. Not that he would have, anyway.

"I did. But—"

The Cardinal waved him to silence. "So much is established. But let us see what other facts there are. Dynae of Knockford, please come forward."

The pretty girl timidly advanced up the center of the hall, dressed much as she had been the last time Christopher had seen her. The audience held their breath; this was clearly where their sympathies lay.

"Goodwoman, you were present during this altercation?"

"Yes, my lord," she said in a stronger voice than Christopher would have expected. "But I did not see them fight. I ran away when Ser Hobilar drew his sword."

"What's this?" the Cardinal said. "Drew his sword?" He turned to the knight. "Ser, surely you are aware that *felonious* assault requires that there be no provocation."

The knight didn't flinch. "The rat insulted me. I merely drew so that he would recognize my superior rank."

"Insulted? What were his exact words? Assuming they are not too indelicate to repeat in public, of course."

Christopher could see a red flush crawling up the knight's neck.

"He butted in where he was not wanted. Then he ordered me out—as if I were to take orders from a peasant!"

"Out? Out of the chapel? This battle took place here, inside?" Faren looked comically surprised.

Hobilar growled. "Inside, outside, what darkling difference does it make?"

"Pater Svengusta, perhaps you can tell the court why the accused was in your chapel."

The old man stood up from his seat halfway back in the hall. "He was, and is, my guest, Cardinal."

"And why do you extend hospitality to this man?" the Cardinal asked with careful innocence.

"He is entitled to it, as a Brother of the Lady," Svengusta answered equally blandly.

Hobilar exploded. "What knavery——?"

"Calm yourself, Ser." Faren's voice was hard as steel now that the trap had been sprung. "You will have your chance to speak." He turned to Christopher. "You are, then, in the service of the Lady?"

Christopher started to say "Yes," but no words came out. He had to change his answer to one that was unambiguously true, and even then the hair on the back of his neck prickled.

"Yes, Cardinal. I pledged to an aspect of the Lady."

The Cardinal blinked but smoothly carried on. "And this device——" He pointed to the guard, who brought forward the shattered halves of Christopher's bokken. "Was this the instrument of assault?" The Cardinal held the two broken ends together and spoke a word. Like a street magician he flourished the wooden sword, now made whole and unbroken. Christopher gaped, but no doubt that was the intended effect. "This seems oddly familiar. Why is that?"

Svengusta raised his hand again. With something like awe, he said, "It is a wooden copy of the favored weapon of Marcius, Consort of the Bright Lady."

Dramatically, Faren turned to gaze upon the wooden frieze hanging over his shoulders. The crowd followed, drawing in its collective breath.

"What were you doing with this holy symbol?" the Cardinal asked Christopher, after everyone had had a moment to contemplate the amazing significance of it all.

"I was practicing a, uh, sword dance, when Hobilar and the girl came in." The word "kata" didn't seem to be in his newfound vocabulary.

The Cardinal turned back to the knight. "I declare your case invalid."

"What?" Hobilar screeched, but the Cardinal stopped him cold.

"You interrupted a priest at his devotions in his chapel. When you drew a weapon on him, he thrashed you. What else did you expect? Attacking a priest in his own church! To avoid further bloodshed, he sensibly fled to Knockford and reported your crime to the authorities."

The knight was dumbfounded. Christopher was impressed, too; the spin was worthy of anything politicians back home could do.

"That's not what happened at all!" the knight shouted.

"Which part," the Cardinal said, "do you dispute?"

"This man was no priest when he struck me, regardless of what costume you've dressed him in now!"

The Cardinal raised his eyebrows. "Ser Hobilar: would you have me believe that a commoner, armed with a chunk of firewood, defeated you, a knight of rank? Is this what you wish to assert?"

Hobilar blinked.

"In any case," the Cardinal said, "he is clearly a priest now. Therefore, the punishment you seek no longer applies. Now that the facts are revealed, all is seen to be a misunderstanding. But no harm is done: your head and your honor are intact. I consider the matter closed."

Hobilar glowered, his jaw slack. Christopher let out his breath, unaware that he had been holding it. The Cardinal had saved him with a magnificent verbal sleight of hand.

Just as he was beginning to believe it was all over, Hobilar rose to his feet in triumph.

"If he is of rank," Hobilar said, "then I invoke my noble privilege."

"Ridiculous!" the Cardinal snapped. "You cannot duel a priest!"

The knight shouted back. "A priest cannot assault a knight! And yet he did! I demand satisfaction!"

Hobilar's incessant bullying finally broke something in Christopher. Unthinking, he leapt to his feet and shouted back.

"I'll give you all the satisfaction you can handle, buddy."

The knight looked at him with surprise, as if he had forgotten Christopher was even in the room. The audience also stared silently, but worst of all was Faren's shocked look of betrayal.

"Impossible!" Faren declared, though his voice had lost its certitude. "I cannot allow such a travesty."

"I know my rights," Hobilar growled. "Either this man hangs, or he dies on my sword. This is the law."

"I am the law here," Faren said. "This court will take a short recess, so that we may all cool our tempers. You," he jabbed at Christopher, "come with me." He stomped off his bench and into the kitchen. Hobilar sat down with a grin, enjoying a celebratory drink.

Karl followed Christopher into the kitchen, as tight on his heels as any sheepdog ever chased an errant ewe. Christopher felt his defiance melting. It was one thing to stand up to a bully; it was something else to be called to the principal's office.

"What," the Cardinal said, "in black blazes were you thinking, boy?"

Christopher hadn't been thinking, really.

"Perhaps you sought to bluff," Karl said. "But you can't bluff a man against the rocks. Hobilar is said to be deep in gambling debt and desperately in need of a ransom."

"He'll not take one from a priest of the Bright Lady," Faren declared. "That is a precedent I cannot allow."

"I'm not sure," Christopher said, "that I am a priest of the Lady."

Faren glared at him, questioning his sanity.

"I pledged to Marcius," Christopher said. The Cardinal looked so surprised, Christopher felt the need to make an excuse. "It was his idea."

"You mean to claim that Marcius personally intervened to select you as his representative?"

"Um. Yes?" Put that way, it didn't sound very convincing.

A rap from outside interrupted them. Karl stepped over to the blanket-shrouded remains of the door and ripped them down, one hand on his sword hilt.

Svengusta frowned at him from outside, looking at his twice-ruined doorway.

"Cardinal, I believe you need to see this," Svengusta said. Behind him was a short, powerfully built man carrying a long package wrapped in a blanket. The man bowed and sweated, far more nervous than anyone else Christopher had seen dealing with priests. But he couldn't be a criminal. By his dress he was clearly a craftsman. By those arms, Christopher was going with blacksmith as his trade.

"Forgive my presumption, Lord Cardinal," the man begged.

"None needed, Journeyman. You have a right to be here," the Cardinal answered. Explaining to Christopher, he said, "This is the girl's father, Dereth."

The man looked guiltily at the bundle in his arms and launched into an explanation. "Some seasons ago, I displeased certain members of the guild by poorly chosen remarks. Hence I found myself with more time than work. My pride was chafed, and I thought to prove something to myself, though I am not by rank licensed to make weapons."

"So you made one anyway." Faren shrugged. "That's not a crime, as long as you don't sell it or stick it in anybody. Why is this relevant?"

"I thought to make something that none could accuse me of illegal commerce yet would still display my skill. Oft times I have visited Pater Svengusta's chapel, to give thanks to the statue of the god for safe travel for me and mine, especially for my daughter, who has walked many times to and from this village, and often alone."

Apparently the Cardinal did not find the heedless ways of

lovestruck girls to be pertinent. His hands twitched, seeking an opportunity to interrupt the smith and send him packing.

Dereth got the hint and skipped to the end. "And so I made this." He unwrapped the blanket to reveal the sword inside.

Not just any sword, but a katana, the naked blade lying on the woolen blanket draped over the man's arms. The *suba* was iron instead of bronze, but otherwise it was a perfect copy of Marcius's weapon from the wooden frieze. Christopher hungered for a closer look. With a weapon like that, Hobilar's armor would hardly matter.

Faren's reaction was surprising. The Cardinal was speechless.

"I thought I served my own pride and pleasure, my lord," the smith said humbly, "but now I dare to think I served the will of the Bright Lady."

"May I see that?" Christopher asked, entranced.

Everyone else looked to the Cardinal for permission, who nodded approval while frowning in dismay.

The smith reverently offered the weapon's hilt to Christopher. Even in the confined space of the kitchen, he could tell it was an excellent match for him. It was exactly the right length and weight for his height. But more importantly, it seemed alive in his hand.

"No clearer sign can I imagine," the Cardinal said slowly. "This must be the work of Marcius. Your coming was prepared for."

"Nonsense," Christopher replied. "You heard the smith, he had his own reasons. It's just coincidence." He could accept alien super-science, but he wasn't about to surrender to mysticism. Christopher was only half involved in the conversation. The sword in his hand kept distracting him, like it wanted to be swung. He studied it closely. "Did you hammer-weld in an edge of harder iron?" he asked the smith.

Dereth looked crushed. "No, Pater. I did not know to do this."

"It's okay," Christopher reassured him. "It's still an excellent blade. But with the superior tensile strength of the steel backing, you can afford to put a sharper edge of brittle iron here."

"You know much about swords for a priest," Karl said flatly.

"It's a hobby of mine." Christopher wasn't sure how to define kendo or explain his fascination with ancient Japanese martial history. "Say, how much would something like this cost?" Traditional Japanese techniques meant six months of work for such a sword.

"I cannot sell it, Pater," the smith said. "I am not licensed. But I gift it to you, as the gods command. Also," he added, "there is the trivial matter of my daughter."

Apparently the daughter was not the only one with a juvenile assessment of the situation.

"Thank you," Christopher said with deep sincerity.

"Clearly my authority is being circumscribed," the Cardinal said with a sour look. "I must respect the will of the gods, assuming I can figure out what that is. It seems at least that I must not forbid this duel.

"But I can demand that you reconsider it. Do you really wish to start your career as a priest with an act of aggression? Will you take up the sword, and perhaps perish by it? Can you see no other way forward? Yes, I know, you are a priest of a god of War. But this does not excuse you from justifying your violence."

"What other options do I have?" Christopher said.

"Money, and letting Hobilar flog you until his arm falls off, should suffice. You can pay us back out of your stipend and heal yourself afterwards. I will swallow my objections to letting a priest be flogged, on account of your newness."

Having just discovered he would be getting paid, Christopher was in no mood to be robbed, despite the Cardinal's noble sacrifice. "Aren't you sending me to war? Then shouldn't I get used to fighting?" The bravado died as soon as it was born, however. Christopher turned to Karl for support. "I can beat him, right? I mean, I did once. And now . . ." Christopher held the sword up to admire it. The others shrank back, save for Karl, who smiled his grim, flat shadow of a smile.

"Not only that, but rank and magic as well."

"Priestly magic," Svengusta objected.

"Still more magic than Ser Hobilar commands," Faren agreed. "And the appearance of the sword is a tangible sign of the favor of a god. Hobilar may yet be brought to his senses."

"If not," Karl said, "it is unlikely either of them will actually die. They are only first ranks."

There was that, too. "You can just revive me, can't you?" Christopher said.

Faren looked truly sad. "I must be honest. I cannot say what Saint Krellyan will do, but my counsel will be to leave you in the ground, as a lesson to anyone else that would challenge Church policy. The political cost of reviving you may be greater than we can afford."

"Consider too," Karl said, "that with death you lose a rank, and you have only one to lose. The Saint will not restore it, even if he returns your life, so you will serve out your draft as a common man, without the advantages of priesthood."

"Maybe we could fight until first blood?" Christopher asked hopefully.

"With that?" Karl frowned at the heavy sword. Christopher looked at it again and was forced to concede the point.

"When fools play with swords, accidents are never far behind," the Cardinal warned. "Perhaps Marcius intends you to fight a duel, but surely you understand that the outcome is not decided. Even if it is the god's will that you *fight*, you may not *win*. Thus, the choice must be yours."

The image of Hobilar's arrogant, bullying face swam in Christopher's vision. "I'll take my chances."

Faren sighed. "Then you must take them alone. I will declare you of the Church of Marcius and thus not under my orders. Understand this means you are not under my protection, either."

"Whose orders would I be under?"

The Cardinal smiled wanly. "I hesitate to answer that, because you are after all a relatively young man. You, as the sole priest of Marcius in the realm, would in yourself incorporate the entire Church."

The knowledge that he had joined a defunct religious order was not exactly comforting. "I can't pretend I can survive without your help."

"You will still enjoy the same protections as any other citizen of the lands of the Lady," the Cardinal admitted, "which I take great pride in saying are considerable. And you will still be subject to Krellyan's orders, as he is the ranking priest of the Lady, whom you also serve."

"For the next three years you will be under the orders of the King," Karl said. "As are all draftees."

The Cardinal took the sword from Christopher and handed it back to the smith. "Dereth, keep this until after the trial. Karl, reconvene the court. I shall continue to hatch my petty plans, despite the gods' disdain."

<hr>

Cardinal Faren glared at Hobilar, who studiously raised his bottle for another drink.

"Ser Hobilar, as Pater Christopher serves the Consort Marcius, god of War, I cannot forbid him from accepting your challenge. But your honor also allows you to show mercy and understanding. Will you not set aside your quarrel for peace?"

Hobilar stood up. "You priests must learn to respect the sword that keeps your borders safe." He set the bottle aside and causally picked up his helmet. "Step outside, Pater. We have business to conduct."

Christopher felt a cold stab of fear. Before he could react, the Cardinal rescued him again.

"Krellyan's law requires that you delay your duel for a full day, which you must spend in reflection of your desire to commit violence. Return here tomorrow, at this time, if you must."

With a snort, Hobilar took his leave, pointing to the doorway and winking at Christopher on the way out.

5.

DUEL

Faren had a coach-and-four, the most impressive vehicle Christopher had seen in this new world. He watched it rolling away, carrying Pater Svengusta and the Cardinal to town. Faren would return the next morning for the duel; Svengusta would return that night, with books borrowed from the head of Novices in Knockford, to teach Christopher what he needed to know of magic. A single evening seemed inadequate to master a field so entirely new, but Christopher was hardly in a position to object.

They did not leave Christopher alone. Karl and a pair of soldiers stayed behind to stand guard over him in the chapel. The men had large wooden shields, which gave Christopher an idea.

"Hobilar's going to have one of these, right?" he asked Karl.

"He is allowed three," Karl said. "Should you succeed in breaking one, he can call for its replacement."

Hobilar's shield was made of steel. He wouldn't need to replace it.

"I think I need some practice. Are you up for it?"

"I am not ranked," Karl said, his voice perfectly even.

What the hell does that matter? thought Christopher. "So? You still know how to fight, right?"

Karl gave him the most peculiar look, one that Christopher simply could not make any sense of. "Yes. I know how to fight."

"Then maybe you could give me a few pointers. For instance, I've never faced a shield before."

"Shields are not used in your land?" Karl showed a glimmer of surprise. So the ice-man had emotions, after all.

"No," Christopher replied honestly enough, "they're not terribly fashionable anymore."

Karl borrowed a shield and a helmet, and armed himself with an ax handle from the woodpile. Christopher belatedly remembered there would be no protective gear or padded weapons. He would have to trust to the young soldier's skill and discipline to not get hurt.

When he performed the traditional half-bow between sparring partners, Karl hesitated before bowing back and raised his shield.

Christopher stepped in for a basic *men* strike, his bokken held overhead and cutting straight down, putting his height to good use. Karl brought the shield up fast, faster than Christopher would have imagined possible, ducking under it and letting the bokken slide off.

Then he clubbed Christopher solidly across the ribs.

"Ow," Christopher said, before he realized it didn't hurt nearly as much as he had expected. The force of that blow should have broken his ribs. He looked down in perplexity, but he wasn't even sore. The only injury was to his pride, as the chortling guards complimented Karl on his technique.

"You are newly promoted," Karl said by way of apology. "I did not think you depleted."

Apparently whatever effect protected Hobilar now protected Christopher too. That was a welcome development.

"Let's not deplete me any more than necessary," Christopher said, and raised the bokken again.

Karl hefted his shield, and for the next two hours they fenced, lunging and parrying. Or rather, Christopher parried while Karl lunged. The young man attacked relentlessly, taking every opportunity to strike regardless of how exposed it left him. This was completely opposite to Christopher's training, which heavily emphasized the value of not getting killed.

Although Karl pulled his blows after the first one, mistakes were inevitable. A number of serious hits left little more than bruises, but eventually a blow slipped through that left Christopher gasping through the pain and seeing stars. He sat down, almost collapsing, the anxiety that drove him burned out with the last of his strength. His muscles were sore, a few probably torn, and a dozen lumps were forming inside and out. Idly it occurred to him that he would not be in any condition to fight tomorrow, but he was no longer physically capable of being afraid.

"Why do you always attack?" Christopher asked, dropping his bokken on the floor to signal surrender.

Karl dropped his shield and club, squatting near him. He struggled out of the chain-mail tunic, letting it pool on the floor in a jangling mess. Christopher was embarrassingly gratified to see Karl had his own share of lumps, at least one of which was seeping blood.

"The goal is to deplete the foe's tael before he depletes yours. Defense is merely giving the enemy free attacks. As an unranked soldier, my only hope is to land one strike before being slain, and trust to my comrades to finish the task." The other soldiers nodded their agreement. "Had we fought for real, you would have absorbed my first blow and then cut me down."

Helga timidly crept into the room, bearing a tray of bowls. Porridge again, but the soldiers dug into it without comment. With considerable relief Christopher observed that as long as Karl was in the room, Helga seemed to completely forget about flirting with him. Karl took this without comment, as well.

One of the double doors creaked open, and Svengusta entered, covered in snow.

"Still alive, I see," the old man said. After dumping a bag on the floor and struggling out of his cloak, he took a closer look. "But only barely. What have you done to him, Karl?"

"Provided an education," Christopher said. "At my request."

"It's likely to be the least painful of your lessons today," Svengusta said, "and the easiest to repair." He spoke a prayer and touched Christopher. Instantly the pains were gone, the bruises healed, and Christopher felt whole and rested again.

"Wow." The surge of good feeling could not be contained. "Can you fix Karl? He's as beat up as I am."

"I don't need him to be able to concentrate." Svengusta went over to the young man anyway. Karl looked like he wanted to object, too, but Svengusta didn't give him a chance.

"Thank you, Pater," Karl said after the prayer.

"How many times can you do that?" Christopher asked. "More to the point, how many times can I do it?" If he could heal himself during his duel, that could turn the tide of battle.

"All will be made clear." Svengusta took a pair of heavy leather-bound books out his bag. "Though I need to wet my whistle before starting. It has been a while since I was expected to lecture to novices."

Christopher picked up one of the books and was not surprised to see that he could read the words without difficulty even while he recognized it was in a different language. He was so engrossed that it took him a minute to notice that Svengusta was staring at him.

"What?"

"You can read?" Svengusta said.

They accepted magic and superhuman endurance as normal, but literacy made them stare?

"No common soldier, then." Karl spoke neutrally; nonetheless Christopher thought to detect the faintest tincture of acid in his tone.

"Well, then." Svengusta handed him the other book. "Read as much of this as you can before dinner. Then we will see."

He swam through the books, taking pleasure in the simple act of reading. It had been days since he had even seen writing. Or paper.

The text was small, handprinted, and dense. One book was in the common tongue, and it taught him that the name of the prayer language was Celestial; the other was written completely in elaborate glyphs of Celestial. Disconcertingly, the glyphs were different every time he looked at them, although they kept the same meaning.

Some of the content was the basics of a liberal education: analysis, logic, problem solving. Some of it was general wisdom: self-discipline, ethics, diplomacy. At forty, with a black belt in a martial art and a college degree, Christopher felt comfortable with those topics.

But what lost him was the context. He could relate to the rituals, like he could relate kata to the art of kendo. He could understand the effects of magic, having experienced it firsthand. But what he couldn't make any sense of was how it all worked. The underlying basics seemed to be missing. There was no discussion of fundamental forces or principles. He couldn't find any reference to a Newton, with his mathematical expressions, or even a Euclid and geometry. All the rules were semantic and contextual, instead of syntactic and formal. This whole attitude, of expecting you to either not care or already know about the underlying mechanics, was the kind of crap he expected from computer manuals, not scientific papers.

Computer manuals. That's exactly what he was reading. How to interface with an incredibly complex system that was largely the product of arbitrary decisions. But not completely artificial: it wasn't law or philosophy. There were inflexible, if incomprehensible, rules that had to be followed.

The rituals were like passwords and procedures, to run specific programs. Each program did its own thing, and in fact was often unrelated to the other programs, as if each one had been written by a programmer with little knowledge of or less concern for what others had done before.

And tael—tael was bandwidth. Tael was how much giga-whack you could get from central computing before they cut you off for the day. The ability to instantly heal some damage was just a side benefit.

Global dissemination, expensive bandwidth, no user-interface standards, and chaos for organization. He'd traveled God-knew-how-many miles from home and found the damn Internet all over again.

There was a ritual for readying the rituals, which turned out to be meditation again. He was alone in the chapel at the moment, everyone else having retreated to the kitchen. Watching him read was apparently not as interesting as watching Helga wash dishes.

He forced the noise of the kitchen out of his head, ignored the snatches of conversation and laughter, and went to his snowy childhood. The meditation was difficult, but the trance it brought on was more than just a state of mind. The hallucination was vivid and real.

In front of him, on the white dark-bright moonlit street, stood an empty suit of armor. It addressed him in chill and hollow tones, although not unfriendly.

"Greetings, Pater Christopher," it said, or rather he, since it was clearly a male voice. "How will you serve the Marshall of Heaven today?"

"I need a menu," Christopher said. "Help? Where's the help key?"

The apparition was a little taken aback. "I cannot provide instruction. You should look to your elders for that. I can only provide you with spells."

"It's my first time. Do you have any default settings? Preferably for a duel or just general fighting."

The suit paused, considering. Christopher couldn't make up his mind if the suit of armor was a program or not. On the one hand, it seemed to interact like a real person, even displaying emotions despite a total lack of facial features or even a face. On the other hand, it felt a lot like talking to Siri on an iPhone.

"The most commonly requested spells before a duel are these."

Pearly symbols appeared in the air next to the suit of armor. They were fantastically complex, like Chinese ideographs gone wild, subtly shifting shape whenever he stopped focusing on them. Yet he could divine their meanings as easily as reading a sentence. The suit took the symbols down and handed them to Christopher.

"Okay, thanks. Anything else?"

"No, young priest," the apparition said with amusement, "you are charged with only this much of the Marshall's power."

The suit of armor and the snowy background began to fade, and Christopher found himself concentrating fiercely on the mystical glowing pretzels in his hands. Keeping them intact and separate without dropping them drained his attention like an open spigot. The symbols slid through his fingers without sensation, and only pure thought kept them from drifting away. But it was a losing battle; eventually they faded like the afterimages of a bright light, and he felt saddened by the loss of beauty.

When Christopher came to his physical surroundings again, Svengusta was watching him. "I intended to offer you advice on what spells to prepare, but I am glad you did not take it. An old village healer is perhaps the worst source of wisdom before a battle. I am not even sure of the rules for dueling."

"There are rules?"

"Many," Karl said, coming into the room, "as any village boy could tell you, no doubt in exacting detail. But in your case, you need only worry about surviving. What will you do for armor?"

"Nothing," Christopher said. "I don't need armor." *Your armor is in your mind*, his sensei used to say. Not getting hit was the key.

Karl stared at him, as if the words were a challenge. Then he shook his head. "Shameful enough that we throw you to wolves with hardly a day's rest. Must we send you defenseless?" He began unlacing his chain-mail tunic.

"I don't want it," Christopher said, but Karl ignored him.

To Christopher's surprise, the heavy armor did not impede his movement. It also fit well; although he was taller than the younger man, he was no broader around the shoulders. The weight of it gave him confidence.

"And how shall you perform your duties without it?" Svengusta asked Karl.

"For an unranked man, armor is merely vanity," Karl said. "But for the Pater, it may slow a killing blow long enough for a healing spell."

"I'll give it back afterwards," Christopher said.

Karl shrugged, unconcerned.

❦

The next day Svengusta charitably let him sleep in, and the household was already up when Christopher awoke. Helga served him a fine breakfast, a ration of bacon on the side. He found that a little too close to a "last meal" for comfort, especially when he saw that no one else was having any.

After breakfast Karl dressed him in the armor, cinching it expertly for maximum protection and minimum interference. He had other gifts, a plain open-faced helmet, the katana safely contained in a simple wooden scabbard so new it still had splinters, and a long cloak to hide the sword until the proper moment, the better to surprise Hobilar. Svengusta watched carefully through these preparations for battle, and then took Christopher into the main hall.

"I trust that Karl has prepared you physically for your ordeal. Now it is my job to prepare you spiritually. For you, a stranger to our land, I have no words of comfort to give. Nor should you, on the dawn of battle, seek advice from one as old and dry as myself."

The old man built up a fire while he spoke, Christopher handing him chunks of firewood.

"But I can give you this much wisdom: you must be of one purpose, in your own mind. Your misgivings are plain to me, and the battlefield is no place for thinking. So sit here and consider, until you are certain what your fate demands of you."

Svengusta left, closing the kitchen door with a sense of finality. Christopher felt alone for the first time in days, with only himself and the wooden gods for company.

Was he really going to do this? Was he really going to try to *kill* another human being? He had never attacked anyone in anger in his life on Earth. He had never even wanted to kill somebody. He had never contemplated it, in the sense he was now, sitting here waiting for noon so he could shove a razor-sharp piece of steel into another man's body and watch his blood and guts spill out while he screamed and screamed and screamed.

He could walk away from this. They would pay the man off, and he would survive. He would be reduced to poverty again, having only just escaped it, but nobody would get killed. It was the rational thing to do, and he was a rational man. Why wasn't he doing it?

Because Hobilar was wrong. But what did he owe Dynae? He couldn't protect her from all the thugs in this world. He couldn't protect all the peasant girls from all the Hobilars. It wasn't his job. Nobody had asked him to do it, and in fact a lot of people were asking him not to. Even Dynae would understand if he walked away.

Because he was proud? But he was reasonable. He couldn't believe he would let his pride get him killed. There were other ways to deal with bullies like Hobilar. Giving up his pride would diminish him, make him less the Christopher he used to be, but wouldn't becoming a killer make him even less? None of the priests he had met would think less of him for not fighting this fight.

Because I want to go home.

The thought sat there, waiting for him to acknowledge it. War and blood had been presented to him as his only hope of return. Was he prepared to climb back to Earth over a stack of bodies? Would Maggie still want him then? Would she even recognize him? Would he recognize himself?

He called back the sound of her voice. In the quiet of the stone chapel he thought he could hear her speaking to him through the crackling flames. He knew that it probably didn't matter. Even if he won this duel, it was unlikely he would survive the next three years, let alone ever find his way home. He knew that she would forgive him for failing, even if she never saw him again. He knew that she would love him, had always loved him, for who he was, had never asked him to be anything else.

Half an hour before noon, Karl came in through the double doors. He left them open to the cold, hard sunlight.

"It's time."

Christopher stood up, followed Karl out into the day silently. His tongue was leaden and he could not speak.

A crowd was waiting, hovering discreetly at the periphery of his consciousness. Faren was there, resplendent in a white cloak, like a lordly snowman. The gold rings on his fingers flashed in the sunlight.

"The rules are simple," Karl explained. "The field of honor is the village square. You go to the center, with Hobilar. Faren checks you both for magic, then asks if you still insist on fighting. If you say yes, then Faren says begin, and you try to kill each other. You stop when somebody dies, goes off the field, or yields."

Christopher wasn't listening. They'd covered all this before. He was listening to the horse neighing, the fresh, sharp snow crunching under his feet, a lonely bird chirping in the trees.

Hobilar was on the other side of the square, armored like a squat, thick beetle. He was alone, save for a huge brown horse. The villagers clustered in knots, leaving a wide gap between themselves and the knight. Hobilar saw someone and called out. The peasant reluctantly approached.

Faren spoke to Christopher, quietly, for his ear only. "I will not ask you to risk yourself, nor hold your blow, yet if it is possible, try not to kill him. Unless it is possible that you have come to your senses and will yield." The Cardinal turned away without waiting for a reply.

Karl pointed him to the center of the square, and Hobilar trudged out to meet him. The two men stood ten feet apart, and Faren glided in between them like an angel.

Faren asked with deep sincerity, "Is there no hope of reconciliation? Is there no peaceful resolution?"

"I have done nothing wrong," Christopher said thickly. "I do not ask for this fight. I hold no offense against Ser Hobilar."

"Give me my money," Hobilar growled.

The wind blew gently through the square, crept quietly across the snow, playfully ruffled the hem of Faren's cloak.

"No," Christopher said.

Faren's face radiated dismay. He chanted his prayer and studied both men carefully.

"I pronounce you both free of magic," Faren said. Christopher took off his cloak, dropped it in the snow. His armor and sword were now clearly exposed. Hobilar's only reaction was a low growl of discontent.

Faren backed up, perpendicular to the men. "Will you not yield?" he cried in desperation, although no one could tell to which man he was speaking.

Hobilar drew his sword, hefted it. The metal scraped on the scabbard, the sound unmuffled by the snow. Christopher didn't bother to draw.

Faren stepped back again, now twenty feet away. "To arms," he barked—angrily, sadly, bitterly.

Christopher spun and bolted back the way he had come, running at full speed. Behind him he heard Hobilar laughing.

He reached the edge of the square, threw himself to his knees facing the chapel. Hobilar roared behind him. Triumph and derision could not fully disguise the relief in his laughter.

"He flees the field," Hobilar shouted. "Your dog yields."

"The field is the square," Karl was already countering, "he has not left it."

Both their voices were drowned out by Christopher's shout.

"If this be your will, Marcius," he raged, blaring the dulcet tones of Celestial jarringly across the snow, "then show me your favor!"

Sparkling confetti appeared, showering the area around Christopher. It sank into the snow, leaving no trace.

Hobilar's roar changed tone, and he lumbered into a charge.

Christopher was still praying. He whipped the katana from the scabbard, pointed it at the chapel.

"If this be your blade, Marcius," he shouted, "then bless it!"

The blade began to shine, a silvery sheen, painfully sharp to look at.

Hobilar clanked and pounded behind him. Christopher sprung to his feet, spun around in midair, froze Hobilar in his tracks with an iron stare, their eyes suddenly manacled together. Now he could see fear in Hobilar's eyes. He held his katana in both hands, in high right guard, like a baseball bat of terrible glowing menace.

Faren's voice carried across the field. "In the shadow of the wrath of god, Ser, will you not yield?"

Greed, stupidity, cruelty. Hobilar's faults were many. Cowardice was not one of them. The cowards were culled out by the draft.

Raging inarticulately at the unfairness of the world that had birthed him, the knight charged, lunged at Christopher, his head tucked under the broad steel shield, his longsword lashing out like a jackhammer.

Christopher stepped back with his left foot, launching his own oblique strike. The longsword burst through his chain mail, sinking deep, but the katana was already in motion, and it did not deign to notice this interruption. It swept a glittering arc across and down, the tip of the arc intersecting Hobilar's sword arm, just above the plated gauntlets, just below the steel cup that protected his elbow.

Christopher struck, without anger, or fear, or guilt. His mind, given over wholly to the moment, could register only that it was a good strike.

Like cutting a melon: first resilient opposition, then flesh like water. The blade passed through Hobilar's arm, leather and cloth. Comically, the hand clung to the longsword as it fell, only releasing its death grip when it sank into the snow. From the meaty stump pumped gouts of bright-red blood onto the pure-white ground, like cherry topping on a snow cone. Hobilar sank to his knees, following his forearm down.

Faren was already there, grabbing the stump in one hand and the remains of Hobilar's arm in the other. Blood went everywhere, stark against the white robes. Christopher idly reflected that cardinals' robes were supposed to be red. Faren sang out in Celestial, held flesh to flesh, and prayed.

"Curse the Dark!" Faren raged. He stood up, letting the lifeless limb fall to the ground. But the blood had stopped, and perhaps the pain. Hobilar looked blankly at his ruined arm lying in the snow.

"You yield," Faren said to the knight. It was not a question but a command.

Faren turned to Christopher, glanced at his wound, dismissed it as unimportant. "Heal yourself," he ordered. Tael had bound Christopher's flesh in the wake of the sword, turning a killing blow only crippling. Christopher used the last of the spells in his head on himself, before his shock faded completely and left him to deal with the full brunt of the pain.

Faren glared down at the knight. "Do you hold your ransom?" he demanded. His voice rang like an iron bell.

Hobilar shook his head, tears running down his face.

"You have no ransom?" Faren roared, shaking with fury. His face turned red, or would have, if red still had any other meaning than that brilliant pigment spattered everywhere. "Your life is forfeit!" Faren bellowed. "*Forfeit!*" He turned to Christopher and asked through seething teeth, "Will you allow the Church to ransom this fool?"

Christopher nodded. Faren, not waiting for his response, turned back to the knight.

"The Church now owns your life." He pronounced it like a sentence of death. "Your arms are forfeit! Strip him!"

Two of the church soldiers came forward and tore the armor off Hobilar with grim efficiency. This was one of the rules of the duel: you staked everything you brought into the ring with you. Christopher had not considered what that meant, until now.

The knight offered no resistance, weeping openly. It was degrading, disgusting, but Christopher forced himself to watch. He had caused this. He could not shirk from its conclusion.

The soldiers stripped Hobilar down to his undergarments, pulling his tunic and leathers off. They claimed his jewelry, pulling rings off the fingers of his left hand and yanking out an earring. For a moment Christopher was terrified they were going to open his mouth and look for gold fillings. They piled the booty at Christopher's feet, retrieving the sword from the snow and adding it to the pile. One of the guards, with cruel humor, stripped Hobilar's gauntlet from his severed hand and put the metal glove on top of the pile.

"Your horse is forfeit," Faren pronounced.

The other guard fetched the animal, led it over to Christopher's growing hoard.

"You can crawl to Kingsrock," Faren ordered Hobilar in bitter dregs, "and beg the Saint for your worthless life. You can beg him for your worthless arm. You can beg him, but do not expect pity."

The priest turned on his heel and strode away, leaving the broken knight shivering and sobbing on his cold blanket of snow.

"Your mount, Pater," the guard said, handing the reins to Christopher.

Christopher realized he should put away his sword. The brittle light had faded from its blade, leaving only a bloody piece of steel. He dropped the reins and looked around for a bit of clean cloth. The guard saw, and with a wicked grin walked to the weeping knight, pulled out his dagger, and cut a patch from the man's linen undertunic. He handed the cloth to Christopher, and went back to help with the booty.

Christopher cleaned his blade, dropped the bloody rag in the snow. He took a few deep breaths and sheathed the sword properly, without looking. He didn't cut anything off, so he must be functioning, but he didn't feel like it. He felt like he was still outside of himself, looking in.

He tried to follow the other soldiers back to the chapel. The horse objected, raising its head and flattening its ears. Christopher tried to calm it, stroking its nose and saying kind words. It was a beautiful horse, a huge chestnut stallion. The horse pulled at the halter, wanting to go back.

Faren came over and talked to the horse. Christopher couldn't recognize the language, although the horse could. It argued with Faren, neighing its disapproval, but Faren was implacable. Finally the horse hung its head and came at Christopher's gentle tugging.

"I told him you are his new master," Faren said, "but he is a horse. He will forget unless you master him in the conventional way."

Christopher could only nod stupidly. The magnificent beast followed him now, so he and Faren led it into the chapel through the double doors, to get out of the cold. The soldiers were piling up the loot and judging it with a professional eye.

Faren looked upset.

"I didn't kill him," Christopher said. "You asked me not to kill him and I didn't."

"Truly, you are 'The Impossible Apprentice.' You pervert every command to punish the master." Faren laughed mirthlessly.

"You can fix his arm, right? I mean, you can revive the dead, so surely you can reattach an arm?"

"If I had been quicker, perhaps. But now, in all the Kingdom, only Krellyan can do this. And the cost is more than a man of Hobilar's rank can pay. You have ruined him."

"If it's any consolation, I didn't plan that. I just took the shot offered to me."

"If I'd had any idea you were capable of such a feat, I would have expressly forbidden it," Faren said with some of his old twinkle. Then his pensiveness returned. "Again I think to see the work of Marcius. The message is plain enough. Raise a hand against the new Church, and it will be cut off. Who will dare oppose you with that kind of imagery?"

"Krellyan will," Karl said. "He won't blink to balk a god."

"Your faith is touching," Faren said wryly, "but even our good Saint is not that dense. No, I fear this is a herald. I think to hear the gong of battle in the distance."

"I'm not trying to cause trouble," Christopher protested.

Faren looked at him with annoyance. "Marcius may be a god of War, but he is still White. He does not plunge us into violence needlessly. I do not fear that Marcius seeks to drive us to battle. I fear that he seeks to warn us of approaching woe."

"But there's a draft. You're already at war."

"There has been a draft for my entire life, yet the gods never felt the need to intervene before." Faren shook his head in dismay. "I fear no ordinary border skirmish but a threat to the Church—nay, even to the survival of the Kingdom."

The soldiers had stopped their looting to stare at Faren in slack-jawed fear. Even Karl watched with closely hooded eyes.

"The Black Harvest . . ." one of the soldiers said, his voice fading to a whisper.

"Children's tales have no place here," Faren growled. "Just a cynical old man reading too much into blood on the snow. We'll speak no more of it."

6.

AFTERMATH

Karl took Christopher and his horse out into the village to find a stable. Turning the animal around inside the chapel was harder than Christopher had expected. The beast was the size of a small car and not inclined to put up with any foolishness.

"You know little of horses, for a man of rank," Karl said.

"Well, I haven't been ranked very long, and there seemed to be other things to focus on." Christopher instantly regretted his snideness, but the horse was snorting in annoyance, and he found it intimidating. Karl rescued him, taking the reins.

Outside, Karl went the other way around the chapel, avoiding the central square. Walking along the backside of the village revealed chicken coops and pigpens, straw-thatched hovels and outhouses, the wood-smoke and animal dung of rural Appalachia. The homey effect was spoiled when he noticed that the sty he was walking past held not two pigs but one pig with eight legs. The stretch-limo-sized beast waddled sinuously to the fence, staring out hopefully for a treat. Christopher found the sight unnerving, although neither Karl nor the horse seemed to find the pig remarkable.

The stable was obvious, the third-largest building in town after the inn and the chapel. Behind it lay a giant, reeking mound of manure so potent it was the only feature of the landscape uncontaminated by snow.

Christopher was just thinking how dominating the dung-pile would be in summer weather when his scabbard banged against his shin, the injury made all the more cruel by the cold. He had not intended to bring the sword with him merely to stable a horse. Karl had insisted, pointing out that going armed was a habit he must adopt. He would now, as Faren had said, live by the sword. The possibility that he would die by it seemed correspondingly increased.

Wincing in pain, wondering how much heat the fermenting manure was generating, thinking about chemistry and swords, he was suddenly paralyzed by an epiphany.

In the valley of the swordsman, the musketeer is king.

"Are you coming?" Karl called from the barn doors.

"Wait," Christopher said, walking to the mound. Its stench could not hold him off; unthinking, he plunged an arm into the black mass, digging deeply, drawing out material from the depth. His reward was a handful of warm gooey filth, speckled with white.

"What the Dark is wrong with you?" Karl demanded from over his shoulder.

"It's already crystallizing," Christopher said. "Don't you see?" He offered his treasure, but Karl stepped back, his hand on his sword.

Christopher finally realized what he looked like.

"Sorry. I just . . ." He struggled to think of an explanation. "This is valuable. No, really." His hand, now covered in wet filth, was becoming uncomfortably cold. "I need to wash up."

Silently Karl pointed to the barn, where a dour, narrow peasant watched in alarm. It was the same man Hobilar had called over before the duel.

"Sorry," Christopher said, walking into the barn with his arm held out at a right angle.

"There's a shovel on the wall and a fresh batch in the stalls, if your lordship desires." The peasant's tone questioned Christopher's sanity even while the words were careful to give no offense.

"Actually, I only want the old stuff." Christopher found a barrel of water and plunged his arm into it. With a yelp, he jerked it back out. The water was near freezing.

"Goodman Fenwick owns the stable and would be happy to assist you, Pater," Karl said. "For a reasonable fee." The last was directed pointedly at Fenwick.

"We live to serve," the stable-master muttered while picking up a huge horsehair brush. Then he grabbed Christopher's arm, shoved it back into the barrel, and began to scrub.

The pain was intense, and he struggled to remain calm while Fenwick worked. How could he be gutted like a fish and not even flinch, but this was enough to drive him to the edge of murder? When his arm came out of the barrel, pink and clean, he saw there was no physical damage. The tael only healed when necessary.

Fenwick finished drying his hands on a square of old horse blanket and tossed the cloth to Christopher.

"Understand," Fenwick said, "he is a destrier. He cannot live on mere hay, like a farmer's nag. He must be fed barley and oats as well."

After a moment Christopher realized the stable-master was talking about the horse.

"How much does that cost?"

The stable-master struggled with an answer, fairly obviously trying to decide whether to charge the local rate or the rich out-of-towner rate. He was spared by Karl's reappearance with a basket of tiny, dry apples.

"Remind the horse of why he is your friend," Karl suggested, handing him several. Fenwick silently took the basket from Karl and returned it to its hiding place, while Christopher went to the end of the barn where the great chestnut stallion hung his head over the stall door.

Christopher fed the apples to the horse, only slightly worried about losing a finger. He scratched the long neck behind the ears, trying to bond with the stately animal. He wished he could talk to it, like Faren had.

"I don't know his name," he said. "I didn't think to ask."

"His name is Royal," Fenwick answered, "and a fine steed he is. Hobilar's pa bred the best and even succeeded in drumming some horse-sense into his boy. This was one of the last foals Hobilar's herd turned before he sold them all off."

"Why did he sell them?" Christopher asked.

"To buy his rank," Karl explained from the next stall over, where he was treating his own horse to one of the apples.

"Aye," Fenwick agreed, turning dour again. "He did his time at war and came back, but not to warm his father's heart and take up the family trade. When old Hobilar died, the boy sold off the stock so he could play at being a lord. He kept the best one for himself, though."

"Royal," Christopher said, and the horse nudged him.

"He's well taught and in good shape. Hobilar took right good care of him, at least," Fenwick said begrudgingly.

Christopher felt a tinge of remorse. This was one thing Hobilar had loved, obviously. How evil can a man be if he loves something outside of himself? On the other hand, Hitler had loved his dog Blondi. If Hobilar had treated people with the same respect he'd shown his horse, he wouldn't be . . .

"Where is Hobilar, anyway?"

"Huddling under a blanket in the coach. The Cardinal is taking him to Kingsrock," Karl said. "He still hopes Hobilar will atone."

"Astonishing that a man so wise can be so foolish," Fenwick said.

"Goodman Fenwick, you are in the presence of a priest of the Lady."

Fenwick reacted to Karl's warning with nothing more than an annoyed shrug. Christopher felt a great surge of relief. The Church he had joined demanded respect but did not inspire fear.

"Forgive my rustic humor, Pater," Fenwick said. "Is the quality of my stable acceptable?"

"It will do," Karl said. "But mind you, the Pater has other duties. You'll care for his horse when he cannot. You'll give it company and plenty of time in the yard."

"No problem there," Fenwick agreed. "My boys are entranced by the beast." Although a dozen horses lived in the barn, not even the huge dray horses could compete with the stallion for sheer presence. "For hay, five copper a day is considered fair, Pater." Karl nodded.

"For the barley and oats your great steed expects with his hay, say five copper a day again." Karl remained still, waiting for more. "Since you're buying the grain from my barn, I'll put in the stable, a paddock, and the loving care of my boys for nought." Fenwick looked sourer with every word, but Karl was finally satisfied.

This was a negotiation that Christopher was inadequate to contribute to, since he did not know the local currency or even how much he was being paid. "Can I afford that on a priest's salary?"

"Yes," Karl said, "although you will not eat much better than the horse."

Not a promising beginning. He would need money to make guns, a lot of money. One always did.

He almost asked how much he could sell the horse for, but he could not bring himself to do it. Although he had only a passing acquaintance with the equestrian arts, the animal felt more familiar and real than anything else he had encountered in this world. It was, at least, one thing he could relate too.

⚬⚬⚬

Back in the chapel, the soldiers had stacked and sorted his booty with admiration.

"Such fine arms will serve you well in the war," the older one said. "If we could send all our lads out so finely dressed—"

"Then they would be too burdened to run away," Karl finished for him. "And they would all die, instead of only half. Plate and horse only mark a man as a target."

Though the younger guard was at least a decade older than Karl, he advanced his argument hesitantly. "The Pater is ranked. Surely he can stand the attention of the enemy."

"Aye," Karl said. "It is what rank is for."

This was not the war Christopher had signed on for.

"Hold on," he said, "I thought I was going to be a healer."

Faren snorted. "You will be. Just from the front lines."

The chain-mail tunic that Karl had lent him was far more discreet. "How about a trade?" he said to Karl. "That junk for your chain mail."

Karl stared at him, flat-eyed, while the other soldiers guffawed.

Christopher had already apologized enough for one night, so he plowed ahead.

"I'm not joking. I don't want it." Never mind the constant reminder of Hobilar's disgrace; Christopher doubted he could even walk in all that metal. "Sell it off or something, and let me buy your chain mail."

Faren was chuckling. "You twist a sharp barb, Pater. Karl ceded his mail to you the instant you stepped into the dueling ring. It was a gift, as it had to be, else Karl would have staked you in the duel and thus been subject to forfeit if you lost. And I see now," Faren said, no longer smiling, "that you've played one on us as well. We can hardly claim a debt for your promotion, for the same reason."

"It does not release him from the draft," Karl said defiantly.

"No, of course not," Christopher said, shamed. "I didn't play anybody. I didn't even know the rules until Karl told me."

"I see your point," Karl said to Faren. "I pity the man who has him for a servant."

"That's what we have gods for," Faren said. "The nobles protect us from monsters, and the gods protect us from the noble-minded. By all means, sell it off. I would just as soon not have a White priest clanking around in plate armor."

"And the sword," the younger soldier said, clearly envious. "It is from Master Sigfried's forge in Kingsrock."

Hobilar's sword was the same style as Karl's, distinguished only by the brass crossguard instead of iron. Christopher leapt at the chance to repay some of his debt. "Karl, you take it. I already have a sword."

Karl hesitated. "I cannot accept arms from your hand, Pater. I am sworn to Krellyan's service. I do not want to create the image of a conflict of loyalty." It was obvious he wanted the sword, though. It was an excellent blade, made of even better steel than Christopher's katana.

"It's a gift, Karl," Christopher said. "Like the one you gave me."

Faren grunted in appreciation. "At least his cleverness runs both ways. True enough, Karl, you gave a gift without expectation of recompense. The Pater can gift you likewise."

In the most awkward movement Christopher had yet seen out of the guarded young man, Karl took Hobilar's sword and sheathed it. He handed his previous blade to the older of the guards, who examined it appraisingly before placing it in his sheath and passing his down to the younger, who in turn replaced his own.

Faren raised Hobilar's purse and eyed it critically. "This should cover your additional expenses, Sven, until Pater Christopher can draw on his account." He threw the leather pouch to the old man, who promptly handed it off to Helga.

"I have an account?" Christopher said.

"You do now," Faren answered. "The ransom for a first rank is three hundred and twenty gold, which we owe you for the miserable soul of that wretched failure of a knight." Christopher marveled at the exactness of the price, even though he didn't know what the numbers meant.

Faren had more instructions for Christopher. "You're subject to the rules of formal society now. In Church lands you need to show cause to force a duel, so you aren't completely exposed, yet I do not think we should put your tact and discretion to the test. In the village you probably won't meet any gentry to offend, so you'll stay here until you report for the draft. Pater Svengusta can finish your education."

Christopher was not quite ready to be abandoned. "I still need Karl to tell me the rest of the rules."

"Perhaps a wise investment of time," Faren said. "If you are willing, Goodman, I think myself and the guards adequate to contain our disarmed prisoner."

"I'll stay on for a few days," Karl said. "My business in town would profit from an absence." He turned to face Christopher. "Your villagers will want to celebrate. Let us join them to raise a pint to the Lord of Luck. The day is done, we're still alive, and there's a warm fire and cold beer. The god deserves his due."

<hr />

If Christopher had been paying, he was certain he wouldn't have drunk so much. But the tavern crowd found it in their hearts to toast their champion and would have none of his money. Which he still didn't have, he reflected drunkenly.

"I need to get some money," he whispered loudly to Karl as the three men staggered back to the chapel. Karl wasn't nearly as inebriated, despite having consumed twice as much, though he was still heavily impaired. Christopher was relieved to see that no cruelty lay under the man's ice. If anything, Karl threatened to turn maudlin.

"Don't we all," Karl muttered. Then he stopped just outside the chapel to relieve himself, leaving Christopher to hold up the semiconscious Svengusta alone.

"What's that yer doing, boy?" the old man slurred.

"Returning a shadow of the favor—" Karl stopped to catch his breath. "—the gods of war have showered upon me." Without his characteristic flatness, it wasn't funny.

"Let me show you how it's done," Svengusta said, and joined him against the chapel wall.

"You people are outrageous," Christopher said.

Svengusta yawned. "What's that, boy?"

Christopher realized he'd spoken in English. The language problem seemed insurmountable, so he went on into the chapel. The others eventually followed him into the main hall, where the flickering chandeliers reflected off the booty piled under the stern gaze of the frieze above the fireplace. The sight chilled Christopher, but Svengusta looked at the wooden god and chuckled.

"Been a while since he's seen that," the old man mumbled, dropped his winter cloak absently on the floor, and went into the living quarters.

"At least it's one of ours," Karl said, and followed.

Left to the last, Christopher couldn't think of anything clever to say.

Helga was still up, sewing by her light-stone. Svengusta fell into bed and was snoring within seconds. Christopher was struggling to get into his top bunk when he realized Karl was standing in the doorway, looking at him, waiting for something.

He looked around to see what Karl wanted, until his foggy brain kicked in. He wasn't that drunk.

"She doesn't belong to me," Christopher said.

Karl grinned—or tried to, but it came out as a leer—and shut the door. Christopher undressed and crawled into his bunk and tried to ignore the muted giggles from the next room.

The noise was not the problem. The problem was that he was still frightened of what he had done today, and of what he had been prepared to do. He needed someone to comfort him, someone to treat him the same even though everything was different now. But his bed held nothing but memories.

<hr />

"Get up, old man," Karl said, and he didn't mean Svengusta. Christopher blinked, rubbed his eyes and his aching temples.

It was morning already. He got dressed, came out into the kitchen where everyone else was eating breakfast, apparently unmarked by the excesses of last night.

Except Helga. Helga was positively glowing, a radiance that flared every time Karl spoke to her or glanced in her direction. His relief that he would not have to deal with Helga's crush was swiftly ruined by concern. He hoped Karl would let her down easy.

"I wish to apologize in advance, Pater. You asked me to teach you to ride," Karl said as they walked to the stable. "If I correct you, it is only for the sake of your horse."

"Of course," Christopher said. "And call me Christopher."

<hr />

Christopher had been on the back of a horse one or two times before. The experience had little in common with riding the magnificent Royal. Especially the way Karl defined riding. Karl's own horse, though smaller and more nimble than Royal, was barely able to keep up with the huge stallion. "Keep up" being the operative phrase, since under no circumstance would Royal allow the other horse to pull ahead of him.

They saw a lot of the surrounding countryside, or at least Karl and the horses did. Once they got to trotting, Christopher mostly saw shooting stars of pain from his spine. When Karl finally decided that any more saddle time would cause Christopher's ineptitude to risk injuring the horse, they turned back to the stable. Christopher was a limp rag that had been through the wringer too many times; Karl was unsparing, and left him to unsaddle and brush down the warhorse under the supervision of a stable boy. The boy was merciless in the way all ten-year-old experts are with incompetent adults.

Christopher waddled back to the chapel, grateful that the ground was no longer rising up to kick him in the butt with every step. Svengusta had a fire going in the main hall, with two hard benches pulled up. Apparently he felt religious education shouldn't take place in a nice, comfortable kitchen while Christopher lay on Helga's bed.

"And don't even think of healing those blisters yet," the old man admonished. "You've got to give your skin a chance to toughen up, otherwise it will be this bad every time."

Svengusta skipped the abstracts and went straight to the practical aspects of healing. Magic, yes, but also mundane things like diagnosis and emergency care. The goal was to determine who needed real magical healing and how to keep them alive until they could get it. The other goal was to not waste the high rank's time on things that weren't important. Christopher kept failing those quizzes. Absent antibiotics and MRI scanners, every symptom seemed important to him. The lesson went on during lunch, Svengusta howling with laughter through his porridge every time he fooled Christopher with a trick case.

Eventually Svengusta ran out of patience, and the party retired to the tavern. Christopher limited himself to one beer, partially out of a sense of poverty, although he seemed to be on Svengusta's tab, but also because the beer was thick, sour, and stringent. He wondered if lager had been invented yet.

He sat around the fire, listening to the men talk. Their discussions were completely unintelligible to him, being strictly limited to farming, husbandry, and weather.

On the way back to the chapel for dinner, a shadowy figure intercepted them. Christopher could feel the electric, automatic response in Karl, as his hand slipped down to his sword hilt. They were both wearing their swords, as always. They only took them off in the chapel and in the tavern, and even then they stayed within arm's reach. But the stalker was revealed by Svengusta's light-stone to be the young man from the chapel, pretty Dynae's handsome boyfriend.

"I wanted to thank you, Pater," he stammered out.

Christopher tried to think of something appropriate to say. "It was no more than she deserved."

"Dereth says when I come back from the war, he'll make me a smith. Then Dynae and I can get married," the boy offered for his approval.

"That sounds good." Christopher was not sure what else he was supposed to say. Then he thought of something. "When are you going to be drafted?"

"Next winter, Pater," the boy said mournfully. "And I'm afraid—I mean, I'm worried that I might never see Dynae again. Begging your pardon, Goodman," he said to Karl, "but I don't think I can measure up to you."

"It is not character you need, but luck," Karl said.

"Don't worry, lad," Svengusta said. "No one is expected to measure up to Karl. A single term is all we are asking, not two."

"Two?" Christopher said. "You were drafted twice?"

"The second time I volunteered," Karl said. "Afterwards, Saint Krellyan made me a civil servant, to prevent a third term. As Quarter-Master of the draft, I now send others to die in my place."

"Two terms, and you still don't have any rank?" That did not bode well for Christopher's plan of advancement.

"He was offered promotion," Svengusta said. "He turned it down."

"I have my reasons," Karl said. "They are not worth your time."

Christopher scratched his chin to cover over the awkward pause in the conversation. "Well," he said to the boy, "then you and I are to be comrades-in-arms. I'll be part of that draft, and I swear I'll do what I can to make sure you come back."

"Truth, Pater?" the boy asked with astonishment. "They drafted you? But you're old!"

Svengusta cackled at Christopher and shooed the boy off. "Go on to bed, son," he said. "He'll be here for the rest of the year for you to gawk at, but your chores won't do themselves on the morrow."

In the chapel, getting ready for sleep, Helga's doe eyes were like beacons. Karl sat on her bed and smiled at her while she stripped off his boots. Christopher and Svengusta retired to their own room, where they had to remove their boots by themselves. Disturbed by the quiet sounds in the next room, Christopher cast his arm over his bed, but there was nothing to hold.

7.

PUBLIC RELATIONS

The next several days passed swiftly, if not painlessly. Spooked by the duel and the upcoming draft, Christopher had become obsessed with sword practice. Karl was always willing and sparred with daunting relentlessness even after a hard day's ride. The regime left little time for self-reflection. What time there was, Christopher spent considering how out of shape he was compared to these people. Unending hard labor was a personal trainer no gym could hope to match. He was a bit relieved when Karl eventually decided that he should be heading back to town. Christopher decided to go along to see what he could buy. The village didn't even have a forge of its own.

"I will escort you for the day and keep you out of harm's way. But you no longer need me here in the village." Karl had conceded that Christopher now understood the basics of riding and just required practice. For his part, Karl already had learned half of what Christopher, the kendo black belt, could teach about swordsmanship. The other half he'd started out knowing.

Dawn had hardly happened by the time they were out of the village. Karl delayed for nothing so trivial as a hot breakfast. But the clear road gave Christopher a chance to talk. Not having to duck tree branches or dodge fences made conversation possible.

"Thank you for the fencing lessons," he said to Karl. "I've found them incredibly helpful."

Karl's shoulder twitched, which would have been a shrug on any less tightly wound man.

"Seriously," Christopher said, "I'm better than I ever was. I can't believe how much difference a week of practice has made."

"It is not practice," Karl said. "It is the rank."

Christopher paused, looking for the right words. Finally he gave up and said, "I don't know what you mean."

"Skill at arms is one of the privileges of rank," Karl explained, "and it gets worse. You want to know what it's like to be fifth rank? I'll close my eyes next time we spar. Then you'll know what a fifth rank feels when facing common men."

Healing, magic, and now skill? The benefits of tael seemed insurmountable. No ordinary man could hope to best someone with that kind of advantage. The only thing they could do against a foe like that would be to overwhelm him with numbers, at terrible cost.

"Are there fifth ranks in the war, then?"

"Yes, and worse," Karl said without emotion. "Let me explain the nature of war. The power of great rank is such that whoever strikes first usually wins. Thus, a battle is a game of hide-and-seek between ranks. The commoners are cast onto the field like sounding stones, to reveal the position of the enemy powers. They do this by dying. To see a crowd of men clashing together with steel means nothing; to see bodies exploding in pieces signifies the presence of rank."

Trying to overwhelm super-swordsmen with mass formations wouldn't work any better than cavalry charges had against machine guns. "What about bows?" Christopher asked. "Can't you just get a bunch of archers to shoot the high ranks to death from a safe distance?"

"Bows are unpopular. Slay a foe at range, and someone else might take his head and his tael before you can claim it.

"Also, bows are expensive," Karl added, sourly. "The Saint will spend thirty gold to equip each boy called to the draft. A crossbow costs thirty-five."

Christopher was alarmed to realize how much his horse and sword would stand out. "What do they get, then?"

Karl barked what might have been a laugh. "That's the business I've been avoiding. Traditionally, each boy is given a spear, a shield, a helm, and a studded tunic." Noticing Christopher's questioning look, he explained. "Studded is leather armor with metal discs sewn in, to give the pretension of a chance to turn a sharp blade."

"Traditionally?"

"Studs are expensive. The armorers charge Krellyan twenty gold for each suit. Replacing it with plain leather would save fifteen gold per boy. With the money saved, Krellyan could send another priest out with the draftees. An extra healer is going to save a lot more lives than that stupid, useless armor."

"So, why not send them out with leather?" Christopher asked. It seemed like an innocent question.

"What? You would send our boys naked to the war?" Karl snarled. "The people wouldn't stand for it. They think the armor helps. They think it protects the boys. You can't tell them it only protects their own pride, to pretend that they are not sacrificing their sons without hope. To suggest such a thing would be unthinkable. Only an immensely popular man could change our vaunted tradition, and he wouldn't be very popular afterward."

A sad realization crept into Christopher's mind. "So what Krellyan needs is a war hero. A man so concerned with the safety of his fellow soldiers that he'd sacrifice his popularity. But of course, he has to have lots of experience on the battlefield, so people believe he knows what he's talking about. He has to have the personal bravery to have done what he's asking others to do. And of course he has to be a commoner if he's going to take something away from the commoners. Where do you suppose he could find such a man?"

They rode in silence for a while.

"Krellyan is a hard master," Christopher said softly. No wonder Karl took no notice of his popularity. He expected it to be a temporary condition.

Karl snorted. "Not as hard as I would be. I'd send them out with nothing but slings and spears. The rest of it's useless, anyway. Don't you see," Karl said with a deep and inexhaustible bitterness, "they're *right*. Commoners really are as useless as stones. If they bunch up in pike squares, one spell kills them all. If they spread out with bows, the knights mow them down like blades of grass. All they can do is die, preferably loudly, and hope someone important noticed."

Christopher could not share Karl's defeatism. Hobilar's enhanced vitality had only stopped a few blows from a stick; it would count for nothing in the teeth of a cannon. Gunpowder here would have the same effect on the nobility as it had on Earth.

"When are you going to give the armorers the bad news?" Christopher asked, wanting to know how long he had to convince them to spend it on something new.

"As late as possible, so they can't do anything about it. When I finally give out the contracts for the leather, too late for the studding to be done, I'll be pilloried in every town as incompetent, dishonorable, and insensitive to boot. Then Krellyan will pacify them by sending out a third priest."

Christopher suddenly understood why he was being told all this. The depth of Krellyan's opportunism was made clear. "I'm the third priest, aren't I?"

Karl gave him a grin that challenged the snowy fields for the title of "wintry." "You're sharper than a slice of bread, Pater. When the complaints have reached their limit, the Saint will placate the people with your head, and you will be the darling of the hour."

"And you'll be Karl the screw-up instead of Karl the brave," Christopher said.

"If you save one boy's life," Karl grated, "I'll count the trade fairly done."

Christopher was hoping to save a lot of lives. He had no idea who the enemy was, but if the war had lasted all of Cardinal Faren's life, then the two sides must be evenly matched. Christopher was pretty sure he could tilt the balance.

On the other hand, tradition was a strong force, as evidenced by the machinations the Saint and Karl were going through to change the simplest of arrangements. Christopher would need vast quantities of genius, diplomacy, and money to revolutionize this society in under a year. What he had was a recipe for gunpowder from a TV show, the ability to insult people without speaking their language, and the change in his pockets.

He hadn't had a chance to take stock of his resources yet. There always seemed to be something more important to do, like avoid being stabbed to death. Here, on the placid ride to town on the gentle back of the broad, strong horse, he dug under his borrowed, tattered cloak and priestly robes to see what he had brought with him.

The answer was not much. Two quarters and a key. The shiny quarters were only nickel cladding over copper. Passing them off as silver pieces would be an act of counterfeiting, and he had committed enough crimes already.

His truck key was aluminum, which might be worth something, if they knew what aluminum was. He seemed to recall it was valuable in Napoleon's day, but he didn't know if medieval smiths even knew of its existence.

"Who would be interested in curiosities from other worlds?"

Karl's face darkened.

"No one sane."

Popularizing technology might be harder than he thought.

"That is to say," Karl continued, "only a wizard, and you would be foolish to deal with them at all. I would suggest selling it to the first magician you see, at whatever price he offers, and forgetting about it. Talk of other worlds can only lead to trouble."

"Why is that?" Christopher asked.

"Because only monsters live in the outer planes, and not by choice. They are banished there, by the powers of the gods, constantly plotting and scheming to trick some poor mortal into opening a pathway here so they may slaughter and plunder."

Saint Krellyan seemed to have been proven right. Chatting about the ancestral home of Man was not likely to win him any friends or influence.

"It's just something I picked up in my travels," Christopher said. "But if you think it's dangerous, then a wizard might think it's valuable."

"You are a priest of the White now," Karl said. "You cannot misrepresent the facts, even by omission. Do not spoil your affiliation before you have discharged your duties to the army."

Christopher wanted to ask what he meant, but that would likely lead to Karl asking him why he didn't already know, and that might lead to questions Christopher didn't want to answer, especially if he couldn't dissemble. Questions like where he and the strange metal had come from in the first place.

"Fair enough," he said.

Karl pursed his lips, as if he had said too much already. Christopher felt a twinge of sympathy. It was clearly not normal for the young commoner to spend so much time explaining basic facts to an older, ranked priest. It must disturb his view of the world.

But then, Christopher had his own disquiets. Wracking poverty on an alien world was only one of them. His thumb went to his last asset, idly spinning it on his finger. A plain gold wedding band. It was the only physical link he had to his wife and the life he had left behind.

A life in disarray by now. How long had he been here? By now they would have found his truck abandoned at the river, his dogs waiting patiently by its side. The police would be unsympathetic; only another husband run off in the middle of the night. She would not believe that. She would wait for him, as she had for all the long years before they met. As he had waited, unaware of what he was waiting for until it burst on him like a surprise party in a darkened room, and afterwards all was chaos and joy.

And now she would sleep in a cold bed, without even knowing the reason why. The pain of it struck at his heart with the force of an ax. By comparison Hobilar's many hurts had been mere pinpricks. He doubled over, clutching at the pommel of the saddle in impotent rage. He would suffer a thousand more cuts, cripple a thousand more Hobilars if he had to.

"Are you unwell?" Karl asked from across the road.

"My apologies," Christopher answered. "I was thinking of the difficulties ahead."

"Fair enough," Karl said.

After they had stabled, watered, fed, and rubbed down their horses—a horse wasn't like a car you could just park—they went into the church. Karl turned Christopher over to a lanky young man who introduced himself as Pater Stephram.

"If you wish to draw on your account," Stephram told him, "you will need to speak to the Vicar Rana. Be warned that while you consider the money to be your own to spend as you like, the Vicar may have other ideas."

A troublesome notion. Christopher frowned, and Stephram goodnaturedly offered an explanation.

"Some of us thought to have a celebratory dinner, in honor of the return of the Church of Marcius. When we went to apply for an advance on our salary, the Vicar denied us and set us to double watchhours as well."

"I'm sorry," Christopher said.

"You have no need to apologize for that," the young man said graciously. "Although when the girls caught sight of Hobilar and his maimed arm, they lost their taste for merriment. So the evening would have been futile."

By this time they had passed several other white-robed members of the Church, whose average age seemed about half of Christopher's. This included at least one attractive young woman who captured Stephram's discreet gaze long enough to interrupt their conversation. The ambience was much like being back in college.

At least until his fellow priests and priestesses caught sight of his sword. Then their smiles turned uncertain. Christopher was surprised the first few times, because he had forgotten he was wearing the thing. The realization that he was comfortable enough with the sword to forget it made him no happier.

Stephram abandoned Christopher at the Vicar's office. Briefly Christopher considered retreating until he could divest himself of the sword, but it was too late. Stephram had opened the door and waved him inside.

The Vicar was the stout woman he had seen on his first trip to the church. She had been alarmed to see him then; now she seemed positively wary.

"I'm sorry," he said, indicating his sword with an open-handed gesture.

"You need not apologize for that," she answered. "It is the symbol of your devotion. But if you are looking for faults to apologize for, I can give you a definite, if inexhaustive, list."

Christopher winced. "I didn't mean to cripple him."

"Again you apologize for the wrong reason. Hobilar must look to Krellyan for succor now, and that may be the only thing that can draw that man into the light."

"What should I apologize for?"

"Dueling in the first place, and winning in the second. Had you lost, Krellyan would have made good your ransom, as he has too much invested in you already. Hobilar would be satisfied instead of enraged, the townsfolk would soon forget the affair instead of gossiping day and night, and the world would roll on undisturbed. Instead you lay your stiff neck in front of the wagon of the world like a log, either to jolt us all or see it crushed."

Christopher wanted to apologize again, but he bit his tongue. He was planning on putting a lot more bumps in the road. He changed the subject instead.

"I was wondering if I could withdraw some money against my salary."

"Why would the Church of the Bright Lady pay a priest of Marcius a salary?"

He found himself gritting his teeth and forced his jaw to relax.

"How am I to survive, then?"

"You have funds," she answered. "At our expense, since we will never recover the money from Hobilar. In any case you need only survive until the end of the year. Then the King will feed and clothe you, although admittedly not in the best style."

Christopher had other plans for that money. He stood, fuming silently.

"Understand," the Vicar said, "I could feed a peasant family for a decade on what Krellyan has given you for Hobilar's ransom. Long enough for a boy to grow into a farmer, or a girl to become a wife. If you wish to parade around in horse and armor, you will find no sympathy from me."

She stared back at him, defying him to refute her logic.

But he couldn't.

"I understand," he said. "Still, I need money." The horse would need to be fed, at the very least.

"Of course," she said. "You will not want to live solely off of Svengusta's charity."

There was that, too.

From a drawer Rana produced a fistful of implements. She opened a glass inkwell and stirred it thoroughly with a round-ended slotted stick. Setting this aside on a bit of cloth already stained with ink, she smoothed out a slip of paper, dipped a quill, and wrote in deft looping strokes, returning to the inkwell after every few words. When she was finished writing, she blew gently on the paper while packing away her tools.

Christopher watched in grave fascination, entranced by the incredible effort involved in such a simple task. This was the world he lived in now.

"Take this to the vault clerk. Be wary. Should you lose it to carelessness or thievery, I will not make good your loss."

He went out into the hall, wondering at her words. They would seem obvious. Karl's admonishment came back to him: the priests of the White were exacting.

A cleaning woman directed him deeper into the church, where he eventually found a bored guard and a clerk behind an iron grate. The clerk took his receipt and gave him twenty-five gold coins.

The coins were smaller than a dime, though thicker. They had ridged edges, implying a somewhat advanced minting technology, and a bearded, crowned face stamped on one side. Christopher couldn't see any denominations or script. Not that a date would mean anything to him.

Fenwick the stable-master had said the horse would need ten copper a day. That didn't mean anything to him either.

"How many coppers to a gold?" he asked.

The clerk looked at him in surprise. "Ten by ten, as it always has been, Pater. Copper to silver, silver to gold."

"It's only five tael to the gold," the guard said.

The clerk grimaced. "You and I need never worry about the price of tael."

Christopher looked down at his coins in dismay. Just feeding the horse would cost forty gold a year. Rana had implied an entire peasant family could live off of that.

Walking back to the stables, Christopher tried to face the fact that the horse might be a luxury he couldn't afford. When he reached Royal's stall, the horse greeted him with a whinny and nosed affectionately at his shoulder.

Karl came into the stable, looking for him. "Would you like to go into town and sell this now?"

Christopher's stomach sank, but Karl was lifting one of the saddlebags packed with Hobilar's ridiculous armor.

"You bet," Christopher said with relief. He grabbed the other bag and slung it over his shoulder. A dozen steps reaffirmed his decision to sell the weighty stuff. "Where do we go?" he asked, hoping the answer was "not very far."

"Only one shop in town works in plate. So we must call on Senior Palek."

Karl strode through the town like a bulldozer, leaving little time for sightseeing. The streets were narrow and stuffed with unpredictable buildings, houses, barns, and workshops all freely intermingled. At least one building looked suspiciously like a grain silo. Children and livestock played in the streets, paying no particular attention to the two armed men.

Palek's forge was a busy place, with three men hard at work and a pair of apprentices running errands. The forge was covered only by a slatted roof, with three open walls. The smith was shirtless despite the weather. Palek, a solid, compact man with a black beard and bulging muscles, pounded a sheet of steel on an anvil, wearing a leather apron and a sheen of sweat.

"Senior Palek," Karl said, after they had been ignored for a bit.

"Goodman," Palek said. "Have you come to buy?"

Karl had to wait before answering, while Palek struck three times at his metal.

"We've come to sell. The Pater has a suit of armor he does not fancy." Karl's toe nudged the saddle bags where they sat in the dirt.

The smith set his hammer down. "Not of his quality, perhaps?"

Karl's eyes narrowed. "The quality is not an issue. In any case it would not fit him."

Palek turned to Christopher. "Is it true you are marked for the draft?"

Christopher nodded.

"Then perhaps you wish to reconsider. You will not bemoan steel between your flesh and the enemy on the battlefield. I can refit it for you, Pater, or if you like, craft new pieces to your order."

"Um, no thanks." Christopher had come here to raise money, not spend it. "I don't think heavy armor is that valuable. I plan to do a lot of running away."

Palek's face, never glowing, now darkened like a banked fire.

"I can only give you one hundred gold," he said, and turned back to his anvil.

"What?" Karl exclaimed. "Hobilar paid you at least six!"

Palek grunted. "The Pater crippled my best customer and now denigrates my craft. I find myself in an ungenerous mood."

"I could get three hundred for it in Kingsrock," Karl said.

"This is not Kingsrock, Goodman."

Wordlessly Karl hefted both saddle bags from the floor and walked away. Christopher had no choice but to follow him out into the wintry streets again.

"Is it really worth that much?" Christopher asked. He'd felt the smith was within his rights to offer so little. There couldn't be much of a market for such elaborate work: the only other armor he had seen was chain mail and helmets.

"Possibly," Karl said, "but Kingsrock is crawling with prickly nobles on the lookout for an easy profit. You would be challenged to a dozen duels within the hour."

Briefly, very briefly, Christopher considered making a career as a duelist. It would be the quickest way to amass money in this brutal world.

Then common sense, and the memory of the gut-twisting fear all three times he had faced Hobilar, reasserted itself.

Karl had noticed his flight of fancy.

"Don't even think it. The Saint will not let you risk yourself so freely. You still owe him three years as a healer."

"Thanks for the vote of confidence," Christopher said, meaning it as a joke.

Karl shook his head. "You are a novice priest. You would be challenged by battle-hardened knights. None of whom would be foolish enough to let you cast two spells before engaging. No one would bet on your victory at any odds."

"So Hobilar . . ." Christopher couldn't finish the sentence. Apparently he had been in more danger than he had known.

"Hobilar was an idiot," Karl said. "Even so, I counted on only your survival."

"Could you take this junk to Kingsrock and sell it for me?" Christopher asked. "I'll give you a cut. Say, ten percent?"

Karl peered at him, as if he were seeing him for the first time. "Yes, if you like, Pater. I can have the chain mail repaired, as well."

"That would be great," Christopher said. "And call me Christopher."

8.

WINDOW SHOPPING

Christopher still wanted to talk to a smith, so after Karl disappeared down the long road to the east, Christopher asked for directions to Dereth's. Unwilling to trust his horsemanship around dogs and children, he left the high-tempered stallion in the stall and walked through the mud and snow that passed for streets.

When he passed a glass-fronted shop, with a neatly arranged bay window display, he stepped inside for a moment to get out of the cold. The tinkle of the bell as he opened the door, the scent of wax and incense, the soft glow of the overhead lights, were so familiar that he forgot what planet he was on until his sword banged against a table leg.

The shop-girl, a striking young woman dressed in a provocative outfit of dark-blue silk, eyed Christopher with all the contempt of a Saks clerk staring at a homeless bum. Christopher started to mutter his apologies but forgot what he was going to say when he realized exactly what was on display in the store window.

Books.

The rest of the store was a magpie's nest of colored bottles, indescribable instruments, and odds and ends as varied as a bag of feathers and a cage of live crickets. But the books were only in the window display.

He was drawn to the window, mesmerized by what knowledge he might find, until he picked up a book and thumbed through it. It was bound in leather, with heavy pages of neatly trimmed parchment.

It was also completely blank. All of the books were.

What kind of shop sold empty books?

He turned to look quizzically at the clerk, but she was watching him with such alarmed puzzlement that he couldn't bring himself to ask what obviously would be a stupid question. Instead, he put the book down and moved to the next shelf.

Here he found paper, stiff, heavy, and eggshell white. He thumbed through a sheaf for a minute before realizing what was wrong. There wasn't enough of it. The whole shelf held a few dozen sheets of letter-sized paper, in small stacks. A single ream of copier paper would put the entire store to shame.

"If you please, lord," the clerk said. Christopher jerked his hand away, like a schoolkid caught reading magazines in the corner store.

"How much?" he asked.

"The standard rate," she answered, "Five sheets for two gold."

He stared at her in amazement.

"You will not have reason to complain of its quality. I adhere to the accepted formula. I collect the materials from virgin plant and earth, and only at the most auspicious times. Each sheet is made on a separate day, so that no contagion occurs. You may be assured that our paper is suitable for either arcane or divine purposes."

Simple lack of industrial process wasn't enough. No, they had to go and add sheer superstition.

"What if I didn't want magical paper? What if I just wanted a thousand sheets of plain old wrapping paper?"

She arched her eyebrows in disdain.

"Master Flayn would not deign to set aside guild regulations. Worse, he would charge you double for an order of such magnitude."

Christopher stepped away from the paper, momentarily dazed by the absurdity, and found himself in front of a shelf of tiny bottles filled with colored powders. They were labeled with curious symbols, which suggested they were chemicals rather than soap powders or seasonings. These symbols were sharp and angular, but unlike the Celestial text they did not change in front of his eyes and suddenly reveal their meaning. He looked to the clerk for help.

She wasn't there to be helpful. "If you cannot read alchemical script, it seems unlikely you could profit from alchemical supplies."

"Just tell me which one is sulfur."

She explained slowly and carefully. "The yellow one."

There was, in fact, only one bottle of pale-yellow powder. With a resigned sigh, Christopher picked it up.

"How much?"

"Two gold, or one if you supply your own vial."

There wasn't more than an ounce in the bottle. Carbon would be free, scraped from any fireplace; he knew where to get potassium nitrate for the mere cost of his dignity. But he would need sulfur by the pound, and at this price gunpowder would be too valuable to burn.

It didn't seem rational. The priests and the peasants treated a gold coin as valuable, yet it wouldn't buy hardly anything in this shop. It was as if he had stumbled into a different world.

Which reminded him. He retrieved the truck key from his pocket and approached the counter.

The girl retreated from his approach until she bumped into the wall, eyes locked on the key in fear.

"Um," Christopher said. "I was wondering if I could trade this." He put the key on the counter. The girl started breathing again.

"I cannot bargain on Master Flayn's behalf. If you would but wait a moment." She slipped through a curtain, leaving Christopher uncomfortably alone.

After enough time that he had to twice stop himself from drumming his fingers on the counter, the girl returned, followed by a thin man in indigo robes with flowing black hair and a nose crooked in permanent disdain.

The girl reached for the key but hesitated; the man gave her a sharp glance, and she snatched it from the countertop. When nothing happened, she handed the key to the man in ill-concealed relief.

"It's just a key," Christopher said.

"To what?" the man, evidently Master Flayn, snapped in a tone as arch as his nose.

"Nothing useful now," Christopher admitted, "but I thought you might be interested in the rare material."

"You claim this is true-silver?" Before Christopher could reply, Flayn forcefully pressed the key on the countertop. "It is naught but dross." Flayn contemptuously tossed the bent key to Christopher's side of the counter.

"Hey!" Christopher picked up the ruined key and stared at it. "It's aluminum."

"I have never heard of such a substance."

"That's how rare it is."

"Indeed. So rare as to have no known value."

"How about an exchange? What I really want is a barrel of sulfur."

Flayn glared in outrage. "You want immense quantities of my finest material components in exchange for a lump of worthless tin? Produce gold or get out of my shop."

Christopher returned the glare. "You bent my key."

"I provided you with a professional assessment at no cost. I now revise that decision and demand the full price of one hundred gold."

Overcome with frustration, Christopher shot back. "Nothing in this shop is worth gold, least of all your stupid opinions."

His face a mask of ice over a boiling fury, Flayn lifted his hand and pointed to the door.

"Go."

Christopher retreated in defeat. Outside, in the cold, he stood and considered the disastrous encounter. It did not seem entirely commensurate with his actions.

Behind him the door opened, and the clerk stepped out, arms folded against the chill. She glanced over her shoulder into the empty shop before speaking to him.

"You must forgive Master Flayn his temper. The wizards exist only at the sufferance of your Church, and he for one finds the strictures cloying. But as the only licensed paper-seller in town, he cannot refuse you."

"At those prices?" Christopher shook his head.

She pursed her lips. "As a mere apprentice, I occasionally produce materials not suitable for sale. I might be persuaded to share some of those, for purely nonofficial uses."

"That doesn't sound . . . regulation."

"I am only an apprentice. Guild rules do not apply to me. Still, discretion would be necessary or I would suffer Flayn's disapproval."

It sounded like she was risking a lot more than her boss's anger. "If you start breaking guild rules as an apprentice, I don't think they're ever going to let you in."

For the first time her face revealed true emotion, a bright and bitter hurt.

"I do not think Flayn ever intends to promote me. He gains too much from having an apprentice. I work for nothing, and—" she stopped abruptly.

Christopher could guess the rest. This time there was nothing he could do. Flayn might be taking advantage, but he wasn't committing a crime. This woman was far too clever to be forced by mere threats.

"He says I am not ready for advancement. But when he tires of me, I shall be pronounced unfit and he will take another foolish girl's guild fee with promises and flattery."

"What can I do about it?"

"Buy my apprenticeship. As Fae the apprentice, I am constrained; as Fae the free craftsman, I will provide you paper and sulfur at prices you find acceptable."

Christopher wasn't sure he could keep a horse. A pretty young clerk had to be a luxury he couldn't afford. But either her or Flayn's chemistry was necessary.

"How much would it cost?"

She was surprised. "One hundred and sixty gold, of course. And then at least eighty a year in salary."

That was a lot of money. Fae saw his dismay and started withdrawing, folding inwardly. He spoke quickly before she could turn back into the shop.

"It will take me some time to raise the money. I might need more than just paper and sulfur. I assume you can read and write. Can you do math?"

"Somewhat," she said. "Though Flayn did not teach me the advanced formulas."

He didn't know what that meant, but he was pretty sure it didn't mean calculus.

"I can't teach you magic," Christopher told her, "but I can teach you things Flayn never dreamed of. Will that be enough?"

"Not if I thought I could be a wizard," she admitted, "but I no longer believe that lie."

Dereth's forge did nothing to inspire him. It was little more than an anvil under a lean-to. Palek's forge at least had workers, which had made the place feel like industry. Dereth's lonely little workshop looked like a hobby. Snow drifted over the unfired hearth.

Dereth answered his knock with a quizzical look and two small children peeping out behind him.

"Greetings, Pater. What can I do for you?"

"I wanted to talk shop. There are some things I'd like made."

"Of course, Pater." Dereth, bare-shouldered, stepped out of the house and went to the forge area, apparently unaware that it was freezing outside. Christopher sighed and followed him.

"Doesn't look like you've been working much," he said, more as a conversation starter than a well-considered comment.

"No," Dereth said. "I've had only enough to keep us from starving. A consequence of ill-chosen words. But once Goodman Karl releases the contracts, I'll be busy enough."

Christopher bit his lip. As much as he wanted to warn Dereth that there would be no armor contracts this year, he didn't want to annoy Karl more. Also, he wasn't sure how to explain that the money Dereth would have made had been spent on making him a priest.

"Have you thought about—branching out? For instance, I could use some heavy-cast steel pipe." It was the best way he could think of to describe a cannon barrel.

"I only work in iron, Pater. For steel you should see the Seniors."

"I have, but they don't seem to like seeing me."

Dereth chuckled in commiseration.

"What if I showed you how to make steel?" Christopher pressed. Some half-remembered college professor had felt it necessary to describe the Bessemer process, on the theory that his mechanical engineering students should know where the steel they used came from. It couldn't be that hard to figure out the details, once you knew the secret. And the secret was simple: the right amount of carbon in the iron, neither too much nor too little. Ancient smiths had either burned it off or ignored it altogether; the concept of moderation instead of purity was modern.

"Assuming you could do so without violating any guild secrets, regulations, or laws, what would be the end? No one would buy steel from us. No one would believe that a priest knew how to make steel in the first place." From the way he said it, Christopher could tell that Dereth numbered himself among that group.

"I'm a priest of War," Christopher said. "War requires weapons, and weapons require steel. The army will buy our steel."

"Then you have won over Goodman Karl? A second victory, even more impressive than defeating Horrible Hobilar."

"Well—not yet. But I'm hoping."

"You have high hopes, then," Dereth said. "I will gladly share them. But I must feed my family, as well as my forge." The smith poked around in the near-empty buckets of charcoal and raw ore. Christopher knew where charcoal came from; cut down a forest and burn it in a hole in the ground. He had an ax, and he knew where to find trees.

"Where does the ore come from?"

"The Old Bog, of course."

Christopher had been hoping for a mine, with rich veins of easily refined ore. Boiling a bog until it yielded up its red treasure was inefficient—which meant expensive.

Apparently Dereth could read the disappointment on his face.

"It's not so bad as that. I'll be the one digging in it."

A smith digging his own ore? The concept defined inefficiency.

"Maybe I should take a look at this bog," Christopher said. Maybe he could work some industrial magic there.

"Just head north, to the edge of town. You can't miss it."

<hr/>

He almost did, though, because it was so pathetic. A handful of dispirited apprentices mucked about in shallow pits in the ground, breaking up the frozen earth. At first glance he had thought they were gardeners.

"Wouldn't that be easier in summer?" he asked one of them.

"Journeyman says it builds strength," the young man replied bitterly.

"Ha!" laughed one of the other young men. "Journeyman says stop looking at my daughter, more likely."

"Bugger off, Trane, you're out here too."

They weren't working together. Each apprentice was filling his own wheelbarrow. At least the dirt was red, which implied it was higher quality than he had feared.

"What if I wanted to buy some of that?" he asked.

"Don't you have enough dirt?" the one called Trane said with a leer, and the others laughed.

"Haha. But I want this dirt now."

"Go see Tom, then," another said. "He'll even dig your night-soil for you, if you pay him." The apprentice jerked his thumb, pointing farther north, and went back to work.

The bog followed the river up and to the right, and disappointment followed with it. A solitary young man was waist-deep in a hole in the ground, shoveling black shale. He seemed poorer than others, dressed in clothes almost as shabby as Christopher's cast-offs. But he was whistling.

"Greetings, Pater," he said cheerfully. "Come to dig some more dirt?"

Christopher smiled lamely. "Has everyone heard about my hobby, then?"

"As the only professional digger in the county, I must confess I paid unusual attention to the matter," the man replied. He was young, a little over twenty or so, and didn't stop shoveling to talk.

"Now that's a profession I haven't encountered yet."

"I'm a second son," the young man said. When that didn't seem sufficient, he added, "Of a farmer." Seeing Christopher's continued blankness, he sighed and explained, "My older brother was graceless enough to survive the draft."

It finally clicked for Christopher. "So you have no farm to inherit."

"Now I heard you were a sharp one, but I didn't expect this," the man said innocently.

Faced with relentless impertinence, Christopher had to laugh. It was nice that wearing a sword didn't intimidate everyone. Actually, so far it hadn't done anything but annoy people. Christopher suspected that was more his fault than the sword's.

"I was told you could sell me some ore."

Tom glanced at him sharply and chose his next words with care.

"I doubt that very much, Pater. Digging iron ore is a craft secret."

"Then what are you digging for?"

"Ah, now that's the very question I have often asked myself. Why dig and delve for ungrateful townies? Why muck out their garderobes and stables? They say there's plenty of good land out in the Marches. Farms for the taking, if you don't mind the occasional band of slavering ulvenmen. So what keeps young Tom here, in muck up to his knees, doing dirty jobs for lazy townsmen?"

Christopher wasn't completely clueless. He knew the answer to this one without being told.

"A woman, no doubt."

Tom stopped shoveling and looked at Christopher with appreciation. "Sharp indeed, Pater. Young Tom Fool, I am. Fool for falling in love with a town girl with a harpy for a mother and an ogre for a father. Pleased to meet you." He tipped his hat, which was a sorry-looking affair that appeared to be two mangy squirrels locked in a deadly grapple.

"Who owns this—" Christopher couldn't call it a mine, as it was just a bunch of holes in the ground, "—this field?"

"The Saint does, Pater, and the coal's free to all who dig it. It's not valuable, like, say, wood or grass. So I dig when others won't and sell it to smiths who don't feel like punishing their apprentices."

"Coal?" Of course. Tom's wheelbarrow was loaded with black, not red. "You're digging coal?" Christopher could hardly believe his good luck.

"That I am. Sometimes the smiths will burn it, as it's cheaper than charcoal, though it's a foul choking to do so."

Christopher scooped up a handful of the soft rock. Poor bituminous, rather than good hard clean Pennsylvania anthracite. It was carbon that made it burn, and sulfur that made it dirty.

Coincidentally, Christopher had need of both.

On impulse he took a gold coin out of his purse and tossed it to the young man.

Tom snatched it out of the air and whistled. "That's a lot of coal. I deliver a wheelbarrow to town for three coppers."

"I need a barrow delivered to Burseberry village. Will that cover it?"

"A long walk, but Tom Fool isn't a fool for nothing." He winked and tapped his head with the coin.

Christopher laughed. "You can take your time to deliver it."

Tom looked a little relieved and then asked carefully, "Only one, Pater?"

"For now. I'll want more coal later, and no, I won't be paying a gold a wheelbarrow then. But I need this one for, um, research."

"So you're a wizard, then."

"No," Christopher corrected him, slightly alarmed. "I'm a priest."

"You're a man with hard gold and loose pockets," Tom replied with a good-natured shrug. "You can call yourself the Queen of Niflehiem for all I care."

Tom dug into his hole with renewed zeal, and Christopher turned back towards town with a more hopeful step. His myriad problems had been reduced to a single vector. Now all he needed was an unlimited supply of gold.

<hr />

The ride back to Burseberry was discomfiting in its mundanity. The horse snorted and steamed in the cold air; the empty road and snow-covered fields simply plain, a picture postcard of a country lane. Absent people, the world seemed too ordinary. It was momentarily impossible for him to believe that he was on an alien world, surrounded by magic, and fighting for his life.

Only when he saw the smoke from the village, and his stomach rumbled at even the thought of porridge, did the sense of unreality return, gradually fading from conscious awareness as he turned his horse over to one of Fenwick's boys and quick-marched back to the chapel before the stable-master could put in an appearance and ask for the money he was due.

Helga sent him off to the tavern to join Svengusta until dinner with serene confidence, the girlish flirtations entirely vanished. Although her transformation had been coterminous with his increase in status from poor, mute beggar to ranked priest, he didn't think that was the cause. Safely ensconced in the tavern, drink in hand, he brought it up.

"Explain Helga to me." He interrupted the old man's laughter: "I know, she's a woman, a creature of ineffable mystery and all that, but I don't understand what happened between her and Karl."

"Good gods, boy, if you don't understand that, I don't know where to begin!" Svengusta laughed so hard beer came out his nose.

Christopher had to wait while the old man sneezed between gales of laughter. "Ha ha. Seriously, I don't understand. Is she in love with him?"

"What woman isn't? He's the bravest of the brave, the best of the best. Doubly tested, you know."

"Is he going to break her heart?" Christopher pressed.

"How do you mean?" Svengusta asked, genuinely confused.

"Is he going to come back?"

"Probably." Svengusta laughed. "You seem to have taken his fancy."

"I mean, is he going to come back to Helga?"

"No, he's not going to marry her. Why would he?"

"But what if she gets pregnant?"

Svengusta put down his beer. "I can see you're truly troubled. Relax, Brother. Haven't you seen Helga lately? She glows. Did you miss that?"

No, Christopher had to admit, she'd been the paragon of happiness.

"Karl made her. She went from being the village orphan to a woman of society in a week. She used to pine to me that the local boys paid her no attention. Now she won't give them the time of day unless they've got a beard. She's had a real man, you see. And a child? A child proves she's fertile. No good man would balk to raise a daughter or two. And if she were to have a son off of Karl, she could have her pick of husbands. Who wouldn't want a whelp of his to call your own?"

"Helga's an orphan? How could she lose her parents if you can bring people from the dead?"

Svengusta shook his head. "Reviving the dead is not done lightly. It consumes a hundred tael with no guarantee of success. Peasants do not expect to be revived. Even knights must be rich or favored by their lord to be brought back. In Helga's case, none of these mattered."

The old man took a drink of his beer, held up his hand to fore-stall questions. "Patience, Brother. I need strength for this next part. A decade ago the ulvenmen overran the March of Carrhill. The town stood against their assault until reinforcements drove the monsters off, but the countryside was devastated. Most folk didn't have enough warning to flee. The ulvenmen slaughtered, burned, and took heads. And they took whole bodies, like Helga's parents, for their victuals. Helga was among a train of children captured for provender, being carted back to wherever the fiends come from. She was rescued by our King, the Lady bless him."

Svengusta stopped to take another drink and steer himself back to the unpleasant topic. "The children were dispersed throughout the realm, to families that could take them. Helga was sent to my village, but she never got along that well with her adopted mother, and so when she turned twelve and my last house-girl got married, she moved in and took over the job.

"But enough of the past," the old man said. "She's riding high now. She's a good woman, and sooner or later some clever fellow will notice, and then I'll have to find a new girl to cook for me. Just as soon you will leave, and I'll have to find a new novice to trouble me. In the end, they all leave."

Before Christopher could respond, Svengusta called for another round and soon had the tavern patrons singing a rough, rude song.

9.

A FLOCK OF GULLS

In the morning he threw himself into his new career, attacking the manure pile with shovel and pickax, and staggered home with a barrel of filth and a head full of plans. Not knowing how to best refine his ingredients or even precisely what proportions to combine them in, he would reduce the problem through brute force: by trying everything he could think of and keeping what worked. Thus was science born.

Science first had to contend with the housemaid, however. Helga took one whiff and drew a bath. The process was unbelievably difficult, requiring repeated trips to the frozen well with bucket and ax, and the amount of firewood involved was horrifying to the man who had to split it.

Helga poured a final kettle of steaming water into the half-barrel laid out in the kitchen and looked at him expectantly. He waited for her to leave, before realizing there was nowhere for her to go. There were, after all, only three rooms in the entire building.

Svengusta intervened. "Why don't you run up to the Widow Fenly's and buy some apples? You can make us a pie for tonight."

Excited at the chance to bake, Helga bundled herself in several layers and bustled off.

"City-bred, I suppose," Svengusta said, handing him a bar of soft soap and a dishrag.

"Yes," Christopher agreed, happy to have an excuse supplied.

"A strange city, by my lights."

"You have no idea," Christopher said, sinking gratefully into the hot water. It was the first time he'd been truly warm since he had arrived.

"And by others'. You mystify everyone you meet. People react with caution or fear to the unknown. You cannot blame them."

"I don't." That the villagers kept their distance did not bother him. He did not want to get close to anything here. His goal was to find a way out, not fit in.

"I have put my finger on your oddness. You carry yourself as one born to privilege. You did so, even before you were ranked."

Christopher came from solidly Middle America, not the one the politicians talked about but the real one, of factories and six packs, small towns and city apartments. Mechanical engineering paid well enough, but he'd never thought of himself as a privileged class. Even being aware of how lucky he was to be born into a rich country, instead of some Third World hellhole, even understanding how lucky he was to be born in the twentieth century instead of the second—although currently he seemed to have backslid on that one—none of this added up to putting on airs. Svengusta wasn't accusing him of being a snob.

The privilege he took for granted was that he thought he was just as good as anyone else.

"I think everybody deserves to be treated the same. Is that really so bad?"

Svengusta grinned at him. "No, but only because of the color of the robe you wear. Were you anything but a priest of the White, you would be dead within hours."

Christopher, luxuriating in the heat, nodded in agreement. That did, in fact, describe his experience so far.

"Yet when you came to us, you were not a priest. How did you survive the first decades of your life with such an attitude?"

Before Christopher could frame an answer, Svengusta shook his head.

"Never mind. It is sufficient for me that Krellyan has accepted your past. I do not need to know, and perhaps I do not wish to know. Knowledge brings danger. Let you and the Saint bear it without me, if possible. Now get out; it's my turn."

When Helga returned, she trimmed his beard while Svengusta

dressed for their usual pilgrimage to the tavern. Tonight three strange men sat at the bar, nursing mugs. An old codger was trying to spark a conversation but failing.

"Greetings, Paters," Big Bob said. "Perhaps you can talk these mummers into a performance."

The men looked Christopher and Svengusta up and down. It did not appear to improve their mood. Christopher couldn't blame them. He looked like a beggar, despite the sword, and Svengusta, in his old, stained coat, was no better.

The men lifted their mugs and drained them. One spoke to the tavern keeper.

"The weather is too cold for a show. We'll settle our account in the morning and be on our way."

"As you will," Big Bob replied. The men stood, and with a polite "Paters," left the room.

"A sorry lot," Big Bob said when they were gone. "Even their womenfolk were nothing to look at."

"Helga will be disappointed," Christopher said. To be fair, so was he.

Svengusta waved away his concern. "We'll have pie tonight all the same. Better than the bawdy, raucous prattle of layabouts."

"For that we have Uncle Abjorn," Big Bob said. "And no need to tip him for it."

The old codger sputtered. "Insolent wretch! And to think I held my tongue and spoke no ill against the swill you've poured today. Enough is enough." He slammed down his mug. "I'll not drink another drop in this hovel!"

Christopher tuned out the argument. They did it every night.

"What would they have done?" he asked Svengusta.

"They had the look of jugglers or acrobats more than players. Perhaps their women would have danced. I fear you would have found it tame, compared to an evening in a townie's tavern."

Christopher wondered what Svengusta and Helga would make of

a movie. But that made him think of popcorn, which made him think of all the things he had lost. Every day he spent here would be another defeat for Maggie. It was the cruelest fate he could imagine: her hope would die the death of a thousand cuts.

Through dinner and pie he struggled to smile, for Helga's sake. With kindness she and Svengusta pretended not to notice, leaving his pain to fade on its own.

～⚬⚬～

Some latent martial-arts skill woke him in the night. A shadowy figure loomed over him, arm raised to strike. The menace was palpable, the wrongness terrifying. He reacted instinctively, putting up an arm to block the downward blow. Letting slip the syllables of the spell imprinted on his brain—he'd been memorizing a different one every day to see what they did—he took his fear in his hand and threw it back, forcefully, into the face of nightmare.

The man shrieked in terror, throwing himself away. He collided with something, fell, scrambled to his feet, and burst out of the door. Christopher came fully awake. They were under attack.

He reached over and grabbed his sword where it lay between him and the wall, courtesy of Karl's training. He caught the haft in one hand and rolled out of bed.

Someone pounced on him like a tiger. He wrestled, rolling to get away, felt the fire as steel sank into his shoulder where his neck had been but a heartbeat ago. He punched up, blindly but with full force. His tael had already closed the wound.

He had to release the sword, its length now a liability. He groped for the assailant's knife hand, tried to apply a lock. The hand slipped away, came back to strike again, piercing flesh. This time copious blood followed it out.

Christopher grabbed blindly for the throat, rolling under the man so he could see, and was dismayed at the sight of a second assailant maneuvering in the firelight shadows for a chance to strike. He brought his knee up, struck his grappler in the face without much damage, but it checked the motion and kept the attackers in each other's way.

Someone touched him from the left and he felt renewed. Svengusta had reached out from his bunk and healed him. The dagger came down again, striking into his exposed belly, but his replenished tael bound the wound and so he struck again with his knee. He felt the solid blow connect with the head, but the assailant shrugged it off and kept fighting.

Even in the midst of the fight he was astonished to see Svengusta produce some sort of farm implement with a short, curved blade. The old man swung it with both hands into the black-clad, black-masked assassin on top of Christopher. It was an awkward swing, from the horizontal position on the bed, but it drew blood.

The man grunted, issued an order. The other one leaped on Svengusta, going over Christopher, who reached up and caught a foot, but he could not pull the man off and fight his own. Again and again the dagger fell, blood spattering in its wake. Christopher realized he was losing everything; blood, the fight, and consciousness. He didn't think he could pull off a spell in these conditions, not without even one free hand. He could hear the old man's cries as the other dagger struck home, on the bed above him, so terribly far away.

Then there were other voices, angry ones. Hands lifted the man off him, clubs raining down. Villagers dragged the assailants into the kitchen, threw them to the ground, and pounded them with clubs like recalcitrant lumps of bleeding dough.

Christopher sat up and reached for Svengusta. He forced his mind to ignore the sounds from the next room, the pain from his own wounds. He touched the comatose old man, said the words of the spell.

Svengusta popped up like a puppet on a string. He looked about wildly, reached down for Christopher.

"No," Christopher said, "I'll live. See to Helga."

He was out of real spells, but he still had orisons, the petty spells that novices practiced with. One was sufficient to stop the bleeding, if not the pain.

Before Christopher could get to his feet, Svengusta returned. "She's untouched." He unleashed his power into Christopher. The relief almost made the pain worthwhile.

Restored to health and vitality, Christopher picked up his sword and forced the crowd back so he could survey the kitchen.

The hoods had been stripped from the attackers. They looked vaguely familiar, but Christopher wasn't sure. Big Bob was there, crying, several men holding him at bay.

"They put my Charles down," the tavern keeper sobbed. "Pater, they cut his throat like a pig." In a flicker his grief turned to rage, his tears still flowing but now of uncontainable hatred. "Give them to me! I'll smash their brains for stew. Give me the beast that cut my boy!" The other men had to struggle to hold on as he lunged at the unmoving bodies on the floor.

"Calm yourself, Robert," Svengusta ordered, kneeling over the bodies. "This one is dead already. This one lives to face the noose."

"But my Charles," the tavern master cried, his face a quivering mass of blubber. Christopher was unnerved by the transformation; normally the man was as cynical and stoic as any barkeep.

"We'll bring him back," Christopher said. "I've still got three hundred gold. Surely we can raise the rest from the village." Svengusta had said a revival cost a hundred tael. It would bankrupt him, but what was a pile of gold measured against a boy's life?

They all stared at him. Big Bob gulped for air, confused.

Svengusta, ever practical, asked, "Who else did we lose?"

"No one, Pater," one of the men answered. "Bob was suspicious of the mummer folk, so he put us in one of the spare rooms in case there was trouble and set his boy to watch their door. In the middle of the night his ma goes to take him a snack and finds him lying on the floor. Bob had to bring him to the Pater just in case. But when we got here the door was hanging open, so Bob dropped the body and stormed the castle, and we had to follow."

"My Charles!" the tavern keeper cried, and rushed outside.

Svengusta turned to the man. "Fargo, where are the mummer womenfolk?"

"I don't know, Pater."

"Find them. Before Big Bob does. Go!"

The crowd cleared out of the chapel, leaving behind only Fenwick the stable-master.

Christopher stood guard while Svengusta and Fenwick turned over the unconscious man and bound him. Then they tore his clothes off.

"It's the only reliable way of searching them," Fenwick explained.

Helga was crying on her bed. "I didn't hear them come in. I didn't wake up. I'm sorry, I'm sorry!"

"It's okay, Helga," Christopher reassured her. "You did the right thing." It made a screwy kind of sense. The girl, having no ranks, was no threat; they'd skipped her and gone straight for the high-value targets, as was the tactics of this world. And they hadn't barred the door behind them, thinking the villagers asleep, and in any case hardly more of a threat than the girl. "And you," he said to Fenwick. "You saved us."

"Of course he did. You're the most exciting thing Burseberry's seen for ages." Svengusta grinned, but it was only a faint shadow of his usual humor. "This one needs to stay warm. Here, girl, let's put him in your bed."

Helga scurried out of the bed while Christopher and Fenwick hefted the naked man into it. Svengusta covered him up with blankets, checked his breathing while sending the other two men into the main hall with the dead body.

"Put it at the end of the hall, where it will stay cool," he told them.

When they had dumped the body, Fenwick pulled out his knife. "Just a moment, Pater." He grimaced and then plunged the blade into the body. Nothing happened, except that Christopher's stomach wrenched at the sound of metal cutting flesh. "Sometimes they fake it," Fenwick said. "Just one of the tricks of the Invisibles."

"The who?"

"The Invisible Guild," Fenwick said, and then recited a bit of doggerel as they walked back to the kitchen, apparently considering it a sufficient explanation.

> *Knight reigns from his castle,*
> *priest from his holy chapel;*
> *wizard rules from his tower,*
> *but we rule the midnight hour.*

Fargo had already returned with news. A handful of women and children had been found only a short way out down the road to Knockford, on the verge of freezing to death.

"I'll come and see them," Svengusta said. "No, you're staying here," he said when Christopher turned to follow him. "If you were their target, blundering around in the dark will only make their job easier. We'll sit tight and wait for light. In the morning we will send for the Vicar."

Fenwick and another man stayed behind as guards, while Helga made them a pot of tea.

The other villager, Jawen, a morose-looking fellow, was all for killing the prisoner. "Who knows what kind of magic he might use when he wakes?"

"If he had magic, he would have used it while were beating him to a pulp," Fenwick said. "He's just a pawn. The masters slipped away, like they always do."

"And if they come back?"

"We'll give them more of this." Fenwick hefted his cudgel. "Plus the Pater's awake now, and properly armed. They'll not strike a man on his guard."

"Pawn or no, the Saint will stretch his neck. He's done murder."

"That's for the Saint to decide," Fenwick said.

"What about the women and children?" Christopher asked with some trepidation.

"No," Jawen sighed with disappointment, misinterpreting Christopher's concern. "Our lord's as soft as a jelly roll. Ought to put the whelps in a sack and drop them in the river, but he won't likely go for that."

"They have the Taint on them," Fenwick said. "Not like our Helga here, she was an honest orphan," he added defensively. "But you can't harvest wheat planted in the Dark. Best that they burn so they can't come back to haunt you."

"Drowning is better. The water confuses their spirits so they can't find you from the other side."

Christopher found the topic disturbing, so he stopped listening, gazing into the fire with his sword comfortably close.

He awoke in panic, until the logical part of his mind noted that the Invisibles would not knock to be let in.

Fenwick was already unbarring the door. Jawen looked around guiltily, still groggy from sleep.

Svengusta came in, stamping snow off his boots.

"You lads go on home now. There'll be no more excitement tonight."

"And this one?" Jawen said, pointing to the body in the bed.

"I stopped him at death's door, but only by an inch. He's no danger to anyone. Now unless you want to further comment on my healing expertise, take yourselves home."

The men left, and Svengusta set himself to heating up more tea. Helga was asleep in the bunk room, so Christopher busied himself with balancing a stone mug on the door's crossbar.

"Don't worry about that. Dawn is only an hour away; we'll keep till then."

"Did you find out why they're trying kill me?"

"The women know nothing. They only took up with this lot a few days ago, recruited as part of a disguise, and abandoned when no longer useful. All they are guilty of is going out a window rather than paying an innkeeper's bill."

"Is this some kind of revenge of Hobilar's?"

"He could not pay his own ransom. How could he pay for an assassination? Speaking of paying, you made a generous offer earlier tonight," the old man said softly. "But what if more had died? Would you have revived Charles and left the others to the ground?"

"I didn't think of that." Christopher blushed, feeling stupid.

"We are lucky. We have one to revive but two to bury." Svengusta nodded toward the bed. "Their tael will go to reviving the boy, so that will offset the cost considerably. But if it had been the other way round, not even your generosity would have sufficed. The Church can't afford to revive every peasant that dies, Brother. You understand that, right?" Svengusta looked at him carefully.

"Not really, no," Christopher answered. Insurance companies back home had figured out how to spread the cost of health care so working people could afford it.

"What do you think happens when good Saint Krellyan finally shuffles off this mortal coil?"

The answer was obvious. "You promote a new Saint."

Svengusta nodded. "And how do you suppose we do that?"

Of course. Tael. Christopher thought about that for a long moment. "How long do you have to save to replace him?" he finally asked.

"I'm not privy to the Church accounts," Svengusta said quietly, "but I've heard it said that if we don't get fifty years of service out of Krellyan, the Church will be short. And that's scraping every penny from the barrel."

"Just how much tael does it take to make a Saint?"

Svengusta looked at him sadly. "You don't want to know. The cost doubles every rank. That doesn't seem like a lot, at first, but it adds up to terrible numbers."

Christopher was well aware of how fast a power sequence climbed. "What rank is Krellyan?" he pressed.

"Saint Krellyan is the twelfth rank, that's no secret. But I remember how tight the Church pinched its purse to promote him. Ah, what a fine young man he was, only twenty-five and barely out of his first rank. The Cardinal—not our Cardinal Faren, but his predecessor—picked him out, called him a gift from the Lady. He was wise and good and strong and pure. Krellyan, I mean."

Svengusta paused, lost in memory. "A paragon of piety. Even the passed-overs like me didn't begrudge him the fine career everyone expected him to have. And then Cardinal Merrian quaked the earth. He revealed the gigantic hoard the Church had amassed over his tenure and gave it all to young Krellyan. He made him a Saint. Our first Saint.

"All those years of saving, skimping, restraint, even on his own promotion. Merrian stayed a Cardinal when he could have been a Prophet. Other churches had Prophets. We had to hang our heads and step aside when their priests walked by, because we were just healers without a Prophet to call our own. But in the end it was worth it, because now we had a Saint, and they had nothing to compare. Krellyan's the only Saint the Kingdom's ever had, except for ancient legends that are told to children."

"Why is a Saint so important?" Christopher already knew that mere Cardinals could raise the dead. He'd gotten that much from the books.

"Weren't you listening, Brother? Krellyan's the only one in the

Kingdom who can grow back Hobilar's arm. He can make your body as good as new. Not young, of course, but it looks the same. I've heard it said the King is regenerated once a year, just on general principle. And welcome to it, as long as he pays the fee. We need both his favor and his money.

"Hobilar's not the first man to lose a limb, you know. Out there over the border, all sorts of beasties can deprive you of loose body parts." The old man twinkled, his usual good nature creeping back. "Under Krellyan's leadership, and with his stature, we've grown. We're now the biggest Church in the Kingdom. But if we lose our Saint, then we'll lose our rein on the high ranks. And that's why we let peasants die. Better a Charles here and there than Hobilars everywhere."

Christopher thought about the thug who had fled in the night, driven out by his spell. "One got away."

"Pray that we never see him again. When next we do, it will be with a dozen thugs instead of three."

⌘

Uncharacteristically, Svengusta turned out to be wrong. In the morning, when they opened the door again to Fenwick's knock, he beckoned them outside.

"You'll want to see this, Paters."

Svengusta and Christopher threw on cloaks and followed Fenwick out into the freezing snow.

The peasant led them along tracks that led from the chapel into the woods. "We didn't see them last night," he explained, "since it was dark and all. But this morning we saw them, and, well, see for yourself."

Only a few feet into the trees the tracks ended at a body, quiet and still. The snow spelled out the story in plain detail. The mummer, running in panic-stricken haste, had plowed into a low-hanging branch and knocked himself out. He'd lain there, unconscious in the bitter cold, and never woken up.

So I have killed a man, Christopher thought sadly.

They carried the frozen corpse back to the chapel and stacked it on the other one.

"Your fortune is safe," Svengusta said.

"What about my life?"

The old man shrugged. "For now, at least."

So Christopher was sent to summon the Vicar. The tension in his stomach was incongruous with the soft white fields and blanketed trees. He kept expecting to be ambushed at every turn, and Royal reacted to his mood by becoming prickly. If he was attacked, his best bet would be to flee, but he doubted he could convince the stallion of that. In any case the only assault he suffered was the weather, which was really too cold for his cast-offs.

By the time he reached the church he was shivering. This sign of weakness pricked his pride, so after dispatching a novice to request an appointment with the Vicar he eschewed curling up next to a fire and instead forced himself to do kata in the empty main hall until sweat dispelled the chill.

He was interrupted by a sour, heavy voice from the door.

"That's not a sight I ever thought to see in my church," Rana said, unsmiling.

He blushed. "I'm sorry, I wasn't thinking." He sheathed the naked blade.

"Again with the spurious apologies? You are a servant of the Lady, in your own fashion, and your worship will not profane Her church. It is only my sensibilities that are abused, and it is your Patron that is responsible."

"Then I apologize on behalf of my Patron," he responded formally. "He deserves a more astute disciple."

Rana laughed. "Pretty words from a war priest. I keep forgetting you are not a heathen warmonger, bent on Red blood and Yellow gold. But then, when I think of you as a Brother, I forget your Patron. You are something I must accommodate, and I am past the age of accommodation."

Christopher winced a little. He hadn't even started making things difficult for people to adapt to.

"But you are here on grave business, I am told, so I must prepare for more unpleasant tidings."

"Yes, my Lady," he replied, "I have to report an attack."

By the end of his tale she was back to not smiling.

"Let us go and see, then," she said. "Though if he really is an Invisible, there is little we can learn. At most we can prevent him from lying; we cannot make him talk."

Christopher hadn't considered there might be Fifth Amendment rights to worry about.

"I didn't realize you extended legal protection to their guild."

Rana looked at him quizzically. "No magic can force an Invisible to reveal his client. It is a privilege of their rank, not a courtesy. Shouldn't you have learned this by now?"

Christopher bit his lip before he got himself into more trouble.

She had already moved on to other topics, however. "We depart in half an hour. Make yourself ready."

<hr/>

It was closer to an hour later that they set off for the village, accompanied by four guards on horseback and a wagon with four more soldiers. The guards in the wagon had crossbows, which interested Christopher considerably. Here was the first sign of complex machinery he'd seen.

The column made a good first impression, but Christopher had become astute enough to recognize that their horses were not warhorses. Even the saddles were only for riding, lacking the high front and back of his war tack. Nor did the soldiers have Karl's whipcord build; some of them were suspiciously close to fat. Royal was equally unimpressed, forcibly taking his place at the head of the column, next to but a few inches ahead of Rana's mount. Improbably the lady had emerged from the church dressed in full chain mail, with a round wooden shield and sickle like Svengusta's strapped to her side.

"Please accept my apologies, my Lady," Christopher said. "My equestrian skills are not yet up to the level of my mount."

The woman chuckled, nudged her horse close, and patted Royal on the shoulder. "It's alright, Pater. If we are attacked—which I sincerely doubt—I'll be happy to have another target up here with me." She adjusted the shield so it wouldn't bang her knees. "I think I might have made a mistake," she confessed. "I only meant to reassure the villagers with a show of force, but the townsfolk will be buzzing to see me off in armor. They'll think we're being invaded or some such nonsense."

"Well, then, when you come home with your prisoners, they'll think you won," he offered.

"Is sophistry now a domain of war?" she inquired with a raised eyebrow.

"I think it is," he laughed. "Rhetoric, and above all demagoguery, are the warmonger's stock in trade. At least, where I come from. Isn't it the same here?"

"Not particularly. The pursuit of tael is all the motivation warriors normally require."

Christopher was going to explain that there wasn't any tael where he came from and only caught himself in the nick of time. Rana noticed.

"No," she said quietly, "don't tell me. Whatever it is Krellyan conceals, I don't want to know. Don't bother to protest your innocence, just let it pass."

10.

OLD-TIME REVIVAL

The village turned out to greet them, watching from the side of the road. Christopher could sense the wisdom of Rana's cavalcade; the bulk of men and armor was a reassuring counterweight to the violence that had been done in the night.

Soldiers carried the unconscious man, wrapped in a blanket but still barefoot and bound, into the main hall and laid him at Rana's feet. She healed him with a word, while men with drawn weapons encircled him. The mummer looked around warily, his eyes sagging in ill-concealed defeat.

"What have you to say for yourself, villain?" she asked.

"What should I say? Your people have beaten me, stripped me, and in general behaved like boors. Have you come to chastise them for their inhospitality?"

"Do you deny attacking the Pater?" she replied, ignoring his banter.

"Only in self-defense. We had innocently wandered into the chapel to pay our respects to the god. A simple wrong turn, a mistaken door, and suddenly we were fighting for our lives." The mummer tried for outrage, but it rang hollow.

"And the boy, Charles? The one who lies there under that sheet?"

The mummer shrugged. "I know nothing of this. We had left the inn, in the middle of the night, for we were quite dissatisfied with the pathetic level of service and the rudeness of the tavern-master. The cooking was none too good, either." He glanced at the boy sadly. "Probably some peasant's squabble over a girl. They're like animals, nothing but rutting and violence on their stunted minds."

"You'll have to lie better than that to fool the Cardinal," Rana said, dismissing the mummer with a sad shake of the head. The soldiers carted him out the double doors to the wagon. "Have the bodies been harvested yet?" she asked Svengusta.

"No, Lady, I thought it best not to disturb anything."

"Well, let's do it. Nothing gained by waiting now." She looked at the three corpses. "We can each do one."

Christopher's mouth went dry, unwilling to speculate on what she meant.

"Ah," Svengusta said delicately. "Our Brother is very new."

Rana snorted. "Time to learn then. He should have done this as a novice. Come to think of it, he should have *been* a novice. In any case, he'll have no shortage of harvesting at war."

"You do have an orison available, Brother?" asked Svengusta. Christopher nodded reluctantly. "Then watch, and listen." The old man bent over the first corpse and chanted a phrase in Celestial. He put his hand on the dead man's head and concentrated, his fingers arched so that his palm did not touch the forehead. As Christopher watched in fascination, a small purple dot grew out of nothing on the pallid flesh under Svengusta's hand, like a tiny lilac blossoming. After a brief moment it stopped growing, the size of a grain of rice, and Svengusta opened his eyes. He plucked the pellet up and weighed it in his hand, his face falling in dismay.

"No ordinary commoner, but an Apprentice rank," Svengusta announced, and gave it to Rana. "Perhaps the mummer's craft—"

"According to your description, they fought remarkably well for thespians," she said sourly. "Perhaps the Guild, after all." She moved over to the next body, but Svengusta cleared his throat.

"Yes, Pater?" she asked mildly.

"That's the thug that Brother Christopher killed. I was thinking, it seemed appropriate and all. And he might feel more comfortable with that than doing the boy."

"I don't want to do the boy," Christopher instantly agreed. "You're going to do the boy?"

Rana frowned. "Of course. His tael won't help him now. And what's wrong with harvesting one of our own? He's giving back to the community. He'd be dishonored if you didn't want his contribution."

"I don't want to do the boy," Christopher said, embarrassed.

She sighed, annoyed. "It's your chapel, and your prerogative. But I'll not have you thinking ill of our sacred ways. Start with the kill you've made, if you must, but abandon any idea that it's somehow more respectable. Quite the opposite, I would argue."

He nodded, tacitly conceding the strength of her argument. He decided not to explain that part of his squeamishness came from the fact that he'd never seen this many dead bodies before. He was tired of being the greenhorn.

Rana pulled up the sheet from Charles's head and repeated the performance, saying the words with extra emphasis for Christopher's benefit. Charles yielded merely a speck.

"Hardly worth the effort," she said. "He was still under the age. No doubt that explains why they didn't take his head."

Steeling himself to the task, Christopher bent over the last corpse and chanted the words. It was easier than he expected, requiring concentration but no particular skill. He drew the tael from the dead man until he felt nothing left, and then he opened his eyes.

He picked up the purple sphere. Like the one Svengusta had harvested, it was as small as a lentil. Weightless, yet he could *feel* its substance, resting in the palm of his hand. He instinctively knew how much it contained. Unfortunately, he didn't know what that meant, so he handed it to Svengusta.

"Also the fourth Novice rank," Svengusta said unhappily. "What an unlikely group to contain two Master mummers."

"But not unusual for an Invisible Guild gang." Rana dropped the pebble into a small silver vial that hung on a chain around her neck. Then she shrugged, dismissing what they could do nothing about. "At least it is good news for Charles. His fee is covered, and the Saint will revive him." She went to the door and summoned a guard. "Bring the parents," she ordered.

When Big Bob arrived, with his wife and a number of other relatives in tow, the Vicar spoke commandingly.

"Be at ease, Goodman. I have already dispatched a message to summon Faren. I do not know how long he will be, but I can tell you this. Charles will not have the door closed on him. I will now enspell him and jam that door. Within the week either the Cardinal will arrive, or I will return and renew the spell until Faren can come. Keep the body safe and you have nothing to fear."

"He is loved," Svengusta added. "He will come back."

Christopher watched in fascination as Rana worked her spell. The body seemed to acquire a light radiance for a moment, as if it had been embalmed with glowing fluid. The mother sobbed her gratitude while Big Bob held her, his eyes wet and shining.

"Does that matter?" Christopher quietly asked Svengusta. "I mean, that he was loved?"

"Considerably," was the equally quiet reply. "The young are lightly bound to this world and often hard to call back. It is reckoned futile to even try with a child under three. But Charles was a happy lad, and well interested in girls already."

"You understand," Svengusta added with a sudden alarm at Christopher's possible depth of ignorance, "that it is voluntary? They cannot be compelled to return."

"Return from where?" Christopher asked helplessly. If there was a Heaven, who would want to return? If it was Hell, or even just Limbo, who wouldn't? And if there was neither, then where were you returning from?

"The other side. The world of the dead." The old man sighed. "Those answers are sufficient for most, but you have a theological mind. So I will tell you what ages of priestly research has definitively concluded to be the answer: we don't know."

Rana had final words for him, as well.

"If this is the work of the Invisibles, you are still in danger. I'm leaving two of my men with you, for the time being. You're to conduct yourself with appropriate caution. Don't go about alone, or unarmed, or unspelled. And for the Lady's sake, try not to kill, maim, or dismember any more people."

"I'd be happy to stop," he said somewhat ungraciously, "if they'd stop sticking bits of metal into me."

"You're a barrel of trouble, Pater," she replied testily. "Just because you're in the right doesn't make it any less troublesome."

※

He had thought he was motivated before; now he worked like a demon bit at his heels. The guards sleeping in the next bunk spent their days in ordinary pursuits, flirting with the village girls and arguing with the farmers in the tavern, but the clink of their armor was a constant reminder of the danger that lurked in the silent, snowy woods. Christopher alternated his time between the chapel, learning chemical engineering from brute experience, and the woodpile, learning the art of wood-splitting the same way. Of the two, he found the wood less galling.

Nonetheless, progress was made, and he was on the final stage of producing a few pounds of clean white crystal when he was interrupted by Cardinal Faren, disembarking from his carriage in a clangor of metal and a foul mood.

"Look at this," Faren said with disgust, pointing to the detachment of soldiers that had accompanied him. "I haven't seen so much armor in our lands in decades. It's almost as bad as a March. And you seem to be at the center of every storm."

"I'm sorry," was all Christopher could say as the Cardinal marched on into the main hall.

"Gods, boy, clean this place up," he sputtered upon seeing the clutter of Christopher's industrial operations, "I've got a ceremony to perform."

Once again Svengusta charged to the rescue. "He died in the tavern, Cardinal. Where his family lives," the old man hinted broadly.

"All right, we'll do it there. Good thinking, Pater." Faren went off to examine the tavern, and Svengusta winked at Christopher.

"No, technically it doesn't matter," Svengusta explained, anticipating the inevitable question, "but if you're superstitious enough to come all the way out to the village, you might as well get the right house."

Several village men carried Charles's body over to the tavern in an atmosphere turned solemn, their hopefulness guarded. The villagers were still awed that the event was even taking place. They did not dare hope for more, like a happy conclusion. It didn't help that Faren's bad mood seemed to stem from his own uncertainty.

The body lay on benches stacked two high in front of the bar, the biggest room in the tavern, packed tight with villagers—all of Charles's family and friends come to invite him back. Faren stood in the center, resplendent in his white cloaks and casual in his absolute authority.

Solemnly he led the villagers in a prayer. Christopher knew it was meaningless because it was delivered in the common tongue instead of Celestial. But Faren was here for the villagers as much as he was for Charles. When he had them prepared to accept any outcome, yet still hopeful for the best, he began.

He put a bead of tael on the boy's forehead and began to pray in earnest, in Celestial. The palpable presence of power filled the room, sending shivers down Christopher's spine. Faren boomed out, his voice shaking the heavens even if the solid timbers of the inn refused to show it. Some of the girls started to cry, quietly, trembling from the intensity. Christopher was not immune.

To heal a scratch, or even a severed limb, was one thing. To learn a language in a day, or ignore a few blows to the body, was one thing.

To see the dead returned to life was something else entirely: a beacon of light undreamed of, unimagined, unimaginable, a brightness so blinding that his eyes began to water. This was not merely the amazing or the inexplicable, it was the miraculous, in the old sense of the word: the upheaval of despair, the victory of hope, the defeat of the invincible. Faren grappled with Death itself, and in a stony voice of command threw the devil down and pronounced his triumph.

"Come back, Charles Aleson," he cried in the common tongue. "Your place is still in this world. There are still girls to kiss, still battles to win. Your mother still reaches out for you. Your father still looks for your hand. Come back, Charles Aleson, to where you belong. Your time is not done. Your deeds are not written. Come back," he beseeched, weeping freely. "Come back, son of man, to the flesh." The words rang in Christopher's head like church bells, deafening in their significance. "Come back," Faren ordered, the command rendered gentle but no less potent in Celestial. "Come back!"

And Charles came, in a blinding rush of light that wasn't really there, like afterimages on the retina of something never seen. The invisible light poured down from the heavens, passing through the roof like glass, filling the body with an invisible glow.

Charles coughed.

The room exploded in bedlam, weeping, laughing, crying, cheering. Faren sagged in relief. Svengusta wiped his eyes with a handkerchief, then silently offered it to Christopher. The parents were stricken dumb with release, wordlessly accepting congratulations while holding the boy in their arms, tears flowing down their faces.

"Let him sleep," Faren prescribed. "Let him rest tonight and all of tomorrow, but then put his lazy bones back to work."

Aunts and sisters shepherded the boy and his mother upstairs, and the wake turned into a wild party. No small blame for this lay on the tavern keeper himself. Made unsteady by the rocket-ride from grief to joy, Big Bob opened his kegs to all for free.

Christopher finally escaped the riot after only two mugs had been pressed on him. Priests were suddenly very popular. He could see why, and he felt reduced by the comparison. Merely chopping people up with a sword was the province of any thug.

Faren had extracted himself as well and was basking in the cold sunlight.

"Can I do that?" Christopher asked. "I mean, as a priest of War. Ever?"

"Yes, of course, though for you it will not come until you are a Prophet. Which, you must accept, seems unlikely, given your age. Do not be jealous, Brother. I remember the first time I saved a man, a woodcutter who'd slipped with his ax and was bleeding out. To save a life always feels like this."

"The only person I've ever healed," Christopher said sadly, "is myself." That wasn't strictly true. He'd healed Svengusta during the fight. But he didn't count that. He hadn't had time to enjoy it, or even see it.

"Your time will come, soon enough," Faren soothed. "Although it will be small balm to patch a man up, only to send him out again into the thresher. For that part, soon enough I'll watch young Charles march to war. It is the way of it, Brother. You are no idealistic sapling. You know the truth. Life and death are two sides of a coin, so spend it well."

Faren was in an unusually pious mood, noted Christopher.

"I know," the old man laughed, "it will be gone again tomorrow. As for that—have you any thoughts to why the Invisible Guild has chosen to favor you?"

"I was hoping you could tell me."

"I doubt it is Hobilar's influence. It's true he spurned the Saint and now roams the streets of Kingsrock, crying for revenge; but he has no money and less sympathy. Possibly the motive was simple murder and robbery. It's not that unheard of, and you are known to have recently become wealthy. The best I can offer you is more guards."

"No, thanks. These soldiers are eating us out of house and home. I'd rather depend on the villagers."

Faren shook his head. "They already have full-time jobs. But evil prefers to strike during the dark. Perhaps just stuffing the chapel with young men at night will be sufficient."

Dinner was a more comfortable affair without the soldiers, who returned to Knockford in Faren's carriage. Svengusta was drunk to the point of silliness. "Never so much commotion in all my life," he laughed. "What will you do next? Summon a dragon and teach it to play dead?" They had to put the old man to bed early.

As they were about to retire themselves, there was a knock on the door. Christopher found himself immediately reaching for his sword, but it was Kennet and three other young men, come for night duty armed with heavy cudgels. All of them were destined for the winter draft, and they found it hugely exciting to be considered man enough to fight for their soon-to-be comrade-in-arms. Several of them hinted they could share the bed by the fire. Helga would have none of it. They didn't have beards to speak of, and she was in a higher class now. Instead they wound up double-bunking with each other in Svengusta and Christopher's room.

The boys fell asleep quickly enough, no doubt due to hard labor and clean consciences. Christopher lay awake for a while, listening to the breathing of the young men he had conned into sharing his danger, for no more reward than the thrill of it.

<hr/>

Unfortunately, all the boys shared was the danger. The work was his own. He had never thought of chemistry as a physically challenging endeavor, but the amount of energy it consumed was phenomenal. Most of his time was spent at the woodpile, and it would need replenishing soon. Splitting wood with an ax was exhausting; cutting down a whole tree with one seemed improbable. Nonetheless he found himself eyeing a particularly large fir at the edge of the woods.

He was taking a breather to consider the problem when a one-horse wagon ambled up, with Tom Fool on the bench seat next to the driver.

"Actually swinging that ax would cut more wood than praying for a miracle," Tom suggested.

"Except my prayers have just been answered." Christopher stuck the ax in the chopping stump and waved Tom an invitation.

"Or you could just burn coal," Tom said, jerking his thumb over his shoulder at a well-laden wheelbarrow in the back of the wagon.

"There's a tree that owes you its life," Christopher said, although the relief in his voice was more for his own sake.

"Perhaps it is the tree's prayer that was answered, then," Tom said. "In either case I am happy to be the instrument of deliverance."

The wagon driver jumped down to help unload, and Tom performed an introduction.

"Please meet Fingean the drayer," Tom said with a little flourish. "He's in my guild, as it were, the guild of second sons. But he drew a horse and wagon out of the deal, so he makes a living hauling. I thought if you were wanting a lot of coal, you might be thinking of hiring a wagon."

The other man bowed, not quite as comfortable with unpredictable priests as Tom.

"How much does it cost?" Christopher immediately thought of a better question. "I mean, how much did you pay?"

"Ah, about that," Tom said with exaggerated dismay. "I'd talked the fellow into coming out here to meet you, and I just tagged along for the ride. I wouldn't know what his ordinary charges are."

"You mean to tell me," Christopher said, "that when I paid you to deliver a wheelbarrow of coal, you recruited a man to haul it out here and convinced him to do it for free?"

"Yes, Pater," Tom answered, a little wary. "I hope that's acceptable."

"Acceptable is not quite the word I'd use," Christopher replied. There was an old adage about hiring the right person when you met him and figuring out what his job was afterward. "How much would I have to pay you to work for me full-time?"

"Doing what, Pater?"

"Manual labor," Christopher answered honestly. "For now."

"Then I am pleased to say I am qualified. An honest wage for a man with no skill or guild certificate is a silver a day," Tom suggested.

"That's forty gold a year." Christopher tried to decide if he could afford it. Were his finances sufficient to maintain a horse and a servant? But there was too much work to be done alone.

"Only thirty a year, if you provide room and board in your fine chapel," Tom countered. "But I get a day off a week, to see my girl in Knockford."

"Deal," Christopher said, leaping at the bargain. "But you get two days off a week." It wasn't as nice as it sounded. Around here a week was ten days long.

He turned to the drayer. "Let me pay for the service Tom tricked you out of, and come on in for lunch.

"Oh, damn," he told Tom, as Helga sighed and got out the dishes she had just put away now that the soldiers were gone, "I forgot, I'm under some kind of death sentence by the Invisible Guild. You might not want to work with me after all."

"I'll not let foxes chase me off from the golden goose." Tom had an uncharacteristic look on his face, and Christopher finally recognized it as seriousness. "I swing a cudgel as well as the next, or even a sword if you've got one to spare."

"Where is he going to sleep?" Helga asked with some interest. She hadn't paid the soldiers any mind, but Tom had a charm that accented his rough-hewn look.

"We'll just have to reduce the number of boys," Svengusta said. "This lad's worth two of them, anyway, and surely half the commotion."

After lunch Christopher paid the drayer with a heavy gold coin. Then he sighed and cornered Helga in the kitchen.

"Tom's going to be eating with us, and I can't expect Sven to pay for that. So how much do you need?"

"Pater gives me a gold a week for the three of us," she said.

Christopher ate as much as the old man and the girl together. Not that he was putting on weight; if anything, he was losing it. Tom would eat at least as much, so that meant another twenty gold a year. Which was ten more than he'd saved by offering Tom a bed in the chapel.

There was no question about it. He'd hired the right man.

He counted over four precious coins. "That's for the next four weeks, then, for Tom and me."

Tom made himself useful immediately, in a way that Christopher had once tried to do but failed. Helga would let him help with the chores she never allowed Christopher to touch. No doubt it had more to do with competence than rank; Tom actually knew what he was doing.

11.

FIRE IN THE SKY

Neither Svengusta nor Helga were willing to tolerate burning coal in the chapel's fireplace, so Christopher cooked his first batch of coke over an open fire. Tom's tongue, normally quick to prod an irony, seemed dumbfounded by the act of burning wood to heat coal. The process took several days to yield a sack of hard gray lumps.

"We'll need to build an oven," Christopher said. "Do you know a bricklayer?"

"If you don't plan to live in it, I can probably manage," Tom said, "though I hope you don't want me to make the bricks myself."

"Not unless you can," Christopher said, but not seriously. Making bricks required firewood.

Now it was time to go to town and burn through his fortune. Buying Fae's freedom would take half his capital; her and Tom's salary and food for the horse would take the other half. That left Christopher a beggar again, depending solely on whatever Karl brought back from Kingsrock. But whenever he found himself fretting over a life of poverty, he reminded himself that he would likely be murdered in his sleep before he starved.

Christopher offered Tom a ride into town, figuring the huge warhorse could easily carry them double. But the horse gave them such a withering glare when Tom put his foot in the stirrup that both men thought better of the idea, and poor Tom had to walk. In town they split up, Tom to find Fingean and bricks, and Christopher to see the wizard.

First he had a friendlier task, paying a visit to Dereth to order a steel tube, about two inches in diameter and a foot long. Before Dereth could complain about lack of resources, Christopher dumped the sack of coke into the charcoal bucket.

"I cannot smelt with coal," the smith said. "Your tube will be useless, as brittle as glass."

"It's not coal," Christopher said. "Well, anymore."

Dereth picked up a lump and examined it more closely.

"This will liquefy your iron. Use a bellows to blow clean air through the melt and watch the flames. When they come out the right color, you'll have steel."

"And what color is that?" Dereth asked.

Christopher shrugged. "No idea. I trust you to figure it out."

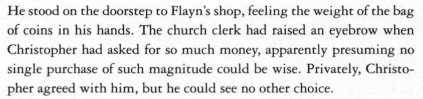

He stood on the doorstep to Flayn's shop, feeling the weight of the bag of coins in his hands. The church clerk had raised an eyebrow when Christopher had asked for so much money, apparently presuming no single purchase of such magnitude could be wise. Privately, Christopher agreed with him, but he could see no other choice.

Svengusta's words of advice from the duel came back to him. There was no room for indecision anymore; he had chosen this path, and now he had to act to a single purpose.

He strode inside, nodded politely to Fae, and dropped the bag onto the counter with a heavy jingle.

Fae's cheek twitched, her only visible sign of emotion. "Master Flayn," she called out in a pleasant, controlled voice, "we have a customer that must speak to you."

They stood there for a few minutes, waiting for the wizard. Christopher marveled at the woman's strength of reserve.

Flayn stepped out from behind the curtain warily, like a man in a strange building, even though it was his own shop. He looked at Christopher, at the money on the counter.

"What do you think you can buy here, Pater?" he said coldly.

Fae answered for him. "Your apprentice."

Flayn had been cold; now he was steaming with fury. Not a muscle moved in his face, though.

"Does my apprentice wish to be bought?" he said, his voice carved out in daggers of ice.

Visibly trembling, Fae stepped forward, stared the wizard in the face. Suddenly she slapped him, a ringing blow with every ounce of strength she had.

Flayn's eyes tightened, and though he did not react in any other way, Christopher was suddenly worried that the wizard was about to blast the girl into the middle of next week.

He cleared his throat, casually hitched his thumb on his sword sash.

"Will you answer for the actions of your apprentice?" Flayn demanded without looking away, his voice flat, ugly, and crawling with menace.

"She's not my apprentice," Christopher said. "She's my employee. But yes, I'll discipline her, if you can look me in the eye and tell me you didn't deserve that."

Flayn turned to face him slowly, like a mobile statue. His eyes raked up and down Christopher with contempt.

"Do you think your sword protects you, fool?" he hissed, a snake threatening to strike.

"No," Christopher said, as mildly as he could under the circum-stances. "I think that big honking church over there protects me. If you wish to bring suit against the girl, then you can. But she'll get up in open court and explain why she thought you deserved it. If you don't like the sound of that, then let's just call it even, and forget about it."

"Get out," Flayn ordered. It seemed an unlikely way to run a business; the more gold Christopher brought in, the quicker he was thrown out.

"I'll collect my things," Fae said. She had aimed for light and breezy. It came out more like a sobbing wheeze as she darted behind the curtain.

The two men stood there, one relentlessly glaring, one gratingly uncomfortable.

"This doesn't have to be so difficult," Christopher said resignedly. "I've no hard feelings toward you, Master Wizard."

"You'll pay for this," Flayn whispered, as if making a promise to himself.

Christopher confined himself to looking pointedly at the wall and said nothing.

Fae came down, carrying a large burlap bag, and edged around the immobile wizard, clutching her cloak about her tightly. Christopher opened the door for her, and silently they escaped into the street.

"That was stupid," he said, taking the bag from her.

"I know," Fae confessed. "It was poorly done. I let my emotions get the better of me. Yet more proof that I am not fit for the arcane arts, he would say." She wilted, but then anger inflamed a rally. "But you were not the one who stood to his groping every night! No," she sighed, seeing his look, "he did not force me. In the beginning I was not unwilling. But then I discovered that it was always about him, and never about me. And then I realized that everything is about him, and never about me. Now I have nowhere to turn, nowhere to live, nothing but your charity. Don't you see, I had to slap him. Or I would turn tail and run back to him and his false promises, even now." She was trying not to weep.

"You're coming to live with me for a while," he answered. "I don't dare leave you in town with Flayn steaming like that. Let him cool down a bit. Once our operations are in full swing, you can come back to town if you want. No," he sighed, seeing her look in return, "do not worry. I have no interest in groping you. You are very pretty, Fae, but I have a wife. She's not here," he explained when Fae looked at him dubiously. "But someday I am going to go back to her and look her in the face and tell her that I missed her every single moment of every single day. And night."

They walked back to the church stables, where Fingean and Tom were waiting with the wagon.

Tom said from under a raised eyebrow, "That was a nice purchase, Pater. I'm glad you made us wait for it."

Christopher was going to defend her, but Fae gave the man such a haughty glare that he burst out laughing instead. Tom waved imaginary flames off of his beard, and even Fingean cracked a smile.

Helga was not as impressed with the addition as Tom was, eyeing Fae with barely concealed disdain. It didn't help that Fae was still wearing her shop clothing, tailored to be suggestive to the point of provocation. Christopher escaped outside to help unload the bricks.

"We have it in hand, my lord," Tom said.

"Why do you keep calling me that?"

"You're ranked, and I work for you."

"I think I prefer Pater . . . or even just Christopher."

Tom's eyebrows shot up, and he pretended to eye Christopher appraisingly. "Not that you're not well favored, Pater, but . . ."

Obviously Christopher was asking for a level of informality that bordered on the intimate. Being able to speak the language masked the fact that he was in a different world, and he kept forgetting the little things. "Okay, Tom, you don't have to make fun of me every time I say something stupid."

"Believe me, Pater, I don't."

"You should have been a mummer," he told Tom with a laugh.

"The only job less respectable than a starving peasant." Tom shook his head sadly. "And it requires travel. I'd never see my girl then."

Christopher could relate to that sentiment.

He didn't want to face Helga yet, so he invited both men into the tavern for a pint and was not surprised to find Svengusta already hard at work on one.

"Our intrepid adventurers return from town, and this time without the Vicar in tow. I trust you've been up to no mischief, then?"

"I guess we better not tell him about the shop-girl we brought home," Christopher said to Tom.

"Good gods," Svengusta moaned, "don't we have enough people underfoot?"

"Don't complain just yet," Tom said. "She's easy on the eyes. Wait till she talks to you. Then you can complain."

"Oh no," Svengusta said with trepidation. "Tell me you didn't bring home Flayn's apprentice. Must you make enemies faster than we can bury them?"

Just to annoy him, Christopher asked, "Flayn looked hot enough to call me out."

"Ahhh," Svengusta moaned. "If you get into another duel, Faren will hang you by your ballocks until you stop squeaking."

"I'll keep that in mind," Christopher laughed. "Now if Tom's done with his beer, we can go home and douse the cats. That's how you stop a cat-fight, right?"

"Or we could just sell tickets," Tom suggested.

But dinner surprised them all. Helga was chatting with Fae like an old friend, and the apprentice was for all appearances grateful for her company. Christopher realized he could hope to master magic and inter-dimensional travel, but some mysteries would always be beyond his reach.

It was becoming a bit of a struggle to fit all of these people into the small living area of the chapel. Fae and Helga would have to share a bed now. Christopher felt comforted despite the close quarters. The Invisible Guild would need grease to slip past all these people.

Fae had not come without gifts: a sheaf of paper, a pouch of sulfur, and skills he had not imagined. And magic.

Uncertain of the exact formula, Christopher decided to make a dozen batches of different ratios. Fae produced a balance scale, mortar, and pestle from her bag and accomplished the task while he was still explaining it. Then she looked at him expectantly. He had to ask her what she was waiting for.

"Aren't you going to tell me the properties of each mixture?"

"I don't know the properties. Hopefully, one of them explodes."

"How can you not know? They are your formulas."

"This isn't my . . . specialty. We have to do some experiments."

She sat back, like a cat arching. Christopher imagined he could see the fur standing up.

"I can't keep asking you to explain things, Fae. Just tell me."

"Experiments are not normally a part of arcane study. A single misplaced syllable can destroy an entire city."

It seemed unlikely that wizards wielded that much power but still mucked about in book shops under the rule of priests. His doubt must have shown, because Fae amended her statement.

"Admittedly, not first-rank magic. Still, we may be in danger."

"This isn't arcane study."

"So it is divine magic. Am I to be a priest, then?"

"No," he said, "it's not divine magic. It's not any kind of magic at all. We'll be safe if we take some precautions."

"But you have taken no caution. I see no wards, you have said no prayers, and as far as I can tell the icon of the god has no power."

"Okay. You can stop telling me now." Fae in explanatory mode was just as mystifying as she was in silent mode. "Look, we just made small batches. So if it explodes, it will be a small explosion. And the stuff's still wet."

"The next step is to dry it?"

"Yes, but without exposing it to fire, since it will eventually . . ."

Fae, not waiting for him to finish, passed her hand over the mixtures while muttering something in a language he almost recognized. When she was done the mixtures had changed color, losing their rich blackness and turning grayer, dry as dust.

"How did you do that?"

"The same way I made your sulfur. I separated out the impurities—in this case, water."

He gaped at the buckets of white crystal he had spent so much effort purifying. But Fae shook her head.

"I am only the first Novice rank. A pound a day is my limit."

"But we'll need barrels of the stuff." Apparently the nascent study of chemical engineering would survive its first contact with magic.

Fae's thin lips closed in disapproval. "Even a great wizard would balk at barrels, and why not? A pinch to trigger the spell is all that is normally required."

"We're not doing magic. And we're going to need barrels of paper, too."

"What will you do with it all?"

"Burn it," he said with a grin and was rewarded with a look of proper horror.

Now came the moment of his own trepidation, however. He had launched down this path with no guarantee of success. Even if he had done every step correctly, it was within the realm of raw possibility that he was wasting his time. Perhaps the rules were different here. He could not conceive of any set of physical laws that preserved the chemistry of the human body and yet banned a simple combustion reaction between oxygen and carbon. But so far his inability to conceive of impossibilities had not proven to be a hindrance.

He made firecrackers out of her fine white paper and his gray powder, and touched them off with a burning twig. Three refused to ignite, two spit sparks, one shot across the room like a rocket, but the sixth one went off with a bang that made Fae jump and fixed a lopsided smirk on his face that threatened to become permanent.

Helga ran into the room, armed with a large wooden spoon. "What was that?" she cried.

"An experiment," Fae said, with what Christopher felt was an unnecessary level of acerbity.

"The sound of the world changing," he answered. The poet may have been right about the world ending in a whimper, but science was right about the beginning: it always started with a bang.

⌇⌇⌇

Over the next few days he exposed Fae to more experiments, setting fire to every salt and powder he could find. Copper dust burned green; iron made gold. Svengusta had an old tub of soaking salts that made orange flames. Mixed with black powder, these would provide the colors of his fireworks. When Dereth delivered the steel tube, Christopher showed her how to make rockets out of paper and glue, inventing corrugated paper along the way.

Tom spent his days mining or logging, and Helga had chores of her own, so that left Christopher and Fae together for hours in the chapel. Eventually Fae stopped working and stared at him pensively.

"You trust me with much," she said. "And yet you do not seek to bind me with oaths or threats."

"I didn't realize that was necessary."

"Flayn thought it so. For the wizards, knowledge is power. They do not share their secrets lightly."

"Knowledge is always power—for everybody," he agreed. "It's just that this is only a small part of my plans. If you leave, you won't find out the rest of them." The girl had a sharp mind, and it had been enraptured with the bits of science he had thrown out. As long as he had new things to teach her, he assumed she would stay.

"There is another tie that binds. Yet you shrink from intimacy." She put her hand on his, and he reflexively pulled away, proving her point.

"I have a wife," he said.

"So did every man I've ever slept with," she countered. "If your wife were a queen or some great power, then men would just laugh at you for being a well-trained dog. But she cannot reach you here, so people assume you're insane."

"Not far off the mark," he muttered glumly. Often he was convinced of the same thing. But then he would stub his toe or something equally mundane and realize it was all too real to be a hallucination. "Wait, what about religious devotion? Surely some priests dedicate themselves to the Lady and forgo other women?"

"Yes," she agreed. "Like I said, insane."

He had to laugh. "At least we agree on that. But then, we also agree that you're not the slightest bit interested in me, and you're only bringing it up because you want to bind *me* to *you*."

She smiled at him, a chess player complimenting her opponent on a well-played move.

It wasn't her that he wanted to impress, though. That night, at the dinner table, he asked Tom if he could borrow his shovel.

Tom politely declined, explaining, "It's a delicate piece of equipment. Best used only by the well-trained."

"I think you can trust him, Tom. The Pater's a specialist in dirt," Svengusta said. "Especially night-soil."

"Fine," Christopher said. "Then I won't show you what Fae and I have been up to."

"I think we already know what that looks like," Svengusta said with an inebriated giggle.

Helga threw the old man a minatory glare. "Big Bob needs to keep closer track of your account, I fear."

"You can help, Sven. I'll need an empty field, one away from houses or stables."

Svengusta laughed so hard he almost fell off the bench. "Your wizardry requires the most unlikely components. You would work miracles with manure and dirt and empty fields. But I warn you, if what you wind up with is a dirty, smelly field, no one will be impressed."

When the boys showed up for night duty, Christopher stopped them before they got their coats off.

"We're all going out," he said, "for an experiment."

The boys' faces lit up, and they went back outside gabbling in excitement. Apparently word of his every act was public knowledge, or at least speculation. By the time they reached the field, they had attracted a flock of villagers.

Tom dug a hole for him in the frozen earth and put Dereth's iron tube in, jamming it down on its spike so it stood straight up. Christopher loaded a rocket in the tube and threaded the long fuse through the hole at the bottom.

"Who wants to do the honors?"

The young man who had carried out the lit candle refused to surrender it, so he got the privilege by default.

"Now set that on fire," Christopher said, pointing to the end of the fuse, "and then run like the devil is behind you." Then Christopher pushed the crowd back a good thirty feet.

The lad bent over the hole, dropped the candle, and ran back on wings of pure excitement. Christopher could relate; village life was boring. Anything new was candy for the young.

The ground erupted in fire and smoke, flames shooting up five feet high. There was a tremendous boom and children screamed.

"The grain size is too large," Christopher said absently to Fae while scanning the sky. He had wanted the slower propulsion of a large grain, not the explosive force of fast-burning fine-ground powder. Now he was worried too much powder had burned outside the tube, and his rocket would hit the ground before it exploded.

It failed to explode at all, landing a hundred feet away like a poor dead bird.

"No, leave it be," he warned the boys. Best to wait in case the fuse was just slow. He went forward to load the next rocket.

Walking back to the safety line, he noticed everyone staring at him. "What?" he said.

"Gods, boy, those flames! It looked like you opened a gate to Hell!" Svengusta exclaimed.

"I know," Christopher said sadly. "I made the grain size too big."

"That . . . cloud . . . is coming toward us," Helga whimpered.

It was true. The huge pillow of white smoke was slowly drifting their way as it dispersed.

"I know," Christopher said even more sadly. "I don't know how to make smokeless powder."

"Is it dangerous, I think the question is," Tom asked with a bit of an edge in his voice.

"Oh, no, not at all. It just smells bad."

With extreme bravery, another lad set off to light the next one. This time he was only halfway back when the ground exploded in a vast plume of white smoke. The rocket was nowhere to be seen, shredded into nonexistence by the blast.

"That," he said to Fae, "is what happens when you make the grain too small." And the fuse too quick, but he could see from her face that didn't need mentioning.

The third attempt burst into a pale-green star globe high above the village, and the audience burst into spontaneous applause. Fireworks, like sex and money, were a universal crowd pleaser. Christopher barely noticed; his hopes had been fulfilled by the violent self-destruction of the second rocket. Like all scientific experiments, the proof lay in the mundane results; the sparkly lights were for the public.

"That's what I'm going to show the Saint," he told his companions. "What do you think?"

Svengusta wasn't terribly sanguine. "It's a pretty entertainment,

I'll grant you, but I've seen wizards do better. I don't think it will get you out of the draft."

"I also fail to see how this will make us rich," Fae said.

"I'm not even sure it can pay for itself," Tom said, watching the crowd disperse. "Especially if you give it away for free."

Leave it to Tom to state the obvious. His original problem remained: an inexhaustible need for money.

<hr />

He set Fae to making more paper, this time by the quarto instead of one sheet at a time. The stench of a paper mill overwhelmed Tom's coal-cooking experiments. Christopher countered with the mound of ripe manure he was collecting. All of this finally resulted in a visit from the town elders, led by Svengusta.

"Gods, boy, this place stinks!" Svengusta exclaimed. The villagers reassured Christopher that they loved their crazy priest, but the smell was getting out of hand. Christopher wasn't terribly sympathetic. The whole village reeked like a pigsty on the best of days, even in the middle of winter. He was dreading warm weather.

"It's only for a little while," he reassured them. "Both Tom and Fae will be moving back to Knockford soon and taking the stink with them. Now please, let me buy you all a drink."

Svengusta cheered the suggestion, and they all retired to the tavern, where Christopher coughed up a pair of gold coins.

Afterward, Svengusta congratulated him on how he'd handled the situation. "We'll make a parish priest out of you yet."

"Only if you're there to lead, and then sell out, every insurrection. Thanks for saving me—again."

"Precious little reward I get for it," Svengusta sighed in pretended despair. "A few beers, a bit of pretty around the house, and exploding wheat fields."

"If I might ask," Tom said, "when are we planning to move back to town?" Fae perked her ears, too reserved to say anything but obviously deeply interested in the answer.

"When Karl shows up with more money," Christopher said. He had been profligate with his fortune; now he was promising to spend money he didn't have yet.

Later Svengusta cornered him alone. "I cannot pretend to understand what you are doing, but I can see you need this more than I." Svengusta put down a leather bag that clanked. Curious, Christopher opened it to find a hoard of coins, copper, silver, and even gold.

"Where did this come from?"

"My stipend from the Church," Svengusta said. "I give away as much as I can without encouraging indolence, but my wants are few and my needs fewer. I had thought to leave it all to the Church, or possibly Helga, when I am gone. But if you need it now, that would seem a better use."

"Why didn't you invest it?" Christopher asked.

"In what?"

It was a good point. There wasn't exactly a managed 401(k) fund around. Retirement planning consisted of stuffing money under your mattress. Or wait—that was what you did with paper money. Nobody would want to sleep on a pile of coins.

"Thank you," Christopher said, "but you have given me something more valuable than money."

Svengusta kicked the bag, eliciting a protesting jingle. "Are you mad? What could be worth more than hard cash?"

"An idea," Christopher said.

"Not another one!" Svengusta exclaimed. "Take the money and be satiated, if you value the quality of my sleep."

12.

DOOR-TO-DOOR SALESMAN

After days of gray skies, cold winds, and hard labor, Karl appeared like sunrise on a three-day weekend. Helga beamed, Tom grinned, and even Fae made a point of being noticed while ignoring him. Svengusta laughed to see Karl casually toss the bundle of chain mail into Christopher's lap, where the weight of it almost knocked him to the floor.

"I leave you alone for a week, and you start killing people without me."

Christopher blushed. "I didn't mean to."

"Gods forbid you should ever intend on slaughter, then."

It seemed like the perfect opening.

"About that," Christopher said. "I'd like to make a presentation to the Saint. And the quartermaster of the draft. I want to commandeer the draft budget."

"Everybody wants to," Karl said. "Why would we care what you want?"

"When you see what I have to show you," Christopher answered, "I think you'll want me to, too."

Karl studied him through narrowed eyes before answering. "The Saint is a busy man. His time is too valuable to waste."

Christopher thought about the twin points in time that ruled his life: the approaching draft and the receding Earth.

"I have less time to waste than the Saint," he said.

"Very well," Karl said. "I will beg an audience and trust you not to make fools of us both. Pack your bags."

"What, now?" But of course now. The layers of bureaucracy he had subconsciously expected did not exist in this world of personal contacts and loyalties.

Christopher hurriedly packed for the trip, Tom and Helga repacking everything behind him so it actually fit into the saddle-bags, while Karl watered his horse. Helga wrapped yesterday's bread and cold bacon in a dishcloth for their lunch.

Returning from the stable, Karl frowned in disapproval.

"Wear the armor," he said. "On that horse you will look a thief without it."

Christopher noticed that Karl had already replaced his own armor, and his horse carried a shield and crossbow as well. The omnipresent sword Christopher could understand; samurai had worn theirs every-where, as a sign of honor and class. But the wealth of rough, well-used weaponry that surrounded Karl at all times suggested an unnerving level of savagery in the world outside the little village. Without further remarks he struggled into the chain mail.

They rode for the rest of the day, stopping only for the horses' sake. It was allegedly spring now, but someone had forgotten to turn off the ice machine. They avoided contact as much as possible, and when they did see people they didn't say hello. Karl wore a scarf over his face so he wouldn't be recognized, almost a bandit's mask. Between that and their swords, the peasants were careful to look the other way. Here was fear, finally, and Christopher felt like an outlaw, the stark contrast to his role as village clown rubbing against him as uncom-fortably as the saddle.

They ate a cold lunch on the road, thanks to Helga's competence. Christopher had been too busy to see how she dealt with Karl's return. It didn't matter. Karl was in soldier mode and oblivious to women. He hadn't even reacted to Fae.

But he had noticed. On a deserted stretch of dirt road, hardly more than a trail, he interrogated Christopher about his living arrangements.

"You've become quite a lordling, Pater. Manservants and pretty girls."

"They're part of my plan of world domination," Christopher replied, trying to be funny but too cold and tired to carry it off.

"How do you know they are not agents of the Invisible Guild?"

A terrible thought he had not even considered.

Karl shook his head at Christopher's stricken silence.

"The correct answer is, because Pater Svengusta has known them all their lives. Still, it would be wise to pay the Vicar for a truth-spell sometime."

They spent the night in a village tavern, Karl conversing brusquely with the innkeeper and paying for a single room that he blocked shut by dragging the bed in front of the door. "Use the chamber pot if you have to," he said, and went to sleep instantly.

The next day they turned into a well-kept country estate just after noon. A pair of stable hands greeted them in the stable, although saving their comforting words for the horses. Christopher didn't see any armed guards until the door of the manor house was opened by the most competent-looking soldier Christopher had yet seen, outside of Karl. Well, and the sickening Hobilar.

The soldier recognized Karl without speaking, but he wanted a name from Christopher.

"Pater Christopher, um, sir," he answered, uncertain of how to address the soldier.

"Ser," corrected the man without any visible offense.

"This is the captain of the Saint's guard," Karl explained.

"Such as it is," the man grunted. He was thirty-something, tall and powerfully built. He had on a light chain shirt and wore a long-sword and oversized dagger. "Knight-Captain Steuben," he formally introduced himself, and inclined his head at Christopher in a way that made Christopher think of Prussians. At least he didn't click his heels.

"Can I ask why I've met the Saint twice but never seen you?" Christopher asked.

"You just did," Steuben said. "But to answer your question, my duties are normally considered ceremonial. I rarely leave Kingsrock, as the Saint is hardly expected to be in danger in his own lands. But your little adventure with the Invisible Guild has everybody in a tizzy."

They followed him into a large dining hall, where Saint Krellyan and a handful of others were finishing a lunch buffet. Karl bowed stiffly to Krellyan, and Christopher copied him, the formality surprising, but the Saint immediately released them from it.

"At ease, Goodman, Pater," Krellyan said. "Have you eaten? No, of course Karl has not delayed for mere necessities of the body. Please, help yourselves."

While they filled their plates, Karl and Steuben speculated on the reasons for the mummers' attack. The discussion led nowhere. Apparently Faren's interrogation had been no more profitable than Vicar Rana's. Christopher didn't pay much attention because he was distracted by the buffet. He had forgotten what it was like to have to choose what went on his plate. There were actual pastries, not sweet like doughnuts but still light and airy compared to the ordinary bread, and once he realized Karl wasn't interested in them, he took the rest of the platter. He could get fat on this kind of food. That would be a problem he'd love to have.

"Are you cursed?" Krellyan asked. "You seem to draw violence and trouble to you from the farthest quarters of the world."

"I don't know," Christopher said, his mouth still full of fruit tart. "Am I cursed? Can't you tell?" He was tired of being blamed for what other people did to him.

"I'm sorry, it was a poor attempt at drollery." Krellyan paused and then spoke in Celestial, tracing a glyph in the air with his hand while peering intently at Christopher. "But no, I don't think you are."

Krellyan had a way of making you regret your petty slips.

"The fault is mine, Saint," he said contritely. "I just don't see how I could do things differently."

"You don't see how you could try to fit in more?" Krellyan asked gently.

"Oh, I see how it could be done. I just don't see how *I* could do it."

Krellyan sighed. "Neither do I. It does seem odd that one first-ranked priest should matter so much. It's not like people haven't knocked heads before, but this seems never-ending."

"Well," Christopher struggled to explain, "I think it's more than that. I'm, uh, I've got different ideas about things. And I think that disturbs a lot of people."

"It always does," Krellyan agreed with resignation. "Now, I understand you have something to disturb me with."

"I do, but it's more impressive at night. Can I make my presentation after dark?"

Everybody in the room was suddenly staring at him.

"It's a light show," he said quickly. "The lights show up better at night, that's all. But I can do it in the daytime, if you want."

"Yes, after sundown will be fine. No, Captain," he said to Steuben with a smile, "do not fret. The Pater is new to our lands. He likely does not even know why you are suddenly alarmed and suspicious."

"It's true," Christopher admitted sheepishly. "I mean, I guess nighttime's favored by evil, or something like that, but I didn't expect you all to be superstitious."

"You'd think the man didn't have demons where he came from," the captain snorted.

"I didn't. I mean, we don't," Christopher said sadly, nostalgia pressing in.

Steuben was startled but looked at him with sympathy. "Then you came from a blessed land indeed. I'm sorry you got lost and wound up in our little corner of misery."

"You didn't . . ." started a young priestess. She stammered to a halt.

"Go on, Sister," Krellyan encouraged her.

"You didn't come from a higher plane, did you?" she asked shyly.

"No," Christopher said, glad he could answer the question honestly. "Absolutely not. We had plenty of monsters. Just not demons." Pol Pot and Stalin leapt to mind. "Our monsters went about in the day."

"So do enough of ours," Krellyan agreed. "Go relax, refresh your-selves. We will reconvene at sundown."

A servant girl led them upstairs to a pair of small rooms. She offered to draw them a bath, if they wanted. Christopher didn't want to impose, but yes, he said, that would be fantastic, and it was. He ran the girl ragged asking for hot water until she finally disappeared on him. He didn't know what Karl did with his time, although the man seemed quite refreshed when sundown came.

Krellyan had set up court on the back porch of the house. The household assembled there, sipping mugs of hot spiced tea, dressed in warm, genteel clothes. The light-stones shone out into the night, and people talked and laughed softly. It was like a cocktail party except that there wasn't a stereo playing in the background.

The porch faced a large garden, covered in thick snow. Christo-pher set his rocket launcher up on the far side of a brick planter, where it wouldn't hurt anybody if the tube failed and exploded. He loaded his first rocket, a simple green burster.

"I'll need a real candle, not a light-stone," he said.

It was a measure of how dependent on magic they were that it took them a few minutes to find one.

"Everybody understands this goes boom, right? And the stable's secure, somebody is with the horses?"

"My captain assures me all is in readiness," Krellyan said. Steuben was standing next to the Saint, looking jaundiced, alert, and suspi-cious all at the same time.

"Here goes." Christopher lit the fuse and stepped back behind the planter. "It takes a few seconds," he explained. "It should be about—"

The rocket shrieked into the night with a whomp and a cloud of white smoke. But the internal fuse didn't light, and it fell silently into the distant woods.

"Interesting," Krellyan said.

"Is that white smoke dangerous?" Steuben asked.

"Oooooh!" the ladies said.

Karl, however, said nothing.

"Actually," Christopher explained, "that one didn't work. Let me try again." He went down and reloaded the tube with a yellow burster. It was difficult because his fingers were numb from the cold, compounded by unexpected nervousness.

But this time the rocket exploded into a star over the dark fields and forest. The yellow was not that different from plain white. He needed stronger salts. Christopher stopped analyzing the color and paid attention to the crowd.

"Ahhh," the ladies said. They liked this one.

"Is that yellow fire dangerous?" Steuben asked.

"Well, no more so than any fire," Christopher said. "I mean, it's not magical or anything. There's no magic involved here." He loaded up one of his untested designs, a multicolored sparkler.

It worked better than he had hoped, pale-blue and green rays streaking out from the explosion, the chemically treated bits of paper twinkling in burning flight. The effect was enhanced by the two colors being on roughly opposite sides of the burst.

"Are those sparkles dangerous?" Steuben asked.

"Not particularly," Christopher said absently, thinking about his next test.

This one was supposed to be a two-stage explosion, the first one green, the second one yellow. It didn't exactly work out. The green burst was good, but the yellow charge apparently came apart too soon and merely fizzled a little.

"I have a few more of these," Christopher said before Steuben could ask his inevitable question. "They are variations on the basic theme, just different colors to amuse people. What I want to show you is how this craft could be turned to weaponry."

He loaded his bomb, its payload a full quarter-pound of his finest milled blasting powder. He winced at the thought of a misfire or the bomb exploding in the tube, but he had a point to make.

"This one will be really loud," he warned. He lit the fuse, instinctively covering his ears.

The rocket streaked up and burst high in the sky, rumbling like thunder after a too-near lightning strike. The porch shook, the audience shrieked most satisfyingly, and even Karl seemed to notice. The boom echoed off some outlying hilltop, and in the starlight the huge white cloud floated peacefully away while the clerks chattered excitedly. Only Krellyan sat unmoved, thinking.

"That was definitely dangerous," Steuben said, raising his voice above the prattle. Other noises leaked around the edge of the house, grooms shouting and the horses acting up in the stable.

"I think we are done here, Pater," Krellyan announced. "You've gotten our attention. Now let us go inside, and you can tell us what it means."

He ushered his giggling flock of servants into the house with his usual gentle smile. To Christopher, it seemed strained.

Krellyan assembled his clerical staff in the main hall while the servants went to prepare dinner.

"Tell us what you intend," he ordered Christopher.

"I want to make weapons based on this craft," Christopher said. "Like crossbows, only deadlier. I don't know yet how well I can do— that depends on the skill of your smiths. But I know I can make a weapon that will supersede all other ranged attacks."

"And you need money."

"Of course," Christopher said. "Tons of it. I want to equip the entire draft levee with these weapons. Then I'll be happy to march to war with them. We'll actually have a chance."

"Nonsense," Steuben declared. "Pater, your lights are pretty, but your alchemical tricks are no substitute for rank. Your men will die just as fast, only more expensively. The money would be better spent on ranking the best ones." He gave Karl a look fraught with significance.

"We don't have the money," Krellyan said, but nobody paid attention.

"You don't understand," Christopher argued. "It's not lights I'll be using for war. You saw how far out those rockets went. I'm going to make weapons that do that, kill people at six hundred feet or more."

"It's been tried before," the captain countered. "They march out, brave and strong in their shining armor, their fine swords, their beautiful horses. And they die, to all manner of ludicrous monsters. Only rank can withstand the power of rank."

"We don't have the money," Krellyan said again, not any louder. This time something in his tone made everyone notice. "Even if I were to accept your scheme, we don't have the money."

"I have a, uh, scheme for that, too." Christopher produced the fruit of his latest novelty, bank notes made from Fae's paper and fine penmanship.

"What are these?" Krellyan asked as Christopher passed them around for inspection.

"It's called a bearer bond. See the date there? On that date, which is ten years from now, you can cash in the bond for that amount of gold. These are thousand-gold-piece bonds. The Church of Marcius is bound to give whoever holds this paper one thousand gold."

"Your Church commands such exalted funds?" Krellyan asked with gentle disbelief.

"No, not yet. But I've got ten years to raise the money."

"How?"

"By investing the money I get now. See, for me to give you that bond, you have to give me five hundred gold first. It's like a loan."

"And you're going to invest the money in your magic weapons and get rich off booty from the battlefield," Krellyan finished sadly.

"That's the general idea," Christopher agreed. "Why is everybody shaking their heads?"

"It is the oldest con in the book," Steuben declared sourly. "You take the money and invest it in a carriage trip to the farthest part of the world."

"But I won't do that," Christopher protested. He played his trump card. "You know I won't do that, Saint Krellyan. I can't. I don't have anywhere to run to."

"What difference does it make?" Steuben asked. "If we don't have the money, then we can't buy your little slips of paper even if we were stupid enough to want to."

"I'm not selling them to you," Christopher said. "I'm going to sell them to everybody else. The townies. The peasants. I'm going to make bonds in denominations of one and two gold, and sell them for five and ten silver. I only need a few gold from each person."

"You'd con our entire nation?" the captain squawked, stunned at the magnitude of Christopher's plot.

Krellyan sat quietly, thinking. "I do not know as much as you think I do. Tell me, what will you do if I forbid this?"

"I'll go somewhere else," Christopher said, suddenly angry, sparked by the fear of rejection and abandonment. "Somewhere on this pathetic planet there must be somebody who understands vision, who can see the value of new things. You keep telling me Marcius put me here, guided my hands, but you balk at my every step. Why am I here if not to change things? Why are you trying to stop me from changing things?"

"Because I fear," Krellyan said sharply, cutting off Christopher's rant. "I fear everything. I fear yesterday almost as much as I fear tomorrow. Twenty thousand people depend on me for protection, guidance, healing, and I fear to fail them. Tens of thousands more cry out to me for justice every day. I fear to fail them. I have far too many responsibilities, Pater, to not fear.

"Silence," he commanded when Christopher opened his mouth. "Your point is made. And I know your mind as well, Captain. I am not blind to either the possibilities or the necessities. There is one person more I would hear. Karl, you are the voice of my common people. Tell me what you think of this."

The young soldier's voice was uncharacteristically soft. "I am just an ignorant farm boy, so stupid he got drafted twice. I do not understand state policy or grand visions. Please do not put this responsibility on me."

"I must," Krellyan said, implacable but not without pity. "I would know your mind."

Karl looked into the fireplace, and Christopher realized that it all came down to this. Karl was the man on the spot, who knew Christopher the most. He was the one who knew what was best for the common soldiers. Now the bond Christopher had begun to forge with the hardened young veteran would be tested to the extreme.

"I can only tell you this, my lord. If Pater Christopher goes to distant lands to pursue his scheme, I will go with him."

Christopher had to turn away, to hide his eyes. He had never conceived of such a loyalty. He was awestruck by the courage this young man had, to stake his entire life, not just his future but even his past, on blind faith in another man.

Even Steuben was moved, blinking in surprise.

Krellyan was convinced. "We cannot risk losing such a servant," the Saint said with a gentle smile. "Pater, I allow you to do as your conscience dictates. I will not oppose you in this endeavor, though I cannot aid you much."

"There is more," Christopher said, feeling utterly graceless. "I want the mineral rights to the Old Bog in Knockford. The current mining methods are hopelessly inefficient. I've consulted a local expert," meaning Tom, "and I've calculated that the smiths are effectively paying two silver pieces for every barrow of ore. They don't know this, because they have to pay their apprentices anyway, so they think the labor is free, but those men could be doing something more productive, like making nails." There were never enough nails.

"And worse," he continued, "in the summer you can even see Journeymen digging their own ore." Or so Tom had claimed. "That's a terrible waste of talent. I am certain I can provide the smiths with ore at one silver a barrow. That means they'll produce more, for less, which will make everybody richer. I'd like you to trade me the mineral rights to Old Bog for the next ten years, for those two bonds, on the condition that I sell ore at half price. I think it's a fair deal for you. And I need more metal than the current production methods can provide."

The captain snorted. "It's the first sensible thing the Pater's said all night. By all means, knock some sense into those guildsmen."

"I'll have to discuss it with our legal expert, Cardinal Faren," Krellyan said, "but I suppose you aren't asking for anything I can't give."

"One last thing, my lord," Christopher winced. "I need credibility. I need to be able to tell the people that you've paid me a thousand gold for my bonds. You have, of course, because you've given me the mineral rights to Old Bog, which are worth at least that much. But they won't buy unless you do, and who could blame them?"

Captain Steuben was frowning storm clouds.

"No," Krellyan said sadly, "I cannot do that. It is too close to a lie. If you must have my name, then you must have my gold. I will send a cheque with you, for one thousand gold drawn from my personal account. I will keep these bonds as fair exchange. You will send me four more of these bonds, made out to the Church, for the rights to Old Bog. Assuming Faren tells me I am allowed to dispense public property so freely."

Christopher stammered. "You have been incredibly generous, my lord. Again. I don't know how to thank you."

13.

ROAD TRIP

In the morning they got a late start, Karl unable to decline a break-fast invitation from the Saint. Krellyan was a wonderful host, and Christopher was remembering what living a civilized life was like. Not *that* civilized, though: there wasn't any running water or central heating.

The journey back was considerably more relaxed. When Christopher mentioned it, Karl explained.

"We are riding away from the Saint. I don't care if danger follows us now."

Reflecting on that loyalty finally forced Christopher to ask the question that had plagued him since the night before.

"I don't want to pry, Karl, but I don't understand. Why did you take my side?"

"Can't I want the draft to be armed, too? If you can truly make these weapons, then it is worth a try. Steuben was right, in his way. Alchemical tricks have been tried, and so have conventional arms. But he's wrong because we haven't tried *your* tricks."

That wasn't what Christopher was getting at. The man had practically sworn fealty. He tried to figure out how to ask about it delicately but failed.

"I don't think that's enough, Karl," he finally said. "I don't think you really believe my weapons will help."

"No," Karl admitted. "I don't believe they'll make a difference. I believe you believe it, but my cynicism remains untroubled by hope."

"Then . . . why?" Christopher couldn't understand. If Karl didn't believe in his plan, why would he pledge his life to it?

"Because," Karl said.

They rode in silence for a while. Karl seemed to be struggling, and when he spoke again, it was as if it were against his will.

"Because I hear it in your voice," he said, "every time you say the word King. Or knight. Lord. Gentry. You hate them. Your eyes flinch every time they are mentioned. Even Captain Steuben, a man of unquestionable honor, made you blink."

"I don't hate Steuben," Christopher protested. The man was clearly devoted to Krellyan, who trusted him implicitly. More impressive from Christopher's point of view was that the man could completely and utterly disagree with him while remaining polite and reasonable.

"No," Karl agreed. "You don't hate Steuben. But you hate *them*."

It was true, of course. American-born, Christopher had an automatic distaste for the aristocratic. He was proud to be from a country that had never had royalty. He couldn't even accept the hierarchy of the Church. His respect for Krellyan and Faren did not stem from their high office or wealth but from the fact that they were honest, moral, and could literally raise the dead.

All the nobility could do was kill people, and Christopher didn't find that terribly impressive. It certainly didn't seem an adequate justification for feudal privilege.

"Is it that obvious?" he conceded with worry.

"No." Karl laughed like a dog barking. "The inconceivable is as good as invisible. How is it possible that one should hate them? They protect us. They put their bodies, their lives, and sometimes their very souls between us and the monsters of the Dark. We exist by their sufferance, by their sacrifice. The reason we're not dog food rotting in a pen until some ulvenman decides we're soft enough to eat is because of the gentry. They fight for us, fight monsters we cannot. Their swords stand between us and degradation, despoilment, and death. How is it possible to hate them, our protectors? How can we begrudge them the prettiest girls, the choice cut of the joint, a few trinkets of gold? They have earned their right to rule, because without them there would be no human beings to rule over."

Christopher realized he might need to revise his original judgment. On Earth, all the nobility had protected the peasantry from were other nobles. Man had no predators left by the time civilization existed. But on this world, the tigers and wolves didn't merely compete with man; they preyed on him. And they had swords and armies, too, and magic. Maybe feudalism made sense here.

"How is it possible to hate them?" Karl said again, his bitterness uncontainable. "No one knows that you do, because to do so is against all sense."

"But you do," Christopher said, revelation striking belatedly.

"I do," Karl said sullenly. "Without rhyme or reason I hate their privilege, their airs, their lofty superiority. They are entitled, but I hate them anyway."

"Which is why you didn't accept a promotion," Christopher concluded sadly. "You couldn't bear to become what you hated."

"You see, Christopher," Karl said, "my actions are those of a madman. For a useless anger I throw away wealth and honors, and pledge to causes that are without hope. You are just my latest insanity."

"But I'm not crazy," Christopher protested. "This is going to work, I know it is."

"They all say that, don't they?" Karl mused.

⧼⧽

They had lunch from their saddlebags, courtesy of Krellyan's kitchen maids, although the comparison with Helga's efforts was quite unfair. As darkness loomed they turned in to another village tavern. Karl wasn't hiding his identity now, and the villagers treated him with warmth and respect, even stabling the horses for free.

Karl still jammed the door shut at night, though.

They set out the next morning in a light snow, the flakes drifting down gently from the hooded sky. They trotted south by open roads, heading for Knockford, where Karl claimed Faren would be waiting for them. Passing between the ubiquitous woodlands and the farms and fields of villages and hamlets, Christopher felt at peace. With his plans moving forward and his grasp of chemistry demonstrated, he could begin to allow himself to notice the quiet beauty of a landscape unspoiled by billboards or concrete.

His nature-trail sightseeing was interrupted when he thought he saw something pop up from the snowy forest hedging the side of the road. Then he was standing on the ground, dumped from the saddle unceremoniously, and blinking while someone behind him screamed in agony, a high, shrill whine.

The snow in front of him moved; in motion, it was revealed to be a short figure, dressed in white leather, reloading a crossbow. Reflexively Christopher drew and struck in a single motion, guessing the outcome to be safe. The figure raised the crossbow as defense; the katana sliced through it, leaving splinters in its wake.

The situation now defused, Christopher turned and looked back to where Royal lay, squealing in pain. The shattered rear stood out in stark highlight, turning the ground red, but he had to ignore it because men were rushing from the sides of the road at Karl, daggers raised. Karl had changed, too, sprouting a white-feathered quarrel from his left shoulder. The young man fumbled for sword and shield while his horse panicked, stamping and rearing.

Christopher turned his attention forward again. The figure had produced a short, thin double-edged rapier and was advancing delicately. From the cold confidence in the eyes—the only part of the face not covered by white leather—Christopher knew he faced rank.

He regretted, now, his initial merciful impulse. He should have struck to kill.

A muffled voice, too guttural for the slight figure in front of him, like Bruce Wayne speaking in a lower register from Batman's costume.

"Gift us the sword and we will gift you your life."

A fool's bargain, to disarm in the face of an unknown foe. He held his katana in high right guard, barked out the words of the spell that covered his sword in glowing silver light. As he had hoped, the act of casting forced the other's hand, and the assassin charged, the thrust piercing his thigh below the protection of the chain-mail tunic.

His tael dulled the pain, so he ignored the thorn and brought his katana down in a sweeping arc. The assassin leaned back to dodge but not enough, and the point of the sharp, glowing blade raked across his stomach, sliding through leather and flesh, bright blood spurting out in its wake.

The assassin continued his backward leap uninterrupted and agilely flipped over, rolling, coming up ten feet away. Blood marked out his path, but Christopher could see the man was no longer bleeding seriously. Only tael could have closed such a wound.

For his part, Christopher felt unusually woozy, struggling to stay awake despite the adrenaline rush of the fight. He loosed his left hand from the hilt, raised the palm, preparing to cast a healing spell.

The assassin started to react but checked his lunge for some unknown reason.

Instinctively Christopher shifted to the right, narrowly avoiding a horse as it barreled past him, Karl's sword passing over his head as the young soldier brought it forward in a charge.

Again the assassin flipped and rolled, easily escaping Karl's charge. Christopher reversed his grip on the katana and thrust backwards, impaling the assailant running up behind him without taking his eyes off of the fencer. The man slammed into his shoulder, with the smell of sweat and bad breath, and then the body was falling, sliding off the sword. Christopher swung the katana about in a great arc, blood flinging off in sparkling droplets, returning to forward grip and high right guard.

Down the road Karl struggled to convince his horse to turn around.

The assassin looked both ways, the mounted warrior to one side and the swordsman to the other. Then he simply turned and walked away, quickly, smoothly, and with a flourish of his white cloak vanished into the snowy woods.

Karl came charging back, slid from the saddle and down to one knee. Christopher reached out and grabbed the quarrel, paused briefly to meet Karl's eyes. Karl inhaled and gritted his teeth; Christopher yanked, ripping the white quarrel out in a spray of red, dislodging broken links of silvery mail. His spell closed the wound before the young man fainted, and suddenly Karl was on his feet again.

"There may be more," he said, "but see to your horse."

Christopher turned back, stepping over the still body at his feet. Farther down the road, where Karl had first been attacked, lay another body in a fan of bright red, but Christopher stopped when he got to the horse.

Royal's back leg was broken below the knee, bone sticking out from torn flesh.

"Hold him," he cried to Karl, who had come after him, sword in and shield held ready. Karl hesitated only a fraction of a second before dropping both weapons and falling across the horse's head.

Christopher reached down, touched the wound, matching the horse's trembling with his own fatigue, shock, and dread. He had to get this right. Svengusta had made it clear that if you healed a bone crooked, it would stay crooked. He could not afford crooked. In this world as in his own, it was an act of mercy to shoot a horse with a ruined leg.

With an orison he stopped the bleeding. In the momentary relief the horse calmed, lowered his head to the ground, and cried gently. Christopher seized the opportunity and took the broken leg in both hands, forcing the bone together with grating snap. With all his strength he held it in place while the healing spell left his lips, the horse squealing in pain and rending Karl's cloak when it fell within range of its snapping teeth.

But as the magic flowed into the horse, the pain vanished and the bone held. Christopher could only hope it was straight. With the last of his orisons he soothed the torn flesh, watching magic knit muscle and skin back into place.

Royal stopped trying to bite Karl and started trying to get up. Christopher did not want to let him—idiotically he wanted the horse to wait and let the leg heal, but he felt faint and weak, and he could not stop the giant warhorse from scrambling to its feet.

Royal cantered away but came immediately back, putting his head down to where Christopher sat in the snow.

"I don't feel good," he said, to Karl or maybe to the horse. He grabbed Royal's head and let the horse help him stand.

Karl, retrieving both their swords from where they had been carelessly dropped, looked at Christopher in concern.

"Mount," he ordered.

Christopher put foot to stirrup and heaved himself onto Royal's back, a process that was surprisingly difficult. Karl started to hand him the katana. After a second look he sheathed it for him.

"Ride," he commanded, and smacked Royal on the flank.

The warhorse broke into a gallop, and Christopher leaned forward, struggling against falling, resting on the animal's long, warm neck.

Without meaning to, without realizing it was even happening, Christopher blacked out.

He woke up when the horse came to a halt in the middle of a village. Unknown hands were helping him down.

"I'm okay," he said, and it was mostly true. He could stand, at least.

A woman with concerned eyes led him inside, sat him down, cut open his trouser leg with scissors and examined the wound.

"It is contaminated," she said unhappily. She healed him with a touch and a prayer. Belatedly he understood she was the village priestess.

"Thank you, Sister." He was still woozy but no longer in pain. He felt almost entirely well, save for a grayness that hung just below his conscious awareness.

With surprise, she replied in kind. "You are welcome, Brother." Then she looked at Karl.

"I'm fine," the young soldier said. "How long do we have?"

"I do not know," she answered. "But he seems to be recovering. It may be that the poison has already done its worst. But you must get him to a Prelate in any case. It is infected."

Karl nodded, acknowledging her command, and turned to go. "We left two bodies up the road, about a half mile. Send a party to burn them. But a large party—we did not kill them all."

"One was ranked," Christopher interjected.

"How do you know?" the priestess asked.

"Because I fought him. No unranked man could have taken that blow and lived."

"It's true," Karl said with sincere approval, "the Pater swings a wicked blade."

"Blade?" The priestess's eyes stared at his sword in confusion. "Oh," she said, as realization dawned. "You are the War priest from Knockford." She looked at him the way someone would look at a tiger in a tutu.

"That's me," he agreed.

"If you're done with the lady, Pater, we have some riding to do." Karl was already opening the door.

Christopher mounted, surprised at how much easier it was this time. Magical healing was disorienting: one moment you were screaming in blood and the next you were fine.

"Thank you again, Sister," Christopher called as Royal took off after Karl's horse.

"Our luck is obscene," Karl barked with mirthless amusement once they were outside of the village. "And your horse magnificent. His strength broke the trip-rope before it brought mine down, even while he set you on your feet. Thus I dodged footmen while you defeated the master assassin despite his poison."

"No, you chased him off with your glorious charge," Christopher countered. "He would have finished me in the next pass." He was recovering from the shock and could analyze things more carefully now. "But why? What did they want?"

"The sword. I had heard rumours, discontent with the idea that a priest could defeat a knight through mere skill. Clearly some believe those rumours and credit the sword with magical powers."

Christopher looked down at the plain steel at his side. "This thing? It's not even properly made."

"I myself would risk much to gain a Sword of Sharpness that sunders limbs from ranked foes in a single stroke. If it were true, it would be worth more than the entire county of Knockford."

"How do we fight a rumor?" Christopher wondered. "They'll just keep coming. Maybe you should have left the damn thing on the ground."

"Maybe you should get a bigger escort," was Karl's response.

Christopher wasn't feeling very well by the time they arrived at Knockford, and it wasn't just his infected wound. He kept thinking about the sounds a man makes when he's been run completely through with a long piece of steel.

Impossibly, Faren was already there and expecting them. Karl handed him a sealed leather portfolio, but first Faren had to hear about the most recent attack.

Faren confirmed the wound was poisoned. "Night-drake root," he declared. "A sleeping draught. Do not feel comforted, though; they did not choose it out of mercy but only because it is cheap. No doubt they would have cut your throat while you dreamed." He also confirmed that infection had also been deliberately injected. "They didn't want you to live long, in any case."

With a word and a spell he made it all go away, even the gray tang of fatigue.

Afterward the three men sat in the little rectory, while Faren read over the paperwork in silence. Karl waited with his usual remote indifference. Christopher was uncharacteristically quiet. His thoughts weighed heavily on his soul.

The old man set down the last of the papers with a sigh. "Why, Karl?"

The young veteran leaned forward in his chair. "The Invisible Guild operates at will in our lands. Nobles tramp over our peasants and challenge our priests. Our boys march out to war, where they are treated like dogs, only less valuable. It's time the Church had some spine."

Faren snorted, shook his head. "You used to be such a sensible boy." But he addressed the rest of his remarks to Christopher. "Do you know how many soldiers the Church employs? Krellyan has an honor guard of a captain and four knights. Each of our four Vicars maintains a dozen common men, but they are little more than police. We directly rule a tenth of the fiefs of the Kingdom, with fewer soldiers than your average Baron's retinue. It is true that our Vicars are not inconsequential figures in their own right, but none of them owns armor any greater than chain mail. We simply do not have a military presence.

"Even our feudal levies are led by foreigners, other nobles appointed by the King. We have no leaders, no regiments, no heroes. We simply do not have a military presence.

"Because we are not a military threat, the King has trusted us. Not just this one, but all of them. Because we are not a military threat, the nobles have allowed us to open churches on their lands, provide healing, guidance, and comfort to their people. Because we are not a military threat, we have been allowed to inherit fiefs that were willed to us by lords who wanted what was best for their people. No other faction would be allowed so much concentrated power, and we are still growing.

"And now you want to change all that. A half century of policy, of careful neutrality, of constant growth, and you want to change all that. You want to march to war with pretty lights and grand illusions of victory."

Christopher hung his head in his hands.

"I would almost suspect you of self-interest. You serve with the next draft, so it stands to reason that you want the levy to be as well-equipped as possible. You want their chances to be greater, because they are your chances." Faren shook his head. "But I know you well enough to know this is not the reason. You don't just want to make your three years safer or more successful: you want to change things. You want to change *everything*."

The smallest muscle in Karl's face twitched. It was enough to transform his perpetual grimace into wolfishness.

"I don't want to upset your national politics," Christopher protested. "I just want to give the boys a chance."

Faren nodded approvingly. "You lie less convincingly than a two-copper whore. I like that in a man, shows he's got a conscience. But you need to learn to not answer questions like that. The only reason you're still alive is that nobody has guessed how much trouble you intend to cause. I suggest you keep them in the dark as long as possible.

"You do understand," Faren said with emphasis, "what happens if this all goes wrong? You'll be all alone on that scaffold. The only neck in the noose will be yours. Krellyan will cut you and your Church loose like an infected hangnail."

"I understand," Christopher said. "I can accept that."

"You do that," Faren said angrily. "If you shit your drawers and the King sends a squad down here to hang you, we won't protect you. We can't. If you piss off one of our allied lords, and he demands your head on a platter, we'll give it to him. We have to. It is only our weakness that protects us. It is only our helplessness that convinces others to fight for us."

"I understand. I can accept that."

"Then what is it you cannot accept?" Faren asked with brutal insight.

Christopher looked down at the floor in shame. "We had a battle today. I killed a man. I killed him and I didn't even think about it. *I never saw his face.* And while he lay there, bleeding to death, I spent my magic on a horse.

"It never occurred to me to heal the human being instead of the animal. Was it because the horse was crying and the man was silent? Or was it because I thought less of a man in a mask than I did of my pet?"

Karl sprung to his feet, his face contorted with disgust. He turned away, radiating contempt, until he gained enough control to speak. "That horse saved your life."

"Karl has a point," Faren said. "Those men would not have thanked you for saving them. Had you healed one, he would have stabbed you while you were still praying. And if you had not healed the horse, then you would have passed out there in the snow, and the assassins would have slain both you and Karl."

"I know that," Christopher said miserably, "*now*. But I didn't know it then. The point is, while it was happening, I didn't even think of saving them."

"No, you thought of saving your horse, and why not?" Faren asked. "He's a good horse. Why should he be put down because some jackanapes chose to do evil? True, he's only a horse, but he didn't do anything wrong. They chose their actions; he didn't."

"Look at it this way," Faren argued. "Could you have done differently? If you had won the field, and the other assassins had surrendered, you would have healed the wounded, right? You did the most
good you had the power to do at the time. You can't be responsible
for other people's actions. The horse was an asset you simply could not
afford to lose at that time. You did what you had to do."

"That's what I keep telling myself," Christopher said with contri-
tion. "But is it enough?"

Faren snorted in disgust of his own. "You'll get no sympathy from
me, boy. If you'd brought them in alive, I would have just had to hang
them. And I'm tired of harvesting your fields. I had to hang a man last
week, on your account."

"You hung him?" Christopher exclaimed, stricken. "I thought he
could atone!"

"He had the chance," Faren grumbled. "Wasted a fifth-rank spell
and the Saint's precious time, for nothing. He chose the noose despite
it all."

"I don't understand," Christopher said, puzzled and hurt. "Why
would somebody choose to die?"

Faren looked at him piercingly. "Why does anybody choose anything?
I don't know, boy, you tell me. Why would someone choose Darkness?"

The perennial question of the heart: why would someone condemn
themselves when others stood ready to forgive? This was a test Christopher could not pass, a question he was constitutionally unable to
understand. Committed wholly to empiricism, to the notion that
truth was something you extracted from the world, he could never
really comprehend those who thought that the world derived from
truth, especially from their private and personal truths.

"I don't know, either," he said slowly, trying to condense a lifetime
of observation and confusion into a few words. "I guess sometimes
people would rather cling to a pretty lie than face an ugly truth. Especially if the lie is one they've told themselves about themselves."

"Indeed," Faren snorted. "Could you be suggesting that a man might do what he absolutely had to do and yet still whine about it afterward? Still expect his friends to tell him he's as gentle as a lamb, as innocent as a babe, as pure as the driven snow?"

Christopher blushed, stung to the core. "I don't want to be a killer," he blurted, trying to erase the memory of facts, to undo the bodies lying in the snow.

"And I don't want to be old," Faren said in a voice of sour wine. "Shit stinks. Who would have guessed? Maybe you shouldn't have pledged to a god of War, eh?"

"But it's so stupid. They think I have a magical sword. They're attacking me for no reason." He was saved by an idea. "I'll sell it. Karl, you take it to Kingsrock and auction it to the highest bidder. We can use the money, and people will stop attacking me. Even if you can't sell it, you'll convince everybody that it's not magical."

"No," Faren commanded, "I forbid it. In fact, I expressly forbid you to tell anyone it isn't magical."

"What? But then they will keep coming!"

"And what of it?" Faren snapped, raising his voice for the first time. "Did you never consider the alternatives? If the Invisible Guild is trying to kill you, then they aren't killing other people. If the gentry are harassing you, then they aren't harassing somebody else. You suck wickedness like a bloodworm sucks poison. Let them come. Better they should trouble you than honest, innocent, *helpless* folk. And what if they kill you and run off with your head? Then everybody's problems are solved."

The Cardinal thundered, "You were happy enough to shake the apple tree, boy. Do you expect me to listen to you whine about a few lumps? This is the price. You want rank, change, whatever the hell it is you are after—this is the price. Are you willing to pay it?"

Christopher buried his head in his arms, crushed under the weight of revelation. He had joined an army without really thinking. Not just any army, but one that fought up-close and personal with swords and spit in your face, not distant and abstract with artillery and jet-fighters. He had formed a plan to make weapons without really considering what weapons were used for. At no point had he pictured mangled bodies torn apart by cannonry, shattered limbs, and splintered houses. He had resolved to gain wealth and power without really accounting for where it came from in this world, a purple essence grown from lives and loves, histories and personalities, from sons and daughters of people he would never meet. He had thought he could take what he needed and go. He had not considered that he might have to leave some part of himself behind.

He had not acknowledged the price.

But here, with it before him in inescapable concreteness, he must also acknowledge what he was buying. It seemed that Maggie stood just outside the room, waiting, and the hollow pain stretched from his heart deep into his bowels. What was she, and the life they had shared, really worth to him?

Finally he raised his eyes, looked across the room to the grim judge who glowered out from Faren's age-lined face.

"I'll need a bigger escort."

14.

ENTER THE TROUBADOUR

With ill-concealed distaste, despite it being his own idea, Cardinal Faren handed over a dozen writs of arms. This meant Christopher could raise armed troops—at his own expense, of course. Karl only twitched at any mention of the Church police, and he wasn't terribly sanguine about hiring mercenaries either.

"They'd just be bought out by the Invisible Guild," he said. "We don't need fighting skill, we need loyalty."

Instead, they agreed to recruit the local boys. These were the ones Christopher would be serving with next year anyway. And they weren't really boys, being seventeen, but the term "men" was reserved for those who came home from the draft. Faren said Christopher could buy the boys off from their parents for the outrageous price of a gold a week as replacement for their lost labor. Then all he had to do was feed, clothe, and arm them, and convince them to risk their lives for him. He had to offer them something besides gold, though, otherwise they'd be bought out by the Guild too. He had to offer them something the Guild couldn't. He had just the thing: Karl.

The Church made official announcements every day at noon. Usually there was nothing to cause excitement. This morning was different. Even the acolyte proclaiming the list choked and had to cough before he could finish.

"Goodman Karl Treyeingson has announced that he will hold a special training class for a dozen last-year boys, to prepare them for the draft. Interested parties should contact Pater Christopher at Burseberry Chapel by next Tenday. Classes will last—" he choked again. "—until the draft. Apprentice buyouts will be provided for quality applicants. Room and board provided."

Karl had insisted on sneaking out of town immediately after the announcement went public. "If they won't walk a few miles, I don't want them," he explained.

Christopher found it ironic that the day he'd ridden in with a cheque for a thousand gold was the first day he'd spent in town without spending any money. He'd barely had time to deposit it with the astonished clerk and make the necessary arrangements. Next to that vast sum, Karl's hard-won contribution from selling the armor in Kingsrock seemed a pittance.

"Go to town," he told Fae and Tom. "Rent a place to live and work. Buy more equipment. And start looking for people you can hire."

"Give us money," Fae retorted, so he did, counting out stacks of fat gold coins that sparkled and reflected from their eyes.

She made the coins disappear and then resumed the conversation. "Why do I need more equipment?"

He couldn't tell if her defensiveness was real or an opening move in one of her secret negotiations. "There are other things I need you to make. I warned you there'd be new ideas. And you too, Tom. Now that I've got money, I've got lots of ideas."

"People to hire?" Tom asked.

"Starting with the drayman, for you." Christopher handed him another stack of gold coins. "I want the two of you to start collecting manure from other villages, the older the better. Just pile it up somewhere convenient in Old Bog. If anybody objects, tell them to take it up with me."

"What new ideas?" Fae demanded.

Block-printing would count as a new idea for her, in this world of the personal and the handmade, but she could never draw enough bonds by hand.

"You'll see."

"That was a profitable trip you took," Tom observed, still fingering the shiny coins.

"I suppose you could say that," Christopher said ruefully, thinking of what it had cost him.

By midafternoon the first boy showed up from town. Christopher assembled his regular crew and told them what the deal was. He explained that Karl would be in charge of the selection, but they didn't seem overly worried. Probably they assumed he would pick them first. Probably he would, because he could trust their loyalty.

Karl ran the five boys ragged for half a day, allegedly testing them for the positions. Christopher suspected he was just having fun. A few other boys showed up before dark, and Karl told them to come back tomorrow. One of them complained about having made the trip for nothing, so Karl told him he needn't bother to return at all.

That night was the last night Tom and Fae would be dining with them. Christopher was going to miss Tom's good cheer. He wouldn't miss having Fae around that much. It wasn't that she was unpleasant, just that she was, well, distracting.

Belatedly he realized he needed to warn Helga. "Um. We're going to have a dozen of those louts living here soon. Can you cook for that many people?"

Helga's eyes widened. She said yes anyway.

⌦⌦⌦

Over the next few days Helga got a practice run, as she fed batches of applicants at Karl's suggestion and Christopher's expense. Any complaints Christopher might have made were silenced by the way their eyes widened at the hams and sausages bought from the tavern.

While Karl ran them through the village like an obstacle course, Christopher struggled to master drafting with pen and ink. Frankly, he felt the boys had it easier.

On Tenday they had the largest crop, as it was the weekend and the last day for the trials. Karl was satisfied with the turnout.

"We've drawn most of the eligible boys in the county. I'll make my final picks tonight. Then we can go to town tomorrow and spend some more of your money."

He had told all the boys the announcement would be made at Knockford Church at the start of the week, and they'd better be there if they were interested. He wasn't thoughtless about it, though. He'd told at least half the boys they didn't need to worry about showing up.

One of those unlucky ones sought out Christopher after the regular afternoon ride. He was a short, skinny kid, missing three fingers on his right hand: Charles, the tavern-master's son.

"Begging your pardon, Pater," he stammered. "Karl said I could talk to you."

"Of course you can," Christopher replied, "but not about the class. He's picking his own students. And aren't you too young anyway?"

"I was born a few days before the cutoff," Charles said. "But I'd rather go out with you, and my parents said I could go early if I did." Understandable enough, given that Christopher had already saved the boy's life once. "Karl didn't pick me, on account of I can't wield a spear with only one finger." Krellyan's regeneration was expensive. It wasn't going to be used on a peasant when he didn't need it. He could still work in his father's tavern. "But Karl said to tell you I can read and write."

That was interesting. Even Karl wasn't literate. When he had signed as a witness on the mineral rights to Old Bog, Karl had laboriously printed out his name like a sacred engraving. It was the only word he knew how to write.

"How is this?" Christopher asked.

"Sister Margaret taught me," the boy answered, "I want to be a priest after the draft."

"You can write with only one finger?" Christopher asked, curious.

"Oh no, Pater, I write with my left hand."

Christopher raised his eyebrows. "Then why don't you use a spear in your left hand?"

The boy looked at him in dismay. "You can't do that, Pater, you'll break the shield wall."

Christopher steered the conversation back to more familiar ground. "Can you do sums?"

"Yes, Pater, a little."

"Let's have a test then. Here, add up all the numbers between one and fifty." He handed Charles a sheet of paper that he'd already ruined with bad drafting.

While the kid scratched away, Christopher discussed his trip to town with Helga. She wanted things, like pots and pans and mixing bowls.

"If you expect me to feed an army," she sniffed, "you have to spend like a lord."

Christopher agreed and suggested she hire a girl or two part-time to help. Much to his relief, she accepted.

The kid was finished, so Christopher went over to check his work. "And the answer is—wait, no, don't tell me—" He closed his eyes, worked the Fibonacci formula in his head. "Twelve hundred and seventy-five."

Charles's eyes grew wide for a moment, then narrowed again. "You knew the answer in advance," he accused, before he remembered he was talking to an adult and added, "Pater."

Christopher laughed. "Okay, pick a different number." The kid rattled off a two-digit number, and Christopher gave him the answer. He had spirit: he came back with a three-digit number. Christopher told him the result and then asked, "Are you willing to check that one? It could take a while . . ."

"Is it magic?" the boy asked in defeat.

"No," Christopher said, "it's craft. And I'll teach it to you, if you want."

The boy's eyes shone. "Yes, Pater, I would like that."

"Then here's your job. You keep track of everything we buy and use for the troop, and tell me when we need to buy more. The last thing I want to do is find out we've got eleven loaves of bread when we need twelve." He didn't actually care about bread, but managing ammunition stores for an army would be more accounting than he could bear. If he could teach this kid how to do it, he wouldn't have to.

The boy nodded again, bubbling over with excitement.

"Go tell Karl what I said. And come with us to Knockford tomorrow."

When he went to the tavern for his afternoon pint with Svengusta, there was a stranger in the bar. Strange, because women were so rarely allowed in the hallowed drinking hall. This exception was understandable, however—long blonde hair, a generous endowment over a thin waist, and a young heart-shaped face with high cheekbones and red, full lips.

She was singing and accompanying herself on a lute. She was very good, and very pretty, but not enough to melt the ice. The villagers had not overcome the memory of the mummers, and remained suspicious and cold. When the song was finished, to a silent crowd, she gave up and approached Svengusta and Christopher's table.

In a sweet voice, she asked, "May I join you, Paters?"

"Of course," Christopher answered. "Have a seat."

When she sat down, he leaned back and casually covered his mug with his free hand, copying Svengusta.

A grimace flashed briefly across her face, but in the same pleasant tone she said, "I've played to friendlier morgues."

"We had a bit of Invisible Guild trouble," Svengusta explained. "They were disguised as mummers, so you can see how the lads are a bit touchy."

"Perhaps you could inform them I am not of the Black Brotherhood, Pater," she said evenly. "I've not made a copper since I got here."

"Perhaps I could," the old priest nodded, "if I knew it to be true."

"I'm certified with the College!" she snapped. Recovering her poise, she tried politeness again. "What makes you think I'm with the Guild?"

"The College doesn't mean much in these parts," Svengusta said. From his tone, Christopher inferred he didn't think it meant much in other parts, either. "And I don't think you are with the Guild. I just don't know you aren't."

"Fortunately, I'm not terribly concerned with what you think," she dismissed him. "I came to talk to Pater Christopher, the first priest of War in the Church of the Bright Lady in over half a century."

"No comment," Christopher said.

"I haven't asked you anything yet."

"Whatever it is, my answer is no comment. You're either a spy or a gossip." Though he'd meant to say journalist.

"Is such suspicion indicative of the nature of your new Church?" she asked pointedly.

"See," Christopher said, "that's why I don't want to talk to you. You'll go away and tell people stuff like that. If I don't say anything to you, then at least you can't twist my words around." He'd been interviewed on TV once, back home, on some trivial local matter, but the experience had taught him a lesson. If you didn't have your own press agency, you were at the mercy of the journalists. On Earth, they were a notoriously merciless profession. He took it for granted this was one of those universal constants that held everywhere.

"I can say good things about your Church, too, Pater," she offered smoothly.

"That would be even worse," Christopher grumbled before he remembered he wasn't talking to her.

"You don't want publicity?" She sounded genuinely surprised. "Every priest wants his Church on the lips of every mouth. Why would I believe you are different?"

"See, more questions I don't want to answer. Why don't you ask me something I can answer? Ask me what color the sky is. Or if I like green eggs and ham."

"Your reticence tells me there is a story here." She smiled, unable to completely hide her triumph.

Despite his best efforts, she'd painted him in a corner. "Fine, I'll give you a story." She would keep digging until she got something, and there were some things he'd rather she not dig up. "Two weeks from now, in Knockford, I'm going to demonstrate a new craft. It's called pyrotechnics, and it's an exciting new business opportunity."

"Pyrotechnics aren't new. Wizards do it all the time."

"Ah, but they use arcane arts. This is just craft." He realized he'd probably just made an enemy of every wizard in the world. "But it in no way competes with wizard stuff. It's different."

"How is it different?" she asked, keenly penetrating his obfuscation.

"First you tell me what you know about wizard pyrotechnics, and then I'll tell you how it's different." That was a good idea. Get her talking so he could shut up.

"I know you summon fire from the ground. I know you have a magic sword. I know you spend money like water, even though you were a beggar three weeks ago."

"That's not about pyrotechnics," Svengusta interjected. "Except maybe the first part."

"What do you want from me?" Christopher asked. "Why are you here?"

"I collect and distribute information," she said. "That's what I do. And I try to make a living along the way."

"Or, to put it plainly," Svengusta said, "you wander around looking for something you can take advantage of. Like looking for gold under rocks instead of working for it."

She grinned. "I prefer my version, although yours is not without merit." She clearly enjoyed the thrust and parry of verbal combat. If she got a hold of the bored and lonely Fae, she'd know everything within minutes.

"I can use some publicity," Christopher announced. "I want a good turnout for my demonstration. I want people to be ready and willing to invest money. I want them to know I am going out next year with the draft, to fight with our boys and to bring back as many as I can. I want people to know I'm honest, upright, and devilishly handsome." He also wanted people to know his sword wasn't magical, but Faren had explicitly forbidden him from saying that.

"Devils aren't handsome," she remarked. "You have a strange way of speaking."

"Oh, yes," Svengusta agreed. "He speaks like a madman. But if you pay careful attention, you'll notice that everything he says is insane."

"If I give you money, will you spread the news I've just told you?" Christopher pressed.

"Depends on how much," she said casually.

"How much would it cost for you to spread just that news and nothing else?"

She grinned wickedly. "Maybe it's not gold I'm after." She started playing footsy with him under the table.

"That's all you'll get."

"So that's true as well, is it?" she smirked. "You prefer the company of your boys?"

He was really tired of this. "Why is it," he said with ugly curiosity to Svengusta, "that every cheap whore you turn down assumes you must be a pederast?" He knew he would regret his pettiness, but right now he was simply angry.

"I'm not cheap," the woman protested with a grin, utterly unstung by his attack.

"The Pater honors his wife's memory," Svengusta said. "The fact that you've never had a man who could remember your name the next day does not speak for all men."

Svengusta's point was not so easily brushed aside. The woman tipped her head and apologized. "I'm sorry, Pater, that was churlish of me. When did you lose your wife?"

"More questions," Christopher said. He could hardly tell her he was the one who was lost. "I'm tired of your questions. You haven't answered any of mine yet. You seem to think I should give you information for nothing."

"Not exactly," she countered. "I have information to trade. I can tell you the names, records, and ranks of four knights who are on their way here to take your sword, and if need be, your head, in a duel."

"I won't be fighting any duels. I'm done with that. But if you can give me the names of four Invisible Guild thugs, I'd gladly chat about my sex life."

"I'm no friend of the Guild. If I had names I would have already turned them over to the Vicar. I could use the gold."

Christopher took a gold piece from his purse. "Then use this. Spread the word about my demonstration. Emphasize how it's a good investment opportunity."

"Give me two gold, and it will spread twice as fast," she grinned.

He handed over another. If it shut her up, it was worth it.

"I am not your enemy, Pater," she said softly. "I came to see if you were Bright or Dark. Now that I know, you will receive one less challenge, on my account."

"He's a servant of the Lady," Svengusta said with disgust. "Of course he's Bright."

"He's a priest of War," she countered. "Who knows what that means? Certainly not your brethren in Copperton."

"Were you going to challenge me?" Christopher asked with some surprise. A woman with tael would be as deadly as a man. She didn't look dangerous, but tael was invisible.

"No," she laughed, "not in a duel, at least. But there is a certain Baronet Gregor who takes my counsel dear, and he will not do violence against the Bright. I am Lalania the troubadour, and I will execute your commission faithfully."

Then she took her leave, like an actress walking off a stage. Everybody watched, despite their hostility. She was extremely attractive.

"I don't think this is what Faren had in mind," Svengusta mused. "Guild thuggery is one thing. An invasion of dueling nobility is something else. What are we going to do?"

"Give them something else to talk about," Christopher said. "I just have to get through the next two weeks."

15.

RECRUITING DRIVE

The next morning Christopher and Karl set out for town, taking all five of their boys with them. They were armed with cudgels and a generous supply of throwing stones. Christopher felt the troop was well-prepared for an ambush by pigeons, or even possibly an angry hedgehog.

"I don't want to hear any whining about carrying rocks to Knockford," Karl admonished them. "This is just the beginning. Welcome to the army." They took this to mean all of them had been picked, so of course it was all right with them.

They were halfway to town when they met a party coming from the other direction. A man and a woman, both shaggy, mounted on horses that were equally shaggy. The woman was dressed in forest-green garlands, with a black crow perched on her shoulder, nestling into her long, curly black hair; the man was in dark-red metal, his horse an equal for Royal. This fact was not lost on the two steeds, who locked eyes and snorted, demanding the other yield the trail. Merely passing them was going to be an ordeal, except of course there was more to it than that.

"Pater Christopher," the man said, "I presume."

"Yes," Christopher answered, "and no, I won't duel you. You have no provocation. If you attack me, you'll fight us all and be arrested to boot. You wasted your time. Sorry, go home."

The woman said something to her man in a low voice, and he seemed disappointed.

"Not even if I wager a purse of gold against your sword?" he asked. "A friendly contest, without killing, and may the best man win?"

Now that was tempting. He could lose that duel, and the sword, and be done with it. But then he wouldn't be a trouble magnet anymore, and Faren wouldn't be happy.

"No, sorry, but thanks for asking." But he had an idea. If this fellow was so keen on fighting, maybe he could be convinced to do some of Christopher's. "However, there are a number of other, ah, adventurers looking for me, or so I'm told. They'll be interested in dueling."

"You recruit me as your champion, untested?" the man laughed.

"Can I do that?" Christopher asked Karl. "Can I hire this guy to fight duels for me?"

"Yes," Karl said, "if he's willing." Karl addressed the other man. "May I ask your rank, Ser?"

"Only a Baronet," he replied, "but don't let that fool you." He was built like a barrel, if barrels were six feet tall. "I can beat any man my own rank in a duel." He didn't sound like he was boasting, just relating a fact.

"That's good enough for me," Christopher said. He didn't really care about losing the sword. His plan only required that it look good so Faren couldn't ride his case. Karl's approval would be enough for that. "Is it good enough for you?" he asked Karl.

"He bears a two-handed sword," Karl said, referring to the five-foot-long monstrosity hanging from the pommel of the other man's horse, "a duelist's weapon. A shield is preferred on the chaos of battlefield, and a longsword is sufficient to slaughter unranked enemies. The greatsword is for bringing down large targets. So, yes, I would bet on him in a duel."

"Excellent!" Christopher started to address the Baronet. "Ser, uh . . ." Didn't people ever introduce themselves by name in this world?

"Cannan," supplied the man.

"Ser Cannan, here's my offer. If anybody your rank or lower challenges me to a duel, you get to fight it. If you win, you can keep their stuff. If you lose, I'll give up my sword."

Cannan looked at his woman, who answered in a delicate voice. "It will at least keep the blade in the hands of the Bright."

"Well, priest," Cannan said, "I agree. For a time, at least."

"I think it's only for the next two weeks, anyway," Christopher said. "After that I hope people will have found better things to worry about."

Cannan laughed at that, obviously amused at Christopher's naïveté, but all he said was, "I'll need five gold a day for expenses."

That was a staggering sum for two weeks of protection—more than he was paying Fae for an entire year of labor. But looking at the huge, armored man, he felt butterflies in his stomach. Cannan was no playboy amateur like Hobilar. He was a bona fide warrior. The idea of facing down more of these was sickeningly frightful.

"Agreed," he said weakly.

They dismounted for formal introductions. Christopher began to appreciate Karl's point of view when the nobleman introduced his horse as Bloodfire and asked for Royal's name, yet failed to notice Karl, despite the fact that the young man was covered in chain mail and armed to the teeth.

The lady Niona, introduced as Cannan's wife, talked to both the horses in what Christopher guessed was the same language Faren had used. The horses paid rapt attention to her, but Christopher was distracted by the creature on her shoulder. He had assumed it was a bird before; up closer, it looked like a cat.

After that they could ride side by side, although Christopher was terrified.

"I'm not a very good horseman," he warned Cannan. "If mine goes berserk and starts a fight with yours, I won't have a clue what to do."

"I think I can control my mount, Pater. As long as you can control your troop." He winked broadly at the four ragged boys behind them. Niona and Karl had fallen to the back of the column, giving the warhorses plenty of room.

"Ha," Christopher said, "that's just the beginning. We're going to town to get more."

He would have explained further, but he was distracted by the sight of Niona's cat launching itself into the air like a falcon, gliding out ahead of them, its broad black wings spread wide.

As they neared town, a rider approached from the east, obviously another duelist, his bright-silver armor glinting in the sun and his great bay stallion running with ease. He galloped up to the party, pulled alongside.

"You're too late, Faulkner," Cannan grinned. "But it's good to see you again."

"Goddarkdamnit, Cannan," cursed the new man from under a bushy mustache. "I rode out here for nothing?" He consoled himself with a cheery thought. "Well, at least I can watch you hack him in half. Maybe I'll learn what it is you've been bragging about."

"Oh no," Cannan said, "I'm his champion. He bought me off, he did."

"Ha ha! . . . Damn, you're serious." He eyed Christopher speculatively. "Just how good is that sword? Maybe I'll challenge you after all."

"It's not that good," Christopher said. "I don't see why everybody's making a fuss over it. I mean, if it were a really super-powered sword, you'd think people would be afraid to face it in a duel. But no, they're just lining up." That wasn't violating Faren's rule, exactly.

"Will he let you use it?" the knight asked Cannan.

"If he wants to, sure," Christopher answered for him.

"Gods! All right, I'll pass. Which way is the damn tavern? This town does have one, doesn't it?"

"Two streets down, to the left, Ser," Karl said, surprisingly helpful. The knight nodded his thanks and galloped off.

"It's not that we aren't afraid of your magic blade," Cannan explained. "I like all my bits and pieces attached. But a sword like that could make a man's career. Now about that gold, Pater." Christopher pulled out his purse, hefted it sadly, and tossed the whole thing to Cannan, who snatched it out of the air with ease. "When you need me," Cannan added, "I'll be in the aforementioned tavern." He galloped after the other man, followed by his lady.

"Are they all like that?" Christopher asked Karl.

"No," the young veteran responded. "Those are the good ones."

<hr/>

Christopher stood in Fae's new workshop and tried not to say anything, since he couldn't say anything nice. The place was a wreck. Fae stood in the front room with the poise of a dancer walking through a muddy street. Tom just grinned at both of them.

"It needs some work, true enough, but I can do that, and your purse will thank me for it."

Like all the other shops in town, it doubled as workplace, retail outlet, and housing. Both Tom and Fae were living in it now.

"Is it safe?" Christopher asked, frowning at the way the roof sagged.

"We have nothing the Invisibles would want to steal," Tom said, misinterpreting his concern. "And when I passed Flayn in the street yesterday, he didn't so much as wink at me."

"That won't last long. About the guild, I mean. I'll make arrangements at the church vault." Once he started printing bonds, he'd need a safe place to store them.

Fae smiled sweetly, which on her was completely unconvincing. "As long as you're going to the vault, we need more money. I've made these purchases on your pledge to pay." She handed him a list of expenses, itself an expensive act since it was written on fine white paper.

Back to the church he went. The Vicar ambushed him there, steaming in anger.

"Do you exist solely to plague me?" she growled.

"I'm sorry," he said, not terribly sorry, "but I am raising the troop under Faren's orders."

"A pox on that," she snapped, still fuming. "Training boys for the inevitable is nothing to be ashamed of. But did you need to bring a *druid* into my town?"

"I'm sorry?" he said again, although he could hardly apologize since he didn't know what was wrong with druids, or even what they were. Rana could see he didn't understand and staggered off, stunned and defeated by his sheer ignorance.

The hall was packed for today's announcements, with curious fathers, nervous mothers, and hopeful boys everywhere. Christopher spotted his new champion laughing and joking with his newest challenger, their heavy, gleaming armor marking them out like lighthouses in a sea of drab peasant cloaks. They were sizing up the boys, who took their ribbing good-naturedly. After all, these were real-life heroes.

Karl took the podium. Without preamble he began. "I've chosen the following. When I call your name, affirm and come forward."

Karl had scored better than Christopher had hoped. Every name Karl called was present. He'd expected at least one to fail to show up, either because his parents overruled him or he'd had second thoughts.

And yet even Karl could not compete with the knights. The boys loved Karl, but they lusted after the knights. All the two warriors had to do was whistle, and Christopher would lose his entire entourage, like rats after the piper. He felt his cheek twitch. Like Karl's so often did.

Karl had made his way to the interior door. He turned, called once to the group, softly, and Christopher was struck with sickening fear. The boys were still gawking at the knights, still pinned by the glittering spectacle of heroism. He knew instantly that Karl would not call again. Worse, he knew Karl would never forgive any boy who did not come now. The men were recanting some war story, and the disappointed boys, the ones not named, were wholly enraptured. Christopher watched with terrible anxiety as the others struggled between the call of duty and the lure of fame.

Christopher was the one who broke first. "Let's go," he shouted, grabbing the one nearest him. "Move it along."

"A weedy crop you've got here, priest," Cannan laughed. "You're picking your beans early."

"Come back in a few seasons, and then tell me what you think," he replied. The boys weren't moving as fast as he would like. He was getting worried again as he made his way to the door.

But Karl's boys came. Some on their own, some driven by parents, a few prodded by their friends. But they all came.

Weak with relief, Christopher released his iron grip on the last one's shoulder and followed Karl into the next room.

Now it was just the boys and their parents. Not all of them had two, and several of them had three. Christopher decided not to ask.

"We've got to fill out some forms, and then I owe you all some money," he announced. The procedure was simple, if expensive. He wrote his and each boy's name in the writ, the boy made his mark, Karl witnessed it, and Christopher handed each set of parents nine gold coins. "That's for the rest of this season. Come summer, I'll pay you again."

"For any boys that are still worth it," Karl added menacingly.

"I'll promise to feed them well," Christopher said, eyeing the ragged lot, "and I'll buy them some new clothes. They'll be well cared for."

"Don't mind that," one father said. "Just make them tough, like Goodman Karl." His unspoken comment hung in the silent air, visible on every face.

So they'll come home again, like Goodman Karl had.

<hr/>

They sent the troop to Palek's to be fitted for simple open-face helms like the ones Christopher and the guards wore. Christopher might agree with Karl on the worthlessness of armor, but helmets were another matter. Even in WWII they wore helmets.

He and Karl went off to the weapon-smith's, figuring their absence could only improve Palek's mood.

"We can't give them swords," Karl explained along the way. "It would be too much of an affront to the men. They're not drafted, yet. They're not men, yet. They'll be disappointed, but we must find other arms."

"You said we should send them out with just spears and cross-bows," Christopher replied, "and I agree. For now." Karl had coerced the Vicar's police into lending him four crossbows, so all they needed were some spears.

Jurgen was smiling to see them, with visions of gold coins in his eyes. "You're recruiting your own troop. Very forward-thinking. You will find my sword-craft an equal to Palek's armor." Apparently the promise of profit was enough to assuage whatever affront Jurgen would feel.

"We want to look at spears," Christopher said.

The smith frowned, taken aback. He led them to a corner of the shop where old stock laid stacked and dusty. "These are the standard spears, Pater, for the ordinary draft."

Christopher pointed to an ugly little stick with a short stubby blade on it. "What's that?" he said.

"That's a half-spear, Pater. A novice's project." He added sourly, "Farmers use them for sticking pigs."

"It's perfect," Christopher said. It was no more than four feet long. "I'll take twelve." He wasn't going to give one to Charles. The boy's literacy made him too valuable for that. "Can you have them ready by next Tenday?"

"You can have them now," the smith muttered, and stamped off, leaving one of his juniors to deal with the unprofitable customers.

Karl was almost grinning as they left, carrying the sticks bound together in a large bundle. "Tweaking Jurgen was worth it," he said, "even if all we do is burn these for firewood." The half-spears had cost a single gold each, the cheapest object in Jurgen's entire inventory. "But I think I'll hide these till the boys get to the village. We don't want them bursting into tears in front of the whole town."

They stashed the bundle under a stack of blankets in Fingean's wagon, Christopher counting out coins to the drayer to carry back to the weaver.

"We'll need coats," Christopher said, thinking out loud. The townsmen were adequately dressed, but the peasant rags would be no more sufficient for the boys than Christopher's were for him. Napoleon had miscalculated the material requirements of fighting in cold weather; Christopher would not make the same mistake. "And boots." He looked down at his purse, calculating.

"I'll pay for the helmets," Karl said. "No one can fault me on that, since it's for the draft."

"Then I can afford to dress them like soldiers," Christopher said. A uniform would help mold a group identity out of his teenage mob.

"And yourself," Karl said. "It is time you dressed like a man of means instead of the village scarecrow."

The idea made Christopher uneasy, even though he was tired of being cold. He did not want a new identity here; he did not want to be anything other than the lost beggar seeking his way home.

***

Christopher almost lost his army on the way back to the village. Half of them ran off into the woods to have a snowball fight. Tom was diplomatic, never losing his smile. Fingean glowered and threatened the boys with a club when their snowballs got too close to his draft-horse.

Karl ignored it all, so Christopher followed his lead.

Cannan stayed behind in town, saying he didn't see any reason to go out to the village. "If anybody wants a duel, send them here." It seemed like a good idea to Christopher. He didn't like the way the boys fawned over the knight.

At the chapel they pushed benches together and threw bales of hay on them for beds; Christopher's workroom was reduced to a corner next to the fireplace. Then Karl nailed the back door shut. Now the only way in and out of the chapel was through the main hall. Christopher wasn't sure if that was to keep the Invisible Guild out or the chaotic mass of boys in.

Dinner exposed an oversight.

"I should have bought a bigger table," Christopher said.

"They'll spend the next three years eating off the ground," Karl replied. "Might as well start now."

In the morning Karl lined the boys up at attention. The indulgence of the night before was gone; Karl cowed the line into silent obedience with a glare so fierce even Christopher stood straighter.

"This is your friend," Christopher said, handing out the half-spears. "You will keep it with you always. You will keep it clean. You will sleep with it. You will live with it. It will never be out of your sight."

Karl had not been wrong. The boys looked at their stubby little toys with dismay. "Beginning your pardon, Pater," said one. "It's a stick."

Christopher forestalled Karl's wrath with a raised hand. "It's a test," he explained. "I don't trust you with anything more valuable than sticks yet.

"And let's get one thing straight right now. You can ask me questions. I'm just a priest. But Karl is your officer. I'll not overrule him on anything: tasks, punishment, or even if he sends you home. You work for me, but you belong to him."

Karl barked, and the boys jumped. "You think I've got all year to make you soldiers? You're wrong. I've got two weeks. We start now."

Christopher fled to the kitchen. He knew if he hung around he'd just get in the way and feel sorry for the boys to boot.

16.

FRIDAY NIGHT LIGHTS

K arl was a monster that never slept, with a thousand eyes that never missed a detail. The boys would have broken down and cried, but they didn't have the time. Christopher attended some of the drills because he needed to know what commands to give. He also needed the exercise. The boys smirked at his poor efforts only on the first day. After that they were too tired to notice.

"We don't actually need them to be able to fight yet," Christopher had tried to explain to Karl on that first evening, wincing as he stripped his boots off his aching feet with aching arms. "They just have to look good, to keep the Invisible Guild at bay."

"I don't know how to train mummers," was Karl's terse reply.

After the second day Christopher was just grateful that he got time off from the regime. True, he spent it shoveling manure, but that activity was less physically taxing. And less embarrassing, since he didn't have Karl standing over him to glare disapprovingly when he did it wrong.

Except today he had a surprise audience. Lady Niona watched him from under her wavy black hair with curious eyes and an enigmatic smile, perched atop her pretty brown horse, her black feathered cat perched with equal poise on her shoulder.

"I did not mean to disturb your work," she said, while he planted the shovel blade in the pile and tried to look like he had just found it there.

"It's okay." He was a little disconcerted that he had no idea how long she had been watching him. If a horse and rider could sneak up on him in the middle of town, his future on the battlefield seemed perilous. "What does Cannan want?"

"The same as any man," she said, "but I am not here on his account. I thought to spare your Vicar my distressing presence."

So this must be the druid Rana had complained about. Christopher couldn't see what was distressing about her; she was neither as scary as her husband nor as immodest as the blonde-haired bard. Unthinkingly, he blurted out the question that came to mind.

"What does the Vicar have against druids?"

Niona's face betrayed almost no reaction, which itself betrayed a carefully adopted pose of imperturbability. Her pet, however, fluttered its wings and hissed.

"Jeger dishonors me with his rudeness," Niona said with a little laugh like the tinkling of bells. "Still, one cannot expect so much from a kittenhawk."

An apt name; it looked exactly like a black-and-white tuxedo kitten wearing a pair of Halloween costume crow's wings. It was as cute as a button, except for the bared fangs and the juxtaposition of unnatural body parts. Christopher stared at it in amazement.

"You have never seen one before?" Niona said, stating the obvious.

"No . . . does it purr?"

"Yes, it is akin to a terrestrial cat in most ways."

Christopher was impressed with how adroitly she had changed the subject, allowing his faux pas to expire silently, but he was already knee-deep in the manure pile, quite literally as it happened, so he pressed the matter.

"Why does the Vicar dislike you?"

"Because I am a druid." Niona's eyes revealed real curiosity now. "Surely you understand—we do not bow to your Goddess, or any god. We are bound to the Wheel of Life; not to a part, but the whole; not to a single nature, but nature itself."

So, hippies. Christopher could see how the uptight Rana would take a dim view of tree-huggers.

"That stuff doesn't concern me," he said. "I won't hold someone's religion against them."

He finally succeeded in breaking through her reserve. With stark wonderment she said, "You would welcome even a slave of the Gold Throne with open arms?" The kittenhawk glared at him and unfurled its wings, crowning Niona in black feathers.

"Those are the bad guys? The ones we are at war with?"

Niona smiled at him crookedly. "Yes, and no. They are certainly Dark, and dedicated to your destruction; but they are also your allies in the perpetual war your King wages against the Wild."

"My King?"

She winced delicately. "I meant our King, of course. We druids are loyal subjects of the crown, even when we disagree with it."

Not just hippies; political subversives. Rana's attitude was looking more reasonable. Niona must have seen his wary calculation on his face, because she offered reassurance.

"A divided heart, yes, but I am testament to its earnestness, wedded as I am to a knight of utterly Domestic pedigree. Cannan, it hardly needs said, is no druid lord."

"How did that go down with the folks at home?"

"I cannot say," she conceded. "We have not been home yet, to face father's disappointment or mother's wrath."

Great. He'd hired Romeo to be his dueling champion.

"And after all these years, I still hesitate. We eloped south, into the Far Wild, ranging afield like any young druid lordling seeking his spurs. And we found them, earning our ranks the old way, but even that seems not enough. So Cannan came running to the rumour of your sword and now seeks to establish his reputation beyond question."

Christopher was trying not to feel sympathetic. He had just discovered that he faced dangers no one had bothered to mention, perhaps because they were so obvious. Between his sword, his religion, and his draft, he'd managed to make more enemies than just smacking Hobilar around would seem to deserve.

But he failed. Niona had made her choices for the same reasons he had made his.

"As long as I have anything to say about it, you're always welcome here," he said.

⚶

She disdained the inn, pitching a camp in the forest outside the village that was little more than a place to tie up her horse. Svengusta accepted her without comment or prejudice, and eventually the villagers seemed to do the same. Her presence was a constant reminder of her husband's pledge, and Christopher began to relax, feeling shielded by her gentle confidence. If she could sleep in the open, then surely he could sleep in peace.

His vacation was doomed to end too soon, and it did when the pretty troubadour Lalania blew through the doors like the pleasant breeze before the storm.

"I like what you've done with the place," she smirked, looking around at the beds and dirty laundry.

"Now what?" he asked, ignoring her baiting.

"Now comes real trouble," she said, not smiling anymore. "Black Lord Bartholomew is on his way to claim your sword."

"You have the name of an Invisible Guild thug now?" he asked, surprised.

"Bart's a lord from the South. Black refers to his armor, and possibly his heart, not his membership in the Invisible Guild. Unless you know something I don't."

"That seems," Christopher said with resignation, "highly unlikely. But as long as you're giving away information, what about my alleged champion?"

"He's coming too, but Black Bart is a Baron." When Christopher did not immediately react with appropriate dismay, Lalania sighed. "Your champion is third-ranked. Bart is fifth. Cannan is out of his league, and he knows it."

"Then I won't accept a duel," Christopher said.

"And that's why I'm here," she said, exasperated. "To prevent you from wrecking the county. You might not appreciate it, but I know the Vicar will. You most certainly will duel him. He's bringing his knights. They are armed, mounted, and utterly without scruples. If you don't give them the sword, they'll take it, and all your police or puppy dogs can do about it is get killed. Yes, the Church will complain to the King. Something might even be done about it, eventually. But the damage they will inflict on the peasantry will never be redressed. So you *will* duel him. I'll not let you provoke a war."

"How does dueling help, exactly?"

"If you lose, he'll have his sword and a ransom, and he'll go home happy. He won't start a war for no profit. And your Church will revive you—you've got the money."

"But what if I win?"

She rolled her eyes. "On the theory that you're just asking out of curiosity, I'll explain. If by some miracle of some unknown god you manage to slay Black Bart, his retinue will not cause trouble. They will only be interested in getting his ugly corpse to the Gold Apostle as quickly as possible."

"What if I just beat him? Without killing him?" That seemed to be his preferred method of dueling, after all.

"I don't think you should consider that option. If you get the chance, you'll kill the monster or answer to every Bright in the Kingdom."

"Then I guess I'll be giving him the sword." Christopher turned to go back into his office.

"That's it?" she said with disbelief. "Just like that, you'll hand over a magic sword for the asking?"

This would make a lot more sense, he reflected, if she knew the sword wasn't magical. Faren was making him look like a lunatic. Well, more like one. He was pretty sure he managed most of it on his own.

"The damn thing's nothing but trouble. I keep getting into fights, most of which end up with me bleeding, and people keep dying. Bad people, or so I'm told, but they just look like poor, desperate losers to me." The ragged men who had attacked him and Karl on the road, and died there, had borne the look of men who did not eat regularly.

"Well, you'll not have that problem here," Lalania responded sourly. "Black Bart's as bad as you could hope for and still be breathing."

He had some work left to do in the office, capping the ink and washing out his pens. Nothing about medieval technology was convenient. Then he dressed for combat, just in case, putting on the chain mail, tightening the laces of his boots, and tucking his helmet under his arm.

When he finally came out of the chapel, he was assaulted by the presence of people. Nothing spoke to his acclimatization to this world like finding a crowd of two or three hundred to be uncomfortable and unusual.

"Who are all these people, and why are they here?" he said plaintively. There were strangers everywhere. There was even a sausage seller's cart set up in front of the tavern.

"You're famous now, Pater," the troubadour laughed. "You've attracted the attention of the peerage. No small feat for a first rank."

More people were arriving on the road from town, following a mounted column at a respectful distance. One of the riders was Cannan, plainly identified by his red armor. The other ten horsemen were dressed in black, but Bart was still easy to pick out. He was the tall man on the gigantic black horse at the head of the column. Even from this distance he looked frightfully dangerous.

Karl joined Christopher in the doorway. "The Vicar won't be sending any police. She won't want to risk offending Bart or causing trouble. But you can be assured she'll tear Faren's ears off about this."

Svengusta came up, looking uglier and meaner than Christopher had ever dreamed possible. "He brings a Gold priest onto our land, and we're worried about offending *him?*"

Karl frowned, staring at a yellow-robed figure hiding in the rear of the column. "He brought his own healer? That's bad."

"The message is clear," Lalania said. "Defy him and you face war."

As the horses came into town, people scattering from their path, Cannan broke into a gallop and pulled up to the chapel steps.

"He outranks me," the big man said, without apology.

"I know," Christopher said. "It's okay."

"I want to fight him anyway," continued the knight. "Killing Black Bart is a good deed in and of itself. But I'll need help."

"Why would killing him be good? Won't they just revive him?"

Cannan looked annoyed, so Lalania explained. "Yes, but you'll knock him down a rank. Weaken the Dark and strengthen the Bright. Cheer one for our side and all that."

So this is what passes for football around here, Christopher thought.

But Lalania was still talking. "Our hero is considering surrendering the sword," she told the knight.

"What!" Cannan exploded. "Give up a weapon of that power to the Dark without even a fight? That's madness, or worse."

Christopher wondered what was worse than madness. Knowing these people, it was probably cowardice, but even Cannan was too polite to use the word.

"Are you a servant of the Dark, or a just coward?" the knight demanded. Apparently he wasn't too polite.

"Neither," Christopher said, "I'm just not that concerned about one sword."

"Bigger fish to fry, perhaps?" Lalania slyly insinuated.

"I'll not stand by idly in this," Cannan said. "Give me the sword, and I'll face him and trust to luck."

Christopher could tell how much this brashness upset Niona by the fluttering of her kittenhawk's wings and the tightness around her eyes, though she did not speak.

"There's no need to die over it," Christopher said. "It's not that big of a deal. Cannan, I need to explain—"

But it was too late. Bart and his retinue had arrived.

One of the black riders broke ahead of the column. From horseback he addressed the group on the chapel steps with insolence and disdain distilled to professional strength.

"Which one of you is Pater Christopher?"

"Here," Christopher said, raising his hand. He didn't see how anything he said or did would affect the outcome, so there was no point in getting all worked up over formalities.

"The Lord Baron Bartholomew addresses you, Pater."

And then the tall man spoke.

"You know why I have come," he said. Christopher wondered if he had to practice that graveyard tone, or if it came naturally.

"To deprive me of my property, I'm guessing." Christopher couldn't help himself. People this full of themselves always made him flippant.

"You are unworthy of such a weapon. You had adequate time to give it to one of your ilk who could defend it. Now you must give it to me."

"I am his appointed champion," Cannan said. "I will defend the honor of the Bright." He gave Christopher a look that said *even if you won't*.

Bart laughed, not at all pleasantly. "That is good news indeed. I had feared I might get no fight at all from these lady-dogs. A long ride without killing makes me grumpy."

"I can't let you do this," Christopher told his wayward champion. "He outranks you, so our agreement doesn't hold."

"If it's only a matter of ranks, Pater, then add a few," Bart said in his gravelly voice. "I'll melee you both. I won't turn down more blood and tael."

"What?" Christopher was startled. "At the same time? That's nuts. I don't care how good you are, you can't take two swordsmen at once."

Bart threw back his head and laughed hard. It still wasn't pleasant-sounding, but the man was truly amused. Christopher noticed that Bart's entire retinue was laughing, as was most of the crowd. Even his own team was looking at him like he'd just said pigs could fly.

"If you won't balk at two, then you won't balk at three," Karl said, his hard face set in stone.

"And what rank are you, brave warrior?" Bart asked, critically eyeing the young soldier.

"None."

Bart was mildly puzzled. "Why would I honor you with death on my blade? It hardly seems worth the effort of killing you."

"I have a masterwork to wager." Karl partially unsheathed his longsword to display the gleaming metal.

"Very well," Bart said, "if the fly brings treasure, I'll swat it. Now to terms."

"There will be no terms, because there will be no duel!" Christopher exclaimed.

"I'm dueling, with or without you," Cannan said with finality. He turned to Bart. "My lady is not involved: she casts no spell or aid and stakes no ransom."

"And you, priest?" Bart asked Christopher, with a casual glance at the glaring Svengusta. "Do you have secondaries to declare?"

"No," Karl answered for them, "we also enter the field of honor unsupported. The Church of the Lady will only heal after the fact."

"Then I declare no secondaries," Bart intoned. "The terms are established." He looked around and by chance and circumstance picked the very spot in the village square where the entire mess had started, then said, "That will serve as the field. I don't mind killing a Bright priest in view of his own altar. Within the hour, then." And he rode away.

Christopher grabbed Karl by the shoulder, dragging him back into the chapel and beckoning Cannan to follow with an angry glare.

"By all means," the red knight said, "let us discuss tactics." He dismounted with a leap and strode into the chapel behind the other two men, shutting the door behind them.

"What is wrong with you?" Christopher hissed at his young friend.

"I'm not a coward," Karl said stiffly, "but you're a fool. Consider this part of your training. I want you to see for yourself what I have been telling you, because you don't seem to believe me. *They are right.*"

"The only thing wrong with him," Cannan said, catching up to them, "is that he lacks tael. He certainly doesn't lack courage."

"Cannan, you idiot." Christopher was so annoyed he didn't care about the flash of anger in the other man's eyes. "The sword isn't magical. It's just a piece of steel. It's not even properly made."

The knight's eyes narrowed as if he suspected a lie before he finally settled for cynicism. "Then all this talk of magic is just a Church ploy? Some game played by you foolish priests?"

"Yes, basically. I'm not supposed to tell people it's not magical, but I'm not going to let you get killed over nothing. I'll give Bart the sword, he'll go away, and people will leave me alone."

"I have already agreed to a duel," Cannan said. "I will not back down. You gave me the right to champion you and paid me with imaginary tael. I mean to claim some of that, at the expense of the Dark. At least I'll have your man with me."

Niona slipped in, shutting the door behind her.

"I risked a spell while you men were laughing." A subtle rebuke. "And I must warn you that he bears some kind of protective device."

"I suspected as much," Cannan said, "which is why I was counting on the magic sword. But I have another string to my bow." He gave Christopher a disgusted look. "So there is still hope."

She misinterpreted Cannan's complaint. "Will you not fight with them, Pater?" she asked in alarm. "You can at least heal."

"Something you need to learn to do," Karl said casually. "Combat healing. We always lose a few men during the first battle, when the young priests are still trying to unpack bandages and wash out wounds."

"Fine," Christopher said, out of patience. "I'll fight." He had no idea why he was agreeing to this insanity. Surely it could not be merely bravado, an unwillingness to appear less than manly in Karl's eyes. "For two reasons. First, because I have a spell in mind I think will be more helpful than a healing, and second, because I refuse to believe that one man can defeat three, if we work together." No swordsman was that good, despite what you saw in the movies. He could not believe that Black Bart could defend against three competent attackers at once.

"Your confidence would be more inspiring if it did not sound so much like madness," Cannan said. "But yes, we must work together, and here is what we will do."

17.

FIGHT CLUB

The other two men dressed for battle while Christopher meditated. Then Christopher ran through a few kata, to loosen up his muscles and the knot in his stomach. Karl grimly followed along.

Cannan watched them silently until the end.

"Dance that well outside, and we may have a chance," the big knight said. As rousing speeches went, it wasn't.

Christopher felt ridiculous, like he was participating in a World Wrestling Federation match. There was a noisy crowd, the smell of beer, contestants in funny costumes, and an absurd fight card of a tag-team of Good guys against one super-Bad guy. He stopped feeling that way when he saw Bart.

The dark knight was standing at the other side of the square, facing one of his men. The soldier had his glove off and was holding his palm up in the air. Bart shoved a dagger through the man's hand, pulled it out, and dropped it to the ground. The man winced silently, but not because tael blocked the pain. His hand was bleeding freely.

Bart raised the man's hand to his face, smeared the blood from his forehead to his chin. He smiled, if you could call it that, a rapturous demonic possession. He released the soldier, who let the priest bandage his hand, obviously saving the healing magic for their lord. Bart turned to the field of honor while another soldier placed a large black helmet on his head.

"It means nothing." Niona tried to sound reassuring but lacked confidence. "There is no arcane or divine significance. He only seeks to frighten you."

The way Christopher's knees went weak belied her words. It was plenty significant. "It means he's one twisted bastard."

"You have no idea," Lalania said with deep sadness. "I could tell you tales to curdle your blood. He rules absolutely in his own land, save for the edicts of the King. But edicts only reach where officers of the crown go, and they don't go into dungeons or villages.

"This is a heroic contest," she told the little group. "I foresee many profitable nights recounting the story. But happy endings are always more popular, so please try to win."

"You'll make me famous?" Cannan grinned. "I've always wanted to be famous."

"I'll try," she said, "but it will be hard to compete with the valorous Goodman Karl. His presence here is inexplicably courageous. To follow his master into battle when he is so utterly outclassed is loyalty beyond measure." Christopher was going to object that he was the one following Karl, but she wasn't paying attention to him. Karl was doing his thing again, where all other men turned invisible. "It is a crime that such a man should be unranked," she said softly.

"I agree," Cannan said. "These lands have become corrupt when such bravery is not rewarded."

"It was rewarded." Christopher felt compelled to defend his new homeland. "Karl turned it down."

Cannan was surprised. The troubadour wasn't. She'd already heard the tale. "Which makes him even more inexplicable."

"I can explain it," Christopher said, since Karl wasn't saying anything. "He's insane."

Karl barked a laugh. "It's true. The Pater and I are brothers in madness."

Lalania stared hard at both of them. Obviously her intuition told her there was more than battle humor here, but she was out of time.

The three men faced Black Bart from twenty feet away. Karl's boys held back the crowd on one side, and Bart's men held back the crowd on the other, although they didn't actually have to hold anything, since no one would get near them. Bart held his side of the field alone, radiating doom and destruction like a pillar of death.

Niona approached Bart, bowed, and began a spell. Bart's priest, an ugly, fearful man, approached the other combatants and started casting his spell.

Bart boomed out, "Priest, swear you and your party are clean of aid. I don't trust my lackey's competence as much as I trust your holy word."

"We are, right?" Christopher asked both his teammates. They nodded, so he called back, "I swear."

Niona came back to them, whispered her findings. "His device maintains the protective field. I still do not ken it, but it lies on him like armor. His blade is enchanted, though no more than the first rank. But these are items and if he stakes them, we cannot object. At least I see no other spells upon him." She tried to kiss her husband. He stopped her, saying roughly that Bart would suspect assisting magic. She retreated to the sidelines with tight lips and clouded eyes.

"Priest," Bart called out, after conferring with his own, "Where is my sword?"

Obviously the magical inspection had failed to detect magic on the non-magical sword.

"Right here, Ser," Christopher called back, drawing the blade and displaying it.

"You swear that is the sword you dismembered Ser Hobilar with?" Bart demanded suspiciously.

"I solemnly swear it. The magic isn't on. Do you want me to turn it on?"

Bart nodded, staring intently. Christopher called out to Marcius for his blessing on the sword, casting the spell that enchanted it. Bart belatedly realized he'd been tricked, and Christopher had gotten a spell off for free. He wasn't amused, though. He was incensed.

With a growl he charged across the short space between them. There was a flutter as the crowd instinctively recoiled, Bart's priest hiking up his dingy yellow cassock and running for the safety of his comrades.

Bart wielded a bastard sword in one hand, like a longsword on steroids, and a large steel shield in the other. He was covered in plate armor from head to toe, not the price-conscious half-plate that lesser knights like Hobilar and Cannan wore, but the real deal. He was also left-handed, which Cannan had explained wasn't as much of an advantage as it might have been, since both he and Christopher were fighting with two-handed weapons. "Still," he'd said, "I'm used to smashing through people's shields. With his blade on my side, he might be able to parry more effectively."

Cannan was on Christopher's right, Karl to the left. The plan was that they would flank Bart from both sides if he charged Christopher. If he turned to face the greatest threat, Cannan, then Karl would have his back. If Bart did the smart thing and eliminated the two lesser threats first, that would give Cannan several free attacks. They were hoping that, and the size of his greatsword, would be enough.

Christopher was already casting another spell, calling down Marcius's blessing for the men fighting on his behalf. Chanting the words helped to ward off the crushing despair that Bart projected. He wanted to prod Bart into recklessness by casting beneficial spells, forcing Bart to advance on him while Cannan and Karl struck from the flanks. But Cannan was fooling around with his sword instead of leaping to the attack, and Bart charged without danger.

As the spell finished and bright winking lights briefly filled the area, glistening off the three men, Bart bore down on Christopher like a freight train, his glowing black sword lashing out, unopposed by the distracted Cannan. Christopher brought his sword up to parry. The dark blade jigged impossibly at the last moment, skimmed over his defense as if it had been rehearsed that way, slammed into the side of his head like a home-run batter, and the world went away.

Cannan bellowed in exploding rage and swung at Bart like he was aiming at a tree trunk. Bart edged away from the blow, just barely. This exposed him to Karl, who brought his sword down like a crowbar squarely on top of Bart's dull black helmet.

Bart didn't shrug the blow off: he didn't even notice it.

The dark knight advanced on Cannan, his blade on his shoulder like a batter about to swing. Cannan held his ground, brought the two-handed sword whirling around in another swipe. Neither man wanted to get hit; they both tried to dodge or parry to some extent. At the same time they weren't terribly worried about it. Like two prizefighters they traded blows to see who could take the most punishment. They just delivered their strikes with gigantic razor-sharp glowing metal blades instead of boxing gloves. Cannan fought with a berserk fury that was awe-inspiring, though it left even less regard for defense. Bart stood like a fortress but never gave up an opening merely because it would leave him exposed.

The black sword smashed into Cannan's shoulder while the greatsword sank into Bart's thigh. Both men shrugged off the blows, shedding little blood, and kept going. Cannan risked a blow to the head, which Bart ducked, and while he was spinning through the stroke Bart stabbed him in the back. It wasn't a total loss, because Cannan made use of the opening once he'd spun all the way around and caught Bart across his exposed left side. The armor squealed as the blade crunched through it. The tall man made no sound. He just hit Cannan again, hacking away with his long black sword. Both men's armor plate was rent in various places, but the bodies underneath were only scratched. The mundane metal was not as resilient as the tael-bound flesh.

Karl had dropped his shield and taken his sword in both hands. Operating freely behind Bart, he laid into the man's back like a sledgehammer. The sword rebounded as if he'd struck a statue.

It was evident that Cannan was losing. Although he was doing tremendous damage to Bart, he was taking almost as much, and it was clear who was going to run out of tael first. Bart seemed unusually outraged with every blow, as if the idea that Cannan could hurt him at all was personally offensive. Perhaps he had expected to be invulnerable to the greatsword, like he was to Karl's thin blade.

Bart whittled away at the red-clad knight, whose costume was now flecked with the red of his own blood. Cannan fought furiously, without concern for his own imminent end, on the constant attack. Bart was damaged, but not enough. Tael still bound the dark knight's wounds. Cannan had begun to bleed freely from the latest cut, and it was clear that he was down to mere flesh and bone. The next strike would be the last and might even be fatal. The terrible power and sharpness of the weapons could kill an ordinary man instantly.

Karl approached again, all but forgotten by both combatants as utterly irrelevant. He raised up high for another two-handed stroke. Something was different. He had traded his sword for the katana left lying on the ground. Still glowing its bright silver shine, the light seemed to prod at Bart, who paused, confused and defensive for the first time, made hesitant by the unseen threat behind him. Cannan threw himself into one last attack, dropping exhausted to his knees to plunge the sword in Bart's chest, a solid blow, but a foolish one, for now he was totally exposed, winded, and immobile, with no defense at all. The black blade rose, its fall and Cannan's death inevitable.

But the sword did not fall, the man did. A majestic tree, straight and solid, he toppled to the ground, the glowing katana embedded in his helmet like an ax blade in a log, its luminance fading back to normal after the flash when it struck. Bright-red blood pumped out of the rent in the helmet, out of the faceplate, out of the neck opening. The yellow priest rushed to his master's side. Cannan staggered to his feet and bodily threw the man away.

"We claim the field," he said, panting. The blood stopped flowing and the point became moot.

At least, that's what they told Christopher later. He missed all of it, waking up on the bed in the chapel, in front of the fireplace. The scene seemed oddly familiar. Before he could remember why, he realized there was something wrong with his right eye.

"I can't see," he said, covering his left with his hand.

"Aye, Christopher," Svengusta said, "there's no surprise there. But the Vicar can fix that for you."

"How bad was it?"

"We almost lost you," the old man replied with uncharacteristic seriousness. "Had the duel lasted another minute you would be dead, bled out despite your tael. But I think there's no brain damage, the eye can be fixed, and you've gotten a handsome scar out of it, so the Lord of Luck has favored you again."

"Brain damage?" But he stopped wondering when Karl handed him the remains of his helmet. It had been cut open like a candy wrapper.

Bart's men were gone, bearing their dead lord back to his own lands but leaving behind his arms and armor. Cannan and Karl had stripped the body first, under the direction of Niona's magical detection, after she drew the tael out of the corpse's cracked skull. Once again booty lay piled before the wooden image of the god of War. Christopher wondered if Svengusta found that as annoying as he did.

"We did well," grinned Cannan, battered but unbowed. "Dark has lost a rank, and we've gained a prize."

"It was not so well done," Lalania cautioned. "To let him bleed out was graceless, when you saved your own."

"He would have done the same," Cannan retorted. "And he wouldn't have had to put up with your tongue afterward."

Niona sat beside her husband, smiling with unrestrained relief. "Graceless was the black knight's acceptance of Karl's participation. He knew his magic rendered the Goodman helpless against him."

"The prize is why we are all here crowding your sickbed," Cannan said, "not a pointless argument over etiquette. I know we agreed I could keep the ransom from a duel, but that was when you weren't fighting it. I feel honor-bound to share the reward with you now. But not unfairly, mind you."

"The standard arrangement seems adequate," Karl suggested. "One share per rank, so Pater gets one-quarter and you get the rest."

"What about you?" Christopher demanded. "You brought the man down!"

"I am your servant, and thus to be rewarded out of your share. I have no rank, and I cannot pretend to be entitled to a troop's share."

"We're not unmindful of the boy's deeds," Cannan said. "But first let us settle the matter of the ring."

He displayed a bright gold ring in his palm, set with small black stones all around.

"It's Dark," Niona said. "This much I know, and I fear it."

"It's powerful," Cannan said. "This much I know, and I want it."

"Unfortunately," Lalania finished, "I don't know much about it, though it is my place to know these things. I am reasonably certain, however, that it was the source of Bart's power and confidence. I believe that the ring shields its wearer against mundane damage."

Christopher was impressed. Magic rings were cool.

"Not completely," she continued. "But combined with his plate, it would be proof against ordinary weapons."

"So how did we win?" Christopher asked.

"Because I cheated," Cannan winked. "I had a potion that rendered my sword magical, much like your spell. I had been saving it against need, and this fight looked to need all the help it could get. That's why he slipped past me to get to you, but if I hadn't stopped to magic my blade, he would have never fallen. Not that I knew that at the time. I was just hoping you could last one pass against him on your own."

"It wasn't cheating," Niona protested. "You brought the potion in with you and staked it as ransom."

"What else did we get?" Christopher asked. He could see the knight was intent on claiming the ring for his own. He couldn't blame him.

Karl finished the list for Cannan. "The armor, which Bart's man will ransom for four hundred gold. That's low, but I don't know that we could sell it for more. Few would wish to be mistaken for Black Bart.

"The blade, for which they've offered a thousand gold. Also low, since it's first-ranked, but it would be a significant insult not to return it.

"And of course his tael."

Niona produced a large, lusciously purple marble.

"That's a lot of tael," Christopher said.

"Yes, it is," Cannan agreed. "Twice enough to put your man here to his first rank, or enough to put you to second. If you were entitled to it all, which you are not. But I will not deny the Goodman a rank."

Everyone looked at Karl.

"No," the young veteran said. "I am not entitled to a share. I will not accept special treatment." He could hardly accept a rank now, in any case. His and the Saint's plan to reduce the armor expenditure of the draft depended on his status as a commoner.

"Your madness borders on insolence, boy," Cannan said. "But your loyalty to your law and your lord must be excused, I suppose."

"What do you think I am entitled to?" Christopher asked.

"We do not know the value of the ring," Cannan said, "but I will concede it is high. Yet if it is as potent as we think, you'll have even more adventurers coming to claim it from you. You are not ranked enough to wield such power. Therefore, I suggest that I take the ring, and give you the rest of the booty. The tael we will divide by standard, a quarter for your rank and three for mine."

Christopher wanted the ring, too, since he seemed to be getting in fights all the time. But Cannan's argument was compelling. It would only lead to more fights.

"The ring is Dark," Svengusta said. "I do not know that any Bright should use it."

"I'm not going to marry it," Cannan growled. "But I do not think my soul will suffer from wearing it in battle. I fail to see how much more evil can touch me when I'm busy cutting people in half. I've struggled with the Dark all my life, and I expect to continue."

"But you expect to always win," Svengusta objected, but not loudly, because it was not his place to say such things.

"I will ask my College about this ring, when I can," Lalania said. "Until then I would beg you do not use it."

"I do not answer to the beck and call of dried-up Eastern scholars." The knight frowned. "I am responsible for my own affiliation, and I will not tolerate any further discussion on the matter."

Christopher looked to Karl for assistance, and the young man nodded subtly.

"Then it's agreed," Christopher told Cannan.

"Since the advice is flowing freely," the knight growled, "I will suggest that armor would make a fine trophy, standing over there next to your fireplace. But I wouldn't give the sword to your stiff-necked young soldier, because I think Bart's going to want to kill whoever has it, just on general principle."

"I don't want to make more of an enemy of Bart than I have to," Christopher said. "I'll take his money if that will annoy him the least."

Cannan looked a little put off. "You could send it home for free, if you are so eager to please him."

"No. I don't want him to like me that much. He might decide to visit."

18.

THE SHOW MUST GO ON

"You'll get no more profit out of your champion, I wager," Tom told Christopher a week later, leaping from Fingean's wagon to unload the latest supplies. Today they had uniforms for the boys and news about Cannan.

"He's too eager," Tom complained. "At first they think he's bluffing, but then somebody tells them about Black Bart and that's the last we see of them."

"Tell him to tone it down a bit, and you might get some more duels," Fingean added helpfully.

"Hello," Christopher said, pointing to the right side of his face, "missing eye here. Not really interested in losing the other one right now."

"You should go to town and have that fixed," Svengusta suggested. "It will only take a moment." Yes, but it was a moment in the Vicar's company, which he was dreading. Besides, he was fiendishly busy getting ready for his tour.

He'd paid Lalania more money, buying more publicity for his tour. Karl had been aghast at setting out a schedule so that everyone would know when and where they were for two weeks of traveling. The security risk was incredible. But that was the point: to provoke a fight with the Invisible Guild when there weren't any villagers around to get killed by it. Karl understood the wisdom of this, even though he couldn't stop shaking his head at the madness of handing out your marching schedule. But once he realized it was quite likely to result in fatalities, he cheered up and modified the training to include security drills, like escorting Christopher through the inn without letting anyone get within arm's reach of him. They also posted a regular guard now, so that at any given time two of the boys were awake and on duty. And woe to the boy who forgot the day's password.

The next morning, bright and early on Karl time, they lined up. The boys were kitted out now, uniforms and winter gear, helmets and bedrolls. The fluted metal helms, long coats, and short spears made them look like some weird version of the Kaiser's Imperial troopers. Christopher and Karl wore the same, although with chain mail under their coats. When Christopher pretended to pull a monocle out of his vest pocket, nobody else got the joke.

They set off for Knockford in a column two wide, the two horsemen in the lead, the boys marching behind with their spears and the handful of crossbows Karl had borrowed. Karl had worked miracles, transforming the boys from rambunctious puppy dogs into orderly, wary young men. True, they were mostly wary of Karl and his exacting standards, but at least they were paying attention now.

They marched into town with a reasonable semblance of martial prowess. The uniforms in particular made an impression, marking them out as a unit, in service to a single master. Christopher could feel his social class rising by the minute.

Sadly, the improvement would not help with the next battle he had to face.

The Vicar glared at him from across her desk.

"My quiet town is now a hotbed of intrigue. Foreign gentry, druids, Gold-robed priests come and go, while mummers, sharpers, and con men of every description choke the streets. Your duel has spread like a taint, as every profiteer seeks to gain your magic sword."

"I'm sorry, my Lady," Christopher said, "but this is not my doing. I would have put the matter of the sword to rest, if not for Faren's orders."

"I'm no happier with him," she snorted. "You might notice he hasn't sent me any additional police, and I've already got half a dozen accused thieves in custody. I'm looking forward to your leaving town. I'm expecting all this to go with you. Including that drunken lout you named a champion. Get him out of here before Black Bart decides to come back for revenge. That's an order."

"I will do my best, my Lady. Our agreement is over, so I think he'll have no reason to stay."

"As a sign of my displeasure," she continued, unappeased, "I'm going to charge you the normal price for restoring your sight. You did not get that injury in performance of your priestly duties, and you cannot plead poverty. Do you have any objections?"

It was quite clear there was exactly one acceptable answer.

"No, of course not, my Lady." But then he had to ask, "Um . . . how much does it cost?"

She pinched her lips in disgust. "You should already know that. You can settle with the clerk. He's got other fees to charge you, as well. We're not a warehouse for your business ventures."

"Of course, my Lady. I am more than happy to pay my fair share."

She sighed, finally running out of steam. "It seems I cannot remain angry at you. Although every step you take discomforts me, you do not act out of malice or stupidity.

"I cannot fathom Krellyan's design," she complained, but not really to him. "The only future I see is you hanging from a noose and your chapel in flames. No, don't explain. If Krellyan hasn't told me, then I don't want to know. But understand, if I show you any kindness, it is out of pity for your eventual fate. Only your imminent destruction makes the disturbances you inflict on my daily life bearable."

He winced involuntarily, thinking of disturbances yet to come. He was reasonably certain nobody had told her yet about the deed he held to the Old Bog.

But she misinterpreted his flinch, responding with, "Now sit still, this won't hurt a bit," in the manner of all medical professionals who are about to inflict unspeakable agony on some helpless patient. She put her hand over his blind eye and cast a spell.

It didn't hurt, though it was quite disorienting when his eye blinked a few times and suddenly the other half of the room came into vision. He hadn't realized how nice stereo vision was until he'd lost it.

"Thank you," he said.

She handed him a mirror. They hadn't let him look in one before, and now he could see why. He had a nasty scar from his temple to the bottom of his nose. The sword had cut absurdly deep.

"How is it I lived through this?" he wondered aloud.

"Because your head is harder than stone," Rana growled. "Like all men who would be famous."

He was struck by her compliment, if that's what it was. "Do you think I'll be famous?"

"Or dead," she said sourly. "Those are the only options open to you. You do not have the personality to live simply in the world, accepting it for what it is."

"I wasn't famous back home, where I came from," he mused. "And no one ever expected me to be."

"That was there, and this is here. The seed grows differently in different soil."

∽∾∾∽

He joined Cannan and Karl in the tavern, wondering if this was how Luke felt meeting Han Solo. Private meetings with rough and dangerous men in dark taverns, discussing violence and treasure, should have been unnerving, but instead it was uncomfortably intriguing. Maybe he'd been spending too much time in the company of excitable young men.

"Our deal is done," he told the knight.

"Aye, it's over," Cannan agreed. "Nobody dares to challenge Black Bart's ghost in front of your chapel."

"But I have another proposition, if you are interested."

Cannan looked at him through narrowed eyes. "You are full of propositions, priest. Do you hatch them like eggs in your funny long coat? But I have one for you."

"Tell us yours first," Karl said.

"I want to go to Kingsrock and see if anybody there has more courage. I've decided to take up dueling as a career, for a time, and having your sword as a prize would attract more customers, so to speak."

Christopher felt like he was betraying Niona, but it wasn't his place to tell the man what to do with his life. "What do I get out of it?"

"What should you get out of it?" Cannan growled. "You stake an ordinary sword, and run none of the risk."

"Not exactly, Ser. I run the constant risk of the Invisible Guild. And I'm staking the reputation of my sword, not just the steel."

"I'll not give you a quarter," the knight declared.

Christopher didn't particularly want to profit from Cannan's killings anyway. "How about you help us with our task, and we'll call it even?"

"Depends on the task, doesn't it? Let's hear it, then."

"I'm going on this trip to invite the Guild's attack, but I'm worried they might take me up on it too well. I want you to travel with me, disguised as an ordinary guard. Karl's borrowed some chain mail and a coat for you. You'll have to leave your horse behind and act like a commoner, not a noble, but I'll still pay you five gold a day." Although that would be another hundred gold, Christopher felt the continued benefit of being alive was worth the price. "It's only for two more weeks, while we tromp around the Church fiefs. I'll give you the same split on any tael we take from the thieves, one share for me and three for you.

"With your ring, which hopefully the guild doesn't know about, you'll be armored well enough to defeat any number of thugs, even in no more than chain mail. And with you leaving for Kingsrock to be my champion there, no one will suspect another common guard in my retinue. At least, that's the idea."

"The guild will never expect it," Karl said. "No ordinary knight would pretend to such a low rank. Yet I think you are more interested in taking heads than turning them." They were hoping that Cannan's strange adventures to the south might have made him less fashion-conscious.

But the knight surprised them both with his reaction. "What does Niona think?" he asked.

"Um, we didn't tell her yet," Christopher admitted. "We figured she would stay in the village and take care of Bloodfire."

"He's a horse. Give him feed and room to exercise, he'll be fine. But I don't underestimate my wife's value in a fight, like you do. She's a lot more dangerous than that horse."

"Can she pass as one of the boys?" Karl asked. "In a coat and helm, she wouldn't draw much attention. No more than one-finger Charles, at least."

"If I do this, then you'll let me be your champion in Kingsrock? For how long?" Cannan pressed.

"Until the end of the year. Then I go out to the draft, so I think Faren will have to admit the sword isn't magical. He can't misrepresent me to the government."

Cannan nodded in agreement. "Long enough, then. Get my wife a coat and another horse. She'll want to leave hers to keep Bloodfire company."

"We can't pay her, though," Karl cautioned. "It's five gold for both of you."

Cannan shrugged, accepting their limited finances. "What about her share of the tael?"

"She can have three shares too," Christopher said, "but then I'm going to claim a share for my troop."

Karl looked troubled, and Cannan looked pleased, at least for a few seconds. Then they both worked out the math. "That comes to the same thing, then," the knight complained. "You get two shares out of eight, instead of one out of four, but that's the same."

Christopher grinned. Apparently these people could do math—when they really cared. And they always cared about tael.

Cannan and his wife would leave for Kingsrock the next day and then secretly return to the village to deposit his armor and warhorse. When Christopher warned the knight to make sure he wasn't followed, Cannan laughed at him.

"Nobody follows Niona," he finally explained, "unless she wants them to. You churchmen have forgotten all your druid lore."

That left Christopher to get ready for tonight's demonstration. He was nervous, suffering a touch of stage fright. It wasn't the fireworks he was worried about. He had a speech to give, and a lot depended on his getting it right.

First he settled accounts with the church clerk, starting with the five gold for his eye. A large sum to a peasant's purse, but the huge stacks of gold and tael he'd been dealing in lately made it seem cheap. He deposited all of the tael he'd gotten from Bart, and most of the gold, keeping a fat purse for expenses. Actually, he kept two, and another one for Karl, because he fully expected to be pickpocketed. In a world where a King's ransom could literally be contained in a golf ball, pickpocketing had to be a popular skill.

When he went to beg some food from the kitchen for lunch, he was surprised to see Cardinal Faren doing the same.

"I've come out to give Rana a hand with her catch of cut-purses," Faren explained. Christopher knew that couldn't be the whole reason. The way Faren fortified himself with several mugs of ale suggested that his task was to placate the angry Vicar.

"She doesn't seem too happy about catching so many," Christopher said, playing along.

"We can't hang them for stealing," Faren glowered. "So there's no profit in it. Not like cracking rich black walnuts."

"Say the word, and I'll stop," Christopher shot back.

"No. Honesty compels me to admit a certain satisfaction in the events of the past week," Faren said, though he didn't seem very happy about it. "Now I go to take my share of the lumps, though I suppose I won't sport such a scar for it."

"I wouldn't bet on that." Christopher gave him a weak smile. Rana was furious, and Faren didn't have sheer ignorance as an excuse.

So he spent the afternoon alone, reviewing the work Fae had left stored in the church. He was impressed, but he didn't want to go visit her or Tom. They didn't deserve to share the black cloud of doom he was trying to stir up.

With twilight came the moment of reckoning. He picked up the box of printed paper and wound his way through the church, followed discreetly by a growing tail of curious clergy. He could hear the noise from inside the main hall. When the guards opened the doors the volume was stunning. The public square at the foot of the church steps was packed with people.

"Did I not promise you numbers beyond reckoning?" Lalania smirked, springing up the steps and flourishing at the crowd.

"No, actually, you didn't," he said. "But I'll be more impressed if you tell me where all of these people came from."

"Mostly just your outlying villages," she said. "But it's a good turnout. I don't know why you insist on visiting each village. They're all used to coming into town for important events anyway."

Because he wanted to give the guild plenty of chances to attack him, but he could hardly tell her that. Also, because he wanted to show his strength to the common people, to lay the groundwork for his future plans and win their trust.

What he could tell her was, "I want to get a feel for the land. Looking at a map doesn't cut it." Especially when the map was as primitive as the local technology provided. "Those people aren't from a village." He pointed to some jugglers and acrobats. They were everywhere, small dogs leaping through hoops, puppet shows, dancers and tumblers, a veritable circus of freelance entertainers.

"What did you expect?" Lalania asked. "You summon a crowd, and the mummers flock. It's their livelihood, after all."

"Oh no," he groaned, "they're not going to follow me around, are they?" How could he win points with the village locals if he brought this plague of locusts in his wake?

"Not all of them," she cheerfully conceded. "The better acts will only be in the towns you're visiting. But the poorer ones will be waiting for you at every village. I hope you already made reservations at the inns."

"How many cut-purses and pickpockets are out there?" Every gold coin they stole would be one less bond he could sell.

"Not that many. Such pursuits are frowned on in these lands. Well, they are everywhere, of course, and usually much more harshly. But not all towns have truth-spells so readily at hand. Your police will likely be waiting at the gate tomorrow, with a priest at their back, to question every stranger leaving town. A simple 'What did you steal?' can be hard to answer when you think they might have lie detections cast. And of course, stealing a few coppers is a minor offense, but lying to a priest can get you in serious trouble. Next thing you know, you're in a tiny room, answering questions about your affiliation and your past."

Christopher could see how a functioning lie detector would have a big impact on jurisprudence. He could only imagine what effect it would have on Earth.

"How accurate is it?" he asked, thinking that she might give a less biased answer than he would get from a priest.

She looked at him curiously. "Like all magic, it can be defeated, and the higher your rank, the easier. But a high-rank thief is not going to be out there picking peasant's pockets."

"No, they'll be picking mine."

"Like this?" she said innocently, handing him one of his purses.

"Am I that easy of a mark?" he moaned.

"Only when you're lost in that wonderland you visit betimes. I don't know what's there, but it must be passing strange, because you go there whenever you learn something that every child knows."

With a sharp pang, he thought of the druid's kittenhawk. Maggie would be entranced by the cute little monster, and it would probably love her, like all cats did. He wished she could see it. He wished he could see her.

"I did it again, didn't I?" he said ruefully, as the bard handed him all three of his purses, shaking her head in dismay.

"In any other man, I would suggest he needed a woman. Yet hold your tongue, Christopher, I will not challenge your virtue tonight. I am wise enough to know I cannot compete with a ghost.

"But do not let your grief consume you," she added softly. "There is yet this world before you."

It's not grief, he wanted to say, *she is still alive, although she does not know that I am*. But instead he put it away from him and turned his attention to the task at hand.

The troop was lined up, letting the townsfolk get an eyeful. They kept good order, despite the jeering from the younger boys. The older men opined that it was the queerest kit-up they'd ever seen, those short, pointy sticks and long, floppy coats. Karl nodded his head as if that was obvious and intentional. Then he stood on the back of Fingean's wagon and addressed the crowd.

"Pater Christopher would like to say a few words," Karl announced simply, and reached down to help Christopher onto the wagon. Christopher was mildly annoyed that all of the chain mail and leather he was wearing made him appreciate the help. Karl, after all, was wearing the same, and he had leaped into the wagon like a cat.

"Um, thank you all for being here," Christopher started. He knew he was supposed to open with a joke, but he didn't have any. "There's a few things I want to say, and then we'll get on to the show."

Everybody cheered at that.

"This," he said loudly, holding up one of Fae's block-printed bonds, "is called a bearer bond. You can see—" he illuminated it with a light-stone "—that it says one gold on it."

"We can't read!" shouted a drunken heckler. The crowd laughed.

"In that case, it says a thousand gold," Christopher responded. They laughed at that, too, which meant it was an easy crowd. "No, seriously, it says one gold. But I'll sell it to you for only five silver." He let them think about that just long enough and then went on. "Now, it's also got a date on it, which is ten years from now. When that date comes, ten years from today, you bring me back this piece of paper, and I'll give you one gold. See how that works? You give me five silver today, ten years later I give you ten silver.

"It's like a loan," he explained. "An investment in the Church of Marcius. The god saw fit to give me a sword. Somehow he forgot the huge pile of gold." That got another laugh, thank goodness. "But you know as well as I do that wars require gold as well as swords. And you all know I'm going out next year, with the draft. I'll take my sword, but I'd like to take something more. I'd like to make some new weapons, for me and the boys, but I'll need money. So I'm going to show you what those weapons might look like, and I'm hoping afterward you'll show me your money."

"Now listen up," Karl barked. "It's loud, it's fiery, and it smells like Hell cracked open. Pregnant women, small children, and dogs are to be sent home."

That got their attention, as Christopher knew it would. They all pressed forward, the better to see.

The boys had formed a square around Charles, who'd loaded the first rocket into the launching tube. Karl gave the go-ahead, and Charles gave a respectable imitation of a salute before lighting the fuse. Some of the crowd were from Burseberry, so they were busy telling everyone else what to expect, but it was still a shock when the rocket boomed up into the air, trailing sparks and smoke in the gentle twilight. Even several of his troopers ducked their heads reflexively.

He'd started with a yellow burster, in his opinion the weakest of his effects. The crowd loved it anyway. Then there was nothing for him to do but worry while Charles loaded and fired the dozen rockets he'd set out for tonight's show. The sparklers almost provoked a stampede before people realized they burned out before reaching the ground. He felt the green and blue double-bursts were suitably impressive. Nothing like the professionals at home, of course. Still, it was adequate for the amateur effort that a small town like this would be able to afford.

"This one is serious," Karl warned for the last rocket. It was the traditional show-closer: the bomb. Christopher had ground the powder finer than ever before. His worst fear was that the launch would fall short and into the crowd, but of course the Church would just charge him to patch them all up again. He was stunned when the rocket worked perfectly. Literally stunned. The boom shook the wagon he was on.

Once the girls stopped screaming, everybody applauded. Karl raised his light-stone, called for silence.

"Those sticks the boys have aren't much, right now," Christopher shouted. "But I'd like to make them do something like that." Not exactly, of course. He wasn't going to make pretty colors. "But I need your help. I'm not asking for charity; I'm asking for an investment. This is a chance for you to do good, set aside some money for your future while doing good, helping out our boys." He felt like a damn TV evangelist, playing to their patriotism, fear, and greed.

An utterly unexpected voice boomed out from the crowd. "Is it true," Cardinal Faren shouted, "that the Saint has already invested one thousand gold of his own personal funds in your Church?" Of course he knew it was, but he gave Christopher the perfect opening.

"Yes, Cardinal Faren, that is the absolute truth," Christopher confirmed, and the crowd drew in its breath. Even though the Saint was a rich man, a thousand gold was a lot of money.

"Then I cannot fail to do my part," Faren answered, catching Christopher totally by surprise. "Put me down for one hundred gold."

The crowd gasped. Yet the miracles were not at an end. Young Tom Fool shouted out his contribution. "Even I can give a gold to the cause! God knows the boys will need it more than I!"

Men started to raise their hands. Christopher could see the glint of gold and silver, hear the clink of coins. They crowded forward, and then Karl held up his light-stone like the Statue of Liberty, a beacon of hope, a dream of pride.

"The Pater put a weapon in my hands, and I brought down Black Bart," he said into the suddenly quiet crowd, their silence a gathering before the storm. "Let him put a weapon into the hands of our boys, and see what they can do!"

Christopher sold out in the first five minutes.

"I'm sorry," he shouted at the milling crowd, "we're out of bonds. I've got some more that I'm taking to the other counties, to give them a chance to buy in. And this is just the winter issue; I'll have some more at the end of spring. But for now they're all gone, and I thank you."

And then he had to run and hide, before they asked any more questions.

Seeking refuge in the church, he was discovered by the Vicar.

"That was quite a show you put on," she said, her voice carefully neutral. "How much did you raise?"

He knew he couldn't be evasive. "Two and a half thousand gold."

"Who would have thought they had so much to spare?" She shook her head unbelievingly. "I am concerned that they have spent emotionally and not wisely. Will you refund their purchase, if they find they are short of money?"

"Of course," he answered, "we'll always buy the bonds back at the purchase price. You know," he suggested, trying to be casual, "they can also trade them to each other. They're bearer bonds, so we'll honor whoever holds the note in ten years. Rather than walk all the way down to the church and cash it in, they could give it to somebody else instead of giving them five silver."

Rana was not fooled. "You would turn paper into gold?" she asked, her brows furrowing. "Will they not wake up from your enthrallment and see through this swindle on the morrow?"

"I don't think so. I know it seems like a new idea to you, but where I come from, nobody uses anything but paper money."

Her eyebrows twitched. "I know you do not have the gall to lie to me, so this must be truth. And is it also truth that you will make weapons of your sky-fire, to arm our boys? Or is this just another one of Faren's public fantasies, which a less charitable person might name as simple lies?"

"No, it's not a fantasy. I don't know how well they will work, yet, but I assure you, my Lady, those weapons are all that stand between me and your battlefield. And, at the risk of exhausting your credulity, I will tell you: where I come from, nobody uses swords anymore."

"You are mad," she scowled, though not really at him, "Charming, in your way, yet utterly mad. Yet the Saint pretends to believe you. So now I must question, is he mad, or is it me? No, do not object, every madman is sincere in his madness, and I do not doubt your sincerity. I must trust that Krellyan works to some secret end.

"One thing I am certain of. You do the work of the gods. Always they seek to trouble us most when we think the danger is least. And for half a hundred years we have done well. Too well, perchance. Have we forgotten that war and death lurk just over the border? Have we grown too soft? I do not know, but I choose to interpret your existence as a compliment from the gods. Obviously I have done too well at making peace and justice, and thus I deserve their troublesome meddling the most.

"But if I find you've gulled us, I'll feed your heart to my dogs," she finished, "and the White be damned."

He didn't know if she actually owned any dogs, but he was sure he could take her at her word. If she had to, she'd buy some just for the occasion.

19.

THICK AS THIEVES

In the morning they got a late start. This annoyed Karl unreasonably, but they needed to give Cannan and Niona time to visibly leave town, circle back to the village, and intercept them on the road.

Karl took out his frustration by lecturing the boys on security. "This was the last honest sleep you'll get for two weeks," he told them. They'd all slept in the church last night, but from now on they'd be sleeping in inns, taverns, or possibly barns. "You'll not leave the Pater alone for even one heartbeat. You'll not notice food, or warmth, or pretty girls. You'll not forget the day's password or challenge, and if someone does, you *will not* tell them what it is. You will immediately tell me.

"Iron discipline is our only defense against magic," he explained to Christopher. "They can change your mind as easily as they can change their face, but they can't change a protocol."

Christopher declined to ask how easily they could change their face. That was obviously one of those things he was supposed to already know.

The day was pleasant, not warm yet but no longer chilled. Spring was still thinking about coming to this land, although the clouds in the east might scare it off for a while longer. Their little column strolled along the road north to the next village—Karl's hometown, as it happened—and even Karl could not keep up a frown. Fireworks, uniforms, and being on the road were the sorts of things that made young men everywhere giddy.

Their cheerful promenade was violently interrupted when a bush by the side of the road roared and leaped out at them, swinging a still-leafy club. Karl drew his sword and shouted orders while the boys scattered like headless chickens.

Christopher had just enough time to wonder why Royal seemed to be the sole creature not reacting before the crossbow bolts started flying. One barely missed his ear, two went in directions that could be called "forward" only by the most charitable stretch, and one lone bolt sank wetly into the apparition on the roadside.

"Ow," the bush said, and started laughing. "By the Dark, Pater, your troop is more of a danger to you than it is to anyone else. Dammit, that hurt. Why did that hurt?" Cannan pulled the crossbow bolt out of his chest, dropping the bush he had skinned and worn like a hide.

"Gods, Ser!" Christopher exclaimed. "Someone could have been hurt!"

The big man looked up at him, too surprised to be angry at the reprimand. "Who?" he said quite reasonably. "I've got the ring on, and if your boys can't be trusted with those bolt-throwers, best we know that now."

Christopher opened his mouth to argue, then shut it again. The knight had a point. The army back home was always extra careful with live ammunition exercises, but they couldn't heal soldiers on the spot, reattach severed limbs, or, if need be, revive the dead. That kind of leeway made for a lot more training options.

Also, life was cheaper here, and violence simply more acceptable. In any case, Karl's glare was for his troop, so the knight must be in the right.

"You idiots almost killed the Pater, you know that, right?" Karl barked at his blushing boys. "Where's your battle line? Why aren't those bows reloaded yet?"

Niona slowly came out of the woods. Her delicate advance seemed to indicate that she didn't think being shot would be fun.

"I told you, husband, it is only partial protection," she explained patiently. "And you are unarmored."

"It's just a scratch," he said defensively. "Although I suppose if it had hit me in the nuts, I wouldn't be laughing." He laughed at that.

Christopher gave Niona a coat and uniform, while Karl unpacked the gear he'd brought for the knight.

"Sword and board," Cannan mused, scowling at the longsword and shield. "Haven't used these in a while, but I suppose the theory is the same."

Karl gave the boys instructions. "You'll refer to Ser as Goodman Barnner. You will not call him Ser or refer to his rank in any way. He is our secret weapon. Do not reveal this secret to the spies of the Invisible Guild." He also told them to call Niona by the name Nick, and to pretend she was one of the boys. She'd cut her long and curly hair, so in the loose coat and helmet she almost looked the part.

⁓≈⁓

They received a warm reception in Treyeing. The entire village was out waiting for them, along with a crowd of mummers, juggling, prancing, and making music, an impromptu festival. No, it was a circus, and he was the main attraction. His group took over the inn, setting up in the barroom where Christopher practiced his politicking, trying to remember the pointers that Svengusta had given him. He wanted these people to like him. The fact that it was Karl's hometown made it possible.

He answered the same questions over and over again, sticking to platitudes and generalities. The strange get-up of the boys was a popular topic, so Christopher expounded on it at length. He discussed the value of good clothing and made clear his intent to equip all the draftees in the same manner.

Karl held a demonstration, showing off each piece of the kit. The ladies all paid close attention to that.

"I'll pay for each piece you send your boys in with," Christopher told them. *Everybody* paid close attention to that.

After sunset they repeated their performance from Knockford, though with fewer rockets. Christopher saw a lot of the same faces from town buying more bonds. He sold out of this village's allotment in four minutes.

He bought his troop dinner at the inn and beer for what seemed like half the village. His generosity was loudly cheered, even though he was spending their own gold on them. Lalania was a surprise guest for dinner.

"I won't see you again till you reach the next town, but I'm pleased to see you've still got all your purses." She'd shown him some clever ways to carry them, where they would be harder to steal. "Congratulations on the addition to your troop." She winked in Niona's direction. "I'm glad you did it. I can't imagine you getting through the next two weeks without bloodshed."

"Let's hope you're right," Cannan growled, already bored and edgy.

The days melted into a blur. Christopher was stretched to the limit, trying to be polite and friendly to an endless succession of farmers and their wives, girlfriends, children, and dogs. Every night they did another performance, and every morning they marched a few miles to the next village, where they started all over again.

They looped around the county and then headed south and east into Cannenberry, which was only technically adjacent, meeting Knockford at a single corner. They hit all the villages there, seeing new faces but not surprising anyone, since Lalania and others had already spread the word. Christopher belatedly realized he should have asked permission of the Vicars of the counties he was selling to. Then he realized he should have asked permission of Vicar Rana before he'd even started his demonstration. No wonder she was ticked at him.

His tour was limited to the northwestern part of the Kingdom, where most of the Church counties were and where the Church had the most influence. Christopher knew he couldn't sell any bonds outside of the Church counties, no matter how friendly. Their young men weren't part of his draft levee, and if nothing else, the rulers would want a cut.

They would be passing through only one non-Church-owned county on the way home, and Karl assured him that its lord was an ally. The Gold Throne that Niona had warned him of was far to the south; the druids and their uncertain loyalties were even farther east. He was restricting his travels to the safest possible path, and even so he ended every day frazzled by tension.

The Vicar of Cannenberry was an elderly man, the oldest person Christopher had seen in this Church of old men, and the friendliest, inviting Christopher's entire retinue to stay in the local church for free.

"You're very generous," Christopher told him over dinner. "And you set a fine table."

"I'm old," the Vicar said, "I've nothing to save for. I'll die before my next rank, so I might as well spend my money." He fed Niona's kittenhawk a bit of meat from his plate, having lured the animal away from her as soon as they sat down. It perched on his shoulder, purring and rubbing its whiskery face into his long white beard.

His Prelate, a middle-aged and efficient-looking woman, frowned.

"Banna doesn't approve," the Vicar crackled. "But she's young, and she thinks it's her rank I'm spending."

The woman blushed. "Brother, do not speak so ill of me to strangers."

"Strange folk indeed," the old priest said. "Did you know I once met a priest of Marcius? Long ago, when I was but a boy."

"No," Christopher said, excited. "Tell me about him, please."

"He died young. They all did, lost on some distant battlefield, sooner or later. He was barely older than you are now." The ancient patriarch's idea of young was apparently relative. "But he was not like you. He despaired, I think, of ever finding peace. And wise he was proved, for here I have lived a long life from that day, and he is gone, but war is still with us."

"It is the cycle," Cannan growled. Niona seemed to have placed herself under a vow of silence, carefully remaining neutral at Cannan's words and the Prelate's deepening frown.

"I am not so old yet that I am blind," the Vicar giggled, smiling openly at Niona. "But you are welcome here, at least while I rule. Bright is Bright. At my age, one can hardly tell the difference anymore.

"But you," he said, turning back to Christopher. "You are something new. You come marching in with a retinue, but not soldiers. You bear a rod of wonder and fire, but not magic. You are something I have never seen before, and that is rare indeed." The Vicar's gaze pierced Christopher, and he understood that the old man had guessed more than he had said.

"I am," Christopher admitted, "something of a novelty in these parts."

"This gives you a little time," the Vicar said cryptically. "But people become accustomed quickly. Your boys, for instance, are laughable, with their leather coats and silly sticks. But that perception could change overnight, for the smallest of reasons, and then we would have to explain why a Brother of the Church leads an armed host."

The Vicar had neatly pointed out the dilemma Christopher was trapped in. The more his boys and his tricks impressed people, the less the Invisible Guild would bother him, but the more the entrenched power structure would notice him. And he'd already had a taste of the trouble that would be, in the style of Black Bart.

Christopher mumbled something inconsequential. He hadn't thought that far ahead.

The Vicar shook his head, amused. "Krellyan was always a cautious lad. Now he has let you grasp the tail of a dragon. As soon as you let go, it will turn around and devour you. I cannot decide if this is because Krellyan believes you can tame the dragon or wants to see you consumed. Let us hope no one else can decide either."

Either conclusion was bad for somebody. If people thought Krellyan was really backing him, then the Saint would have to answer for his growing disturbances. If people thought Krellyan wanted him dead, he was likely to wind up that way.

"It's only a matter of the draft," Karl said, pushing the party line.

"Of course," the Vicar agreed. "And we will be happy to give you gold for your pretty lights and vainglorious dreams. The people assume Krellyan will refund their money when you die. I know, Brother, you said nothing of the sort, but people see what they want to see. You cannot speak truth to a man who will hear only a comforting lie."

These priests were quite prickly about the difference between truth and falsehood. Christopher agreed with them: a lie of omission was just as bad as a lie of commission. The Vicar was looking for assurance that Christopher was not allowing people to deceive themselves on his behalf. But how could he give that?

At a loss for anything better, he answered, "I'm too young to die."

The old Vicar nodded, as if that was somehow an adequate response, and called for the next course of the meal.

Dinner was merely three courses, not seven or more like a gourmand from Earth would have. But it was still the best meal he'd eaten since he got here. Fresh greens—Christopher assumed there was magic involved in that—delicate sauces, bits of unidentifiable meat on skewers with unidentifiable fruit. And real bread, fresh and light, with herbed butter. Even Cannan felt compelled to admire it, in his way.

"You're going to spoil those boys, feeding them like this," he growled. "They'll get fat and soft."

"You don't have to eat it," Karl said. "You could set a heroic example."

"But I want to get fat and soft," Cannan grinned. "Especially at someone else's table."

"We do not eat like this every day," the Prelate said. "Only on special occasions."

"Which I make up as fast as I can," the Vicar smiled. "I fear that my funeral will be the last special occasion these parts will see for some time."

"The peasants never eat like this," Niona said, but softly.

"They will at least once. I've made explicit instructions in my will. The one thing I am saving for."

"You'd have them celebrate your death?" the Prelate said reflexively. This was obviously an old and practiced argument between them.

"I'd have them just celebrate. But if I do it while I'm still alive, I'd have to listen to them beg for it again. This way I get the pleasure of the idea without the cost." He winked at the table and his discomfited Prelate.

His generosity did not end at dinner. After the performance he had his clerk announce to the crowd that he would personally buy fifty gold worth of Christopher's bonds. Since he would certainly not live to collect on them, this was an act of real faith. The crowd noticed and responded accordingly.

In the last village of Cannenberry, just before they passed north to Copperton, they relaxed in an inn after another performance. The weather was turning toward pleasant, and the saddlebags of bonds and rockets were steadily being replaced by saddlebags of gold.

Christopher found himself at a table with a mug of ale—not the usual bitter black beer, but a smooth pale lager, and an extremely pretty and flirtatious young woman. The hour was late, so the small barroom had fewer than a dozen people in it, half of whom were from Christopher's company. He was exhausted from politicking and at ease from the success of his endeavor so far.

The girl was friendly. More than friendly. It had been an awfully long time since he'd picked someone up in a bar, and he was pretty sure it didn't used to be this easy, but he was too relaxed to worry about it. Every time she spoke, her teeth sparkled and her eyes flashed, and Christopher felt warm and comforted.

She was telling him a story about a recent break-up, or an absent boyfriend, or something. The details slipped away in a fog of alcohol, but the message was clear. She was a human being, she had needs, and she for some incomprehensible reason found Christopher to be fascinating, handsome, and fun. He returned the favorable impression. This girl was sharper than the usual peasant girl, with a quick wit and a sophisticated outlook. She also promised to be a lot of fun, in a very specific way.

They'd just agreed to find someplace a little more private and stood up from the table, when they found Karl blocking their way.

"Going somewhere, Christopher?" he asked evenly.

"It's okay, Karl," Christopher said, trying to walk around him.

"No, I don't think so," Karl said.

"Your lord is gentle, to suffer such insolence," the girl said. "Would you deny him even a little comfort?"

"He's not interested."

"Um, yes, I think I am," Christopher said. "Look, I don't care what you make the boys put up with, it's been a long time. We're all adults here. I don't need you to babysit me."

"You're married," Karl said, his tone still flat.

"Not even his wife would ask him to suffer so long," the girl answered. "He'll still be married tomorrow. Just happier."

"It's true," Christopher argued. "It's a natural and healthy function. I don't want repression to build up and twist my head around. I won't be any good to anyone then."

"You're married," Karl repeated.

"I know that, Karl," Christopher said, beginning to get a little snappish. "I know that better than anybody. But . . ." he trailed off. He wasn't sure what was supposed to come after the "but."

"I mean his wife no harm," the girl said. "She will thank me for showing him comfort when she could not."

"Exactly," Christopher said. "Maggie's not unreasonable. She's probably . . ." He was going to say she was probably seeing someone else too, but that made him stop and wonder exactly how long he had been on this world. It seemed like forever, even though it was only a few months.

"You're married," Karl said.

Christopher was becoming angry, but the young man's words could not be denied. However much he wanted it now, he would regret it later. He should be thankful that Karl was so faithful. Mostly he wanted to shove the man aside, but he knew he was supposed to be grateful.

"My lady," he said to the girl, still flirting with her, "I'm sorry, but I think he's right."

Her eyes grew wide, then wet.

"Do not I also deserve some comfort?" she cried, clinging to Christopher.

Christopher began to have ugly thoughts. He'd finally found a girl that preferred him over the irresistible Karl, and now Karl was throwing a fit.

"You're being paranoid, Karl. Just because she likes me more than she likes you doesn't mean it's a trap." But then gears started turning in his head. Didn't it almost certainly mean that? It wasn't inconceivable that a woman might prefer him to Karl. Just inconceivable that a woman like this would.

She really was too pretty.

"You can wait till you're off-duty, like everyone else," Karl said.

Christopher leaped at the compromise, unready to give up all hope. "That might be best," he said to the girl.

Her face did not respond with sadness or regret, only ugliness.

"Idiot," she snapped, and touched her wrist. Karl reached out to stop her, but his hand was still in motion when Christopher struggled against the onrushing blackness, failed, and sank beneath the wave of darkness.

～◇◇◇～

Someone kicked him, not gently. Cannan, wearing a sour face.

"What happened?" Christopher moaned, and sat up, looking around at all the unconscious bodies filling the room.

The knight did not deign to answer, reaching over the bar and pouring himself another mug instead. A few feet from where he stood drinking, the girl sagged against the bar, her head hung low and unmoving. It took Christopher a moment to realize she was held against the wooden paneling by a sword through her chest.

He struggled to reconcile his surging emotions. His lust for her was still strong, not yet balanced by the memory of the blackness. "Did you have to kill her?"

"She was armed and had magic," Cannan growled, kicking a dagger across the floor at him. "How was I to judge her rank? I only hit her once."

Staring at the evidence of the girl's perfidy, he could feel the insensible lust fading. He still felt sickened by her death, but the dagger on the floor brooked no argument. "Why didn't it affect you?" he asked.

"An excellent question," Niona said, entering the room warily, the kittenhawk riding on her fist like a weapon ready to be launched. She looked around the sleeping room, her face filled with dismay. "This is powerful magic." And well used; the assassin had struck while Niona and half the troop were elsewhere.

Cannan snorted, his counterargument obvious.

Niona went to the body, her eyes bright with curiosity. She muttered a spell, staring intently, and then pulled a small gold chain with two mangled, crushed ornaments from the woman's wrist. Niona sniffed the bracelet, her face curling up a like a cat's, and then she tossed it aside. Placing her hand on the corpse's forehead, she drew out the tael and examined it.

"A single rank," Niona said. "Insufficient for a spell of such potency. Your assassin was merely a tool, delivering a stroke prepared by others. It seems the Invisible Guild has decided to escalate their efforts."

"Thank goodness Cannan was here, then."

"Thank more than that," Niona said, eyeing her husband critically. "Even his rank should not have stood against such a spell."

"Wife," said Cannan, "you are not doing my reputation any favors."

"You are wearing the ring." It was the closest to disapproval that Christopher could imagine coming from the carefully nonjudgmental Niona.

"Aye," Cannan answered. "I forgot to take it off this morning. I like sleeping with it on. Not only because I no longer fear a knife to the throat, but also because the bedbugs are powerless against it."

"It protects against magic as well as swords?" Christopher felt a pang of envy. He, too, would like to sleep soundly and without paying a blood-tax to a different population of insects every night.

"A deal's a deal," Cannan said. Christopher couldn't argue; the more powerful the ring was revealed to be, the more dangerous owning it would be. At some point it would even be dangerous for Cannan to keep, a fact clearly not lost on his unhappy wife.

"At least I can safely say the bracelet has no power left," Niona said. "And we are doubly blessed; its compulsion did not affect you, though its lower rank makes that explicable."

"It did affect me," Christopher answered. "But not Karl. Him and his protocol." He went to wake his young savior, who was snoring peacefully beneath the table, before Cannan could get around to kicking him. Karl deserved better than that.

20.

ON THE ROAD, AGAIN

The enemy waited for their next strike until after the very last village. Perhaps they wanted all the money, or were waiting for the crowd of mummers to disperse, or wanted the troop as tired as possible. On the morning of the last day, as Christopher's party headed for the border to County Fram, Niona's kittenhawk came swooping down to her shoulder and she cried out in alarm.

"Bart comes, riding hard behind us, with horses and men!"

"We can't fight cavalry," Cannan snapped. "Get off the road."

Karl leapt from his mount, smacked it on the flanks to drive it on ahead. No such luck with Royal, of course, who would not leave Christopher behind when he could smell a fight brewing. The big warhorse followed Christopher into the woods, pushing through bushes and branches.

"You do understand that there will be no reviving this time," Karl said, apparently concerned that Christopher was not frightened enough. "He will burn our bodies and scatter the ashes to the wind."

"Shouldn't we try to hide?" Christopher asked.

"I suppose that would be a good idea," Karl mused, looking at the massive equine head hanging over Christopher's shoulder, "but I don't think it's possible."

"No," Niona agreed, "I fear not. Look: he comes."

Out on the road they could see the black column already turning into the woods.

Christopher gathered everyone together, a desperate football huddle, calling upon Marcius's blessing for the battle ahead. The spell had helped alleviate the fear that Bart projected into the duel. Christopher was ill with the prospect of facing that despair a second time; he was sure it would shatter his untested boys. But the twinkling lights of magic stiffened their backs. Gray-faced but not trembling, they turned to face the incoming threat.

Behind them Christopher drew his blade and waited, trying to match Karl's icy calm. Cannan was grinning wildly, which meant the danger was extreme.

The three men would be hard-pressed to beat Bart again, especially with Cannan in chain mail and longsword instead of his superior equipment, a deficit barely erased by the ring changing hands. That left thirteen poorly armed boys to fight eight first-rank knights. Impossible odds. Niona was their only advantage. He did not see how it could be enough.

A salvo of crossbow bolts flew out from Christopher's battle line. Most missed, but one struck Bart squarely in the shoulder, and the black knight cursed in annoyance.

"Ha ha, it hurts now, doesn't it?" Cannan laughed.

"Fool," Bart snarled. "That ring was not meant for you!"

"Drop your trousers and I'll give it back, though I warrant you'll change your mind after the first three knuckles." At least the knight was reloading while he bantered. Christopher would have preferred that he remain silent altogether. It might have benefited them if Bart had not known exactly who he faced until the last minute.

The boys stood their ground, held only by the anchor that was Karl. They got off a second salvo before the cavalry closed through the trees, but against ranked knights it had little effect.

Niona chanted in her unknown tongue, and the forest came alive. Bushes clutched at the horses' legs, tree branches grappling for the riders. One knight was pulled from his horse and held, struggling, five feet off the ground. Their horses screamed in panic. Christopher almost joined them; this was magic on a scale he had not yet witnessed. He took a step back but was blocked by Royal's stalwart shoulder.

The remaining knights dismounted, which wasn't much of an

improvement. The underbrush clutched at them, too, but several pushed free and attacked the line of spearmen.

Karl had the boys in teams, two with spears protecting one with a crossbow. Christopher wanted to stay with them, but Bart had forced his horse through everything and bore down on Cannan.

Bart's sword was magical, so the ring would be of no use. Cannan flew into his tael-fueled rage, but it would not make up for plate and steel. Presumably he knew this, but he did not seem to care.

Christopher fired his sword with the silvery enchantment and ran forward into the battle before he could allow himself to reconsider.

He didn't make it to Cannan. One of Bart's retainers intercepted him, lunging with his longsword and missing his face by a hairsbreadth. Christopher counterattacked, slashing his katana across the man's steel shield, but his enchantment was not that powerful. The shield was scored but did not fail.

Christopher was driven back by the man's flurry of thrusts. His two-handed sword was awkward in the woods and the close press of combat. At the last second he avoided accidentally stabbing someone coming up behind him. This was good, because it was Royal. The horse reared and lashed out with his front hooves at the enemy knight, teeth bared in a fearsome snarl.

Christopher started to feel a little hopeful. He was pretty sure that he and Royal could take this guy. Letting the horse block the man from one side, he sidled to the other and advanced, blade at the ready. The knight was in a pickle. He needed to have his shield between him and the katana, and his sword between him and the horse, but right now it was the other way around. Suddenly he dashed straight between them. Christopher's strike was slow and bounced harmlessly off the shield. The knight spun in place, and now he was arrayed as he wanted to be. He only had a second for his smile of triumph, though, before a curved blade came up behind him and tore his throat open.

He fell, a gushing fountain of blood. Niona stood over him with fiery eyes, her bloody sickle in a professional grip. Without a word she moved on into the battle.

Royal wasn't convinced, stomping on the dead body with sickening crunches. Christopher could not afford to react, so he turned around and charged blindly into the fray.

The boys were losing. Even with half the knights struggling with the flora, the boys were outclassed. At least one lay unmoving on the ground already, and more were in bleeding heaps. Cannan wasn't fighting Bart but was trying to avoid him, dancing carelessly through the lesser knights. They couldn't hurt him, but he dealt out terrible damage, uninhibited by their nullified weapons.

Karl was stalking Bart, but the black knight ignored him, pursuing his real foe. He let his horse battle Karl to a standstill.

Before he had time to think about it, Christopher sprung on a knight extricating himself from the grasp of several saplings. He lunged and thrusted, trusting to the tael to guide it between the chinks in the armor. The knight cried out and lashed back with his own sword. But he had dropped his shield, so Christopher ignored the weak blow that skittered off his mail and chopped savagely against the knight's neck. The enchanted blade sank into the meat, came out red and dripping. The knight fell and Christopher turned away, ignoring the unreality of it all, the terrible feeling of having cut into living flesh, and sought out the real enemy.

The black knight had won free of the area where the plants were active. He drove Cannan before him like a calf to the slaughter, back out to the open road where the warhorse could ride him down. From the road came two more horsemen, and Cannan was trapped as they plunged through the woods at him, but he was not their target. The unknown riders flew past the beleaguered knight and crashed into Black Bart.

One rider was armored in blue half-plate, with a sword as large as Bart's but glowing like a cobalt torch. His warhorse eagerly challenged Bart's coal-black mount. The men whaled on each other in the peculiar offensive style of this world, ignoring blows that would have felled an ordinary man. Bart seemed to be dominating, but now Cannan was back into the fray, stabbing up from the ground. The second rider hung back, the smaller horse unwilling to join the clash of hooves, but the rider stood in the saddle doing something unusual. Christopher realized she was aiming a crossbow only when he saw the bolt sprout from Bart's shoulder.

He had not recognized her with a weapon in her hand. Lalania the troubadour, making a grand entrance. As usual.

"Cannan! Save the boys!" Christopher cried.

The knight glared angrily but did not hesitate. He sprinted back to the line, threw himself bodily into the black knot of armored warriors. Their swords rattled on him like sticks on a broken drum, but his blade flew in bright-red arcs as they fell around him.

Christopher ran forward, feeling small in the midst of the huge horses and iron-clad men. Unnoticed, he stabbed at the seam in Bart's armor where the leg joined the hip. A weak strike, but the sword flashed brightly and the black knight shrieked in pain. Bart urged his horse forward, as if in a panic.

The warhorse plunged out of Christopher's reach, so he chased after it. It reared on its front legs and kicked him squarely in the chest with two hooves. His tael absorbed the blow like a spring, transforming organ-crushing force into merely broken ribs, but nothing could dampen the kinetic energy, and he flew twenty feet through the air until he crashed into the trunk of a tree, which immediately wrapped its branches around him and held him tight.

It didn't matter; the battle was decided. The horses screaming against the unnatural ground that pulled at them, the groans of men, the clash of metal carried on, but the fight was done. Bart had forced the stranger's horse into the circle of grasping shrubbery, and now his own black mount gathered itself for escape. Nothing could check his flight, but Niona appeared, singing in a high, beautiful voice. The black warhorse slowed, stopped, turned its head and stared at her, entranced. Bart raged on top of it, lashing out, striking it with his fists and feet, but it ignored him and did not move. The strange knight freed his horse and charged, his long blade held out like a lance, aimed at the rider. Bart snarled in fury, but his men were down, his horse was paralyzed, and his foes advanced upon him. He looked away, to where freedom lay, and then . . . was simply gone.

His saddle was empty, the blue-clad knight's sword passing through still air. Niona sang a different song, soothing and calm, and the panicked horses began to quiet and still, while the blue knight galloped around the circle of writhing shrubbery, looking in vain for the vanished foe. Lalania advanced carefully to the edge of the circle, took leisurely aim at a knight trapped in the trees, and shot him in the throat. He twitched once, twice, and then the tree, no longer sensing life, dropped the corpse to the ground in a heap.

Then all the plants relaxed, returning to their normal placid torpor. Christopher fell forward and whimpered with the effort of drawing breath. He had to ignore the pain. He was not going to die, but some of the boys might.

He managed to stand, but every step constricted his shattered chest like a vise. Never mind the way his sight faded with every flash of agony; he simply couldn't breathe. With hand signals he waved to two of his boys, who carried him between them like a mannequin.

"Show me the worst," he whispered. They brought him to a corpse, mangled and still. Morbidly curious, he rolled the body over. It was Kennet.

Three more boys were unmoving, one from shock, but the other two were dying. Being a priest of the Bright had its advantages. Although his last remaining spell for the day was the fear-inducing one that had claimed his first casualty in this world, he was able to transform it into a healing spell, and bound up the wound of the boy before him.

"Niona," he tried to cry out, but she was already there. She bent over the other critical case and cast her spell. The boy opened his eyes and blinked.

"I am down to orisons," she told Christopher. He saw her costume was cut, and there was blood on it.

"Me too," he choked, coughing up blood into his hand. He looked at his reddened hand with horror.

Niona reacted more practically, touching his chest and casting a spell. The pain faded, only flaring when he tried to walk.

"You cannot heal them if you are dead," she said, the nicest possible way of chiding him for his stupidity. Together they scanned over the remaining boys, spending their magic to stop the worst of the bleeding. The rest would have to depend on mundane bandages.

Lalania helped, binding open wounds and in one case setting a broken arm. The boy sobbed in pain but did not scream, and she rewarded his bravery with a kiss.

The blue knight cantered up, but not empty-handed. He dumped a whimpering yellow-clad figure on the ground. Christopher recognized the ugly little man as Bart's priest.

"I caught this rat sneaking away, though I could not find even a trail of his master. But I dared not search too far afield." The blue knight's voice was strong but not hard.

Cannan stood guard, glaring at the knight on general principle.

"Who are you?" he demanded.

"May I present the Baronet Gregor," Lalania said, "late of Tomestaad. More recently, late of Goodman Parno's wretched little inn."

"We've been shadowing you for days," Gregor said. "But only this morning did we catch wind of Bart. We came to warn you, but you had already departed. We chased after you and found ourselves chasing Bart. And now he's given us the slip."

"Not without a few tail-feathers," Cannan said with satisfaction, glancing around at the corpses. "But what's this mewling putrescence?" He kicked the yellow priest lying on the ground.

"A loose end to be tied up," Gregor said as he dismounted.

Niona spoke to her kittenhawk, and it took to the air. "Bartholomew stands alone, and we have gained his mounts. If we have good and capable horsemen, we might still give pursuit. We should not let this predator escape to kill again." Christopher was a little unnerved by her manner. He knew she was right, but he couldn't shake the image of her cutting the knight's throat.

"Agreed," Gregor said. "Will your pet find him?"

"If he is near, yes. I do not know what magic he used or how far he traveled."

Gregor looked to the troubadour, who shrugged unhappily. "My spell-craft is certainly no better than the Lady Niona's. All I can tell you is it was a device of some kind."

"Perhaps this can tell us something," Cannan said, looking at the yellow priest Gregor had hauled to his feet.

"I know nothing!" the priest whimpered. "I only follow orders. The Lord Baron tells me nothing."

"I know a question you can answer for me," Gregor said with a dangerous ease. "How many children did you murder last year?"

Christopher started to object to this slanderous accusation, but the man was already confessing.

"On Lord Bartholomew's orders!" the priest squealed. "He demands the secret rites, and I must obey."

"Then perhaps you can tell me this. Did you rape them before or after you killed them?" The blue knight casually drew his dagger with his right hand, while his powerful left kept its iron grip on the little man's throat.

"You cannot hold me to account for my religious duties!" the priest squeaked in wide-eyed terror.

"Just watch me." Gregor ripped open the front of the priest's robes. Underneath the stained and tired yellow were more robes, as black as night.

"I beg the justice of the Church," the priest choked out, futilely struggling against the vise.

"We are on Church lands," Karl said softly.

"Shouldn't he get a trial?" Christopher asked uncomfortably.

Lalania's pretty face was twisted. "He'd be set free. Your Church does not prosecute priests of other faiths. It does not dare warfare."

"Exactly!" the priest squeaked like a yellow-headed blackbird under the cat's paw. "You must respect your Church law."

"I object," Christopher said to the blue knight. "I formally demand that you surrender this prisoner to the nearest officer of the Church."

"Dark take you," Gregor replied with a fake smile, like he was saying, "Have a nice day." But the phrase was the local equivalent of the F-bomb. It didn't get any ruder than that.

"Hmm," Christopher said to the priest. "It appears that the weakness that prevents the Church from prosecuting you is the very same weakness that prevents it from protecting you. Apparently I cannot punish or prevent your crimes, any more than I can punish or prevent Ser Gregor's."

Despite his anger, the blue knight grinned at the sophistry, and Cannan laughed out loud. If the women had reservations, they kept them to themselves.

With grim exactitude, Gregor drug his dagger up the priest's exposed belly, and then across, in a grotesque cross. Blood and guts spilled out, long, gray, slimy loops splashed in red, as the man fell to the ground, grasping in futile agony at his internal organs. Christopher's head spun, and his knees went weak at the sight, but no one else, save the boys, seemed to be particularly affected.

The priest squealed and bled on the ground while Gregor watched him with bleak satisfaction. Cannan was amused, Niona indifferent, Lalania disgusted but not unapproving. Only Christopher found anything wrong with the sight.

"End it," he grated.

"It's exactly what he does to the children," Gregor said. "Well, minus the raping part, but I'm not interested in that. Help yourself, if you are."

Christopher could feel his blood rising and pounding in his temples. He glared at the blue knight so fiercely that Lalania intervened.

"This is no less than he deserves."

"I. Don't. Care." Christopher could not prevent their revenge, but he did not have to tolerate wanton cruelty.

With a sigh that might have been resignation, or possibly even relief, the blue knight put his armored boot on the back of the priest's neck. He reached down with his hand, caught the man's greasy black hair, and cranked, snapping the neck like a twig. The body convulsed and then lay still.

Cannan was looking around appraisingly. "There's too many to harvest," he said. "We'll have to boil them." He bent over the dead priest, and without further ado twisted the head off the corpse.

Christopher was going to object, but he fainted instead.

<hr/>

He was out for mere seconds, but the ground was comfortable, so he stayed there while the troubadour knelt over him.

"You are the most puzzling enigma," she said with an ambiguous smile. "You fight like a swordsman, talk like a priest, and flutter like a virgin on her fourteenth birthday. You know things esoteric even to me, yet toddlers confound you with their wisdom. We troubadours cannot resist puzzles. I would think you tease me purposefully, but I know better now. So instead I am confused, and frustrated." She ran her hand down his chest, lightly, but not lightly enough.

"Ow," he said. "Ribs. Broken. Ow."

"Stupid chain mail," she grumbled.

"He can't fight like that," Gregor said, leading two horses over to them. "Leave him. The druid's pet has not returned. We must scout a wider circuit."

Christopher raised his head enough to see that Karl was mounting a steed from Black Bart's retinue. Cannan was still making sickening noises around corpses, filling up a sack with disgusting bulges, but then he was done and leaping into a saddle.

"I can ride," Christopher forced himself to say. It was just pain. His tael would not let him bleed to death, at least not from this injury.

"No you can't," Gregor objected quite logically.

"Don't leave us alone," one of the boys whispered, but Gregor overheard.

"No need to worry, lad. We're pursuing them now. You'll be safe enough until we get back. But load your bows, just in case."

"We need him," Niona said. "Eat," she told Christopher, passing him a tiny handful of berries. He was going to ask, but breathing was harder than eating, so he did what he was told. Unsurprisingly, the pain receded quickly, and he made it into Royal's saddle before the party left without him. He was going to ask if there were any more for the boys, but the druid shook her head.

"Why do we need him?" Cannan asked, innocently curious, as they rode out to the highway.

"Because he might still be the target of assassins, and we can't leave him lying around helplessly," Lalania explained with a trace of exasperation.

"Because he is insanely lucky," Karl said.

A hundred yards down the road, they found a roadblock. Two trees had been felled and strung with ropes. It was the work of a moment to open a path, but that was a moment they would not have had if Black Bart had been behind them.

Lalania's sharp eyes made a sad discovery. She slid from her horse and gently lifted the black-and-white body of Niona's kittenhawk, now broken and stained with red.

"I'm sorry," she said to the other woman in genuine sympathy.

"It is the cycle," was Niona's response, but her eyes were glistening and she turned away abruptly.

"It is a crossbow quarrel," Karl said, examining the tiny corpse, his ironed flatness the only hint of his emotion. "A white one, fletched in goose feather."

Christopher and Karl exchanged glances. They had seen this color of quarrel before, although last time it had been impaled in Karl's shoulder.

"My enemies combine against me, it seems."

"So he had reinforcements waiting," Cannan said. "Damn, but I'm good. If we had tried to flee, we would have been in Dark water."

"Horses have been this way," Lalania said. "Niona, can you see?"

"Yes," the druid answered. "Karl's, and many others besides."

"We've lost him, then," Gregor complained. "With plenty of horses, a head start, and an unknown number of reinforcements, we don't dare chase him across the countryside."

"Assuming he is even out there," Lalania said. "For all we know, his spell took him home."

"Well, there's one less Dark priest in the world. I suppose that will have to suffice for a day's work," Gregor said, but he clearly wasn't ready to suffice.

"And a sack of heads," Cannan said encouragingly. "We've made a tidy profit."

"He stole Karl's horse," Christopher complained.

"We stole his back," Lalania pointed out. "Ten to one."

"And you've got a nice pile of armor to add to your Black Bart collection," Cannan laughed. "But let's get to the point. I claim six shares of the tael, for myself and Niona."

"I claim four, for myself and Lalania," Gregor said.

"The Pater claims two, one for himself and one for his troop," Karl said, when it was clear Christopher hadn't realized he was supposed to say something.

"Fair enough," Cannan said. "We'll pass on the arms. I don't fancy hauling that crap around. Unless there's any magic?"

"I doubt it," Lalania said. "Bart seems like the type to take it with him, but I'll check. His men didn't even have purses. Except the priest." She produced a leather pouch, tinkling with coins. "Not much, but it's gold."

"We'll take half of that, then," Cannan suggested, "and leave the arms to our valiant troop. Gods know they need them. And the horses for Karl, since the Goodman lost his." Royal snorted, perhaps in approval.

Christopher was deeply annoyed that they were even having this conversation. There were more important things to think about than loot.

"If you're quite finished, what are we going to do? I have wounded, I have dead, and a long day's march through unfriendly territory."

"It's a short march, and Earl Fram is as friendly as you can get for being a cheapskate," Gregor said. "But I'll be glad to escort you."

"We'll take you home, Pater," Cannan said. "We'll get no more fun out of Bart today."

"Ser is right," Karl said. "Black Bart flees the field, for now. With your permission, Pater, I ride to Kingsrock."

"Why?" Clueless, Christopher had to ask.

Karl almost revealed an emotion. "This was an act of open war. The Saint must be informed. Something must be done."

"Don't get your hopes up," Lalania cautioned. "Your Church ever walks with a light step."

Karl did not deign to respond, simply looking at Christopher for release.

"Of course, Karl. Whatever you think is best." Christopher was too tired to wonder why Karl was even asking him. Shouldn't Karl be telling him what to do? But the young man bowed his head, wheeled his newly gained horse, and was gone.

The rest of them rode back to the impromptu camp. Luckily for

Christopher, Gregor took over command and set the still-functional boys to stripping bodies and boiling heads. All Christopher could do was sit next to Kennet's cold body and worry. What was he going to tell Dynae?

"Your share," Niona said, delicately handing him a tiny purple stone.

It was about the right amount for a revival. Niona saw him looking speculatively at the corpse and shook her head.

"Your sympathy touches me, but is it not childish?" she said softly. "The cycle cannot be denied."

"I'm not big on cycles," he said. "I tend to think more in lines."

More riders came from the road to join the camp, but they wore white. The town was only a few miles east, and Karl had stopped off long enough to alert the Vicar. Christopher felt stupid for not having marched there in the first place, but the man had made him feel so unwelcome, he hadn't thought of it as a place of refuge.

The Vicar had brought only four men with him. Either that was all he could mount, or he was counting on his moral and political authority. Either way, Christopher couldn't fault his personal bravery.

And he couldn't fail to be grateful after the man single-handedly healed all of the boys.

He didn't heal the knights, though. They weren't seriously injured, just scratched, since the combat had not completely exhausted their stocks of tael. Christopher's curiosity got the best of him, and he asked Cannan how long it would take for him to be at full fighting strength again.

"Tomorrow," the big man laughed.

"It comes back that quickly?" Christopher was impressed.

"I don't know. I've never waited before. I just have to wait on Niona."

Gregor was more helpful. "A week or so, Pater. Unless you see fit to hasten the process, when you are able."

"Of course," Christopher promised. "It's the least I can do." He was a little unhappy that the Vicar hadn't already done it.

But Gregor excused the other priest. "He's probably low, Pater, and he wants to save some for emergencies."

"He probably doesn't want to become involved in foreign affairs," Lalania said, less sanguinely. "He'd like to pretend this was a fight between ranks that just happened to be on his land, instead of an attack on one of his Brothers. And in a way it was. I think Bart is more focused on the ring now than the sword."

The boys had been building a funeral pyre and stacking the corpses on it. There was one body left, and everyone looked at Christopher expectantly.

"No," he said. "We'll take him home with us."

"I understand. His family will want to bury him in his own village," the Vicar said, not understanding.

The Vicar's soldiers stood guard over the burning pyre. They would scatter the ashes later, leaving nothing identifiable. There would be no second chances for these men. The fate that Christopher had narrowly avoided reached out for him in the tendrils of foul smoke, sickening him.

As they group departed, he saw Cannan toss something small and black on the flaming pyre. When Niona thought no one was observing her, Christopher saw that she wept, and Cannan held her tenderly.

◆◆◆

In Knockford his allies deserted him. Niona took Bart's warhorse with her, a fait accompli since she was the only one who could approach it, let alone ride it. She left her well-trained saddle mare in its place, adding to Christopher's newly acquired herd. It would be a good training horse for the boys, a way to work up to the less-forgiving cavalry horses.

Unnerved by the loss of the man who had been his shield for the last four weeks, Christopher tried to bribe Lalania and her slice of beefcake into replacing them.

"I need an intelligence agency. How much would it cost to put you on the payroll?" he asked.

She snapped her head in sharp exasperation. "What is it with men? Must you vase the flowers while they are blooming?"

He was pretty sure his lack of comprehension was not due solely to language issues.

"I am too young to settle down," she sighed. "But I serve your cause, even if I am not your servant. And I serve your cause best on the road."

Ser Gregor, at least, was convinced to stay.

"My blade is pledged to oppose the Dark, and thus I must follow its lead. However, you do seem to be attracting more than your fair share of Darkness, so if you'll feed me, I'll stick around for a while."

It was a bargain price for a knight of the same rank as Cannan, so Christopher readily agreed. The boon was double; in Karl's absence, Gregor automatically took over command of the boys, putting them to work on drills and standing watches. He just couldn't bear to see them standing around idle.

The boys kept dropping hints that they would look dashing in all the armor they'd liberated from Black Bart's troop.

"That's the problem," Christopher told them, "you would. The Vicar is angry enough that you even exist, following me around like a retinue. Imagine how annoyed she would be if you looked like knights."

That shut them up. They may have fought desperate battles in distant lands against dark foes, but they were still afraid of annoying the Vicar. As was he, to be honest. The next conflict he would have to face without them. He was going to ruffle enough feathers as it was.

Helga washed his clothes that night and trimmed his hair and beard. The preparations were not missed by the sharp-eyed Gregor.

"Expecting a confrontation?" he asked. "Shouldn't you be trying on some of that fancy armor instead?"

"I'm confronting tradesmen, not soldiers. And no, you can't come. I'd leave my sword behind if I thought I could get away with it. They'll be angry enough as it is. I don't want them to feel like they're being invaded."

"Why are they going to be angry?" Gregor asked with undue concern.

"The Saint gave me rights to the Old Bog. The townsmen aren't exploiting it efficiently, so I'm going to shake things up."

This explanation worked as well on Gregor as it had on Captain Steuben, winning his immediate approval.

"Don't be too happy," Svengusta warned the knight. "Give him time, and he'll get around to upending your whole way of life, too." Svengusta laughed, but Christopher didn't. It was too close to the truth.

21.

SHOWDOWN AT OLD BOG

Looking over the crew of diggers Tom had hired, Christopher briefly considered calling for his troop again. But they were still back in the village, and he reminded himself this wasn't going to be a battle. The dirty, ragged, and not overly bright men before him weren't supposed to be impressive.

"I've not made you any friends," Tom told him in a private voice. "Save of course for these men themselves. All of them were employed yesterday, though not happily. Now it's their employers who are unhappy."

Christopher wanted to sigh, but he was saving all of his sighs for later. Briefly, ever so briefly, he felt a fleeting desire to be facing simple problems, like gangs of murderous swordsmen.

"I don't expect trouble," Christopher told the men, "but I don't want you to run away. Just stand your ground, okay?"

The men looked a little confused, and even Tom was rendered curious.

"These men are tried and tested, I assure you, my lord, the bravest of the diggers in the Kingdom. They're not afraid of any patch of dirt."

"How about angry crowds? I'm taking over Old Bog today." Christopher showed them his deed. They couldn't read, but they recognized the Saint's stamp.

Tom winced. "I think I liked it better before you explained."

They rode to battle in Fingean's wagon, a pair of wheelbarrows and a cluster of picks, shovels, and hammers their tools of war. The day was pleasant, being the middle of spring, and there were half a dozen young men hard at work in the bog. They watched the wagon approach with mild curiosity.

"Having fun?" Christopher asked them.

"Not really, Pater," said one of them. "We know you're crazy and all, but even you should have known the answer to that one."

Another apprentice commented on the men and equipment being unloaded. "So you've found recruits for your church of night-soil?"

"Ah, you're a witty lot," Christopher said. "Such verve and intelligence is wasted digging dirt. Go home.

"No, seriously," he said, when no one moved. "Go home. You're done. You'll dig no more ore today or any day."

"We're going to argue with a priest?" said one young man, tossing down his shovel. "When he tells us to stop breaking our backs?"

"With all due respect, Pater," the first apprentice said, "Palek is unsurpassed as a smith, but even he cannot smelt without ore."

"If he wants ore, he can buy it from these men here." He pointed to his team. "I've the legal right of it." He showed them the deed.

They couldn't read either, but they knew he wasn't lying.

"They'll kill you," the apprentice said simply.

"They'll have to go through this paper first," Christopher said, "and it's signed by Krellyan himself. Now look, whose side are you on? Do you want to be out here digging dirt, or do you want to be in your shop working metal?

"Go home, and tell your masters that I've cut the price of ore in half. It's now ten coppers per wheelbarrow, delivered to their door. Not the twenty they pay you to waste a day digging it."

Tom whistled as the men trundled off disconsolately. "I only charged three, Pater. It looks like you'll be getting rich off us."

"Not really, since I'm paying you five times as much as you were making."

"But we don't know how to dig iron ore," one of his men objected.

"It's not so hard. The sharp end goes into the ground." Christopher pointed at the blade of the shovel. "And then you kind of scoop it into the wheelbarrow.

"I'm sorry," Christopher immediately apologized. "I'm just nervous. It's true there are some craft secrets to mining, but let me let you in on one. The smiths don't know them either. I do, and I'm going to teach them to you. Once you understand them, you'll double production, and I'll be able to give you a raise. Now let's get started."

Tom knew a lot more about ore than he'd let on, showing the men how to identify good from bad and where to dig for the best results. He didn't explain where he got the knowledge, and Christopher didn't ask. It was an easy guess that, on the sly, the man had done his share of digging before but was sticking to his promise of secrecy. Even more discreetly, he didn't point out to everyone that Christopher, who had just represented himself as a master miner, was as clueless as the novice diggers. Christopher decided, for the hundredth time, that he was underpaying the man.

Now he couldn't do anything but stand around uselessly and wait. He hated that. At least he didn't have to wait long.

A crowd of angry men flowed back out of the town to the bog. On a positive note, they weren't carrying torches and waving pitchforks.

"Welcome," Christopher cried. "Come to buy some ore?"

They ignored him as the senior smiths stiffly greeted each other and then briefly noted the lesser smiths. Only after that did they acknowledge his existence.

"What is the meaning of this?" Palek demanded, already lapsing into hostile.

"Can you read?" Christopher politely asked.

"I can, Pater," said a younger man.

Christopher showed him the deed from the Saint. The man read it slowly, carefully, and then read it a second time.

"It is true," he told the crowd. "The Saint has given him this right."

"Not given, exactly," Christopher corrected him. "I paid four thousand gold."

"And now you mean to make it back out of us? Did you not take enough of our money for your pretty lights?" Palek asked.

"You shouldn't be digging iron, you should be hammering it. Paying smith's wages to dig dirt is ridiculous. And you're no good at it. These men can dig twice as much for half as much. We all win."

"They cannot dig without training," Palek said, shaking his head. "Let us see their guild certificates."

"Ore is ore," Christopher said. "You don't need a certificate to dig it." Luckily for Christopher, Palek had blundered directly into his trap, making the argument about skill rather than law or tradition. "See these two piles? One came from a wheelbarrow left by one of your men. The other was just dug by mine. Can you tell me which is which?"

Palek sniffed in disgust, but the young smith bent down and fingered the piles.

"This is no adequate test," Palek said, when the younger man did not immediately declare an opinion.

"Then what is?" Christopher asked. "Give me a test, and I'll pass it."

"You cannot carve ore out of the ground willy-nilly!" Palek complained. "It must be dug in the right frame of mind, with the appropriate obeisance to the gods."

"You're telling me what the gods want? Because they told me different." It was, in a sense, true. The hallucination of Ostara had told him to be true to himself, and this ridiculous industrial inefficiency was the sort of thing he would have to be dead to ignore.

The argument stalled there, as the crowd tried to decide which authority had more weight.

"This one," the young smith said, standing up and pointing to a pile. Christopher had no idea which was which. He'd turned his back while Tom had arranged the piles so he wouldn't accidentally give it away by an unconscious reaction.

"Tom?" he asked, and the young man stepped forward, unable to conceal a smirk.

"Journeyman, you say that pile is of quality adequate to your needs?" Tom asked, sweetly innocent.

"He is only a journeyman," Palek snapped, suspecting the worst. "He is not qualified." He bent over the piles, made a cursory inspection. "This one is clearly the correctly dug ore." Of course, he picked the other pile.

"Thank you, Senior," Tom said, now smiling openly. "Though the Pater ordered it otherwise, both piles came from my shovel. This I swear on the Lady's breast."

Christopher decided he was *seriously* underpaying the man.

"Anybody can get lucky once," Palek growled.

"Don't your apprentices dig ore, too? Men without a guild certificate? Do they succeed through luck?" Christopher demanded.

"They are supervised by a certified smith," Palek objected, falling back to what seemed like solid ground.

"That's a good point," Christopher admitted. "So I'll have to hire one to oversee our operations. That way you'll know the quality is up to standard. The job pays a hundred and sixty gold a year, and requires eight days a week of supervisory capacity. Dereth, did you speak? Why of course, I'd be delighted if you would take the job."

Dereth coughed, the first sound he'd made.

"He is not qualified to teach others! He is not a Senior!" Palek said, dragging anchor in the winds of unfamiliar logic.

Christopher had done quite enough surrendering. "Then I'll promote him," he snapped back.

The crowd collectively blinked.

"He must pass the test," Jurgen objected with surprising venom. "We would not want anyone to think his rank was merely bought." Inexplicably, the young, literate smith blushed at the older man's words.

"What's the test?"

Dereth answered. "The test, Pater, is to produce an item that shows one is worthy of advancement."

"And Senior grade is when you can make weapons, right?" Christopher said. Jurgen's face started darkening. "So if you had a made a weapon of superior quality, then that would show your potential."

Carefully, slowly, Christopher drew the katana from its sheath. "May I present Dereth's senior thesis."

"He is not licensed to make weapons," Palek said.

"He is not licensed to sell weapons," Christopher corrected. "He did not sell it. He gave it to me." But this story was already well-known to the audience. "Go on, take it," he urged Palek.

The smith reluctantly accepted it, examined it carefully. He turned to Jurgen, who only shook his head, his face black, but younger smith took the sword and considered it.

"This is not the time or place." Palek was backpedaling as fast as he could. "We have not done the rituals. We cannot approve this blade without questioning its maker, and that means discussing guild secrets."

"That's fine, Senior," Christopher said. "I'm not trying to disrupt your rituals. You can take your time, schedule whatever you need. My point is only that Dereth has both the tael and the skill to be advanced to Senior. And thus, can oversee my mining operations. And make weapons, too, I suppose." He had to struggle not to gloat over that last bit. Two birds with one stone, and all that. He was planning on making a lot of weapons.

"It's a very good sword," the literate smith said softly, before handing it back to Christopher. Even more inexplicably, Dereth blushed furiously.

"Well, I'm very happy for all of you Seniors," said a different man. "But what about us independents? What about the ore?"

"Half-price ore means twice as much product," Christopher repeated. "You'll all thank me later. And if it doesn't work out, the Saint has the right to revoke my charter. He's not going to let you starve, and neither am I."

An apprentice raised the important point everyone else was interested in. "Who is going to pay for Dereth's advancement party? And are they going to stint on the ale?"

"I will pay," Christopher sighed, "and I promise no stinting will be allowed." Money really was the answer to everything.

"Then three cheers for Dereth!" another man yelled, and the crowd took up the cry. It wasn't until later that Christopher realized the cheerleader had been Tom.

<hr />

The crowd dispersed, leaving behind a red-faced and confused Dereth.

"I've got something that might help you understand," Christopher explained, producing a sketch of a primitive Bessemer furnace. "It's not just digging I need you for."

"So I'm not to spend my days cracking a whip over apprentices mucking in the dirt?" Dereth was not particularly saddened by this twist of fate.

Christopher grinned. "You'll do your share of that, too, at least enough to keep the other smith off our backs. Speaking of which, what was the deal with you and that other guy?"

Dereth blushed, a different color of red.

"I need to know, Dereth. I just pissed off virtually every smith in town. I need to know why they're angry at you, too."

"I can answer that, Pater," Tom said. "Dereth has a penchant for speaking unpleasant truths."

"Understand," Dereth pleaded, arguing to someone other than Christopher and Tom, to some invisible audience that had never let him speak before, "Jhom is a good man. I like Jhom. Everybody likes Jhom. But he is not a good smith. I voted against his promotion when the smiths were assembled to judge his test. But his father Jurgen is a Senior smith, so others voted to curry favor instead of their conscience.

It angered me to see a poor smith elevated when there were other good smiths held back only by lack of tael. And my anger moved my tongue." He hung his head in shame.

"Jurgen's tongue was no less moved by spite," Tom said.

"It is true," Dereth agreed. "He spoke ill of me, and for a year I got only enough work to survive."

"Jhom is the one who could read, who blushed when the topic of bought ranks came up," Christopher confirmed.

"Yes, and in the gods' own way, I have been punished for having broached that word, for now you buy my promotion and I will spend the rest of my days defending my skill against that very charge."

"Should I hire someone else?"

"Oh, no," the smith said, "I want the advancement. It means wealth and prestige for my family. It means I can do more with metal. It is the achievement of a lifelong dream. The sniping of petty tongues is a small price to pay."

"Don't you think Jhom felt the same way?" Christopher said as gently as he could.

"Of course. But he is still no decent smith. He is an embarrassment to the craft, a waste of tael. He means well, but his hands are unfeeling and he does not have the art." Dereth was contrite but still unwilling to retreat from the truth. "He should have followed his mother, not his father."

"What do you mean?"

"Jhom should have become a priest," Dereth explained. "He trained for it as a boy, but when he came home from war, he chose his father's work instead."

"Jhom's mother is a priest? Who is it?" Christopher tried to think of all the appropriately aged female priests he'd met but came up short.

Dereth raised his eyebrows in surprise.

"But how can you not know this? It is the Vicar Rana."

Over dinner, ensconced in his chapel and surrounded by his own people, Christopher relayed the story of the day's events solely so that he could end by demanding, "What else does everybody know that nobody's told me yet?"

"Well, we can hardly know that, can we?" Svengusta laughed. "I'd give you the genealogical history of everyone in the village, including horses and pigs, but there isn't enough beer in the world to keep me awake through the telling."

"Your Church is exacting," Gregor observed, "for you to not have noticed this yet. She shows the boy no special favor." Gregor approved of this, it seemed. Well, so did Christopher.

"I need Lalania," Christopher said. "She'd know what I need to know. Why does she keep running off? Maybe I should chain her down next time I see her."

"I've tried," Gregor said with uncharacteristic moroseness, but then he changed the subject. "Pater, might I request your charity?"

"Um, perhaps. What?" Christopher tried to stifle his automatic reflex to spend money.

"Not to detract from my gratitude for your healing, but my armor needs some repair as well."

"I guess I do employ a smith now, so sure, I can have him look at it when I go into town next."

Gregor was confused. "Can't you fix it yourself?"

"I'm not a smith."

"But you are a priest."

They stared at each other in mutual perplexity.

"Ahem," Svengusta said, and the table looked to him for rescue. "Perhaps you should consult your books, Brother."

An intense hour later, Christopher ran his finger over a rent in the blue armor, whispering words in Celestial. The metal flowed like wax, ran together, and smoothed. It wasn't a weld, it was an undoing. The metal was restored perfectly, as if it had never been torn.

"Normally we leave this to the smiths," Svengusta explained. "Our Church does not compete with them for services, and they kindly agree not to compete with us for ours."

"The smiths can do this?" Christopher asked, still in awe.

"Of course. What did you think their Novice ranks were for?"

Christopher started grinning uncontrollably, a lopsided smirk that twisted his face into a clown's mask. Making guns was going to be a lot easier than he'd ever dared hope.

"Is he all right?" Gregor asked.

"He does this all the time," Helga said, embarrassed.

"How often can they do it? Are they limited, like me, to a few times a day?" Christopher fired out questions. "What about the carpenters? Can they do this too?"

"Peace, Brother," Svengusta demanded. "We're not privy to the secrets of the guilds. But I assure you, they must be limited. And yes, every formal craft has its own powers."

"There's even one for cooking," Helga said, surprising everyone. "Well, that's what I heard. But only rich men's wives can ever get that."

Svengusta frowned. "A frivolous use of tael that would be," he said, in counterpoint to Helga's obvious envy.

⁓

"No," the miller said, the instant Christopher walked through the door. "Absolutely not."

"But I haven't asked anything," Christopher protested.

"I see the way your eyes move. I have the lease in perpetuity. If you've come to grind grain, you are welcome, but otherwise get out."

"Can I look at your water wheel, at least? If I have to build my own, it would be helpful."

"You looked at Old Bog once, and now it's yours," the miller said sourly. But he couldn't resist the chance to show off his machinery to an appreciative audience.

Christopher was duly impressed. It was only wood with iron fittings, but it was sturdy and reliable, twelve feet tall and groaning in an inexorable pirouette. Unfortunately, it was also well situated, on a spur of ground at the narrow point of the river. There was no room for another. What grain the water could not grind was ground by horse-driven stones, a tiresome and expensive affair.

But Christopher needed a source of constant power, and the mill sat idle half the time. The iron fist of efficiency was about to descend on these pastoral, unsuspecting people, and Christopher was its top hatchet man. He tried not to think about that on the way to Dereth's party.

The event was as tedious as a medieval coronation. It seemed half the town had crowded into the church hall to witness boring speeches and meaningless prayers. At the end of it all Dereth ate a small purple ball, everybody cheered, and kegs were knocked open, transforming the event into Oktoberfest in an instant. Christopher hoped the free-flowing booze would earn him a little forgiveness.

As it was, the smiths were less concerned with Christopher than they were with Karl. The contracts were still not issued, and no one knew why. Unable to discuss the matter without lying, Christopher attached himself to Dereth's side, enjoying the smith's family. The smith's daughter was remarkably cheerful, considering her fiancé was lying cold and stiff in the church morgue.

"I have faith, my lord," Dynae said, when he indelicately broached the topic. "He will have many brushes with death at your side, but you will never lose him."

Christopher did not feel it was fair to call it a brush with death when somebody actually died, but he chose not to quibble. The girl might explain who she had faith *in*, and Christopher did not want that burden. Let Faren carry it, and the grief, if the boy did not come back.

Escaping the girl and her radiant complacency, he trapped Jhom in a corner alone when the man went to refill his mug for the seventh time.

"What do you think of this?" Christopher asked the young smith, handing him a schematic.

Jhom studied the paper with appreciation. "Drawing this lathe looks like it was almost as much work as building it would have been."

"Could your father's shop make it?"

"Of course. . . . What's this part?" Jhom pointed to the bearing sleeve.

Christopher handed him another drawing, a schematic blow-up of the part.

"How many more of these are there?" Jhom asked with dawning comprehension.

Christopher grinned. "About two dozen," he answered. "Still think your shop could make it?"

"Yes," Jhom said loyally. "But it would take some time."

"Time is one thing I hear you've got these days."

"We won't once Goodman Karl finally puts in his order."

"Then you'd better get started."

"How is it powered?" Jhom asked, leafing through the drawings. The young man was an engineer at heart. That didn't mean Dereth was wrong, though. Christopher liked to think of himself as a pretty good engineer, but he handled a drill press like a pregnant elephant danced the ballet. Great machinists were born, not made, like artists and musicians.

But power was a topic Christopher didn't want to discuss at the moment, so he changed the subject.

"I hear you trained for the priesthood as a boy."

"A youthful indiscretion." The smith's joke could not hide his embarrassment.

"Nothing wrong with being a priest," Christopher said with a wink, although he knew it wasn't considered a particularly virile profession like soldiering or smithing. "But it's even better to be a smith who can read and write. How are your sums? Do you do the books for your father?"

"Adequately," Jhom said, close to blushing.

"Do you enjoy it?" But Christopher had gone too far, and Jhom's face turned hard. "Journeyman, I did not come to mock you," Christopher pleaded. "This is Crazy Pater Christopher here, who never means what everyone else means. I came to hire you. I want you to oversee building this lathe, and then I want you to oversee running it."

"What has that got to do with sums?" Jhom asked, softening a little. Christopher apparently still had some credit left on that crazy card.

"Because I don't want you to run the lathe, I want you to supervise it. I want you to hire other men to run this lathe and the other tools I'll be making. I want you to take orders, pay salaries, buy raw materials, deliver finished goods, settle disputes, encourage the workers and satisfy the customers. I want you to run a shop. Not be a shop, but run one. One that can work according to drawings.

"Everybody likes you," Christopher pointed out. "They don't particularly like me. There's a chance for both of us to gain here."

"How big of a shop?" Jhom asked, reluctantly curious.

This was a delicate moment. "Pretty big. I'm thinking of hiring a few Seniors to work in it."

Jhom was not unappreciative of Christopher's ambition and grinned wryly. "That would be a shop worth running. And a challenge, too, to keep such noble horses pulling in the same direction."

"There would be a salary involved. And a share of the profits." But Christopher wasn't going to offer to promote any more smiths.

Jhom was tempted but not yet ready to hop the fence, so Christopher stalled for time.

"Just think about it, Journeyman. Build this lathe for me and think about it." He was trying to be subtle and patient, but it wasn't his strong suit.

At the end of it all, when he was tired and ready to go home, he was ambushed. He walked through a door, heading for the stables, and found himself face-to-face with the unsmiling Vicar Rana.

"First smiths, and now millers? Is there no satiation for your greed?"

Small towns and secrets. He should have known.

"I'll pay for it. Name a fair price." Although, since he would be paying with paper, he wasn't sure any price could be fair.

"No. We need merely wait until you are drafted, and then our lives can resume their normal course."

Christopher shook his head reflexively. The machine economy he built to make weapons would, inevitably, revolutionize the making of other things. Nothing would be the same in his wake.

"The wagon of the world has changed direction, Sister," he said in as neutral a tone as he could manage, "and now it is I who seek to keep your head from falling under the wheel."

"That is not for you to say. This is my county and my responsibility. I must look out for its people to the best of my ability. I say, no more."

He stood, blocked by her immobility, but only temporarily. She saw his calculation on his face and dared him on.

"Do it. Go over my head and yank on your pet saint's chain."

"I'll have to." He already had, with the seizure of the Old Bog. If he stopped to think of all the ways he had insulted the Vicar, he would be lost; she had every right to be angry, and he knew it. That his insults were the result of ignorance rather than malice was no more balm to him than it was to her. "And he will do it. It is for the good of the realm, Vicar. Not just the county."

She stared at him, basilisk-like, slow and impassive.

"We should have barred our doors and let you freeze in the snow. But instead we showed you mercy, and now everywhere I look there are men with swords. Blood and death run riot in my streets, and my people burn with a fever of discontent I cannot cure and I cannot understand. The Lady does not reveal her path to me, and I fear of losing my step."

Her gaze had drifted and now seemed focused on something in the distance. Christopher, unnerved by the dark tone, tried to shrug it off.

"Change isn't always bad."

"Like the man you are," she said, shaking her head, "you do not understand. I do not understand either, but I feel. And I would throw you to the cold myself, except that I feel it is too late. The dam has burst, far, far upstream, and now we must prepare for the flood."

***

A sharp spring storm blew through his village the next day, and when it passed, letting the sun shine unimpeded in the bright-blue sky, Cardinal Faren's carriage rolled into the square.

Like a clown car, the vehicle disgorged a surprising number of unlikely figures, half a dozen hard-faced men in rough clothes. Karl followed them, unsmiling, and then Faren, even less so.

"Mercenaries?" Christopher guessed. The men had that look.

"Police," Faren said, his lip curling with the lie. "Our churches have guardsmen, and yours is entitled as well."

"Trash," Karl said, "swept from the gutters of Kingsrock. For food, shelter, and the booty you've won from Bart, they will protect you until the draft."

"Squires," one of the mercenaries said, kneeling and drawing his sword. He offered the weapon to Christopher, hilt first. "All at least the first Apprentice rank, none above the third. And we are Bright enough, as the Cardinal will attest, if not so lily-pure as Goodman Karl." The rest of the men knelt behind him, though they had no weapons to offer.

Christopher recognized the sword as the one he'd taken from Hobilar and given to Karl. He turned a questioning look to Karl.

"They cannot serve me," Karl had said. "They must be tied to your Church, not mine. And I cannot serve you. I told you I could not accept a sword from your hand, so do not chastise me for giving it back."

Gregor had been appraising the men, and now he spoke approvingly. "A squire in armor is half a knight, and a knight inside stone walls is worth three. Bart would not dare attack you now with less than an army."

"Then let us hope he does not bring an army," Faren growled. "Our allies are sworn to our Church, not yours."

"Can't I appeal to the King for protection?" Christopher said.

"Not without pointing out that the Vicar is unable to provide it," Faren answered, "which we would strongly prefer you not do. Indeed, Bart murdering you on her land could be cause for the King to unseat her.

"If you're really worried," Faren said, as an afterthought, "you could come stay in the Cathedral."

Christopher shook his head. He wouldn't be able to accomplish anything hiding in a monk's cell.

"No thanks."

Faren nodded, as if the answer was expected, and went inside to undo the most recent casualty. With a minimum of ceremony the Cardinal reached out and stuffed life back into Kennet's body. It was, in its way, a compliment: Kennet received a man's resurrection, not a boy's.

Lalania stopped by on one of her intermittent visits. She breezed into the chapel, kissed Gregor warmly, flirted with the boys, and frowned at the mercenaries.

"What's this lot?" she asked. The men eyed her with equal suspicion. *A bottomless pit that I shovel food and beer into*, Christopher wanted to say. But instead he answered, "Karl felt I needed a bigger escort."

"Supposing Bart does attack, how will you tell his army apart from yours?" Dressed in the black-enameled armor, the men did look like evil henchmen.

"It gets worse," Christopher sighed. The pressure from all quarters had been too great, and Christopher had been forced to try on one of the suits of half-plate. Karl had appropriated the remaining one.

"Is Bart going to attack again?" Karl demanded.

Gregor, knowing the troubadour better, waited patiently for her to get around to it on her own.

"I don't think so," she said, turning serious. Effortlessly she managed to arrange things so that only Karl, Christopher, and Gregor could hear her. "You've stung him twice, Pater, and each one hurt. He knows you don't have his ring, and he wants that more than your sword. I wouldn't give a copper for Cannan's health, though. Bart's fifth rank again."

"How is that possible?" Gregor could not conceal his dismay.

"He harvested two entire villages," she answered, her voice angry and defeated.

"He cannot!" Gregor moved directly to outrage, skipping shock and disbelief along the way.

"He can do whatever the Dark he wants, on his land," she snapped. "No lord will war over peasants. Yes, technically it is illegal, but that hardly seems to be a concern for him these days.

"He was already fifth when he came for you the second time. After he was revived from your duel, he spared no time in lowering his people. But killing his knights put a real crimp in his stride. He was close to the point of rebellion with the harvesting, and now he has hardly any loyal servitors. He wants to harvest another village and make more knights, but he needs the knights first to keep the villages under control."

"How do you know all this?" Gregor demanded. "Tell me you did not go into his lands to do your spying."

"Ask me no questions, and I'll tell you no lies," she said breezily, but Gregor was white-eyed and angry at her terrible risk.

"How did he get away from us?" Karl always focused on the pragmatic.

"That I don't know yet," she said. "Obviously he has powerful friends to provide him with magic. But it was a low device. I am certain it transported him no more than a few hundred feet. He was away from his estate too long to account otherwise."

"So if we had pursued him hard, we might have had him then," Karl said.

"Not at all," Lalania said. "You forget his army of Invisible thugs. The good news is, they never back a losing horse. Bart's defeat has forfeited their support."

"He has forfeited his right to rule," Gregor declared with impotent anger.

"We should take the fight to him, then," Christopher said. The best defense was always a good offense. "Can we?" But everybody was staring at him. "What? It's an honest question."

"You want to increase your holdings already? You've barely finished decorating this one." Lalania was laughing at him. "No, you can't. Assuming you could march your gang over there without interference, you'd still have to face his men-at-arms. And assault his keep. And on his lands, his powerful friends could show up and disintegrate you, and no one would object. Finally, who would you put in his place? Kingsrock looks the other way when a lesser lord inherits or buys land, but they won't stand for a knight rank taking it. We'd need a peer to hold the title."

"The rules seem rather stacked against me."

"They are," Gregor said. "That's the point of rules."

"Look at the bright side," Lalania said. "You've beaten him every time you've seen him and made a handsome profit in the bargain."

"I didn't make so much profit the second time. In fact, I spent all of it getting ready for his next attack."

The troubadour twisted her pretty mouth into a sort of smile. "Welcome to the game of thrones, Pater."

"And at the expense of a lot of villagers," Christopher said, getting to the real root of his objection. "Not ours, but his—but human beings nonetheless."

"You can't be held to account for his actions," Gregor said instantly, but Christopher could see that the girl wasn't so certain.

Karl was even less sympathetic than the knight. "You sound as if the death of those peasants was a bad thing. Their suffering is over, and they're not toiling to enrich the Dark anymore. With any luck we can get him to harvest his entire county." The young man was the only peasant here. No one dared to object to his bitter assessment of life as the property of a wicked monster.

"When you're drafted, Pater, you'll be protected somewhat by the commander of your regiment," Lalania soothed. "And more protected by sheer anonymity. Eventually the word will get out that you have neither the sword nor the ring." He'd told both of them the truth about the sword. Nobody was going to die for a lie on his account. Well, no more than already had. "Until then we will stand by you," she swore. He noticed she didn't hesitate to volunteer Gregor's help, which was particularly galling since she never stayed long at the chapel.

"I appreciate that," Christopher said, grateful for whatever she chose to give. "If you can keep me alive until the draft, then I'll take it from there. I've got plans of my own. I just need time."

"And money," she said pointedly.

"Well, of course," Christopher said. "That goes without saying."

22.

FIGHT OF THE LIVING DEAD

Less than a week later, Karl's paranoia was validated. When the two boys on watch at the front door quietly slipped into unconsciousness, the backup watch—a mercenary taking his ease at the fireplace—silently raised the alarm.

Christopher was shaken awake by Karl with a hand over his mouth. He pulled on pants and boots, grabbed his sword, and went out into the hall.

The boys were helping the mercenaries with their armor, Karl and Gregor in their midst. No one was talking. The two young men at the doorway were still asleep, undisturbed.

Karl signaled to wait, pointed at Christopher's armor. Christopher shook his head. He didn't have time for that. Instead he grabbed Charles and went back into his room. His digging crew had appreciated the invention of blasting sticks; now it was time to see what this world thought of the classic nail bomb.

He got his satchel, pulled out a hooded lantern and gave it to the boy. While Charles lit the candle in the little tin box, Christopher found Kennet. He pulled a cardboard tube wrapped in a layer of nails out of the satchel, made throwing motions, and handed Kennet the satchel and the tube. Charles came up, and the two silently nodded their understanding.

Another boy made the mistake of passing too close to a shuttered window. In the dim glow of the one light-stone they always left uncovered in the ceiling, he cast a gentle shadow, and the thunk of a crossbow bolt impaling the wooden shutter was startling.

"They know we're up," Karl said. He was only halfway into his armor. Christopher looked around, but all his boys already had helmets and pants on, so he peeked through a window.

Two large wagons were pulling up south of the village. In the starlight he could see figures moving. He stepped away from the window before they decided to shoot him.

"A lot," he announced. Another peek and, "Dammit, they're opening the barn!" He stepped away again rather than watch his fortune in horseflesh run out into the hands of the enemy. At least they wouldn't take Royal.

No, he realized, *they won't take my horse, but they might kill it.*

He cursed the armored men. "Get a move on."

"Can we shoot, Pater?" asked one of the boys, a loaded crossbow in his hands. Karl had brought more with him, so now all the boys had one.

Christopher looked to Karl, who nodded.

"For god's sake be careful," Christopher said, although he knew it made no sense. This was war.

The boys began opening the shutters, nimbly stepping away in time for the hail of crossbow quarrels that rained down in response.

"At least two dozen," Karl said.

"Put out that light," Gregor ordered.

One of the lads clambered to the top of a bunk and covered the light with a cloth. The room went dark, and starlight streamed in through the narrow, open windows.

Christopher's own crossbows began firing back, with rattles and clunks and bolts slithering through the air. The boys had spent a lot of time practicing. He hoped it would pay off.

"When they get close enough," Christopher told Kennet. "It's supposed to be a three-second fuse." He risked a quick peek again. What in the hell was up with those wagons?

A boy cried out in pain, fell down with a bolt sticking out of his shoulder. Svengusta was already on him, pulling out the bolt with one hand and casting with the other. The boy stopped bleeding, but he was still white-faced with pain. Svengusta was saving his big heals for the important assets.

"The door, you fools," Gregor cursed, struggling into the last of his armor.

The bar across the door was jiggling, trying to pop open. Two boys rushed to it, held it down, and then collapsed, asleep, along with another one who had moved to a nearby window. Whatever wizard was on the other side of that door wasn't giving up yet.

"They're charging," another boy cried, looking out a window.

Christopher was going to ask what he meant, but the boy fell to the floor as a bolt bounced off his helmet and spiraled through the room. He sat up immediately, uninjured except for the stun, and looked toward the door in fear. Christopher could hear the tromp of feet and something else, a clicking sound that was sickening and eerie and electrified the hair on his neck.

Svengusta was almost to the door, drawn automatically to the fallen boys although they were only asleep instead of injured, when the bar fell off. For a brief second events stood still, while everyone turned to the sound of the bar clattering to the floor, and then the doors burst open to nightmare.

Skeletal figures surged forward, their bare bones clicking on the stone steps, clawing at the wooden doors. Christopher realized they were actual skeletons when he could see right through their rib cages. He might have fled in fear, but it was too much like a horror movie, so instead he stood paralyzed, waiting to see what the next scene would be.

Svengusta raised his rusty sickle, a candle in the darkness, an old man in a nightshirt standing against a tsunami of death and evil, and cried out in Celestial.

"I abjure thee!" His voice roiled with emotion, anger, outrage, hatred, but not fear. "I abjure thee!" he repeated over and over, impossibly advancing a step with each chant.

Incredibly, the monsters shrank back, the empty, grinning skulls chattering in bloodthirsty madness but falling back.

But only the front rank. The next rank surged past them, spilled into the church, groped for the small white-haired figure in front of them.

Without conscious thought, Christopher moved, rushing forward to the old man's side, drawing his sword as he ran, but not to strike. He held it before him like a signpost, adding his voice to the chant.

His sword shone with its own light, and the monsters quailed, falling back, their mad chattering somehow fearful instead of hungry. They backed away from Christopher, who advanced on them, wholly given over to the power he wielded, mesmerized by the faces of nightmare fleeing before his every step.

He might have followed them out of the chapel and into the yard, but the boys were already throwing the doors closed. Out through the shrinking crevice flew a sparkling, smoking torch, and Christopher only had time to recognize it as one of his blasting sticks before the knot of boys slammed shut the door and hugged against it, white-faced and trembling, holding out the creatures of the dark.

Christopher tried to tell them to move, to get away, but he couldn't find the words. His tongue was confused between three languages and two cultural contexts.

Shielded from the light of the sword and the sickle, the monsters rallied, pushing and clawing at the doors. They were winning, the doors opening a crack. Christopher finally acted with reason again, shoving Svengusta and himself away from the gap, when the dynamite went off.

The doors surged open, boys spilling everywhere, and a rain of shattered bones and dust blew through the chapel.

The remaining monsters, utterly unaffected by fear or shock, pushed forward again eagerly, but the mercenaries charged past Christopher with what would have been blood-curdling yells if his blood was not already cottage cheese. The armored men crashed into the forest of bones, Gregor's sword glowing with its own blue magic, and the forest was already thin and tottering from the blast.

In heartbeats the skeletons lay in broken pieces like discarded toys on Christmas morning, and Gregor looked back at him, his face flushed with excitement and righteous anger and life, burning bright against the icons of death scattered all around.

The armored men followed Gregor out into the yard and staggered into a rough line as they charged the wagons. Behind them came half a dozen boys, Kennet and Charles with them, laughing madly, sparkling in the night. Before them quarrels came snarling, but the heavy metal shields and plate bounced them aside with ringing rebuttals.

Christopher followed them out, drawn in their wake like flotsam. Belatedly he charged his sword with its killing magic. Somewhere out here was Bart. A stray skeleton staggered up to him, and he knocked its skull from its neck without conscious thought, his attention searching for the black knight. The monster rattled to the ground like a puppet with its string cut, the skull rolling over and staring up at him with empty eyes.

There was still covering fire from the chapel windows, and now a boy was shooting from the steps. Christopher's armored men surrounded a wagon but had to duck and hide from the hail of fire from within.

Christopher shouted something; he wasn't even sure what, but Charles looked at him and so he pointed to the wagon. As the two boys ran toward it, Gregor understood and ordered his men to fall back. The horses were frightened now, lunging in their traces, but the brake was fixed and the wagon did not move, even while the sparkling stick of dynamite arced inside.

Christopher could not understand why the men were not trying to escape, forgetting that they did not recognize the danger, and then one of them came sailing out, propelled by fire and smoke as the wagon exploded. The blast overwhelmed the brake, and the horses bolted forward, dragging the flaming and shattered wagon behind them as bodies and wood fell from it with every jolt.

Kennet fell to the ground without a sound, Charles screaming in fear and shock for him. The boy had grown a quarrel in his chest. Christopher yanked it out and healed him, but he used the wrong magic, a ranked spell instead of an orison. Kennet sprang from the ground, fully healed, his face aflame, and reached into the satchel again, dragging Charles after him.

Christopher himself sank to his knee, crumpling over a brutal gut-shot. He looked down, stupefied, at the quill feathers stuck in him. He only had time to register that the feathers were black, not white, before the pain arced through his mind, shutting out all other thought.

But then he was standing again, alert and ready, Svengusta tossing the bloody bolt to the ground beside him.

"Find Bart," Christopher bellowed.

A bolt clipped his ear, and he realized he should have at least put on his helmet. A single shot to the head could kill a first rank, as Lalania had shown in the forest battle. He ran for cover, finding some in shadows before wondering why there were shadows at night. But the battlefield was lit by fire from the south. His barn was in full flame.

He moved out from the corner he'd hidden in, tried to advance to the barn. In his way was a battle, three of his boys against one chain-mail-armored foe who had gotten ahead of his fellows. The boys were being driven back, the man swinging the sword with deadly menace, when one boy, possessed of insane courage, leaped upon the man's shield and clung to it like a dead weight.

He dragged the man to his knees. The man stabbed at him, the boy now using the shield to protect himself, but not well enough. The boy screamed in pain as the blade found its mark, but he did not let go. His comrades rushed forward, thrusting with their spears. One stepped on the sword as it slid over the ground and trapped it.

The man let go of the sword and grabbed the boy's leg. Instantly the boy froze, toppled like tree. The man grabbed at the other one on his shield, and immobilized him, too. But the boy hadn't let go of the shield yet, so the man had to leave it on the ground, locked in the frozen grip. He stood, unarmed save for the chain mail he wore, and in the light of the fire Christopher could see his hand was deformed and discolored, a putrid green with long black nails that glistened.

"You," growled the creature in Hobilar's voice. The two men faced each other again in the village square, and this time there would be no mercy.

"You," Christopher said, still amazed. "Your hand . . ."

"Do you like it?" Hobilar snarled. "You'll like it better when I shove it up your—"

But he stopped talking and started gurgling. A crossbow bolt had appeared in his chest. Reflexively he reached up with his terrible hand to pull it out, but the black nails accidentally cut into his flesh, and he froze, too, a look of horror on his face, and fell to the ground.

The last boy screamed in rage for his fallen comrades and plunged his spear into Hobilar's body, leaning on it until it went all the way through and into the ground. Then he started kicking the corpse. Christopher thought about pulling him off but went to check on the casualties instead.

The boys still breathed, their eyes tracking him. They just couldn't move. He stopped the bleeding of the injured one. Then he reassured them, told their still forms that magic would free them later, hoped he wasn't lying, and moved deeper into the battlefield.

From somewhere came another blast. Christopher could hear shrapnel ringing off metal armor. The mercenaries were deep into the territory held by the enemy archers, the boys coming out of the church and backing them up, firing constantly. Bart had started out with more crossbows, but Christopher's boys had started with better cover.

And then the second wagon surrendered, the men throwing out their bows and raising their hands when Gregor knocked on the wagon side, threatening fire and doom in a voice that could not be doubted.

Christopher bent over an armored mercenary lying motionless

on the cold ground. He was still breathing, so Christopher used a small spell to stop the bleeding and continued on, trying to get to the burning barn without getting killed.

Then there was a melee, a thick knot of men with spears and shields, the handful of mercenaries hesitant to throw themselves into the thorny hedge, until Kennet ran up, fire in his hands, and the wall crumbled under the threat, the men throwing their weapons and their bodies to the ground, crying for mercy. Kennet had a difficult heartbeat before he managed to pull out the fuse.

"The barn!" Christopher's screams were hardly less shrill than the screams of the horses.

He ran to the flaming building, threw open the door, but was literally forced back by the wave of heat. Inside he could hear someone keening in fear and pain, and he wept in rage, helplessly listening to the dying horse. He pushed against the heat, but it would not budge. He had no spell that would let him walk through fire, and so he sank to his knees as the barn fell silent, save for the roaring of the flames that mocked him.

"Bart is gone," Gregor said without sympathy. "Get up, you have wounded to tend." He pulled Christopher to his feet, threw him away from the fiery wreckage.

Belatedly Christopher realized the blue knight's horse was in there too. He staggered back toward the village where the enemy sat on the ground, their hands over their heads, fenced in by the mercenaries' swords and glares.

Svengusta's normal personality had been replaced by efficiency. He directed Christopher to bleeding men and boys, told him what to do. When they were out of magic he started binding wounds with long, clean strips of cloth. By the end the paralyzed boys were recovering on their own, moving in slow fits and starts.

Karl was injured, the left half of his face dotted with red like a pepperoni pizza. There was something wrong with his eye, too, but he stopped Christopher with an upraised hand.

"I'll live," he grated, "and the eye can wait. Bart is gone."

"I know," Christopher said. "He stole my horses and ran away. Again. He killed . . ." Looking at Karl's face, suddenly the horse didn't seem so important. "How many did he kill?" he asked instead.

"Svengusta says none." That was the way of this crazy world. No matter how bloody the battle, if you carried the field, your losses would be light. Wounds were rarely fatal instantly, usually killing through organ failure, blood loss, or infection. The astonishing healing powers of the priests made victory cheap at any cost.

"How many did we kill?"

"We're still counting body parts."

It took Christopher a moment to realize the young veteran wasn't telling a gruesome joke.

"Your fireballs were quite effective," Karl said. "I just wish Kennet would learn to throw them with a little more caution." But this was too much like an actual emotion, so Karl went back to the facts. "It looks like Bart brought forty men and a dozen or more of those horrors. We've got at least ten corpses, but Svengusta says we'll have more by morning." The healing magic had not lasted all the way through their own men. There was none left over for the enemy. "That still leaves you over two dozen prisoners to deal with. All commoners, as far as I can tell. If Bart had knights, they left with him."

"And we know he had a mage," Gregor said, coming up to join them, "and I've found no sign of him either."

"What do I do with them?" Christopher looked out in dismay over the prisoners.

"Have mercy," cried one, seeing that they were the object of discussion. "We had no choice but to serve our lord."

"You killed my horse!" Christopher's anger snapped like a string, and he was suddenly standing over the cringing man with his sword in his hands.

The realization that he had almost killed a helpless man did not chill him as much as the fact that Gregor and Karl stood by, watching, without any particular comment. They weren't going to stop him.

He made his brain function. Would he do this if Royal still lived? He put away his sword slowly.

"It's just a stinking horse!" the man cried, his fear replaced by fury once the dreadful blade was back in its sheath.

"You didn't have to kill it," Christopher answered.

"We did as Lord Bartholomew ordered. What choice did we have?" The man was groveling again, the switch between anger and fear instantaneous.

"You did not have to become a soldier," Karl said. "You could have remained a peasant."

"And left our women and children at the mercy of his whim? Do you not know he beheaded two whole villages to boil their brains?"

Karl was unmoved. "That does not justify the violence you have inflicted on others."

"If your goal was to protect your families," Gregor said with brutal ice, "you've failed. He'll drain them first, now."

"Let us go!" the man cried, and several others joined him. "Let us go home to save our wives and children!"

Christopher was torn, but Gregor was unyielding.

"You're boot-lickers," the knight said. "If we let you go, you'll lick Bart's boot the minute you see him."

"Mercy!" they cried back, and Christopher agreed. He turned to the knight, the question in his face.

"You want to show these men mercy?" the knight barked. "Kill them now. Kill them before daylight. If you turn them over to your Church for prosecution, Bart will have a spy in the courtroom. He'll kill the families of every man who surrendered, whether he needs their tael or not. He'll torture them to death as an abject lesson. If these men die now, then perhaps Bart will be concerned with other things. But if they are named as cowards, then he'll punish their families in ways no sane mind can dream of. Send them home to Bart and he'll do the same, but in front of them, before he kills them for being deserters."

With a cry of inarticulate rage, the kneeling prisoner charged Christopher, who stepped aside and knocked him down with a well-placed knee. On the ground, the man writhed in pain, but not from the force of the blow. The silence of the prisoners confirmed the terrible words of the blue knight, and they hung their heads in despair.

"Every one of them is guilty of rapine, murder, and torture, Pater," Gregor said. "Your Church will hang them all, anyway. Give them a warrior's death. Conceal their cowardice from the world. That is all you can do for them and their families."

The prisoners didn't look like they wanted a warrior's death.

"Why did you put me in this position?" Christopher asked them. "Knowing all this, why did you surrender?"

"Because they are cowards," Gregor said with contempt.

Karl had more insight into the peasant mind. "Because they were hoping you'd gotten Black Bart."

"So if we'd killed Bart, then I could turn these men over to the Church for judgment, and possibly atonement." *And I wouldn't have to choose between fueling terrorism or running an abattoir*, his mind whispered. "He's got a long ride home. If we had horses, we could chase him. If you hadn't taken so damn long to get into your armor, we could have saved the horses." He could not keep the bitterness out of his voice.

Gregor was too insulted to respond, so Karl did. "Without our armor, we would not have carried the field, Pater." He might have been angry, but with his face torn up like that, it was simply impossible to read the taciturn man.

"I'm not blaming you," Christopher said, apologizing. "I'm blaming the armor. It's stupid and slow. The fault does not lie in you, but in the armor." The fault lay in this whole stupid world and its stupid habits.

"It's good armor," Gregor said defensively.

"Not the armor, itself," Christopher said with exasperation. "The fact of armor, any armor, at all."

"Would you change even how we dress?" Gregor asked in surprise.

"Of course," Svengusta said. "I told you, Baronet, the Pater would get around to you too, in time."

Karl, ever pragmatic, set aside anger and futility, and spoke to the moment. "There are horses in Knockford." Christopher must have let his dubiousness show, because Karl felt the need to explain. "The Vicar will aid you, Pater. This was open war on her land. She can no longer pretend to be neutral."

Christopher still wasn't so sure. After all, no villagers had been hurt, and the only building burned was his.

"He brought those *things* into our lands," Svengusta said with uncontained disgust. "She'll throttle him with her bare hands for that alone."

"But how do we get to Knockford?" Christopher asked.

Reflexively they all looked north, to Fenwick's stable. Impossibly, Fenwick was already leading two horses toward them. Royal spotted Christopher and trotted up to him, nuzzling him with a long, soft nose. His mane and tail were badly singed, but otherwise the horse seemed unharmed.

Christopher was too overcome with emotion to speak, clinging to the horse's mane like a drowning man.

It's just a horse, his mind said. It is a warhorse, a machine of battle, a military asset. Do not get attached. But he could not help it. He was struggling to not get attached to these people, who he must leave someday when he went home. The horse was the one living thing in this world he dared to love. After all, he might even be able to take it with him. It would not feel out of place in the wrong world, homesick and useless.

Do not get attached, repeated his mind, implacable. But he noticed that Gregor tenderly stroked the muzzle of his own great warhorse.

"When Royal kicked his way out of the barn, he went looking for a safe, comfortable place, so he came back to my stable," Fenwick explained. "I guess Balance followed him." Fenwick always knew the horses' names.

"Then who?" Christopher could not finish the question.

"How many horses did you leave in the stable?" Karl demanded of the prisoners.

"Lord Bartholomew left three," said one of them. "The warhorses, of course, and another he spat on, saying he would leave the druid to burn if he could."

Christopher was ashamed that the thought of Niona's gentle mare dying in terrible agony did not affect him like the thought of Royal had.

"The ghoul-hand knight tried to claim that destrier," offered another prisoner, pointing to Royal. "But when it smelled his new hand, it would not let him near."

No wonder Hobilar had been so angry. Christopher had stolen the heart of the only creature on the planet that loved him. Or rather, Hobilar had thrown it away by making some kind of unholy pact with Darkness. It all depended on how you looked at it. But that was in the past, now, and it was time to move forward.

Stroking the warhorse's long neck, his mind started working again.

"Lock them in a barn and nail it shut. Let no one in or out. Sven, make sure our people understand how important it is to hide these men's identities, even the fact that we have prisoners at all." Hopefully the peasantry here would feel some sympathy for Bart's peasants. "Karl, bring the mercenaries in that wagon."

They still had one of Bart's wagons, with its two draft horses. Come to think of it, Fenwick had a stable full of draft horses.

"How much tack do you have?" he asked Fenwick. A horse without a saddle wasn't worth much to a cavalry man.

"We won't be fighting. We can ride bareback to Knockford," Karl said.

"Gregor and I will go on ahead and get things started." Christopher was enough of a horseman now to know that the draft animals couldn't hope to keep up with the warhorses. The plow horses were bred for strength and placidity, the warhorses for stamina and spirit. The warhorses were also fed expensive grain instead of cheap hay, a fact that had not gone unnoticed by Christopher's purse. But they would repay him now, reward him with speed when he needed it.

༺✦༻

Galloping without a saddle was deceptively easy, but all it took was one mistake and you had no chance to correct before you were on the ground. Christopher could barely manage it in his light chain shirt. He could not understand how Gregor could do it in full armor. Well, not quite full armor. The knight had taken off his plated leggings and strung them over his shoulder. He looked ridiculous, but the horse's naked back was spared the hard metal.

Thinking of the armor prompted an apology.

"I'm sorry," he shouted at Gregor over the pounding hooves. "I didn't mean to insult you."

The blue knight had been surprisingly complacent since the horses had appeared. Christopher wasn't sure if that was because he was hiding his anger or just relieved to have his horse back.

"You owe me no apologies," Gregor shouted back. "You are favored by the gods and must follow the path they have set you on."

"We got lucky," Christopher objected. "It was just luck."

"That's what I said," the knight repeated mildly. "The luck, bye the bye, is not that our horses escaped a burning barn. They are trained not to panic, and an ordinary stall cannot hold an animal this strong. The luck was that Black Bart holds no free loyalty. His barns are built like fortresses, to trap the creatures he owns. So he did not see that your barn was built to house, not cage. If your other horse had not panicked, she might have followed ours out."

If Bloodfire had been there, she would have followed him, Christopher realized sadly.

"This is how we defeat Evil," Gregor said with satisfaction. "It cannot comprehend Good. Well, that and fireballs. I had no idea you were a wizard of such rank."

"I'm not a wizard."

But the knight was chuckling. "I'll bet that put a weasel up Bart's butt. He wasn't expecting fireballs. His mage could only do sleep. In one stroke you wiped out his secret army of soul-trapped and shattered his battle plan."

Christopher shuddered to think what would have happened if the monsters had gotten into the chapel while everyone was asleep and unarmored.

"But Svengusta drove them from the chapel with his . . ." Christopher didn't know what he'd done. He'd skipped that chapter in the book. It hadn't seemed important at the time. "How could they help Bart if Svengusta could drive them out?"

"How did Bart control them in the first place?" the blue knight growled. "Who knows what plans that twisted mind laid? But I grant you, his recklessness stinks of desperation."

"Where did he get them?" Christopher was still drowning in questions. He could deduce that magic had animated the bodies, and presumably Bart numbered a practitioner of the necromantic arts among his allies. "Where did he get so many corpses?"

Gregor looked at him, surprised or perhaps envious of his innocence.

"He had two whole villages' worth at hand, last I heard."

On that ugly note they fell silent, the sun rising on the horizon, a promise for the end of the darkness in the sky, though not for the day.

23.

AS THE CROW FLIES

Vicar Rana was waiting for them in her office, despite the early hour.

"I dreamed badly," she explained. "Like a child, of the Black Harvest. Monsters of the Dark come to take all our heads. I left my bed chamber to escape the nightmare, and now here you are."

Her stony face showed no reaction to Christopher's report. Perhaps her dreams had been worse. At the end he broke down in desperation.

"We have to catch Bart. We have to," he pleaded.

"Is your appetite for blood and tael so great now?" she asked, a stone speaking.

"If motive is the issue," Gregor said, "I'll forfeit my share. We must stop Bart. He is gone, Lady, sunk into Black. He no longer acts from profit or even fear but only violence. I fear his retribution on his people will be terrible, a blow to the strength of the Kingdom itself."

"Then the high lords will replace him," she answered.

"Only after," Gregor said softly.

"Me too," Christopher said. "I'll give up my share. Just give me horses."

"Mere horses cannot catch him," Rana said. "My stable does not hold zephyrs."

She had a point. The prisoners had told them that Bart had brought eight horses with him. Adding Christopher's, or rather Bart's original, eight meant he would be doubled up on the ride home. Christopher wasn't even certain how they could find him, let alone close the gap. He really missed the druid and her kittenhawk now.

"And if you could catch him, then what? Can your band of mercenaries defeat him and his knights?" The prisoners had also told them that Bart had six knights, although they were newly promoted and poorly armed.

"Probably not," Gregor said, "but we'll try. If the Pater has any more charges in his wand of fire, we have a chance."

"I don't have a wand," Christopher said with exasperation. "It's just the sky-fire stuff." But he checked his satchel while he was talking. "I've got three left."

"He knows I will send messages to Cannenberry and Copperton. He will not dare to pass those lands. So he must go twenty miles south before he can go east." Rana seemed to be talking to herself.

"Can't you send riders to the other counties?" Christopher asked.

"That would involve a discussion, and by then Bart will be home. We have only this day to act.

"Are you both committed, regardless of the danger?" she suddenly asked them. "For no gain but to save men and women you do not even know and owe nothing to? To strike against the Dark now that it is exposed, regardless of the risk?"

"Yes," they both said in accidental unison.

"Perhaps I have sat too long," she said to herself. "To bring the soul-trapped into our lands is an insult no one will deny." Her glare blazed out at Christopher. "If I must be driven before the lash of your Patron, I will not spare you. Prepare yourselves for a day of hard riding and harder deeds. Just the two of you. I cannot support more. You have one hour."

She folded her hands in meditation, and they were dismissed.

Outside her office Christopher was mystified, but the knight was grinning.

"Get a comfortable saddle, Pater. Don't bother to pack food or water, but bring your bag of tricks."

"She's going to send us after him alone?" Not that he was going to back down now, but the venture seemed unlikely to succeed.

"No, Pater. You've stirred the mountain to move. She's coming with us."

An hour later, Christopher and Gregor stood outside the church in the cold light of the spring morning. Karl and the men were there, disappointed that they would not be accompanying the chase. They had brought Christopher's armor, and so he was arrayed in the heavy plate and chain, a steel engine of woe.

"You'll need it, Christopher," Karl said. "Without your magic you'll need every edge." Christopher's spells, exhausted in the night, would not renew for many hours yet.

"How can the horses run with all this weight?"

"Little good it will do to catch them if we are naked," Gregor answered. "The horses are trained to this. It is only for one day."

Once again Vicar Rana came out in her armor, her guards leading her horse. Christopher's mind could not reconcile the transformation from middle-aged woman to warrior, no matter how many times he saw it. Nor, apparently, could anyone else's. The crowd of guards and priests watched in silent confusion, unsettled by the loss of their well-known Lady and this strange replacement. Only Gregor seemed comfortable with it.

"I cannot fight well," she told them matter-of-factly, "but I am still sixth rank. And I have my magic. You must dispatch his knights quickly, either with death or fear. Then you must help me with the monster."

She turned to each horse and cast a spell. Royal seemed to swell up, and his ears twitched with eagerness. When Christopher mounted, the horse moved under him like he'd just been let out of his stall.

The horses turned to the south, their heavily laden hooves ringing hollow on the bridge.

Next to a small wood they paused, while Rana called a huge black crow down from a tree to her open hand. She spoke Celestial in heavy concentration as she locked eyes with the bird.

"Here is bread, feathered friend. See that I call you to share in my bounty. Will you call me to share in yours?

"No," she said when the bird answered her in squawks, "I do not want fresh berries or aged meat. I seek no worms, fat and tasty as they are. I seek a party of horses, many horses, with not enough men. Go, find them, and lead me the way. You will have bread for the rest of your days and my eternal gratitude."

The bird preened, cackled, and took to the air. The horses took to the ground, and they flew south, over tracks and trails, through fields and pastures. The horses were not in full-out gallop, merely cantering, but even twenty minutes of that should have left Royal wet and foaming. Royal ran on and on and on, long past Christopher's experience and past his own endurance. His butt was getting sore. But it was just pain, so he ignored it.

They stopped to water the panting horses in the middle of a field of stubble. Rana handed out empty leather waterbags, then held her fingers in an "O" over each one in turn. Water gushed from her hand like a magic trick.

While the horses drank she spoke to Christopher.

"Do not seek to appease me by flattering my son."

"I do not flatter him," he answered automatically. "I need him. He is like me, in a way. He works with metal in his head, not with his hands."

"It is true he obsesses over your scrollwork. I caught him wasting good Church paper trying to do his own. I would think him enspelled if I did not know better."

"I'm sorry. I'll replace the paper." Paper was something Christopher had plenty of now.

The coldness he had come to expect from her suddenly cracked, as if his simple apology had been a piton driven into a block of ice.

"No, you owe me nothing," she said. "I owe you, for you have given my son what I could not. Day by day he summons your machine into being, turning paper into metal. With each part his father's respect grows. Your gold fills the shop's coffers, wrung out of your papers like water from rags. Jhom does no metalwork but directs the men, and as your machine takes shape so does their respect.

"I fought your changes, in everything. And now here I am, lashed into war, punished for my intransigence. You have taken my Saint, my town, my son, and now my peace."

"I didn't mean to," Christopher said helplessly.

"Your Patron has much to answer for," she said equally helplessly. "But I forgive you now. I can do this because we likely ride to our deaths. Thank you," she said humbly, "for the light you have put in my husband's eyes and for the spring in my son's step. Should it all end here, those moments were worth it."

What could he say? So he said nothing.

The waterbags were empty. Rana went to each horse and cast a healing spell on them.

"A shameful use of power," she said. "But it is to need."

And they rode again, cantering through the sunny day, the horses fresh as if they'd just left the barn.

Their feathered guide circled them late in the morning, cawing, and winged to the east. They followed as best as they could.

"I should not have sent him out so soon," she told the men, "but we are in luck. No hawk took him."

"Will Bart know he is followed?" Christopher asked.

"He'll assume it," Gregor said. "We'll not catch him napping."

But it was starting to look like they would catch him. The horses had run for an unnatural length of time, and still they pressed on.

Shortly before noon, the horse-magic faded. The horses were merely mortal again, and Rana had no power to spare to refresh them, saving the rest of her spells for battle. But they had covered an incredible distance.

Bart had barely more than two hours' head start on them. He had double horses, but they had magic ones, and they had a guide. The sun was still high in the sky when the crow squawked, calling attention to the herd of horses traveling east.

They were spotted, too, and the herd broke into a gallop.

"Idiocy," Gregor declared, as their own horses burst into pursuit, but then he saved his breath for the coming fight.

Bart did not seem to have a plan, just a panicked flight. He ran his horses brutally, but they simply could not keep up the pace, not after a long day of hard traveling. When one of them simply stopped running, and then a half-dozen began to stumble, he came to his senses and stood his ground.

The black lord and his six knights pulled their panting horses into a wide, ragged line as Christopher's party slowed to a trot. The men were in chain mail, with cheap wooden shields.

"I do not see the mage," Gregor said with a frown.

"I rejoice at your coming," Bart shouted at them, his voice tinged with maniacal frenzy. "I will take your head to the altar and be redeemed. I will show I am the stronger servant."

Rana ignored his lunacy, addressing his troops instead. "Flee now and we will not pursue you. We seek only your master."

"Stupid bitch," Bart growled. "I'll not hesitate to burn your corpse. Get away while you can." At least now his words seemed to be relevant to the occasion, as if the unexpected presence of the Vicar had steadied him.

"You brought soul-trapped into my lands," she answered him. "You have gone too far."

"Her tael will make one of you a captain," Bart promised, and he kicked his exhausted horse into a canter, charging at them, his men following with ragged shouts.

The grass rose up on one flank of Bart's line, grabbing at the tired horses. Bart looked around wildly for the druid, and so did Christopher, but it was Rana chanting the spell. Gregor cut across in front of her, charging the other flank. The blue knight ignored Bart, who ignored him also and drove straight to Rana. Christopher would have been worried about her if there wasn't a sword in his face demanding its own attention. One of the knights had closed with him.

Neither of them was a great horseman, but Christopher had a great horse. Royal instinctively went to the man's shield side, making his attacks awkward. Christopher didn't have a shield, so he didn't care which side his foe was on. He started beating on the man's shield. It was wood. It might come apart.

Gregor battled two other men. On horseback he had a great advantage, since they could not press against him tightly. He kept slipping out of the reach of one or the other, making it practically a one-on-one fight, where his rank would guarantee him victory.

Bart bore down on Rana, who stood her ground. Christopher heard her cry out in Celestial, turned enough to see her thrust her hand out at the black knight. The knight shuddered but shook off the spell, cursing at her.

He charged upon her and slashed his huge black blade across her head. Her plain, open-faced helmet disintegrated under the attack, falling in pieces to the ground with lengths of her hair. Absurdly, she took the blow with little more than a shrug and repeated her command in Celestial.

"Hold!" she ordered, her fingers gripping the air in front of her as if it was his throat, and this time Bart held. He went rigid, like a person pretending to be a statue. Only then did her desperation become apparent, by the quality of her relief.

She leaned forward, caught the halter of his horse, held it still next to hers. She did not speak but waited patiently against the ticking of the clock.

Christopher's foe held his shield above his head and swept his blade under it horizontally. The blow failed to penetrate Christopher's half-plate despite the ringing force, and it gave him room to slide his katana under the shield and thrust up into the man's armpit. The man squawked, but the chain held. And then Royal sidestepped, putting his weight behind the katana, and it burst through the chain and slid deep into the man's body.

The man fell from his horse like a rag doll. Christopher urged Royal around to Rana's side. Gregor was winning, one man down, but then he had to wheel about to face another rider who had freed his horse from the circle of grasping vines.

Christopher raised his sword and took aim at the immobilized form of Black Bart.

Rana spoke: "Strike hard, for the spell ends with your first blow."

Christopher looked again at the thick armor and lowered his sword. "How much time do we have?" he asked.

"Seconds," she said flatly. "And I cannot repeat the spell."

Not enough time to take off the man's armor, and even if they did, they might not cut through the tael-reinforced neck in a single blow. Not enough time to tie him up. They could take his sword, but just his plated fists were probably enough to beat them all to death. Christopher was already depleted, the blow that had not broken armor would have broken ribs but not for his tael. Gregor had cuts of his own and was still fighting two men. And Rana could have little tael left. Bart's one strike had been awe-inspiring.

He dropped his sword, grabbed for his satchel, steering Royal alongside with his knees. Pulling out a stick of dynamite, he leaned over and wedged it firmly under Bart's helmet, in the neck-hole of his breastplate, with the fuse dangling out. He drew the flint-stone from his satchel and struck at the fuse, a short, sharp rap that would not harm the man but would spark the fuse.

His first blow smashed his finger.

"Block," he ordered Royal, and the horse pressed closer, pinning Bart between himself and Rana's horse. Christopher struck again, the flint sparked off the metal plate, and the fuse began to sputter. He yanked Royal back and slapped the black knight's horse on the flank.

"Flee," he yelled to Rana, and tried to gallop away from the spooked horse, a task made difficult by Royal's desire to chase it down and make it submit. He had a bad moment until the warhorse acceded to his demands, pulling away a few dozen feet, and then the bomb went off.

Bart's helmet flew thirty feet into the air as his horse panicked and ran blindly into the grasping weeds, where it tripped and fell with a sickening crack.

"Yield," Gregor ordered.

The man who had joined the fight late turned his horse to flee, and Gregor cut him down. The other, wounded and demoralized, threw his sword to the ground and started pulling off his helmet.

Gregor rode around the circle to the other two, who were still trying to free their horses.

"Yield," he ordered them, "or the wizard will use his fireballs against you."

They did not believe him until Christopher rode over, holding a stick of dynamite in the air.

"You said we could flee," argued one.

"That was before the fight," Gregor responded.

"Then blast away, for the bitch will hang me anyway," the man cursed back.

"Suit yourself." Gregor put away his sword and began cocking his crossbow.

"I yield," the other man said. "But I fear to step into the choking grass." He threw down his helmet.

"Give me a warrior's death," the rebellious one demanded. "Fight me man to man."

"No," Gregor said, and shot him.

"Dark take you!" the man screamed in pain and rage. He pulled out the bolt, kicked his horse madly. "Move, you foul beast!"

"Yield," Gregor said, reloading.

"The spell ends soon," Rana said, and Christopher decided he ought to go pick up his own sword.

Then the grass relaxed, and the wounded rebel charged Gregor with a victorious yell. Gregor fired but missed, dropped the crossbow and tried to get his sword out, but he had to duck as the man swung at him, the blow crunching on the blue knight's armor. And then the man fell, spitting blood. Behind him the other knight pulled his charging horse to a stop and carefully threw his red sword to the ground.

"That is only one of many foul deeds I have done," said the traitorous knight. "Yet it was on your behalf. Will you hang me all the same?"

"You will be given a chance to atone, I swear," Rana answered. "We will not hold your past against you, if your future lies with us."

"Truly," said the wounded knight who had surrendered first, "you will forgive us?"

"It's not quite that simple," Rana said. "But you will see."

***

They bound the two prisoners' hands behind them while Rana used her last healing spell to fix the fallen horse's broken leg, since the alternative was killing it on the spot. The other horses were easy to round up, given their state of total exhaustion. Rana spent her orisons making water for them.

"So much magic for mere beasts," said one of the defeated knights.

"Stop your whining," Gregor told him. "You'll not bleed to death, and you might notice she's not healing us either."

"The beasts are innocent" was Rana's only comment.

Christopher noticed the crow pecking at the face of one of the corpses. And not alone; it had already summoned others with its cawing.

Gregor laughed darkly and chased the birds off, and then Christopher had to help him bind the corpses on the least-tired mounts. Seeing Bart's corpse for the first time, while knowing he had already died once, was surreal. And not entirely reassuring. Christopher wouldn't relax until he saw it burned and scattered. It might not stay dead, otherwise.

The original crow squawked in annoyance to be denied its prize, bravely flying up to them to deliver its scolding. Rana gave it a chunk of bread.

"I will have to send a novitiate out to its tree every day, now, to deliver bread." She sighed. "And crows can live a long time. But he has earned it, I think."

The three of them each led a string of horses, Gregor's string bearing the prisoners. Christopher didn't know what to do to keep the horses in line, but Royal did, so everything worked out. Slowly they walked northeast, headed for Cannenberry.

"We'll not arrive till long after nightfall," Rana said.

"Let's hope there are no other predators on the plains," Gregor said.

At first Christopher was confused, but from the way the blue knight scanned around them, he realized the enemy mage had not yet been accounted for.

"Where's your mage?" he asked the prisoners.

"How can we trust their answer?" Gregor said, but one of them answered anyway.

"He did not travel with us. He met us at your village, along with the rogue who opened your door." It was the traitor knight, pitching hard for his new team.

"Describe the rogue," Christopher demanded.

"A woman, tall enough to pass for a short man. She dressed in white and carried a sword. She was exceedingly angry with you, Pater." The knight grinned. "Give me my freedom and I'll give you her head."

It certainly sounded like his assassin from the road.

"Do you know how to contact her?"

"No," the knight admitted, "but if it will gain me favor, I'll gladly try. If you wish, I'll even torture her for you."

Christopher winced. This whole atonement thing was going to be a big attitude adjustment for the man. Assuming he survived it, of course.

24.

A BIT OF POETRY

The worst part about getting to Cannenberry after midnight was knowing they'd missed dinner at the Vicar's table. But even the cold basket of food he sent to their rooms was rich with meats and cheeses. Christopher felt real gratitude, even while he was ashamed at how cheaply he was bribed.

They slept in, had a wonderful breakfast that could barely be recognized as porridge, and got a late start the next. The Vicar lent Rana his carriage and lent Christopher and Gregor fresh mounts, along with a handful of horse-wranglers for the tired herd. The prisoners he dispatched to the Cathedral in Kingsrock. The corpses went into his charnel house, and only black smoke came out again.

"Magic seems awfully strong," Christopher hinted to the blue knight as they ambled along. "Rana defeated Bart quite easily."

"Not really," Gregor said. "Fighting is about whittling down your opponent, and arms, and tactics, but magic is about staking everything on a single cast. If her second spell had failed, we'd all be dead now. But I'll grant your fireballs came in handy. I've often wondered what would result if the wizards and the priests worked together."

"I'm not a wizard," Christopher protested again.

The knight laughed. "Then I guess I'll never find out. Pater, I know you're not a wizard, and they're not really fireballs, but I don't know what else to call them. By the way, they're weak compared to real ones. They're harder to deliver—throwing them, come now, that's ridiculous—and they don't pack as much punch."

"How do you know so much about magic?" Christopher asked, genuinely curious.

"I've seen my share on the battlefield. Fireballs are particularly popular, as you can imagine. Also, Lalania won't shut up about the stuff. She seems to think she should impart the wisdom of her College to me. Claims it will keep me alive."

"Does it?" he had to ask.

"Evidently, so far."

Knowledge like that would help Christopher a lot. He needed to find a way to gain the troubadour's trust without getting more than that. He didn't want more, and he didn't want to upset the blue knight, whom he was pretty sure would take a dismal view of any romantic overtures.

"I can teach you the most important lesson about fighting magic, one that I knew long before I met any troubadours," Gregor continued. "It is this: fast or slow. You either kill the wizard quick, before he can cast, or you wait until he's out of spells. Priests are a lot hardier than wizards. One well-aimed strike might have killed Rana if she'd been ranked as a wizard. If Bart had been wise, he would have hit you first, but in all your armor, nobody expected you to be the wizard."

Great, so the battlefield was a game of "pop-goes-the-weasel," with everybody looking for the hidden landmines. Actually, that matched Karl's description.

"How do you wait out a wizard's spells?" Christopher had a sinking feeling he already knew the answer.

The blue knight confirmed his fears. "That tends to involve a lot of low ranks and commoners dying. The quick way tends to involve a lot of dead high ranks, if it doesn't work. You can guess which way the issue is usually resolved."

<hr />

He stabled his growing herd in town, renting space in private barns until he could build another one of his own. He would have complained about the expense, but he didn't have anybody to complain to. Rana had given him and Gregor their share of tael from the battle, Bart's helmet conveniently holding his crushed and burnt head in one piece. She gave Christopher all the horses but kept the captured chain mail and swords. She was going to be hiring more guards.

Bart's sword and armor went to Christopher. Again.

"I've already got a sword, thank you," Gregor had said, "and besides, you've earned it."

Since Christopher also already had a sword, that left no one but Karl. It was agreed all around that he had earned it, as well, so the blade went to him despite his reluctance to accept a magic sword in place of the mere masterwork he'd given away.

Faren caught up to them on the road to Burseberry and offered them a ride in his carriage. Since they were walking rather than taxing the warhorses so soon, they accepted.

Gregor was very satisfied with the latest events, as he explained to Cardinal Faren in-between bounces. Christopher was having trouble following the conversation because he really wanted to take the carriage apart to see how it worked and then hang whoever had designed that travesty of a suspension.

"Your Church needs to take a stronger hand," Gregor argued. "You'll not get any more easy fiefs, like the ones you have. Everybody knows your name now, and the Dark is united against you. As much as they can unite against anything, I mean. You have the manpower and the money. Why won't you field an army?"

"Under who?" Faren was particularly grumpy today. "We don't have the tael to make lords, even if we were willing to keep that many jackanapes around. And we are not suited to battle, despite Rana's heroics. She took a terrible gamble."

"Well, there's this fellow here," Gregor said. "He seems suited to battle. Promote him to the peerage. And then see if you can find more like him."

Christopher suddenly realized they were talking about him.

"Um, no," he said automatically. But wait: wasn't this his goal? To be promoted to power?

"More like him?" Faren's eyebrows were dancing violently. "This one priest of War has all but started a war. Two of him would wreck the Kingdom. And we dare not promote him. We cannot intervene so directly. I know you disagree, Ser, but it is our Church and our future, so we must play our hand as best we see fit."

Gregor was in too good of a mood to admit defeat. "Black Bart's corpse is ash scattered to the winds, I've got a pocket full of tael, and your Vicar and the Pater raise armies in spite of your fine speech. This is a good day for the Bright, whatever you say."

∽∾

It wasn't a good day for Christopher. When the carriage rolled into Burseberry, Karl and the mercenaries broke open the barn. Now the prisoners stood beside the chapel, three lines of dirty, ragged, unhappy men. They grumbled and looked askance at the guards they outnumbered, until Karl threw down the twisted helmet and giant black sword. After that they hung their heads in silence.

"What am I supposed to do with them?" Christopher asked in despair.

"By the King's law, you can take their heads for tael," Gregor said.

Christopher couldn't do that. He couldn't kill men for loot just because they had lost.

"What about Church law?" he asked Faren.

"The Church has never had prisoners of war before." Faren was even more rancid than he had been in the carriage. "We cannot atone so many at once. We cannot send them all to Kingsrock."

"If you feel generous, you can enslave them until they work off their ransom," Gregor suggested. "A few years of hard labor will do their spirits good."

"But then who will feed their families?" Christopher asked. Hadn't they just done that wild ride to save the men's families?

Gregor shrugged, not with indifference but in defeat.

Christopher turned to Faren. "Help me."

Faren looked at him, sighed heavily, and turned away from the prisoners to have a quiet conversation.

"Your assistance to date is deeply appreciated, Ser," he said to Gregor. "But if you would be willing, we would ask more from you."

Gregor's lip curled in distaste, but he nodded. While the Cardinal bent his head and muttered a simple prayer, the knight stepped over to the woodpile and fetched the ax.

Then Faren waved at the first prisoner in line, who shuffled forward and without even being told, knelt in front of Christopher's wood-chopping stump and laid his head on it.

Christopher was too stunned and horrified to object.

The ax rose and fell, sinking into the wood next the man. He flinched, slowly opened his eyes in disbelief.

"Goodman," Faren said, his voice deep and sad, "we will not punish you for the sins of your master. Nor can we address all the sins of the world. I am going to let you go, on the understanding you will never again take up arms against our Church. I would also counsel you to look to your affiliation, but that is your affair. Suffice to say, do not allow your Yellow to lead you into foolish acts again, or you will lose everything."

He offered the man a hand, helping him to his feet.

"It's a long walk home. I suggest you get started." From his purse he handed the man a silver piece. "Pay for your lodging and meals. Do not beg, steal, or tarry, or I'll have you to Kingsrock."

The man bowed, scraping the ground as he retreated, and ran from the village without looking back.

"He's evil," Gregor said, although without force.

"We cannot address all the sins of the world," Faren repeated under his breath, and then he called forward the next man.

The ritual went on for a while, but then it changed. The ax still missed, but when the man stood, Faren shook his head.

"Your Red is more danger to your family than is your absence. You go into the wagon, to Kingsrock, to either atone or hang."

Christopher had just gotten comfortable with the judging, pleased to see that less than a quarter of the men were being classified as Red, when the ritual changed again.

This time, when the man put his head on the block, his eyes burning with hatred and fear, Faren froze him in place with the Celestial command Rana had used on Bart.

"Do not miss this time," he told Gregor sadly.

"Why?" Christopher asked. "Doesn't he get a chance to atone?" How could the Cardinal have judged this man without even asking him a question?

"He is Black," the Cardinal said. "They never atone, and I am not certain I would let one if they would."

"Have no sympathy for him," spoke up one of the prisoners still in line. "He was our sergeant. When Bart was displeased, he would let Bugger Bill abuse us."

"Yes," another agreed, "and worse. The only reason we did not kill him in the barn was fear that Bart still lived."

"In fact," said one of the prisoners from the wagon, "you should return us to the barn for a brief period, so that we might rectify the imbalance of the world. Bill has given much and has much to receive."

"One time he—" another prisoner started, but Christopher cut him off.

"I get it," he said resignedly, and the ax fell.

There was only one more Black in the group.

"If Black Bart were truly evil, then why so few truly evil men?" Christopher asked the Cardinal as he was getting back into his carriage.

"Perhaps you already killed them all, when you slew his knights," Faren said, unconcerned.

"Or he killed them himself," Karl answered. "Blacks do not make good soldiers. They are undisciplined. Even the Darkest fiend prefers an army of Yellows, or at least Reds."

Then Karl idly recited a bit of doggerel.

> *White for right,*
> *Blue for tame,*
> *Green for name,*
> *Yellow for gain,*
> *Red for pain,*
> *Black for none.*

"I've never liked that ditty," Faren complained. "Tame is a poor choice of word. Law would be better."

"But that doesn't rhyme," Karl said.

"Spare me your literary critique," Christopher said in exasperation. "What does it *mean*?"

"You have never heard the Color Poem before?" Karl asked in surprise. Even Faren raised his eyebrows.

"The Pater is new here, remember," Svengusta said. He had been uncharacteristically silent so far. Christopher was guessing the old man was a little upset at having his wood yard turned into an abattoir. Christopher agreed; he was planning on burning that stump and getting a new one as soon as Faren left town.

"It means," Svengusta explained, "those are the reins that drive the affiliations. White works for the right of everyone. Blue serves the law. Green is driven by honour. Yellow seeks gain. Red can only be compelled by threat of punishment. And Black does evil for its own sake, even sometimes to its own undoing."

Now it made sense. The five stages of moral development: universal rights, social contract, peer approval, desire for gain and fear of punishment, and then absolute amoral sociopathy—not a stage, but the lack of any moral compulsion at all.

"There was even a Green in that lot," Faren said. "But I did not want to make his life harder by exposing him to his fellows. Perhaps their next lord will be less Dark. It wouldn't be hard. It was only a matter of time until something drove Bart over the edge, into madness."

"The loss of his ring," Christopher said. Then he couldn't remember if anyone had told Faren about the ring. "Did we tell you about the ring?"

"I heard about it, no thanks to you," Faren said, while Svengusta blushed. "This is a secret that should not be bandied about, agreed. But in the future, keep me better informed. Speaking of secrets," he added, suddenly cranky again, "you are released from my command. You may dispose of your sword, and its truth, as you see fit. Possibly we overplayed our hand. We did not intend to start a war."

Christopher breathed a sigh of pure relief. And immediately moved on to the next problem.

"I'll need that mill soon." He was eager to get back to industrializing people instead of killing them.

Faren rolled his eyes, even grumpier than before, if possible. "The answer is no. It would be easier to redirect the river than to undo so many years of legal contract. But be silent, Pater, we are not deaf to your needs. The Saint has sent you an offering, a loan from our church to yours of valuable property. I left it at the Knockford Church. Make it work or do without."

Christopher wanted to ask more, but Faren would have none of it. His carriage trundled away, followed by Bart's wagon with the prisoners marked for atonement.

"You've let an awful lot of tael run off," Gregor said, referring to the majority of prisoners that were released. "But I find I cannot be unhappy with your choice. And we should still see a little more from that wagon-load. I doubt any of them will atone."

"Does anybody ever atone?" Christopher asked darkly. So far, every person he'd sent to Kingsrock had wound up on the wrong end of a rope.

"Sometimes, Brother," Svengusta soothed. "Sometimes."

That night, after dinner, when he and Svengusta had a moment alone, he asked another question that had been bothering him badly.

"We barely got enough tael out of Bart to promote someone to second rank. But he was fifth rank. I don't get it. You're the only one I dare ask, Brother. Please help me."

Svengusta's eyes grew wide as he studied Christopher's clueless face. The old man shook his head in disbelief.

"I had thought your past mystifying; now I find it unimaginable," Svengusta said softly. "But do not elaborate. I am content to let you and the Saint bear that knowledge.

"But your answer, which every child knows, is that while death reduces a man by a whole rank, it enriches his slayer only by a fraction of his rank. One-sixteenth, to be exact."

The precision of the number did not bother Christopher as much as the magnitude. Trading tael was not a zero-sum game; it was a losing game. For every knight created, sixteen commoners would have to die. To create all those knights, Bart really must have slaughtered whole villages.

The blood on his wood stump suddenly seemed inconsequential.

25.

BOTTLED WATER

Standing in the Knockford Church vault, Christopher scratched his beard, annoyed. He'd asked for a watermill and gotten five bronze bottles. He was just a little confused.

Svengusta wasn't. "Faren said it would be easier to redirect the river than unmoor the mill from the miller's hands, and so he has. But do not ask him for a second miracle; these have stood in the Cathedral fountain for at least a century."

The bottles were not graceful enough to qualify as art in Christopher's opinion, being heavily cast out of inch-thick metal. But each one did bear an image of a god, Ostara, and her four consorts from the tapestry back in Burseberry.

"How is this supposed to help again?"

"Perhaps an experiment, since you're so fond of them," Svengusta said with a laugh. "But not in here—outside!"

Christopher struggled with one of the heavy metal bottles. It had a bronze stopper screwed into the top, with markings carved into it. He couldn't quite read them, and the bottle was too heavy to hold up to his face, so he unscrewed the stopper and looked more closely at it while they walked through the halls.

The words were in Celestial. "Stopper" was the first word. Well, yes, it was a stopper. Nice that they labeled it.

He read the second word aloud, because it was so unexpected. "Stream," he said. "What does that mean?"

But then he noticed water was gushing from the bottle.

"Ack . . ."

He tried to stick the stopper back in, but Svengusta screamed at him and waved his hands.

"No!" yelled the old man. "Read the command word, the command word!"

Christopher looked at the bottle cap again. "Fountain" was the next word, but that couldn't be right. The last word was "Geyser," so he read it aloud before his brain considered the wisdom of such an act.

The bottle kicked him in the stomach like an angry mule. Water gushed out of the bottle like, well, like a geyser, knocking Svengusta to the floor and washing him flailing down the hall.

"Stopper," Christopher shouted, wrestling with the bottle, and the flow stopped. "Brother, I'm sorry." He sat in the pool of water where the bottle had knocked him down. "Are you all right?"

Svengusta sat up, soaking wet, watching the water run down the hall. Novitiates and servants stuck their heads out of doors. They did not succeed at stifling their giggling.

"Now you know what it does," Svengusta said, "and I know why Helga squeals when you use the word 'experiment.'"

"How did all that water come out of this bottle?"

"Brother," Svengusta said with exaggerated gentleness, "it's magic."

"Well, duh, but how does it work? How long will the effect last?"

"Last? I already told you the bottles are at least a hundred years old."

"You mean," Christopher said with amazement, "they were pumping water for all that time?"

"Yes," Svengusta said. "The fountains of the Cathedral. Bathed in colored lights, they were a beautiful sight. And now they are stilled. The Saint favors your cause. He signals to the city that no beauty can thrive when unjust war rages."

"Or more likely, he feels guilty." Rana glared at them, having been summoned by the commotion. "He rewards you for surviving his unintentional war. Note that he does not send any pretty presents to me, seeking my pardon for the uproar he has caused in my town."

Before Christopher could utter his usual apology, she spoke again.

"You must learn more caution, Pater. Not all magical devices are so benign."

Then she was gone, in an imperial splashing.

~~~

Dereth was not overly impressed with the results of the new blast furnace.

"A Master could make better steel," he said.

"It's not supposed to be better," Christopher answered, "just cheaper."

And it was, which was why they now had sixty feet of heavy steel pipe standing up in the air, supported by scaffolding that cast the new buildings going up around the Old Bog in an industrial light. Christopher sent an apprentice scrambling up the side and coached him through the pronunciation of the command word for the bronze bottle's screwed-on top.

The pipe rumbled under the pressure of the geyser. Then the falling water hit the wheel attached to the bottom, and Christopher's new lathe began to spin like a demon.

After a brief moment of shock, the assembled smiths broke into spontaneous applause for Jhom, who stood with his hands behind his back and tried to look modest, but failed.

"You did well, Journeyman," Christopher said. "Very well. Here you go." He handed the smith a sheaf of papers.

"Is this my reward?" the young smith asked, but then became enraptured in the drawings.

"No, it's the next one. It's an inverted lathe, called a mill. And these things, these are ball bearings. The first set you make goes on the lathe." The squealing of the axle was already driving him nuts. "You'll need the lathe to make them, though."

"But Pater, you own the lathe."

Christopher put his hand on the younger man's shoulder.

"I will pay you like a Senior and treat you like an equal. You'll hire and manage at least a dozen other men. Will you take the job?"

"My father needs me," Jhom said. "I cannot abandon him."

Christopher took a deep breath. "Your father is one of the smiths I want you to hire. Along with every man in his shop."

Jhom was dumbfounded. "You would buy my father's shop and give it to me?"

"I can't afford to buy it. I don't have that much cash. But if you convince him to join our operations, I'll give him a share of the profits. And you, too."

Jhom got right to the point. "How big of a share?"

Christopher didn't care about the money; he just needed the men. "An equal share. Me, you, Dereth, your father, and Palek. All equal shares."

"That is a mighty shop you assemble," Jhom said, stars in his eyes.

"And you can run it for me. All you have to do is convince them to join it. I'll pay everybody standard guild rates. They'll have to work for another man, but then, most of them already do. And they'll get paid regular and only work eight days a week, ten hours a day, with an hour off for lunch."

Christopher's conscience would not allow him to faithfully recreate the dawn of the industrial age. It remained to be seen if it was possible to build a commercial empire without savage exploitation.

"Can you make it happen?" he asked the young man.

"They are proud," Jhom said dubiously.

"They are idle," Christopher said. "I'll let you in on a little secret: when the draft contracts are finally released, they'll *all* go to one shop."

Jhom was properly scandalized.

"They'll kill you, Pater."

Christopher winked. "They're nowhere near as mean as Bart, and he didn't kill me."

Jhom laughed. Christopher's final victory over Bart had made him the local hero. The townspeople's attitude was more in line with that of Karl and Gregor than with official Church doctrine.

"I will do my best," Jhom told him, "but I might not have much clout until you award the contracts. The bird in the bush always looks tastier than the one in your hand."

"As long as you get the lathe running. We'll need those ball bearings." Ball bearings were one of those things you took for granted, until you didn't have any.

His new popularity paid off in more ways than one. Fae told him that people kept asking her if they could buy more bonds.

"Why won't you sell as many as you can?" she wanted to know.

"We want to keep demand up," he told her. "If we flood the market, we'll have trouble selling them. They're only worth anything because there aren't very many of them." He could see she was struggling with the concept, but it looked like a fair fight.

Lalania, back again from one of her many jaunts and sharing dinner with them all in his chapel, confirmed the wisdom of his restraint. His bonds were trading at face value. Although they couldn't be redeemed for another ten years, people were accepting them in lieu of a gold piece.

"And now what will you do?" she asked intently.

"Spend it. Unless you tell me we can issue more bonds without collapsing the market."

"What makes you think I support this scheme?"

"I offered to put you on the payroll. Do you want a cut instead?"

The girl was getting angry. Christopher was a little mystified until Gregor sighed in the background, and suddenly it came to him in an epiphany.

"You've been spying on me. You left Gregor here to watch me."

"Now what makes you think that?" Lalania asked, impossibly innocent.

"Who are you spying for? Your College? The Saint? Tell me, dammit." He didn't care that she was spying; he just wanted to know who his enemies were.

"Myself." She glared at him. "I undertook to protect the common folk of my own accord. Does this surprise you?"

Now he was back to being mystified. "Protect them from whom?"

"From you," she snapped. "Look at you. You live like a lord with chapels and armies, and yet last year you did not even *exist*. How should I not be suspicious?"

"Like a lord?" He looked down at the chicken leg he'd been stripping with his teeth.

"It's true, Lala," Gregor said gently. "The Pater eats from the same pot we do. His money does not buy him luxuries. Nor does he revel in the command of others. If anything, he shirks it."

Well, of course he did. Telling other people what to do was a lot of work. He had better things to do with his time, like figure out how to increase iron production. He wanted to start selling efficient Franklin stoves before the cold returned.

"Tell me where you came from," she demanded, point-blank.

"A distant land. Where things are done differently," he fired back. "Do you disapprove of my changes?"

"You take their gold and give them paper. You take their shops and give them work. You take their hopes and give them dreams," she said menacingly. "They believe in you, Pater. They believe you will arm them with your sky-fire magic and overthrow the Dark. They can live without money or shops, but they cannot live without hope. If you steal their dreams, I will find a way to kill you, your luck be damned."

"If I fail their dreams," he answered, "you won't have to, because I'll be dead. They're my dreams too, you know."

"Pass the butter, please," Svengusta said.

"I see your mark," Lalania snapped at the old man, tears in her eyes. "Your Saint has declared for him, so who am I to question? What matter is the opinion of a foolish young troubadour?"

"I keep trying to pay for your opinions," Christopher said, "so obviously they matter to me."

"I just want the butter," Svengusta protested. "I don't need to argue the Pater's case. If you'd stick around long enough, you'd see for yourself. Like your man has."

Gregor hung his head in silence. Apparently Christopher had won the man over, passed his tests, without even knowing it.

"I'll argue it then," Karl said. "Who are you to question the Saint? He carries twenty thousand on his shoulders. If he thinks the Pater can ease that burden, who are you to object?"

"Peace," Helga said, "there'll be no more politics at the dinner table."

"Lalania, what can I do to prove myself to you?" Christopher said earnestly. "Ask me any test. Let me show you what I've spent the money on. Heck, you can go over my books. In fact, could you go over my books for me? I don't want to make Fae feel slighted, but I'd sleep a lot better at night if I had an independent audit once in a while."

"Tell me where you are from," she said, but instinct made her cloak this dangerous repetition, and she spoke in Celestial. Christopher was impressed, again, with her staggering array of skills. One of which was keeping secrets. The mere knowledge that she wanted the answer to this particular question above all else would naturally draw undue attention to the question.

"Anything but that," he said sadly, in the same beautiful language. Krellyan had told him not to reveal his origin, and nothing that had transpired since that first day had given him any reason to doubt the Saint's wisdom. "But I promise you this, someday I will tell you. When the Saint gives me leave to, then I will tell you." A promise made in Celestial felt terribly binding, like he'd just sworn on his mother's grave.

"Pass the butter, please," Svengusta said in the same musical language. It sounded rather silly in that holy tongue. But he made his point. They were not the only two in the world who could speak it.

"I'm sorry," Lalania said to the table, in the common tongue. "That was rude of me."

"I don't mind," Helga said. "I've always loved the sounds. Pater used to sing to me, when I first came here and could not sleep."

"You should hear how he sings to the widows in town," Karl smirked.

Helga blushed, Gregor chuckled appreciatively, and Lalania rolled her eyes.

Svengusta put his hands up in defeat. "What in blazes does a man have to do around here to get the butter?"

<hr />

The first day of summer crept toward them. Christopher was busy, riding into Knockford most every day of the week. He couldn't believe he had an hour commute, but that was the price of living in the suburbs. Royal needed the exercise anyway.

Building the new machinery went a lot faster with the lathe. Jhom had it running full-time, using his father's men. Technically, everybody still worked for Jurgen, but the lure of machine tools was stronger than family loyalty. Christopher could see the men getting into the habit of walking to his shop every morning. Any day now, Jhom was going to make his move. It would have to be soon. The tension was becoming ugly.

Christopher had the rest of the town on his side, though. He spent a lot of money on buildings, so the masons and carpenters were happy. He had to buy food and beer for his army, so the farmers and brewers were happy. And he was a local hero, so everybody else was happy. The strain between the still-prestigious but out-of-work smiths and the rest of the town threatened to tear the community in half.

Finally, the deadline for giving out the armorers' contracts lay before them like a snake in the path. It could no longer be put off until tomorrow, because it was today.

"Do we take an army or not?" Christopher asked Karl, only half-joking.

"The Vicar would not thank you for doing her police work," Svengusta said, but Karl ignored the question as unimportant.

They rode into town, just the two of them, eschewing Christopher's normal escort. Word of their arrival spread quickly, and by the time they left the stables, there was a crowd of angry men waiting for them at the church steps.

They tried pity first.

"Goodman Karl," said an independent smith, "I have had no real work for weeks, only making nails. I cannot feed my children on nails."

Christopher had put off buying anything metal, trying to make the market collapse, but the carpenters always needed nails.

"Making nails is Apprentice work," complained another one.

"So is digging ore, but you complained when I took that away from you," Christopher said. "Do you want me to make my own nails now?"

That shut up that line of questioning, but perhaps not in the best possible way. Christopher wished Svengusta was doing this, or even Tom, while the crowd glared at him. But that attitude was a tactical error on their part. Pity was the one argument that would have worked.

"If you do not hand out the contracts today," another smith demanded, "then how can we finish the work by year's end?"

"I have not yet decided on the contracts," Karl said.

"What do you mean?" the smith shot back. "They're the same as always. What's to decide?"

"This year they may be different. Pater Christopher suggests he might have some ideas, which I am considering." Karl was unflappable.

"Pater Christopher isn't a smith!" The man was outraged.

"No, but I am a priest of War, so weaponry is in my domain," Christopher countered, and it worked. These people were too used to trusting priests. He'd have to work on that.

"But Pater, you don't have a shop," said another man.

Christopher looked to the north, where his buildings were, although you couldn't see them from here. "Hmm . . . what do you propose we call that big building full of machinery and forges?"

"A shop is not tools and buildings; it is men," Palek said, and the skirmishing was over. Now the big guns were engaged.

"Are you saying I need men? Then I will hire them. You all know my working conditions. Anybody interested?"

The crowd muttered, uncertain of its cohesion, but it did not break. His offer was tempting but not overwhelming. Smithing was an elite craft, and these men had a guild, even stronger than a union. Just money wouldn't be enough. He needed political support. He needed an inside man.

Slowly, reluctantly, moving like he was stuck in molasses, Jhom stepped out in front of the crowd.

"I'm interested," he said.

The crowd shook, stunned at this betrayal. Christopher tried to read Jurgen's face but could not decipher it. Then he realized that the lack of outrage meant he'd already won.

"You've all seen Pater's machines," Jhom told the crowd. "I want to work on them. I want to make more."

"But how can you leave your father's shop?" someone asked. Jurgen had the best shop in town, and Jhom would inherit it. How could he turn his back on his family and his fortune?

"I'm not," Jhom said. "Senior Jurgen and Senior Dereth have agreed to form a partnership, with Pater's money. I will oversee the shop as Master of Novices."

"Then there are no jobs after all?" the first man said.

"There are. Even if all my father's men join us in the new shop, we still have more work than they can do. We have need of another Senior, and his trained men. Senior Palek, will you not join us? We will offer you an equal share."

Christopher hadn't been sure about this open-air bargaining, but Jhom had chosen it anyway. The young smith felt that the public knowledge that they had offered Palek a fair deal would be worth more than anything they could gain by secrecy.

"I'll not dance to another man's tune," Palek spat out. "You'll not get away with this scam, awarding yourself the contracts. The Saint won't stand for it."

"You doubt my authority?" Karl said, and his voice almost had emotion in it, if ice-cold steel was an emotion. "I'll give the contracts to whomever the Dark I please."

And that was that. The argument was instantly over.

Palek boiled, but he did not burst. He turned and walked away. The crowd dispersed, escaping the dangerous Karl, but soon re-formed around Jhom, clamoring at him for attention. They wanted the jobs that Palek had just turned down.

Christopher was happy to abandon the young smith to the wolves. That was what he was getting paid for, after all.

⁓

They waited a few days, but soon enough Karl and Christopher had to make a call on Palek. The smith met them with a glare.

"Why do you darken my door, priest?" he growled.

"I've come to eat crow," Christopher said. "We want to give you the contract for the helmets."

"So my methods are good enough now?" Palek's fury was undiminished.

"They always were, Senior. I hoped to use your skills in a different way. But we each serve the cause as best we can, and you make helmets."

"I'm thinking of raising my prices." Palek just didn't accept apologies.

"Go ahead. But if you do, you'll find the price of iron goes up, too."

"You've won," Karl said. "You get to keep your shop and your old ways. What are you still fighting for?"

"Will he change nothing else?" When neither of them could say yes, Palek continued. "Then I will keep fighting."

"Well, as long as we understand each other," Christopher said, accepting defeat. "I've got this absurd suit of armor everybody wants me to wear. But it's too large and it's too black. Can you fix it?" Before the smith could answer, a number of Christopher's boys hauled Bart's clinking plate into the shop.

"I did not make this."

"No, but you are the only one I trust to fit it to me," Christopher said quite honestly.

"It is fine work." Palek fondled the dented helmet. "Masterwork from Kingsrock. I cannot do this kind of work," he said sadly. The smith's eyebrows twitched when he saw the breastplate, torn like a piece of paper. Christopher had used his magic to patch all the holes from the nail bomb, but he couldn't twist the metal back into shape by hand to weld it down.

"But can you fix it?" Christopher didn't care about the stupid armor, although everybody else did. He was just trying to find a way to give the man some business. He felt bad for all the independents who hadn't been hired into his shop. They were still hurting financially. Making helmets for Palek would help, but not if Palek took his anger out on them.

"Yes, I can repair and resize it," Palek answered. "The standard charge is one hundred fifty gold."

That seemed cheap, given the amounts he dealt with these days. No, wait, it didn't. That was a year's pay for an ordinary smith.

"Can you fix the color?" Christopher was going to pay, anyway.

"Yes. What color would you like?"

"White," Karl said.

"You presume much," Palek said sourly. "White won't stay white in a war."

Privately, Christopher agreed, feeling bad for whatever recruit would wind up polishing the stuff, but Karl reacted like he'd been slapped.

"For your own sake, pray you are wrong."

The two men glared at each other, and Christopher decided discretion was the better part of valor, since he had no idea what they were going on about.

26.

BULL BY THE RIFLE

"Cannan and Niona have gone into the Wild again," Lalania told them when she breezed back in at the end of the week. "He overstayed his welcome. A fellow Bright took exception to his manner, and they dueled, which is common enough, but Cannan killed him, which is not common. People began to question his devotion to the cause. And when rumor began to circulate that your sword was mundane, and merely a device to entrap Black Bart, then other people began to blame Cannan for his part in the deception. So they stepped out for a while."

Christopher was torn between relief and sadness. "I'm worried about Cannan, too." Actually, more about Niona. "But I am happy to hear my sword is no longer an issue."

Lalania smirked. "As long as you were merely ignoring the rumors, that seemed to confirm them. But now that people have an alternative explanation, that it was all a jape at Bart's expense, they can believe it. The fact that their alternative explanation is itself false only helps." They shared a grin at the madness of crowds.

"What about the ring? Did you find out anything?"

She sighed. "Not yet. It is low on the list of the Loremasters' priorities. They have other more pressing topics to research. Or more personally interesting, I suspect."

She made it sound like they had a supercomputer they had to budget time on. Well, heck, maybe they did.

"I'd really like to see this college of yours."

She studied him, searching for sarcasm. "Traveling out of your own lands seems rather too dangerous for you at the moment."

Unfortunately, he had to agree with her. And he didn't have the time to waste. There was plenty of work to do before the end of the year.

The smiths had finished the other machines in much less time than the first one had taken, the lathe already proving its worth in increased productivity. Jhom's men now stood idle, watching while Christopher handed Jhom his prize creation, a sheaf of papers he had labored over for many days.

"What kind of machine is this?" the young smith asked.

"This," Christopher said, "is the whole point. This is a sky-fire weapon."

The men had been curious; now they were electrified.

"Now let me explain something: I've gone for broke. I decided to start at the top. If you can't make this device, then I'll simplify it."

He was hoping they were motivated by the challenge. If they couldn't make a decent breech-block, he'd have to fall back onto muzzle-loaders.

Jhom studied the pictures carefully while his men waited in respectful silence. Nobody even thought to remark on what a change that was from just a few weeks ago.

Finally Jhom announced his verdict. "We can make this. A Senior will have to do this particular step, and that one, but we can make this."

Christopher bowed to his shop manager. He'd taught the man as much as he knew about operating a machine shop or running power tools. From here on out, Jhom and the men would have to figure it out themselves.

"I am prepared to be impressed," he told them.

And he was. He and Karl stood together in the shop, looking over Jhom's creation. It had taken a dozen smiths ten days to make the first gun, but only because they were still learning how to work in an assembly line.

He ran his hands sensuously over the rifle. It was absurdly heavy, since he hadn't been sure of the strength of his steel or his powder, but it was beautiful. It was clean and smooth, straight and even. It was *machined*.

It made him think of home.

"Excuse us, Pater," Jhom said. "Now that we've made it, perhaps you can explain it. Dereth says it's a kind of pipe, but we don't understand what the grooves are for."

After they had milled the tube from its raw casting into a precise diameter, they'd carved out six grooves that made a complete twist from beginning to end inside the barrel.

"That's what makes it a rifle," Christopher said. "Rifle," he pronounced for them. "You all might as well get used to the word." He opened the breech and closed it again with a smooth click.

"How does it work?" Gregor asked, always interested in weaponry.

"I don't know," Christopher said. "I mean, I don't know if it does. We'll have to test it. You need to make a bench to hold it and a string to pull the trigger. If the tube fails, it will blow up in your face like a stick of dynamite."

They all knew that word, now. Tom had a new nickname, from all his mining. They called him Booming Tom.

Karl took the rifle. "Have a little faith in your smiths. Give me a charge."

Christopher had explained the basic theory of firearm operation to Karl many times now. He was trying to write a manual, and Karl was the one who could tell him if his instructions made any sense to a farm boy.

"Karl, it's dangerous," he objected, and then sighed. That comment guaranteed the young man would go through with it. In defeat he handed over the small box of rounds that Fae had manufactured.

Everybody filed outside. Christopher couldn't help himself—he told Karl to pick a safe backdrop, despite the fact the veteran was a crack shot with a crossbow. He already knew how to safely handle a missile weapon.

"It's gonna be loud, isn't it," said one of the apprentices as Karl loaded the rifle. Christopher grinned and the crowd laughed. Everything Christopher did was loud.

"That stump," Karl said, pointing. He raised the gun to his shoulder as the crowd backed up a few steps and covered their ears.

"Pull it tight," Christopher warned. "It kicks a lot more than a crossbow."

Karl sighted down the barrel and squeezed the trigger. As usual, Christopher was shocked when it actually worked. Fire and smoke and deafening noise came out of the barrel, and dirt kicked up a foot to the left of the target.

Karl was displeased.

"The sights are off," Christopher told him. "No surprise there. We'll need that bench to zero them in."

Christopher could tell Karl was slightly mollified because he changed the subject. "It seemed louder," he said. "The sky-fire is loud enough and makes lights besides. Why is this one louder?"

Christopher decided not to try to explain the concept of sonic booms. The good news was the sharp crack meant his bullet had broken the sound barrier.

"That means it's working," he told Karl.

"But how much damage does it do?" Gregor asked as Karl, like all young men everywhere, reloaded the rifle while glaring at the stump.

"I don't know," Christopher said. He'd patterned it after the old Sharps .50 caliber from the Civil War, which he knew had become popular with big-game hunters afterwards. "It's supposed to kill large animals."

"It probably won't kill me in one shot," Gregor said. "Let's try it out on me."

Christopher was too stunned to speak at first. "Absolutely not," he finally got out, grabbing the knight's shoulder before he walked over to the stump.

"Why not?"

Christopher was hard-pressed to answer. Why shouldn't he let one of his friends shoot one of his other friends with a buffalo rifle? *Because it's insane* didn't seem like it would convince these lunatics.

"It might kill you in one shot. I don't know, Gregor. It might be that strong."

Gregor nodded, dubious but not completely reckless, while Karl took another shot at the stump. He hit it this time, sending a shower of splinters into the air.

Gregor wasn't overly impressed. "I would have survived that. But still, a strong weapon, I agree."

"There's really only one way to tell," Karl said, turning to one of the smiths. "Your uncle has a bull ready for slaughter, does he not?"

Christopher had no idea how Karl would know such a detail, but the man nodded.

Work was over for the day, apparently. His shop emptied, the younger men running ahead. By the time they got to the farm in question, a crowd was gathered around it.

The bull was in a fenced pasture with its herd. It watched silently while the farmer drove the cows out. Then it walked to the center of the pasture and pawed the ground.

"It's almost like he knows what's going to happen," Christopher said, saddened and surprised at the same time.

"He does," Karl said. "He is old and wise, for a bull."

"He has had a good life," the farmer said to the crowd, reciting some kind of formula. "But now he must contribute to the greater good."

"Who comes to end his days?" the farmer asked, and a number of men with spears moved up to the fence.

"Whoa," Christopher said. This was no painless slaughter, this was a bullfight. Dangerous to the men and inhumane to the animal. "You can't do that. Just put him in a stall and use a sledgehammer." They could get an adequate ballistic report by shooting the carcass.

"We cannot," the farmer said. "He already knows." After a second, Christopher realized the man was talking about the bull.

"He'll not let us drive him to slaughter, Pater," said another man. Then he grumbled something under his breath that sounded suspiciously like "city folk."

"So the lot of you are going to go out there and stab him?" Christopher asked.

The crowd was mystified at his horror.

"Of course," the farmer said. "We are no knights, to face the bull in single combat." The man apparently thought that what Christopher was objecting to was their ganging up on the bull. Christopher was at a loss to cross the gulf. "Unless Ser wishes to do the honor," the farmer added as he nodded respectfully at Gregor.

"Not particularly," Gregor said. This was the cue Karl had been waiting for.

"I will." He jumped the fence.

"Karl, you idiot! Get back here!" Christopher was terrified. The bull was huge. Gigantic, even.

"Would you like assistance?" Gregor called, grinning. He always approved of courage, even the suicidal kind.

"Not yet, Ser," Karl answered.

Christopher wanted to argue some sense into the young man. What if the rifle misfired? What if he missed or the gun couldn't kill a creature of that size? There were a thousand things that could go wrong. This wasn't a scientific test; it was a spectacle.

And a compelling one. The crowd was mesmerized, all attention on Karl.

"Karl," Christopher called, knowing it was futile.

"Have a little faith," Karl called back, and then he bowed to the bull.

The animal snorted, pawed the ground again, and lowered his head in return. Karl brought the rifle to his shoulder, aimed at the bull.

"To arms," he said, and the bull charged.

The massive creature pounded across the pasture in a growing thunder of hooves, its head bowed and its terrible horns pointed directly at Karl. Christopher panicked and closed his eyes. A buffalo skull could bounce a .30-caliber rifle bullet. Who knew what powers this strange world had given this beast? And what madness made Karl think he could hit a moving target with only his third shot from a rifle?

Karl waited until the last second, letting the bull get so close that missing was hardly an option. The gun barked, and Christopher opened his eyes in reflex.

The animal sank to its knees like a battleship, majestic but silent, two paces from where Karl stood. It fell in a heap and did not twitch. Karl had shot it right between the eyes.

"I wouldn't have survived that," Gregor said, finally impressed.

The crowd watched in a subdued murmur, staring at the white cloud of smoke as it dispersed, as if it bore a message they might comprehend if only they studied hard enough.

"I don't understand," Gregor said, on the way back to their own village. "It does not seem like magic but more like a weapon. Striking the bull in the head seemed important. It's as if it matters where you aim it."

"Well, of course," Christopher said. "How could it not matter?"

"A wand of missiles does not care. It never misses, regardless of how you aim."

Great. They already had magical guns.

"Mine does," Christopher conceded dispiritedly. "It's not a magic weapon. It's just a better version of a crossbow."

"The smoke and noise are not desirable," Gregor argued, "but then, it does possess more power than even the biggest arbalest."

"And it reloads faster," Karl added.

"Still, if you think to change the world with expensive, noisy crossbows," Gregor said, "then I fear you are in for a bit of a disappointment. Why not arm your knights with wands of missiles?"

"What knights?" Christopher said, confused. "And why don't they arm all the men with these wands, if they're so great?" He was upset that magic equivalents to guns already existed and nobody had bothered to tell him. True, he hadn't exactly asked, but still.

"The knights you promote to wield your rifles," Gregor said, equally confused. "Unless you are going to squander such weapons on your mercenaries, like you have plate and masterwork swords."

"The rifles aren't for the mercenaries. They're for the boys."

Gregor got it. "I see. Very interesting. Yours are not as good as magical wands, but you'll have a dozen of them."

"Not *my* boys," Christopher said in exasperation. "All of them. The whole draft."

Gregor blinked.

"Oh," he said. "Oh my."

Karl actually snickered.

Gregor finally said good-bye.

"I wish you well, Pater," the blue knight said, "but I think I'll get no more tael in your service." He was joking, of course. He wasn't really in it for the money.

"As long as you stay in your own lands," Lalania explained, "you should be safe. Bart's allies seem to have deserted him; you no longer have anything the guild wants to steal. And I do not feel you are a danger to the people. At least, not intentionally," she clarified. "Your shopkeepers are now busy all week. I am unable to explain how your taking their money makes them richer."

"So you want to know my secrets? Very well, but someday I will come to your College seeking my own answers and expect you to pay." Christopher grinned at her, but the more he thought about it, the less it sounded like a joke. He really did want to talk to whatever passed for a scholar around here. Wizards and priests just didn't seem interested in mundane ideas. "They use my paper like gold. I suspect you had a liquidity problem, not enough gold pieces to go around. And since prices are fixed, deflation can't correct it. And you won't allow forgery"—the classic medieval solution to illiquidity—"or adulteration of the metal. So short of digging up more gold, there's no way to increase the money supply."

"That's what monsters are for," Gregor said. "We import their gold, though not at prices favorable to them."

"That only lines the pockets of the lords," Lalania said. "It doesn't help the peasantry."

"It does if the lord spends it," Christopher said. "In fact, if he spent more than he had, that would help too, at least temporarily."

That was what Christopher was doing, spending money he didn't have, a trick no other lord could match. The increase in demand was making everybody rich, at least until he had to figure out how to pay it all back.

"You have strange ideas," Lalania said, looking at him carefully.

He winked. "You're not the first person to tell me that."

27.

BOOT CAMP

Once the first dozen guns had rolled off the assembly line, Christopher started a boot camp, calling the entire draft for five weeks of training in a rotating schedule that saw fifty or more boys in the village at any given time. The village would have crumbled under so much teenage energy, but for Karl.

Karl was born to be a leader. Instinctively he assigned the boys in batches to the mercenaries and handed out prizes to the teams that performed best. Their eyes on the gold, the men drove their charges mercilessly. The boys hated them blackly, of course, but all Karl got was worship.

He treated the original crop like subalterns, junior officers, and eventually they became them—extensions of Karl's hands, eyes, and ears. Christopher watched as Karl stole the army, turning it into his own, and said nothing.

The boys had to share rifles for the first class. Christopher was frantically trying to get production up. The smiths didn't understand why until he showed them his other drawings. Rifles wouldn't be enough.

The days slipped into autumn, unnoticed. The chaos of the drill yard turning slowly into order drowned all other signals of passing time. Christopher trained with them, too—all the skills Karl thought they would need to know. They all had to be able to drive a wagon, cook a meal, bind a wound, pitch a tent, build a fort, and a hundred other things they would have to do on their own from now on. Of course, most of that they could already do, the bulk of them being farm boys used to self-reliance. The cooking was the one real sticking point.

"We're not taking a bunch of women to cook for us," Karl told them. "And you can't walk home to your mama's every night for dinner. So unless you want to starve, pay attention."

His lecture didn't take until he forbade Helga's girls from cooking for a week, and it was learn or go hungry.

But mostly Karl taught them to work together, to trust each other and their officers. Out of random boys he made teams, squads, platoons, finally . . . an army.

And then there was quiet, except for the cool autumn winds, the boys gone home for the harvest break. Christopher found himself in the fields, like everyone else. Backbreaking labor, but he was stronger now than he had been when he first came to this world. It had shaped him, kneaded him like dough to a different consistency. Only when the trees turned red and gold did he remember that he was once a subtly different person, a man whose life included more than horses, men, and guns. He held a crimson maple leaf in his hand and thought of scarlet hair.

What was she doing now? What must she think? Was it years or months before they declared you dead—not just missing, but gone, irretrievably lost to the people who once loved you? He had not reached for a phone at the sound of a bell, tried to put leftovers in the fridge, or stretched his hand out for the light switch in ages. Eight days a week wasn't funny anymore, just an easy workweek.

He could not remember what chocolate tasted like.

It was with relief that he welcomed the next class of boys, plunging once more into the task at hand.

"You're lucky," he told them. "Some of you will become gunners."

They didn't know what the word meant yet, but they got excited anyway.

The boys, of course, loved the cannons. Boys everywhere, for all of history, have always loved cannons. Even the mercenaries could be found hanging around the range during practice time. Christopher wished Gregor were here to give his assessment of the weapon's utility, but Karl's gleam of approval would have to be enough.

Later, Karl demonstrated his wisdom and intimate knowledge of the battlefield with nothing more than an approving twitch of his eyebrows. Christopher grinned to himself, ignoring the whooping boys. The boys and men were thrilled merely with the new toy, but Karl understood it was more than merely another way to go bang.

"Layers," he said to Christopher that night, during dinner in the chapel. The stone room had become the center of a building, as wooden extensions sprouted around it. Helga ran a whole crew of young women now, and with shameless hypocrisy kept them from fraternizing with the troops. But she still ate dinner at the officers' table, along with Svengusta. Christopher wanted that, needed that sense of family, of home. The mercenaries were transformed from hardened veterans into polite but taciturn guests by the mere presence of Helga.

"You have layers," Karl explained. "At long range you use the cannon. At medium range you use the rifles. At close range, you use the grenades." The rifles also came with bayonets, for extreme close-range work, but that was a weak weapon. As weak as those silly short spears he'd made the boys carry, what seemed like so long ago.

"We'll still get slaughtered by cavalry," Christopher said. "Unless they break and run." Cavalry was his nightmare, his constant nagging thorn.

"Cavalry is not that popular amongst the monsters," said one of the mercenaries. He was the one with the third Apprentice rank, so the others deferred to him automatically. They called him Bondi, but Christopher had never figured out if that was a name or a title. "Some kinds don't even have any."

"Ulvenmen don't need it," said another. "They can run like the Dark on their own. Begging your pardon, miss," he added, apologizing to Helga for his coarse language.

"Our best bet is a wall," Christopher said. "That's why I stress fortifying so much. If they have to stop, even for a second or two, we can break their rush and then we have a chance. So we should always strive for a defensive position."

"Yes," Bondi agreed, "that's what we should do, all right."

Christopher stopped himself before he corrected the mercenary. He appreciated the solidarity, but these men weren't actually going to go to war with him.

But Karl was silent and pensive the rest of the meal.

<hr />

Winter came on, inexorable, inching up on them day by day. Christopher had withdrawn as much as possible from his businesses in town, preparing for his departure. The shops could not look to him for problem solving very much longer. His visits to town were only social now.

Tom had come to him, a few weeks ago, in desperate straits. He wanted an advance on his salary for the next few years so he could buy a house. It was an unexpected request from the severely competent young man, especially since Christopher had already given him so many well-earned raises. He agreed only because he could pay in bonds, although printing money on demand gave him a queasy feeling.

"I'm not in a position to be a bank, though, so don't tell anyone else," he told the young man.

"Pater, they'll just think you're sweet on me. They won't expect you to do the same for them." Tom grinned at Christopher's lack of political savvy.

Christopher laughed back at him.

"But I am sweet on you, Booming Tom Fool. Isn't everybody?"

"So it would seem," Tom said with uncharacteristic sourness. But he didn't explain.

Now Christopher was having dinner in Tom's fine new house and meeting his girl for the first time. She wasn't very articulate, and she was obsequious to a fault, afraid to meet his eyes. But she was a good cook, thank goodness, so he could honestly praise the meal.

"She's not used to royalty," Tom explained when she cleared the dishes and left them to have a manly ale.

"Neither am I." Christopher looked around the spacious room. "It's a nice house you have here. Am I really paying you that much?"

Tom laughed. "Yes, Pater, you are. But you'll not regret it when you're out there in the field, freezing your arse off. You'll think of Tom, warm and snug in his fine house, and be glad somebody is getting the use of all your money."

"As long as your wagons come running when I whistle, I won't begrudge you a warm bed." They'd built a whole fleet now, and Fingean had hired a crew.

"Too warm, perhaps," Tom said, and then Christopher understood.

"You have to look out for Fae for me," he told the young man, baiting him. "Protect her from Flayn." Although this seemed unnecessary. The wizard had apparently decided to pretend Christopher and his people didn't exist. "Try to keep her honest on the books. And make sure she doesn't get into trouble with any young men, get in over her head or anything like that."

Tom turned a different shade. Red, Christopher suspected, although in the firelight it was hard to be sure.

"A little double dipping?" Christopher said quietly.

"A lot. Enough that a man might have to buy a house three sizes too large to make up for."

"Be careful," Christopher said sadly. He hated to see people make wrecks of their lives. "Her veins run pure ice. She'll break your heart in the end."

"It's not my heart she's breaking," Tom said. "But I'll not fail you, Pater, you needn't worry about that. I can keep my hens out of your shoes well enough. There will be no egg on your feet."

Christopher had to trust him, just as he had to trust Jhom, and Fae, and all the people who would stay behind and manage his industrial empire while he was far, far away. He would depend on them utterly: a technological army required constant deliveries of ammunition, spare parts, and new equipment. If they failed him, he would die; if the guns failed him, he would die; if the monsters turned out to be immune to bullets, he would die. Sticky feet hardly seemed like a sufficient metaphor.

And then it was here. Impossibly, it was all over. The training, the preparing, the building—all done. Christopher felt like something had been stolen from him, because, of course, it had. He'd spent a year of his life doing this. And now it was all being taken away. His shops, his employees, would all be gone; distant memories while he slogged around in mud and blood, trying not to be eaten by monsters for three years.

Draftees did not get leave.

Fingean and his wagons would have to be regular visitors, resupplying him wherever he was stationed, and carrying letters, although few of his employees could read. But he would not see home again for three long years.

Home. The word reminded him of why he was doing this in the first place. He went back to packing.

The village was overflowing with boys. The last training class had ended that week, and the others were streaming in, getting ready for the march to Kingsrock. His pasture was full of tents, his buildings were stacked six feet high with the materials of war, and every barn was stuffed with horses. Karl had been buying horses all winter. They needed two horses for every wagon, and a wagon for every one of the platoons, plus another wagon for luck. They needed a horse for each platoon's cannon and ten horses for scouts. That added up to a lot of horses.

And of course Royal. Christopher had been tempted to leave the horse behind. Why expose him to danger? But he had been bred for battle. When Christopher recognized that as a cheap excuse, he told himself Royal had saved his life too many times to stop now. Eventually that wore thin, and he had to admit he just didn't want to go to war alone.

Helga was inconsolable, red-eyed and weeping for the last three days. Even Svengusta struggled to crack jokes. The most visibly affected was Karl, because nothing ever visibly affected Karl, but these days he was snappish and angry with everyone. They'd had an actual shouting match over the armor.

"You have to wear it," Karl had ordered. "You will be a prime target for the enemy. It will be all that keeps you alive."

"It will make me stand out like a beacon," Christopher had argued back. "I'm better off being invisibly anonymous. I'll have my chain shirt on underneath."

"Chain mail won't save you. They'll know you from your horse. Wear the armor!"

"Then I'll leave the horse behind." Christopher could threaten to do this because he knew Karl would never, ever accept that.

"You are impossible!" And Karl stormed out of the building, red-faced and confused.

Now the hard young man stood in Christopher's room, watching him pack.

"I cannot accept this," Karl said finally, and laid Black Bart's huge sword on the bed.

"You're giving away my sword again? I keep giving you better and better swords, and you keep giving them away."

The young man blushed, a truly unique experience for both of them. Christopher decided to stop torturing him.

"I'll pay you twice what Krellyan does. Plus room, board, and equipment."

"Draftees do not get paid." Karl's face was a mask of pain.

"Dark take that. I'll put the money on account for you. Sign up with me, Karl. Do an impossible third term. You wanted to save these boys; here is your chance. You know your expert leadership will make the difference."

Christopher should have felt bad, asking the man to risk his life again when he'd already done twice what anybody could expect him to. But he didn't feel bad. He wanted Karl's help too much to feel bad. He needed him.

"I can't ask you to do this, Karl. Nobody can. You did your time, and it's impossible for anyone to ask you to do it again. You did your time twice. Nobody can ask you for more. But I'm asking you."

He picked up the sword and held it out to the tormented soldier.

"I want to tell you that it will be different. But I can't, because I don't know. All I know is I need you. They need you. And I'm shameless for asking you, but I'm doing it anyway."

Karl took the sword, sighed in utter resignation, a man defeated by his own immutable nature.

"Was there ever any doubt?"

Christopher shook his head. "No" was all he said, but the word carried much with it.

"Do I get a rifle?" Karl asked as he helped Christopher carry his belongings out of the room.

"Only if you give up that ridiculous armor," Christopher bantered with him, but he stopped when they came across the six mercenaries standing together in the chapel.

"How much are you paying him?" asked one. "We'll work for half."

"But only if we get to pick our own platoons," said another.

"You don't know what you're saying," Karl said with easy hypocrisy. "It's the draft you'll be joining, not a lord's personal regiment.

We'll be under the command of gods know who, subject to his will. You can't come along as a private army but only as slaves, as boys without rank or merit, sentenced to three years of hard labor."

Their response was a simple question.

"Do we get rifles?"

<hr>

The regiment fell into marching order, winding its way out of the village. The columns of men in uniform, their helmets sparkling in the bright, cold sun, were a moving sight. Christopher could not help but feel strong, riding at their head, his officers ranging up and down the line on their black horses. The boys felt it too, their strength in organized numbers, and they marched with proud steps and high heads, as did Royal, finally in his rightful place.

"Karl, send out our scouts."

The young veteran called orders to the boys they had chosen for this duty.

"Show me what you've learned," he told them. "I don't want a crow to cross our path that I wasn't warned about."

The scouts had been the hardest picks. It was a dangerous job and required many skills, of which riding was merely one. Karl had not given them rifles, at first, just spears. That had reduced the willing pool of applicants dramatically.

He finally relented, arming them with guns, but only on the express understanding that they never use them.

"I don't want you to kill anything," he told them. "I want you to tell us about it so we can kill it. If you try to shoot at something, you might get shot back, and then where would we be? Deaf and blind in the enemy's grasp."

They came into Knockford like a victorious army, and they got a hero's welcome. This was what the people had paid their gold to see. Their boys were not a helpless rabble sent out to servitude, but a single entity, a long and sinuous dragon with two hundred fire-breathing mouths.

Vicar Rana was uncharacteristically emotional, tears cracking from her eyes when she saw Karl in uniform.

"Does it never end?" she mumbled, but then shook it off with iron discipline. "We are sending one of our own with you, as we always do. Pater Stephram will accompany your regiment to provide healing and wisdom, though no one ever listens to first-ranked priests. Treat him well, if you can."

Christopher hugged the young man tightly, grateful for this tangible sign of support. "It's good to have you, Steph." Stephram didn't look so happy, but he hugged back. "We're going to be okay," Christopher whispered.

But of course Stephram had already been drafted once and no doubt did not find Christopher's empty promises very reassuring.

There would be no third priest. Karl had spent all the Saint's money on guns. Christopher had spent twice as much, but those who sold tael did not part with it for mere paper.

"We'll be marching on," Karl said. "Technically we have another week to report for duty, but I do not wish to be the dregs of the barrel. Unless Krellyan already knows who we are to serve?"

"If he does, he does not tell me," Rana said unhappily. "But avoid the city as much as you can. Its iniquity is terrible, and many a young man has lost his way there. These boys are not yet fixed in their affiliation, and they face a terrible future. Do not let despair entrap them."

She gazed out over the column of young men. "This is the first time we have ever seen our draft assembled. I do not think we realized how much we sacrificed each year, when it was hidden in towns and villages sending their children to the city in little droplets."

And then she kissed Christopher on the cheek, and Karl and Stephram too, then fled.

Christopher had to say good-bye to all his employees, gathered together in a small crowd. He felt much like Rana had described, realizing for the first time just how many people now depended on him.

"Make me rich while I am gone," he told them, trying to grin.

"We will, lord," they swore, solemn and grave.

The goal was Copperton, not the town but the county, a twenty-mile march from Knockford, and they'd gotten a late start out of the village. But the highway passed through Fram, so they could camp there if they had to. Karl didn't think they could do twenty miles in one day, and of course he was right.

They barely made Fram by nightfall, and the boys fell out to pitch camp on a field outside the town. They were terrible, getting in each other's way even though they'd all done this as smaller groups before. The crowd of sightseers didn't help, laughing at general chaos and egging on the flaring arguments.

In the morning Christopher lined the men up and showed them his latest invention, a number of cloth stripes, three inches wide and half an inch long. He handed them out to his officers and subalterns, and while the army decamped, women from Fram town sewed the stripes onto their coats.

Christopher tried to explain the concept of military rank, hoping it would reduce the number of times a draftee ignored a mercenary's command simply because he was from a different platoon, but the men couldn't get past the word.

"There aren't ranks in the draft," Karl said. "And the mercenaries outrank me, anyway, since they have Apprentice ranks."

"It's not *rank* ranks," Christopher said. "It's military ranks. How high you are in our military organization. The original boys are all the first step, the mercenaries are all the second step, and you're the third." Finally he got through to them when he gave up on the word "rank" and called them "levels."

"I'm going to do three drafts too, so I can have three levels like

Karl," boasted young Charles the quartermaster, completely misunderstanding the point. He was carrying a satchel full of papers and armed only with an ink pen, so perhaps his idea of soldier duty was a bit different.

Nonetheless, the older men laughed. "That's a lot of pain for a bit of cloth."

They made their twelve miles the next day, camping at the fork in the road that led north to Copperton. Amazingly, they still got visitors, not only from the surrounding hamlets but a few from Copperton town as well.

"I shouldn't let them in," Karl said, "but this will be the last time these mothers see their boys. When they come home, they'll be men." Superstitious as any soldier, he was careful to say "when" instead of "if."

Some of the alleged mothers seemed suspiciously young, and Karl had to check all the tents that night to make sure there weren't any unapproved guests.

The middle of the next day they passed into Kingsrock county. Christopher felt like Caesar crossing the Rubicon. He had nowhere else to go but forward. He wondered if Caesar had felt that unreasoning pang of fear, that desire to turn and bolt for safe home and old familiar ways.

They reached the city the next day at the edge of darkness. There was still enough light for Christopher to see why it was called Kingsrock. The city was built on a spire of rock sticking out of the ground, like Stirling Castle in Scotland. It was a magnificent natural fortress, and as the night fell, the sparkling lights from the city made Christopher dizzy with nostalgia.

They camped at its feet, in an open field next to a series of squalid barracks. From his tent in the heart of his temporary hamlet, he listened to men and horses snoring. He felt like a debutante on a blind date, waiting for the inevitable faux pas, certain that the morning would dispel the mystery and glamour of the distant city.

But it wasn't the city that shriveled in the light of morning, it was their camp.

"This is where the recruits train?"

"Yes, Pater," Bondi said. The field was mud, the buildings were dilapidated, and the smell of manure clung to the ground and everything it touched.

"It's filthy."

At least it was winter and the ground was frozen solid. The place would be a muddy hellhole of disease and infection otherwise, Christopher complained in disgust.

"It usually is." Bondi was indifferent, and Christopher wondered if it was because the Church could heal any disease, or whether it was just ordinary military-style indifference.

The situation was not helped by their neighbors. A handful of dirty men lounged in the doorways of the barracks, watching them with indolence.

"Who are those riffraff?" Christopher asked.

"The regimental commanders park all sorts of trash here, Pater. Keeps the farm boys out of the city. The real troops, the personal retinues and what-not, they got quarters in the city usually."

Bondi stopped to spit on the ground, although whether he was offering his opinion on the riffraff or on the regimental commanders wasn't entirely clear.

"Most counties field a regiment under their own lord," he expounded. "Sometimes it's a band of professionals, sometimes it's a rabble of commoners, usually a little of both. These fields are for the free use of the regiments while they train, or while their lords practice dancing and foot-waxing up in the city." The man had a rather jaundiced view of lords. "But every day in camp is a day you're not being eaten by an ulvenman, so the veterans learn to enjoy it." He had a pretty jaundiced view of army life, too.

A wagon was working its way down the dirt road toward them. Christopher met it at the edge of his camp, expecting some kind of official greeting.

"You don't get no food," the wagoner said, "until your Saint pays up. But we'll feed you today if you got money in your pockets."

"The Saint won't be paying you," Christopher said. "He's entrusted the maintenance of the regiment to me."

"And who the Dark are you?" the wagon-rat snarled.

Christopher was done. He was saving all his politeness for later.

"Go away, or I'll have my men beat you." He was mildly curious what was in the wagon, but Karl had said the draft usually ate barley porridge, not even oats. Nor three times a day, but twice, and never mind the grub-worms. Christopher was afraid that if he looked at what the supplier had brought, he might lose his temper and actually have the man beaten.

The wagon-rat looked down at Christopher's sword and went.

Then there was nothing to do but sit around all day.

"Karl, this sucks." Christopher was at a loss, having spent so much time doing so much and now doing nothing.

"Welcome to the army, Christopher. Hurry up and wait."

Gosh, that sounded familiar.

"We've got to go out sometime and exercise the horses." Christopher was looking for something to do. He desperately wanted to visit the city, to see what it was like, but he was convinced an assassin would leap out at him from every corner. Besides, it was time to stop thinking about civilian life. It was time to focus on war. But it was a hard transition to make, and he was very grateful when Lalania came down to see him that night.

"I like what you've done with the boys," she said.

"I don't know. It seems like a lot of brown. I was thinking, maybe some pink to lighten things up?"

"Your wit is still as sharp as it ever was," she laughed, "which does not say as much as one might think. But I have some things to discuss with you, so if your honor will not be besmirched by my forwardness, perhaps we could retire to your tent."

Inside the tent, he sat on the one luxury he allowed himself over the men: a narrow cot with rope springs and a thick mattress.

"I need my sleep," he explained. "I always have, and I'm old now. I'm not as sharp without a good night's sleep." He felt bad about it, but since it was true, he had to deal with it as best as he could.

Lalania threw herself down on the cot and contrived to look inviting.

"Not the softest, but then I rarely pick a bed for the mattress."

She smiled at him, and he wrestled against his reflexive arousal.

"Christopher," she said more seriously, "it is not natural for a man to go so long without a woman. You cannot think straight. Not that men can, in general, but surely you agree, you need this. Just once," she cajoled. "Your wife would not hold that against you, surely."

"I'm an addict," he said. "I can't have just one. Marry me, and then we can be together every night."

He'd finally found her weakness. She made a face at him, disgusted.

"You're already married. I'm not offering to do your cooking."

He laughed but stopped abruptly. "Wait . . . how did you know my wife was still alive?"

"I am not completely stupid. I worked it out. It is not your wife who is lost, but you. Whatever land you come from, you think your wife waits for you there. Why this place must be a state secret, I do not yet know, since everyone knows you are a lost traveler."

"Be careful, Lala," he pleaded with her. "You must be careful with that knowledge. It could get me killed." He had no idea how people would react to the information, but it would either make him look crazy or dangerous. Neither of those would advance his plans.

"I am the mother of caution. I prepare for eventualities that will not come to pass in a thousand ages. Consider, for instance, your wife. What if she is not made of adamantium like you? What if she gives in, from loneliness and despair, and seeks solace in the arms of another, even for one night? Will you not be angry at her, when you are reunited? Would it not be better that you should be the guilty party, or at least not innocent, so that your union is not burdened by her shame and sorrow?"

She leaned forward as she talked, until she lay in his lap, looking up at him with tender, bright-green eyes.

"No, Lala," he said softly, "I will not be angry with her."

"You are truly not a man of this world."

For a brief instant he did not realize she was only jesting.

"At least I have fresh, warm news for you, even if all you give me is the same cold shoulder. Duke Nordland will be your commander. He is a good man, if somewhat stiff-necked and unimaginative. His county lies northeast of here, and he is an ally of your Church. But his lands have their own faith, an old one, so do not preach theology at him."

That was a safe bet. Christopher didn't know any theology.

"When will I get to see this august personage?"

"When he is ready. Do not think to upbraid a lord, Christopher. You must curb your tongue and bide your patience. Not all are so informal as your Church, and even it demands respect from those it does not call Brother."

"What of my assassin? Does she lurk in alleys, ready to spring on me the minute my back is turned?"

"Probably. Don't do anything stupid. Like going into that cesspit of a city." She stroked his arm absently.

"Well, thanks for the news. And now you must go. It's getting late."

"I don't have to go yet."

"Oh, yes, you do." He shooed her out of the tent. "Yes, you do."

It was a full week before their commander came down to see them. Karl and the officers struggled to maintain discipline during the long, boring, cold days. They had the boys marching and drilling, but the city lights beckoned every night and the boys were getting frustrated. Christopher could empathize, as could the officers, since they were all enticed by the lure of the city, and consequently they rode the boys even harder, trying to drown their own frustrations.

So everybody was happy to line up when they saw the riders coming down from the city. Two men, one dressed in green leathers, the other in shining blue armor, on horses that screamed nobility. Christopher grinned. He had a horse like that.

He tried to ask about the proper protocol, but Karl told him to just speak when he was spoken to. No fancy salutes or anything. Probably just as well, since he was sure they would have screwed it up.

The blue man dismounted from his horse, a thick, squat, barrel-chested mass of muscle. And that was the horse. The man was even more so.

"Who is the oldest boy?" he asked the neat lines of troops.

The green-clad man did not dismount but scanned the area carefully. He had a longbow on his back. Christopher stopped staring and stepped forward.

"I am, sir. Uh, Ser." What was his name again? Lalania had told him, and he'd already forgotten.

"You address the Lord Duke Nordland," the green man said, but without anger.

"You're not a boy," Nordland said. Oh, he was a sharp one, he was.

"No, Lord Duke. But I am responsible for this lot." Christopher decided he could have phrased that more diplomatically.

"Where are your priests?"

Stephram was up at the Cathedral. He said he'd know when they were moving out and would come join them then. Christopher was annoyed that the man didn't make regular visits to the camp so he could have a communication line to the Cathedral, but he couldn't blame the priest for not wanting to sleep down here.

"I am one," Christopher said, "and the other is up at the Cathedral."

"You're not a priest of the Lady. You've got a sword." The man was not smiling. This was not going well.

"Yes, Lord Duke, I know. I am a priest of War, pledged to Marcius."

"Oh, that one. I knew you were in the camp. I just expected someone younger." Nordland was thirty-something himself, and Christopher had to bite back a snide response.

"Is it true, then, that your sword has no power?" Nordland asked. When Christopher nodded his agreement, the Duke shook his head in disappointment. "That is too bad. A weapon like that would have been most interesting."

Nordland started to look around the camp, which Christopher thought was suitably orderly, especially given the competition, but he didn't get any farther than Karl.

"What is that?" he asked, pointing to the huge sword Karl wore on his back.

Karl said very carefully, "It is a sword, Lord Duke." Christopher had to bite his lip and clench his hand so as not to laugh or smack Karl upside the back of the head, or possibly both.

But Nordland did not seem overly perturbed. "It is Black Bart's sword, is it not?"

"Yes, Lord Duke."

"What rank are you, man?"

"None at all, Lord Duke," Karl said, and Christopher was sure he was the only person there who could hear the satisfaction hidden deep in Karl's voice.

"Who arms you with such a weapon, Goodman?" The Duke was not happy, but he wasn't taking it out on Karl.

"The Pater Christopher, Lord Duke." When the Duke didn't look enlightened, Karl wiggled his eyebrows in Christopher's direction.

"I know his name, boy." The Duke was not as clueless as he let on. "Pater, explain to me why you bear a common sword, yet your servant wields a ranked blade."

That was a good question, but Christopher had an airtight answer. "The sword I bear is the symbol of my god, Lord Duke."

"But why give such a blade to an unranked man?"

Christopher couldn't explain why, in words. "He needed a sword" was the best he could do.

Had he just called Marcius his god? What an unnatural feeling. He realized his mind was drifting again, and he forced himself back to the present.

"He does that often, Lord Duke," Karl was saying. "We like to think he is communing with his god." In this case, it was vaguely true. At least he'd been thinking about Marcius.

"I was led to understand you were a missile regiment," Nordland said. "Yet all I see are spears."

This was another question Christopher could answer. "They are both, Lord Duke. The weapon is called a rifle, and it is a combination of half-spear and crossbow."

Nordland actually looked like he approved. "I heard you were contriving some folderol, but I did not realize it was as practical as this. Very good."

"Would you like a demonstration?" Christopher asked eagerly. They hadn't fired a single shot since they'd left Burseberry. A little shooting would release some of the frustration.

"Not particularly. I know what crossbows do."

Christopher wanted to argue, but the Duke froze him with a glance and continued talking. Christopher did not dare interrupt.

"This is the Baronet D'Arcy." He obviously meant the man in green, although he didn't bother to point or anything. "You will accept his orders as my own." Then Nordland mounted his horse, shared a nod with the green knight, and rode away. He didn't wait for Christopher's agreement or understanding. It wasn't optional.

"We march north," D'Arcy said from his horse, "into County Romsdaal, on the morrow."

"May I ask what our orders are, Baronet?" Christopher needed to know where to have Fingean send his wagons, and when.

"No," D'Arcy said. "You will be told only what you need to know." He dismounted lightly and stood stroking his horse. It whinnied softly, and from the paddock Christopher could hear Royal answer. "I will inspect your camp now."

Christopher had had his fill of lords and didn't trust his patience to hold out much longer. "My lieutenant is at your service," he announced.

D'Arcy did not recognize the word, but he obviously understood the concept well enough. "Conscripts can hold no office."

Christopher was going to object that Karl was a two-time veteran, but then he remembered that legally Karl was indistinguishable from the draftees. They weren't soldiers in a troop; they were a peasant levy.

Karl objected for him. "These men are not conscripts, Ser. They are trained soldiers, not hapless farm boys."

"We were not informed of this change in your Church's policy," D'Arcy said neutrally.

"We were surprised by it ourselves, Ser."

D'Arcy grinned, and Christopher was impressed at how easily Karl's insolence was tolerated by these high ranks.

"Then they will be disciplined and well-behaved? The Duke would not have Romsdaal be given cause to complain."

Christopher started to relent a little. D'Arcy wasn't that bad; he was just expecting the usual. The people around Christopher had become so used to his changing everything that he had forgotten how unsettling his methods were. Now he had a whole new world of people who needed to get used to change.

"There will be no cause for complaint," Karl stated. "Now, if you wish, I will show you your provisions, so that you may judge if they are adequate to the need."

The two men left together, sharing a common bond despite their differences in rank. Both of them had seen more than enough combat to know what mattered and what did not. Christopher was torn, wanting to be in that special club, but not really. The price of admission was high.

28.

INTO THE WILD

They reached the hamlet of Tyring an hour after dark on the first day of their march, their practice and discipline finally coming together. D'Arcy was impressed and not too proud to mention it.

"Your wagons are surprisingly fleet of wheel," he told Christopher as they watched camp being pitched.

"Thank you, Ser."

The man looked at him a little oddly, and Christopher realized he probably didn't know they were, in fact, Christopher's wagons. He'd designed the suspension. Mentioning it now would seem like boasting, though.

"Still, they will be difficult in the Wild. We will make slow progress."

Christopher couldn't argue with that. There were two other wagons waiting for them in the village already, the old style, full of horse-feed. These people didn't seem to understand that an army moved at the speed of its slowest member.

But again he wasn't being fair. D'Arcy didn't know there were better wagons to be had.

"When will the Lord Duke be joining us?" he asked, to change the topic. "Or is that a secret, too?"

"It is, but I can tell you now. My Lord will meet us at our destination. We wait for the signal and then have twenty days to arrive at our position. In the meantime, see to the discipline of your men."

That wasn't easy, since they were basically confined to the camp. Christopher even had to buy firewood from the locals, instead of gathering it. Too many days of this would be positively grating. But still better than that filthy pit outside the city.

They only had to wait five days, though, and three of those were spent coping with a tremendous blizzard. The locals were overwhelmed and let Christopher's men "help" them gather firewood, even though Christopher still paid the same price for it.

"That should be the last storm of winter," D'Arcy told Karl and Christopher. "I expect the signal any day now. Timing is critical. This is a coordinated action, of which we are only a small part."

Christopher didn't approve of the condescension, but at least the man was talking to them now. His time with the boys had loosened him up. They were good kids.

The signal came in the form of a large hawk. No kitty parts here, just pure bird. It landed on D'Arcy's outstretched arm, screeching in complaint at anyone who tried to come within twenty feet. D'Arcy opened a small pouch hung around its neck, took out a green marble, and put in a blue one. Then he sent the bird back to the sky.

"We march in the morning," he announced.

Karl was deeply unhappy about going into the Wild alone, so much so that he brought it up to D'Arcy.

"You are not alone," D'Arcy said. "I am here."

"With all due respect, Ser," Karl said, "you are only third rank."

Apparently it was a legitimate complaint, because D'Arcy was not offended. "These lands are well patrolled," he said with a smile, "and I expect no threat. Still, I take your mark. If mere soldiers can march around hither and thither in the Wild, what do we pay those lordlings for?"

Karl couldn't answer this without committing insubordination, so he didn't say anything at all. Christopher could see that the young man was stretched tight, disgusted at his own reliance on the high ranks he despised.

⚬⚬⚬

Crossing the border into the Wild, the boys fell silent. Automatically they sought to hide their presence, tiptoeing and whispering so as not to attract attention. Christopher felt the same instinct, but he did not want to let it slip into fearfulness.

"The men seem kind of subdued," he said to Karl and D'Arcy. "I'm worried about morale. Shouldn't we be singing marching songs or something?"

"Gods no," D'Arcy said. "They make enough noise as it is."

"They're right to be subdued," Karl said sourly. "Here there be monsters."

So even Karl was affected. The one person who seemed comfortable was D'Arcy. Ever since they had lost sight of the last building, the green knight seemed to have relaxed, actually smiling when he thought no one was looking at him.

"I suppose you have a point," D'Arcy said after a while. "If you will not find my absence too disturbing, I will go a-hunting. Meat will do much to raise their spirits."

"Please do," Christopher said. "I only ask that you take two of my scouts—not to help you, but so you can teach them. Someday we might have to forage on our own."

Surprisingly, D'Arcy agreed. He took four scouts with him, showing them the path the army must take that day, and sent two back as guides. He could do this because the horsemen could travel much faster than the wagons. On the open ground the wagons were invaluable, transporting tons of supplies at a fast walk. But cutting a path through woods or thickets was time-consuming, and several times they had to unpack the wagons, carry them by hand across a gorge or ravine, and reload them on the other side. With all this effort they were lucky to make eight miles a day, which struck Christopher as incredibly slow. But none of the professionals found it unreasonable.

The venison roasting over the fire did not excite as much comment as Christopher had hoped. If anything, the boys were more fearful, looking out from the campfires into the darkening gloom.

"The first night is always the worst," Karl said. "Sleeping in the dark Wild, you keep expecting something to leap out and eat you."

"You know what would make them feel better?" Christopher said. "A little target practice."

They still hadn't fired a round since Burseberry. Christopher was getting unreasonably worried. What if the rules of physics were different out here in the Wild?

"Not a bad idea, Pater," D'Arcy said. "We'll make some time for it in morning."

D'Arcy almost put a stop to the practice after the first shot.

"What in the Dark was that?" he demanded furiously. The white smoke drifted up while the blast still rang in their ears. Christopher had made everybody wear earmuffs while practicing back home, but they didn't have baggage room for such luxuries in the field.

"Perhaps the Lord Duke should have accepted that demonstration," Christopher said, a little annoyed.

"The Lord Duke would not have been impressed," D'Arcy answered. "Your spear-bows are not worth this much noise and stink. You can hear this from a mile away, at least."

Christopher decided not to schedule any target practice with the cannons.

"They are what we have," Karl said.

D'Arcy could not argue with that, so he took his hunting party and left.

But the exercise lifted the pall of helplessness and fear, and the boys started to recover their normal spirits. As the days wore on, and nothing leaped out of the woods at them, the march of doom gradually turned into a Boy Scout adventure, with D'Arcy as the wise Scout Leader. He fed them meat every night, taught them how to find soft ground for their tents, how to bank a fire so it made no light, or how to burn it clean so it made no smoke, and a dozen other bits of wood-craft. He took different teams of scouts out every day, and Christopher began to feel that he should pay the man for all the training he was doing.

"Thank you, Ser," he said one night, as the long week marched into the next one. "Our lives will depend on those scouts when you are gone."

D'Arcy was surprisingly dismissive. "Scouting is a dying art. Everybody uses birds these days." But he clearly enjoyed teaching his craft to appreciative students.

They got to their destination early, breaking camp at the foot of a small mountain chain.

"We have a few days," D'Arcy told them. "We should not attract any attention, on this side of the mountain, but we should not invite it, either. There will be no more shooting practice."

"Can we build a fort?" Christopher's boys could use some practice in that, too.

"No," D'Arcy said, with a tinge of exasperation. "We only wait here. Must you advertise your presence at every turn?"

He spent the next two days trying to show them how to make their camp blend invisibly into the forest, without much success.

And then a cavalry troop rode into camp, armor glinting in the sun, and Christopher sighed. The fun was over.

Nordland was not unhappy, but you could hardly tell.

"So far, so good," he growled, and fed his horses from the clunky wagons Christopher's men had all but carried here. He had brought twenty men with him, all armored in blue enameled full plate, with blue ribbons on their heavy warhorses. They were gorgeous.

And ranked, according to Karl. "All second rank," the young man told him.

"That's a lot of money." Christopher was a little envious.

"Tons. Literally, two tons of gold, I've heard it said."

"It is true," said a light voice. One of the armored riders had come over to them, helmet in hand and a long gold braid across her shoulders. "My Lord husband has spent a fortune on them. But you will not begrudge that expense when we close to battle."

The two men bowed their heads to the Lady Nordland. She was movie-star beautiful and shared that disconcerting agelessness that Krellyan had.

"I thought we should discuss healing," she said to Christopher. "I understand you represent the Bright Lady in this regard?"

"I do. Well, sort of. Yes," he finally settled on. "But not very well. I do not have as much healing power as Pater Stephram."

He introduced the young priest. Christopher had a little trouble adapting to the context. For the moment, he was a priest having an amiable discussion with fellow clergy, instead of a junior officer in an army.

"I am ranked as a Curate," the Lady said. "But I also lack the special distinction of your Church, Pater Stephram, for which I am most envious."

Stephram blushed at her flattery. "We do not march to war in armor, My Lady, for which I am perhaps a little envious."

The young man had agreed to dress like the soldiers so that he wouldn't stand out to the enemy. The only visible signs of rank in Christopher's army were the stripes on their sleeves and the handful of swords. The mercenaries had been persuaded to leave their heavy armor behind, but nothing would pry those valuable swords from their sides.

"If I had to march in this," she said, "I don't think I would get very far. I depend upon my valiant steed's indulgence and strength."

"I rode, too," Stephram confessed. "So I can't even be whining about that."

A huge hawk fluttered down from the sky, tried to land on the tip of the spear Lady Nordland held in her left hand, noticed the razor-sharp point, and abruptly changed its mind. In a buffet of wings it moved to her shoulder.

"I can see why you need that armor," Christopher said, looking at the bird's thick talons clawing for purchase. He was guessing it was the same hawk that had visited D'Arcy.

"Another creature I depend on," she said as the bird glared at the two men. "But now you know that I can cure fevers, so do not hesitate to ask. However, I am called upon to do more than healing during a battle, so do not look to me for aid then."

She was warning them that her troop came first, and his men would get whatever magic was left over. Christopher couldn't object to that, but he strongly suspected it didn't go the other way. They probably expected to monopolize his healing power, too, if they needed it.

The next morning they struggled up a mountain pass that got narrower and narrower, until late in the day they came out the other side onto a broad shelf overlooking a valley that stretched for miles, surprisingly flat and open. Not until many miles north did it turn into thick forest. Christopher did not particularly notice that, because his attention was drawn to a wooden fort sitting in the middle of the plain, about half a mile south of where they were.

Even from here it looked dirty, but what trapped Christopher's eye was the way it radiated alien-ness. He couldn't put his finger on how it was so different, but the shapes of the buildings were subtly uncomfortable, like there was an unknown purpose to their ramshackle and dishabille. The oddly shaped tower in the center of the round fort focused the strangeness to a sharp point.

"Never mind," D'Arcy called, "they've already seen us."

"Well, then," Nordland said, and they made camp.

"Permission to fortify, Ser," Karl said.

Nordland shrugged his shoulders. "If you wish."

Then he came to stand at the edge of the cliff with Christopher, looking out over the fort in the valley.

Christopher couldn't see anything moving. "Is it abandoned?"

"I hope not. This is what we came here for."

"Excuse my ignorance, Ser, but what is it?"

Nordland answered him absently, mulling over the valley below. "It's a goblin fort."

Christopher nodded sagely, then with perfect timing asked, "Begging your pardon, Ser, but what's a goblin?"

That got the Duke's full attention.

"Is it possible that you are mocking me?" Nordland sounded more surprised than angry.

Christopher backtracked. "Ah, no, Ser. But I am new around here, and there are a lot of things I don't know."

"Imagine a hobgoblin, only man-sized, and twice as cruel." The Duke went back to studying the fort.

This was probably not the time to ask what a hobgoblin was.

Something moved down below, but he couldn't make it out. Dammit, why hadn't he invented telescopes?

"Will they attack us? Or are we going to attack them?" Christopher thought it was about time to let him in on the plan.

Apparently Nordland agreed, because he answered. "We wait for our allies. I do not fancy digging out a goblin fort by myself. If they choose to attack us, they must come up the slope there—" He pointed to the south. "—and your archers will have the height and the range."

The pass they stood on, trapped between cliff and rising mountain, was lightly wooded and thus offered little cover to advancing foes.

"What if they climb the cliff face?" It seemed unlikely to Christopher, but he didn't know if goblins could climb.

"Then your archers will have it even easier." But Christopher could see he approved of the cautious thinking. "You need not put a strong guard on the rear, though. There is no other pass through these hills than the one we just took."

"Our allies must be coming from somewhere else, then," Christopher guessed.

"Yes, they come from the south. We have marched a long road to flank the fort. When our allies take the field below, we will cut off the retreat. Your men should not suffer too much. The enemy will be demoralized and fleeing. My cavalry can do most of the work, but if the enemy gathers together to make a stand, then your archers must break the knot loose.

"Your cavalry may ride with mine, if they are capable," he added.

"I don't have cavalry," Christopher said. "Those are my scouts and officers."

"I'll take that to mean they are not capable," Nordland said with a hint of exasperation. He looked at the activity in the sparse woods, as men attacked it with axes and saws. "Send a squad of your men back down the mountain to refill the water wagons. We'll find no springs up here, and we might be a day or two."

"We don't have water wagons, Ser."

Instead, they had the last bottle from the Cathedral, appropriately enough the one carved with the symbol of Marcius. That had been part of the reason they had made such good time. They didn't need to carry water or pick their camps based on the availability of it. D'Arcy had been openly impressed with the magic water bottle. Christopher was afraid the Duke might be impressed too, to the point of acquisitiveness. It would be incredibly handy for a cavalry troop.

"You have a surprising amount of magic for a Church draft," was what Nordland said when he saw the bottle. "But it was a foolish expense. A wand of fire would do more to kill the enemy than a slaked throat. You spent your money unwisely."

He didn't seem open to argument, so Christopher let it be. Soon enough he would give the Duke that demonstration of his weapons, and then maybe the man would take him seriously.

The boys labored late into the night building their walls. The sight of the fort in the distance had motivated them like nothing Karl could say. They worked by the flickering glow of the dozen light-stones Christopher had swiped from his chapel. Nordland shook his head at this additional waste of money on draftees, but his knights all had light-stones of their own, which they also lent to the activities.

The Lady's hawk was sleeping, but a huge owl had found them just after dark. Christopher felt a pang of sympathy for D'Arcy when she sent it flying south to reconnoiter. He looked around for the green knight but couldn't find him. Then he tried to sleep, lying on his cot, but he was terribly nervous. Maybe even a little frightened.

⚬⚬⚬

He woke to the sound of chopping wood. Karl had let him sleep in—a whole hour. He felt guilty, but Karl would have none of it.

"We didn't bring you out here for your strong back, Christopher. We brought you for your spells."

The boys were gathered round something during their breaks from construction. Christopher got a bowl of porridge and went over to see what it was.

It was a head, or rather, two of them—ugly, green, and too small to be human. Yellowed fangs stuck out from under a flat nose and pointed ears, but the creatures were clearly humanoid.

"They're hobgoblins," one of the boys told him. "Ser D'Arcy killed them in the night. Said they were spying on us."

Karl had the boys hard at work, building up fortifications so they wouldn't sit around and get nervous. Christopher decided that activity was an excellent plan and found an open spot where he could do kata. He felt silly, at first, doing kata around all these laboring people, but then the magic of his bond with the sword swept him away.

"If you are finished with your devotions," the Lady Nordland said, "we have something to discuss."

He blushed and started putting his shirt back on. "My apologies, Lady."

She was watching him with an appraising eye. "You need not apologize. Your obeisance to your god trumps our war councils. It is I who must apologize, for staring, but it was only professional interest. You are remarkably unscarred for a warrior."

"I'm no warrior," he said absently, sliding into the chain mail.

"No, I suppose not. Then your skill is through devotional practice and not actual combat?"

"Yes." That pretty much described it accurately.

"You will have no shortage of combat now," she said sadly.

⌘

Nordland's tent was spacious but not fancy. It had been in the baggage Christopher had brought, being a luxury rather than a necessity. He thought about getting himself something like it for a command post, but then he had to pay attention to the meeting.

"My owl has not returned," the Lady said. "This troubles me greatly. Nor have we had messages from the other captains."

"They're late," Nordland said. "They should be in the field by now."

"Do you wish me to reconnoiter south?" D'Arcy asked.

"No, it is too dangerous. And we need your bow to kill their spies. We will wait another day, and see. How are our supplies?"

Christopher opened his mouth to answer, but apparently the question was meant for D'Arcy.

"Adequate, My Lord," the green knight said. "We can tarry five days without concern."

Nordland was still displeased. "They are goblins, but their cowardice is not that strong. If we sit up here for five days, surely they will attack us by then."

"Why do they not attack already?" the Lady asked.

"I agree with My Lady," D'Arcy said. "We are in their territory, but we have had nought but a few night-spies. Why do they let us sit and fortify?"

"Perhaps they are under-strength," Nordland suggested. "If so, we should press the attack. Send out the hawk, my love, and espy their fort."

Outside the tent, the Lady Nordland spoke to her bird in a screeching gibberish, but the hawk answered in the same tongue and then took to the sky and headed for the fort, staying well out of arrow range.

Christopher was watching the fort so he did not see where they came from, but when the Lady cried out, he looked up and saw two black shapes wrestling with the hawk.

"Amana," the Lady cried, tears in her eyes for the fate of her pet. More black shapes were rising from the fort. Her hawk fought valiantly, but it was doomed and soon tumbled from the sky.

"Shrikes," D'Arcy said, and his voice was bitter.

Nordland's face was a thundercloud. "Why do they have shrikes?" he demanded, although no one could possibly have an answer for him.

Christopher wasn't in any position to tell how bad this was, but Karl drove the boys with redoubled whips and spurs. Soon they needed Christopher's help in designing small towers to hold the cannons, and he was glad to have something to occupy his mind for the rest of the day.

He was awakened before morning, D'Arcy summoning him and Karl to the command tent. On the way there, under the cold stars, he felt dislocated and lost. Did every soldier have this feeling, the first time? Did it ever go away?

"The owl has returned, severely wounded," D'Arcy told them. "Her Ladyship has healed it, but the news is bad."

"The bird found no sign of our allies," Nordland announced. "We will withdraw at daylight. A single tribe of goblins probably does not dare to challenge me, but I do not wish to storm their fort."

"I brought siege weapons, Lord Duke," Christopher said. When Nordland looked surprised, Christopher explained. "Those long iron tubes." What the hell did the man think Christopher had been hauling them around for?

Nordland's mind was already made up. "All the same, Pater, my troop is cavalry, not heavy infantry. I'll not waste them on this foolishness. Get your men up and ready to move. And prepare this fort to be burned. I'll not have it left to defy us when we return."

Outside, as they went to wake their sergeants, Christopher asked Karl why he wasn't happier. "We're leaving, so there won't be a fight, right?"

"Withdrawals are always fraught with danger," Karl said. "The enemy may harass us as we march. Men will die, and for nothing."

Still, Christopher was glad that this foray would return without having fought. Every day without battle was a day to be celebrated, the veterans kept saying. But the morning light crept over the mountains and changed everything it touched.

<hr />

The Duke's face was black in the pale dawn, full of fury and disgust.

"So many," the Lady said, at his side, her voice small and wounded.

"Two full tribes, at least, My Lord," D'Arcy said, shaken. And then he swore, pointing. "Wolf cavalry, my lord!"

The tiny figures streamed out from the goblin fort. They kept coming and coming.

"Saddle the horses." Nordland's voice was ironed into perfect flatness.

"And trolls!" D'Arcy shouted. "How can they have trolls?"

Even Christopher could see the figures in chains. He hadn't paid them much attention because they weren't any larger than the figures holding the chains. But then he saw that the slaves and slavers were both twice the height of the armored goblins.

The unreality of these strange creatures did nothing to diminish their fearful aspect. The eight-legged pig had been so strange as to be unsettling; these creatures, with their purposeful marching and glinting array of weaponry, were simply terrifying.

"Four bands of wolf riders, two tribes of goblins, and two battalions of ogres. With trolls." D'Arcy was in awe. "Where did it all come from?"

"Is that a lot?" Christopher asked. He estimated there were about a thousand figures down there. That was four- or five-to-one to his two hundred or so. Not impossible odds.

"Are you mad?" Nordland said. D'Arcy was too stunned to speak.

"We can take them." Christopher was in a fort, with cannons and grenades. It wouldn't be pretty, but they could do it. "Unless they have magic. Do they have a lot of magic?"

"Take them?" Nordland exploded. "You can't even take the trolls. They'll swarm over your walls and eat your men like berries on the vine."

"What's so bad about a troll? I realize they're big and ugly, but is that it?"

"They cannot be killed," the Lady said, when none of the men could recover enough to speak. "Save by magic or fire, and we have little of either."

That sounded bad. But not hopeless. "I have plenty of fire."

"You're going to knock them down and then have your boys hold a torch on them?" Nordland asked, incredulous. He turned to Karl. "Your Pater is insane."

"Yes, we know," Karl said, "but he has a way of surprising you. I humbly suggest you hear him out."

"Insubordination," the Duke snarled. "I would have your head for that, but for pity."

D'Arcy's face was grave. "The trolls are not the problem. The wolves are. Lord, they run like fire in the woods. On open plains they cannot catch our horses, but in the woods they will run us to the earth."

"I know," the Duke said, his voice flat again. "We ride within the minute. We must be away before they reach the foot of the mountain. This is retreat. We flee for our very lives."

"We were betrayed," the Lady hissed. "We thought to set a trap, but the trap was set for us. That fort is bait, and our foes knew of our coming. Our allies are delayed, destroyed or diverted, and we are fed to the mill like wheat. This could only have been arranged from inside the Kingdom. One of the Dark has betrayed us to the Wild." She gripped her spear with white knuckles.

An ugly thought crept up on Christopher "Wait a minute. My men cannot ride. We don't have that many horses."

D'Arcy winced and went to share the Duke's orders with his troop. Nordland turned to Christopher and in a hard, dull voice, explained the facts.

"Your men are destroyed. They must flee, each to his own. It is possible the wolves will miss some of them, if they concentrate on us. Possible, but not likely. I am sorry, but your men are already dead. Now get to your horses. Mount all you can, but only one to a horse. I suggest drawing lots if you cannot choose."

"No," Christopher said, stunned. "We will not run. We can win this, if we stay and fight."

"Do not argue!" Nordland ordered, his patience fraying. "I do not like it any more than you do, but we have no choice. We must retreat and save what we can for the next battle."

"We have a choice. We can fight."

There was a ringing in his ears, and his face burned. The Duke had slapped him.

"Come to your senses, fool," Nordland demanded, flat and ugly. "We cannot fight. If we had all our allies here, we could not win. We were betrayed. I have spent ten years building my troop. I will not waste it, and my own life, in a futile gesture. To flee is hard, but to defy reason is to feed the enemy. We will come back for vengeance, but first we must survive."

"I have spent only a year building my troop, but I will not throw it away. I will not flee while my men cannot. I will stay and fight." When Nordland reflexively raised his hand again, Christopher stopped him with a glare. "You have ignored me since the moment you met me. But I tell you, we can win this fight. If you keep the magic off of us, my men can take ten times that number. We have rifles and artillery!" His voice was rising, despite his best efforts. "We are in a fort! They are savages, armed with swords and bows. We can win this!"

"One more word of insubordination," Nordland said, "and I will take your head." He stormed off, ignoring Christopher.

"All who can ride, get to your horses," Nordland shouted at the army. "Bring us your pay-chest, quartermaster," he told young Charles, "and your magic items. We will see that they are returned to your Church. For the rest of you, I say this. Go back down the mountain, head due south. If you can reach my lands, you will be safe. Do not go together, but one by one. Most of you will die, but some may slip through. We will angle southwest and try to draw them with us. You must do as best you can. Take food and water, and make no fires. Leave your weapons: they will aid you not. Your only hope lies now in stealth.

"Do not stand there!" he bellowed, angered beyond control over his own helplessness. "Run!"

But the boys looked beyond him, not to Christopher but to Karl. Nordland turned to see what they were looking at. Even Christopher looked to Karl. The camp paused, all eyes on the young soldier.

"The Pater says we can win," Karl said. "I believe him." There was no way of telling what the suicidally brave young man really believed, but it was unmistakable what he was going to do. He was going to stand and fight.

"Then you will die," Nordland said. "A foolish waste of the Kingdom's resources."

The boys quivered, ripped between fear and loyalty. They wanted to bolt. The approaching horde screamed at them to flee, and even their commander ordered them to cast off their arms and run.

"I'll save what I can. You six, get on your horses. Your tael belongs to the King." Nordland pointed at the mercenaries, the ones with Apprentice ranks. Slowly they walked toward their horses, looking at the ground. "And you too, Pater, your tael belongs to your Saint." Stephram, white-faced and dizzy, moved to obey. "You, boy, fetch me that water bottle. It belongs to your Church."

Charles jerked like an unwilling puppet. The boys could not bring themselves to disobey a direct order. Their rifles began to slip from their hands, and they cast furtive glances to the north, where the mountain pass beckoned.

And then Nordland went too far.

"And your sword, Goodman. If you choose to throw your life away and feed your tael to the enemy, I cannot stop you. But I will not allow a weapon of rank to fall into their hands."

Karl, who had so freely and frequently given away so many swords, reacted with immediate and easy hostility.

"You can have my sword," he said, "when you pry it from my cold, dead fingers."

Duke Nordland snapped, his patience exhausted, his soul shredded at playing executioner to all these young men. He drew and advanced on Karl, fire in his eyes and death in his hands.

What is the sound of one hundred rifles cocking?

The Lady whimpered, and the Duke stopped. He looked around at the weapons aimed at him, the terrified but angry faces behind them. He understood that he would serve very well as a scapegoat for their imminent disaster.

"You are all mad," he said, despair overwhelming his anger.

"We are all dead men," Karl said. "What does madness matter to us?"

"We can win this," Christopher shouted. "Listen to me! I didn't cross the galaxy to die on the end of a pointed stick."

"You cannot win," the Lady said. "We cannot win. Our troop will sink like a stone in that ocean of evil. Will you not give your men leave to go and let those with horses be saved? Will you not send your magic back for others to use, instead of giving it to the Dark?"

Charles stood paralyzed by indecision, clutching the valuable bottle.

"We'll need that water," Karl said, "to walk home with."

Christopher, steeled by Karl's steadfast example, turned to the Curate. "Lady," he begged, "protect us from their magic. We can do the rest."

"You'll not kill my wife with pity," Nordland said. "And you'll find no pity from me. You have become insolent and delusional in the face of death. I am disgusted.

"We ride!" he commanded, and strode toward his horse.

Christopher watched him walking away and was consumed with a disgust of his own.

"If you leave now," he called out to Nordland, who spun and glared at him, prepared to cut him down for any hint of a charge of cowardice, for any challenge to his honor, however slight. The entire camp hung on the next words, paused in mid-step, watching the drama play to its climax. In this moment Christopher's army, his reputation, and possibly his life, would be made or broken.

"If you leave now," Christopher said, "you're not getting any of the tael."

29.

THE PRICE OF VICTORY

D'Arcy rattled in a staccato monotone, delivering information about the habits and abilities of their enemy while the Duke's troop thundered out of the gate and up the hill. Karl absorbed the lecture like a sponge, until an invisible string snapped and the green knight leaped to his horse and galloped after his lord, in mid-sentence.

Stephram, head hung low, rode out with the Duke. So did Christopher's mercenary sergeants, stony-faced and avoiding eye contact. His scouts might have gone too, but one glance from Karl and they froze. Better to die a horrible death than be thought a coward by Karl Treyeingson.

"What the Dark are you standing around for?" Karl growled. "Get to work."

In a frenzy the boys threw themselves back into the task of fortification.

A few minutes later, the guards opened the wooden gate again. Back into the fort rode the six mercenary sergeants. They dismounted, tied their horses to posts.

"Not a word, Karl," Bondi said. "Not a Dark damned word, or I'll cut your tongue out and shove it up your arse."

Karl did not speak, but something in that wintry face might have suggested a smile.

But Stephram did not come back. Christopher was left alone, the only source of magic or healing in the camp. The responsibility was crushing. He stood on the wall, watching the monstrous horde cross the plain and funnel up the mountain pass.

Christopher had two hundred and twenty-three men, counting his officers, scouts, and artillery crews. Karl had seen to the disposition of their forces, and Christopher could not fault his deployment.

The young man had been working with crossbows long enough to understand how to use rifles. A hundred on the south wall, facing the enemy's advance. Three cannon stood on towers along the wall, their steel arrow-shields deployed. Another fifty men manned the west wall, where the gate was. The remaining two cannon faced the gate, a backup for if—or more likely when—it was breached. A handful of boys kept watch over the north, and two lonely lads stared out over the east cliff. The last two platoons, their youngest and greenest boys, waited in the center of the fort as reserves.

Every man had a rifle, except for Christopher. He always figured he would be too busy healing to shoot, but now he felt naked without a gun. He stood with Charles and Kennet, overseeing the supplies laid out for the coming battle. They dug holes in the earth and filled them with the explosive stores. If one accidentally went off, it wouldn't destroy the rest of their ammunition or kill everyone in the camp. He had taken Gregor's lecture on magic to heart and brought a lot of stores. As a first-rank priest, his magic wouldn't last more than three minutes, but if the enemy tried to run him out of fireballs, they would be in for a nasty surprise.

When there was no more point to fortifying, when the eve of battle was imminent, Karl stood on a wall and addressed the camp.

"Boys," he told them, his voice richer and more vibrant than Christopher had ever heard it, "all your life you've feared the Dark." They listened to him, nervous, eager, sad, or angry, each to his own disposition. "The monsters prey on us, like wolves on mice, and we hide in our hovels and pray. All your life you've been dismissed by high ranks, by lords and wizards, by the creatures of the Dark, by the ones that matter. Today," he shouted, "that changes.

"Pater has given you strength, in arms of steel and fire. Pater has given you wisdom, in training and craft. All that is left to need is heart, which you must give yourself. Too long have we cowered from the Dark. Too long have we feared them. Today, we will teach *them* to fear." The men roared. "Today, we will teach them that *we* matter." They roared, louder.

"Stick to your training. Hold your position. Do not fail the Pater, and he will not fail you." Karl let that sink in, and then finished, his face flushed with more emotion than it had shown since Christopher had known him.

"Today," he shouted, "we will teach them *a little respect.*"

And then the time for preparing was over, and all they could do was wait.

⌘

"The wolves seek to bypass," shouted a sergeant. "Do we let them?"

The wolves and their small green riders streamed ahead of the advancing army, coming up the slope and making a not particularly wide berth around the fort.

Christopher didn't care about covering Nordland's retreat, but he did care about his own. "We don't want dogs nipping at our heels on the way home," he shouted back. "Kill as many as you can."

Like popcorn, a scattered few at first, then a rapidly increasing crescendo, the rifles began to fire. In the heat of the moment, the smoke and fear, the flashes and bangs, Christopher felt a tinge of exhilaration. Now was action.

He carefully worked his way to the west wall, peeked out through a firing port. The ground was littered with bleeding wolves, massive animals three feet high at the shoulder. The grotesque creatures riding them were hobgoblins, green and nasty, firing back with short bows. The rifles were barely adequate for the wolves, taking two or three bullets to drop them, but they were overkill on the diminutive hobgoblins, ripping them to shreds in a single hit and scattering ugly green body parts like confetti across the field. Still, the little horrors fought bravely, hiding behind their fallen mounts and popping up to fire arrows.

Some of Christopher's men were screaming now. The battle looked almost equal until someone threw a grenade, and then it was over, the hobgoblins and wolves racing back down the hill like water.

"By all that is Unholy," the sergeant said, looking over the carnage outside the wall, "the crazy priest might be right." The man sounded shocked, as if the possibility of not dying horribly in the next hour was too incredible to grasp.

Karl sent a party with rifles and axes out to harvest the fallen, while Christopher saw to his wounded.

"I'm saving the magic for the dying," he told them, and patched the cuts and arrow holes as best as he could with bandages. He had plenty of bandages. Svengusta had insisted that he would run out of magic at some point and want them. He said a silent prayer of thanks to the old man.

The damage wasn't too bad. Ignoring the risk of infection, there were only two serious cases. Two boys had taken arrows to the face. One was dead. The other shrieked in wrenching agony when they pulled the arrow out of his eye, but he calmed down after it was bandaged.

"If you can take the pain, soldier, then you'll make it," Christopher told him. "And you'll be in a very special club. Both Karl and I have lost an eye, at one time or another."

"I can still fight, Pater," the wounded boy said. "Don't take my rifle away."

"I wouldn't dream of it."

The goblins were angry. You could see it in the way they marched up the slope, like ants boiling out to defend the nest. Two hundred yards short of the fort they stopped to arrange themselves for battle.

The north wall guards cried out, and Christopher looked up in the sky where they were pointing. Black winged shapes were battling what might have been an owl. The bird killed at least one of the foul creatures, but then fell into the forest as black shapes circled down around it.

"They'll come back," Christopher said. "Once they realize the wolves aren't after them, Nordland and his lot will come back to see how we're doing. If they're nice, we might even let them in."

The boys, flush with their first victory, whooped it up.

"Pater," Bondi said, "come look at this." Karl joined him at the south wall, and they gazed out at the horde. The monsters were arraying themselves for a frontal assault.

"They're in a hurry," Karl said, "and we are in their way."

"Excellent," Christopher said. "It couldn't be better. Hold your fire. Let them get into killing range."

The boys started getting nervous, watching the monstrous host fall out into skirmish formation and begin advancing up the hill, but Christopher was merely annoyed they weren't bunching up in nice easy-to-hit lines.

"Why are they all spread out like that?" he asked Karl.

"Have you not given them reason to fear magic?"

Gregor had talked about fireballs. Artillery was not unknown in this world, just uncommon. Still, Christopher couldn't get too worried. The sun was shining, the field of fire was clean, and the enemy was advancing uphill and on foot.

The human-sized green creatures had large wooden shields held in front of them, obviously considering them adequate protection against arrows. Christopher had trained his men to simply aim right through shields. The only thing that would stop his bullets was a quarter-inch of iron, and anything that could carry that much weight they'd just have to shoot with a cannon.

The yellow and brown ogres eschewed shields, favoring large

clubs and two-handed axes. They looked impressive in some kind of thick hide armor, but Christopher was more concerned about the horribly deformed green and gray monsters that wore nothing but chains. They strained at their bonds, eager to rush forward and attack, like slavering dogs.

"A pile of ugly, that is," Bondi said.

The trolls were nine or ten feet tall. Christopher's wall was eight feet.

Christopher looked for something positive to say. "They don't have any bows."

The only bowmen the enemy army seemed to have were the little hobgoblins, and they were hiding at the rear.

"No, Pater, but they can throw a mean javelin. And there's more out there than you can shake a stick at."

"Ha, watch me." He called to his artillery men. "Focus on the big ones. Riflemen, concentrate on the little ones or anything that gets closer than a dozen paces."

"Get off the wall, Christopher," Karl ordered, and he had to go. He couldn't afford to be exposed to their return fire.

When the first cannon went off, it was a shock. A two-inch gun wasn't something you ever got used to. Then the other guns on the wall opened up, and all the rifles began to fire.

"Take your time and aim," Karl bawled over the noise.

The gun crews loaded efficiently, too jarred by the concussion of their guns to do anything but operate by habit. Watching from a firing port, Christopher could see the enemy advancing at a slow jog, holding their sparse formation. For some reason he thought of the Alamo. But that wasn't the image he really wanted at the moment.

The rifle fire settled down from a single thunder into a steady tattoo, men loading and firing at different rates. The goblins began to notice that their shields were worthless as they fell like Christmas lights, blinking out one by one. A troll-handler had been torn in half by grapeshot, and his charge came bounding and leaping toward the fort, dragging its chains and keening in a most disturbing way.

At ten yards the rifles finally turned on it, and it went down in a hail of bullets. The men barely had time to reload before it got up again, and this time they brought it down only a few feet from the wall. Kennet leaped up to the railing and hurled a sputtering stick of dynamite at the prone body.

"Fire in the hole!" he yelled, and the boys ducked their heads behind the protection of the wall.

The dynamite went off, the troll remained still, and the rifles resumed firing. The hobgoblins had made some progress in the lull, but now they were closer and the boys weren't missing many. The creatures fell like grass before the wind.

They could not comprehend. In the way of this world, they pitted their strength against strength. They set their tael against the enemy's, to see who would fail first. But they did not understand Christopher's technological cornucopia of destruction, and so they threw themselves into the fire, trying to quench it with blood, while Christopher fed it with gasoline.

At fifty yards the mass of troops broke into a charge, shrieking in hatred. They drew swords and javelins, not stopping to aim but throwing on the run. Their rush was terrifying, and if it hadn't been for the presence of the wall, Christopher might have fled in a panic. As it was, he flinched, and so did not see them hit the wall, but felt it, as the entire fort shook under their weight.

Others quailed behind the wall, but Karl was already screaming for the grenades. Every fourth boy in the army had been made a grenadier and carried three of them as part of his kit.

The goblins did not even blink at the first fireball. They did not flinch at the second. They did not quail at the third. But when the twenty-fifth grenade went off outside the walls, shaking the air with its concussion, hurtling lead shot in every direction, they had had enough.

"Hold fire," Karl yelled as the creatures fled. "Hold the grenades, you idiots, keep shooting!" he bawled when men looked at him in confusion. But they couldn't see anything to shoot at, because acrid white smoke hung over the wall like a blanket.

By the time it cleared, the enemy army had withdrawn two hundred yards down the slope.

"Give them something to think about," Christopher told a cannon crew, and they sent an exploding round into the midst of the creatures. Limbs and parts flew into the air, and the boys cheered madly. The enemy fell back to three hundred yards.

Karl sent a team out front to harvest these heads, Charles and Kennet with them in case any of the trolls were faking it. They had got only two of the foul creatures and a handful of ogres because the goblins had broken discipline at the last and charged ahead.

There were goblin parts everywhere. The boys found it gross and amusing, as boys will. Karl merely complained that he couldn't get an accurate count because of the disorder.

"Another problem with your magic," Bondi said, "is that sometimes it blows the brains to smithereens. We can't be sweeping the battlefield with a mop to get your tael, Pater."

They plunked the bags of heads down by the boiling iron kettles. Christopher was sickened by the smell, but it had to be done.

"We did little damage to the giants," Karl said, "but we've slain perhaps a third of their foot and a quarter of their cavalry."

Karl was flushed with excitement. Their own losses had been light, relatively speaking. The last assault had resulted in seven men struck by javelins. Christopher patched up the least with cloth and the worst with magic. Even this trivial effort left him depleted, with only a single spell left. He bit his lip to stop himself from cursing Stephram's cowardice.

The enemy army withdrew to the bottom of the slope.

"Damn," Christopher said. "Now they've gotten smart."

⌒∞⌒

The day passed slowly. The officers tried to get the boys to sleep in shifts, but without much success. Between excitement, fear, and cold, sleep didn't come easy.

The monsters were obviously waiting for nightfall. Under the cover of darkness, they could approach the fort much more closely before the rifles could find them. Christopher wished he'd invented parachute flares.

"This one will be bad," Karl told him. "The giants will reach the wall and sweep it clean. Our only hope is that the men underneath will bring them down."

"Well," Christopher said, "I can think of one surprise we can give them."

"Do it." Karl went to check on something else.

Christopher went out to survey the south wall and saw a squad picking over the dead.

"What are you doing?" he asked.

"Prospecting for gold," their sergeant said, cutting off a ringed finger and tossing it into a sack.

"Forget that." Christopher looked around at all the javelins. "Bring in as many of those as you can. And any spears or swords you find."

There was a time they would have asked him why, but now they just did it, trusting he had some good reason.

"It's not much," he said, after he demonstrated their use. He'd lashed a javelin to the top of the wall, pointing outward. "But it might slow them coming over the top."

It wouldn't hinder a man climbing up, since he could go between the bars, but Christopher was thinking of all those giants just hopping over. Once he got a few crews going, cutting strips from the thick leather armor of the goblins and lashing up their impromptu spikes, he went back to his first plan, finding six young men and arming them with hooded lanterns.

Twilight was brief in the mountains, a moment of fading light and then sudden darkness. The sun crept to the horizon, prepared for its final dash from the sky, and Christopher was as sorry to see it go as he had ever been.

"Remember," Karl told the army, "if you see a troll moving, throw a grenade at it. If you don't have a grenade, shoot it, and shout for Kennet."

They nailed half the light-stones to the outside of the wall so the light projected outward without blinding the men on the inside, but the dim illumination reached only twenty or thirty feet. At least they did not have to hope for a full moon, merely for brilliant starlit clear skies.

"Marcius smiles on us," Karl said in the pale dark.

Visibility was still low compared to daylight, but they could pick out human-sized figures at fifty yards easily enough. This was proved by the crack of a rifle.

"They've sent out their spies," a sergeant yelled, reloading.

Christopher stood next to Royal, stroking the horse's nose. Of all the horses, he was the only one untied. The stallion could smell the coming battle and insisted on being free to fight.

Another rifle cracked.

Christopher thought about telling them to conserve ammunition, but there wasn't any point. If it turned into a siege, they would run out of food before they ran out of bullets.

From the south came the sound of drums, dolorous echoes of doom. In the starlight he glimpsed flittering shapes, the shrikes flying high above their camp.

"This is going to go on for a while," Christopher guessed. "Those of you not on watch, try to rest as much as you can."

He went to lie down in his tent, but Karl stopped him.

"You'll need a guard," the veteran said. "We can't let you out of our sight. Assassins."

So Christopher pulled his cot out into the camp, a few yards away from the south wall.

"Shut the hell up," he told the boys, and lay down under the stars and the watchful eyes of his soldiers to take a nap.

Royal stood over him, napping as well. Somehow they slept through occasional gunshots and drums and a little construction work, waking only when Bondi shook Christopher gently by the shoulder.

"They come, Pater," the sergeant said, and Christopher stood.

He stretched, checked his sword, cleared his mind, and petted his horse. Then he was ready.

"Magic, Karl," Christopher said to the young veteran. "Where is their magic?"

"They usually don't have much. Goblins rely on cleverness, not magery. Besides, they have trolls. What's that, if not magic? Still, Christopher, you are right. We must expect some kind of arcane assault tonight."

"Like what?" Christopher hoped D'Arcy had given Karl some warning.

"Sleep spells, at the least. Perhaps invisibility or fireballs. We should have built the walls with partitions, so that one blast could not kill many, but we did not have time."

"What other tricks do they have?"

Karl shrugged helplessly. "I am hoping their spells were depleted healing their wounded. They should wait until they can renew, or for cloudy weather, but they are still in a hurry." A pity; Christopher would have had a chance to renew his spells as well.

"Steady," called a wall sergeant. "Hold, boys, hold." Then, belying his own command, he aimed and shot into the darkness.

The darkness worked against the enemy in a curious way. The only figures the boys could see at long range were the big ones, the ogres and trolls. The trolls swatted at the bullets, annoyed but not terribly bothered by a few stray shots. The ogres, however, were made of ordinary flesh and bone. Nine feet and six hundred pounds of it, but still mundane creatures. After two or three bullets, they fell down and stopped moving.

And of course, what the riflemen could see, the cannons could too. The boys were mostly using grapeshot, but every so often they would aim at a troll and use an explosive round. In the flare of the shells Christopher could see the unreal advance, the terror of unleashed violence redoubled by figures of nightmare.

They moved quickly, dispensing with shields or protection, counting on speed. They had learned from the first battle. The hundred riflemen on the south wall loaded and fired steadily, but they didn't get off more than a few shots before the enemy was at the wall.

"They flank," screamed the west wall sergeant, and the boys on that side began to fire too. They had no cannons up, and only fifty rifles, but it was just the dogs again, trying to get past the fort.

A dozen boys slumped at the wall, unmoving. Christopher gasped in horror, grabbed a stick and ran over to them, walloping around like mad, waking them up with his blows.

"Now!" he screamed, "now now now!"

His lantern crew began to respond as the wall groaned under the weight of the trolls and ogres pushing at it, pulling at it, snapping javelins off like toothpicks and clearing wide swaths of the wall with each swipe of their clubs. The ogres, that is. The trolls grabbed men and pulled them over the top, biting necks in half, tearing off limbs, cackling gleefully. The ogres you could at least duck, but the trolls were fearless, exposing themselves to rifle fire without concern.

Then the boys put flame to powder, and the shaped charges Christopher had hung on the wall, their bowls filled with rocks and pebbles, went off. The wall shook with every blast, but the buttresses held, and many of the ugly heads leering over the wall abruptly disappeared.

Now grenades began to go over the top. An ogre batted one back like a badminton serve, and men scattered, some falling under the blast. But reserves rushed forward, took their place. The ogres were suffering terribly as the men on the ground shot at them whenever they stuck their heads above the wall.

Then green humanoids began to appear on top of the wall and got shot at, too. And of course the grenades never stopped.

A troll pulled down a cannon, squealing and spitting, and the exposed gun crew fell back. Kennet appeared, pushed the box of cardboard-encased cannon rounds over the wall, held a stick of dynamite behind his back, and threw it over as soon as Charles had it lit.

Christopher didn't think that was a very good idea, but the wall held under the massive blast. In the lull the gun crew rushed back to the wall and started firing their rifles.

Screams from everywhere: the chaos was unbearable. Only by sheer chance was Christopher looking to the north, at the very spot where a troll appeared from literally nowhere. One minute there was nothing, and then there was a troll, snatching up a man and biting at his spine, tearing him in half, his guts spilling out like jelly from a doughnut. The horses squealed in terror, Royal stomping in front of his herd, defending it, but the troll was not that stupid. He ignored the animals and loped for the south wall and the exposed backs of the men, all but ignoring the scattered rifle fire from the few guards on the north.

Not good, Christopher thought, *not good at all*.

He tried to get the boys to turn around and face the danger, but they had their hands full already and could not hear him over the constant explosions. It was only one troll, but it could do terrible damage. It could clear a section of wall, and then more would come over that. Christopher sprinted for the cannons facing the gate, shouting for their crews to attend him.

As he struggled with a gun, turning it around alone, wondering where its crew was, he saw an unlikely figure running to intercept the troll. Rifle in hand, little Charles advanced to the side of the troll like he was going to poke it with his bayonet. Christopher raged silently at the foolishness of boys and the stubborn cannon that fought him, but his words were impotent. The troll saw Charles, stopped and reached for him with gibbering madness, and the boy stuck out his rife and fired at point-blank range.

Not into the troll, but into the ground. Into the ammunition store the troll happened to be standing over. The blast blinded Christopher for a brief instant, but his sight came back in time to see the troll's head still going up, fifty feet high, and then blood and parts rained down on the camp like a spring shower. He could not see Charles anymore, but in the fading sparks of paper and powder he saw a ter-rifying man-shaped figure hovering in the smoke over the south wall.

It was huge, twelve feet tall, but it was invisible. Christopher only saw it because of the absence of smoke, an empty shape cut out of the solid air, floating twenty feet above the ground and inside the wall. Horrified, he yelled and yelled, but Karl could not hear him, so far away, manning a cannon that had lost its loader. Christopher pounded on the barrel of his own cannon as its crew finally arrived, helping him wheel it around to face the new threat.

There was a laugh, an evil and dark chuckle, that somehow could be heard under all the noise. The creature became visible at the same instant something awful and awe-inspiring happened. A miniature blizzard formed in a conic section stretching out from the monster, tiny ice particles falling from the suddenly frozen air. Even so far away, Christopher could feel the wash of cold.

Karl and all the men around him, up and down the wall for thirty feet, turned white and stopped moving. A thin layer of frost covered the area, comically peaceful and clean in the midst of the bloody, fiery carnage.

The monster laughed, his fat belly shaking and spittle dripping from twisted yellow fangs, but not for long. Bullets flew at him, gouts of blood spouting when they struck. He promptly disappeared again.

But the bullets kept coming, and little splashes of blood plopped out of the empty air carved out of the wall of smoke. The monster flickered, wavering between visibility and invisibility, and then stopped at the halfway point, transparent. Now the bullets winged through him without effect, and he laughed some more. Rendered insubstantial, he could no longer do damage, but he called encouragement to his soldiers, ordering them to the attack in a brutal, grunting language.

Behind Christopher came shrieks as the wolves simply leaped the walls in a single bound, their maneuver to bypass the fort exposed as a feint. Some got stuck on the impromptu spikes, but others slipped through, falling amongst the men with vicious savagery. The west end of the main wall was still and quiet, covered in ice, and figures began to crawl over it unopposed. The gate behind him shook under the weight of wolves and hobgoblins, from both sides. And Karl was dead, an ice sculpture, a piece of frozen meat.

The possibility that this might be the end began to wander around the empty places in Christopher's mind, small and distant, a well-behaved child humming to itself patiently.

The cannon was finally ready, the gunner aiming at the hovering apparition, acting from training and not rational thought. As the gunner reached for the chain that would release the hammer and fire the cannon futilely into the insubstantial horror, Christopher leaned down and kissed the barrel of the gun.

Instinctively, without thinking, he whispered in Celestial, "If this be your blade, Marcius, then bless it."

The cannon fired, the recoil tapping Christopher in the mouth and bringing the taste of blood. Rays of light streaked out from the cannon, tracing the path of the grapeshot. Where they intersected the ghostly figure, ghostly blood sprayed out, turning into solid liquid in the air and falling in a bright-red shower.

The creature wavered between illusion and reality, and then, of flesh and blood once again, fell heavily onto the ground like a sack of potatoes gone bad.

Beside him the other cannon fired, shredding wolves and hobgoblins and men against the wall. Royal reared and squealed, beset by wolves, battling to save his herd, and men rushed to his aid. The wolves were losing, too many of them trapped by the wall spikes. The assault on the south wall seemed stalled, somehow, though the frozen part of the wall was still unmanned.

And then the giant creature twitched, an absurd horror film, the villain simply unkillable. The cannon was not even done reloading, yet the monster sat up, bellowing in uncontrollable rage. With one hand it grabbed a man and crushed his skull like an egg, blood and gray matter spurting out either end of its huge fist, gushing between its grotesque fingers.

From the wall Kennet came running, his arms open, his satchel slung forgotten at his chest. Moved by incomprehensible insanity, by mindless bravery, he leaped onto the monster, a child tackling a football linesman. The monster laughed in appreciation of the absurdity, opened his arms to accept this farcical challenge, and the two grappled, hugged for a brief instant before the monster crushed Kennet's body like a rag doll.

And then the satchel went off.

Even from halfway across the camp the blast knocked Christopher off his feet. He found himself wrestling with a white-eyed hobgoblin that stabbed blindly at him with a dagger. Grabbing it by the throat, Christopher banged its head against the carriage tongue of the cannon until the creature stopped moving. He climbed to his feet amid snarling dogs and shouting men, a forest of gunfire around him. The men had fallen off the wall from the blast, and for some reason they were not getting back on it. He screamed at them, his voice lost in the noise, or maybe he was still deaf from a dozen sticks of dynamite exploding all at once. They ignored him, abandoning the wall to its own fate, shooting and stabbing at the howling wolves.

A hobgoblin leaped onto his back, grabbed at his throat, waving a short sword clumsily around in the tight quarters of the grapple. Before Christopher could react, it shrieked, and something dragged it off his back. He turned to see Royal drop the creature to the ground and stomp on it like a rat. Christopher drew his sword, pointed to the wall, and forced more sound through his raw and burning throat.

But the wall remained empty and still. The sudden quiet was deafening, the occasional rifle shot almost comforting.

"They flee," said a sergeant, his face bloody, his helmet and an ear missing. "Their master is slain, and they flee."

"Command the defense," Christopher told the man. He turned to the wounded and was lost in bandaging until the sun crept back over the horizon, its wan light small comfort in the cold.

***

He ran out of bandages.

They had lost eighty-four men. Charles he found, cold and dead, his entire arm gone to join his missing fingers. Bondi lay amongst the corpses, his throat torn out. And Karl, whose body had not thawed in the night, still stood frozen in place, his face unmoving for the last time.

"It's not much, Pater," a boy said, with tears in his eyes. "But it is all we could find."

The boy handed him a bag with a broken pumpkin in it. Christopher was confused by the surrealism until he realized it was Kennet's head.

"I need orders, Pater," said the older of his two remaining sergeants, almost apologetically.

The kettles were boiling again.

"We'll need that," the other sergeant said gently, hesitantly. He meant Kennet's head.

"No," Christopher said.

"We cannot leave them for the Dark to harvest," the sergeant argued, but not forcefully.

Christopher was suddenly alarmed, but the pile of heads next to the kettles contained no humans. They would not start without his permission.

"Let me think." He sat down on his little cot, which was, oddly enough, somehow still intact. He held the sack in his lap and thought furiously, forcing his mind to crank through logic. Royal stood over him again, stoically ignoring the pain of his torn flesh, the wounds not serious but ugly.

The men waited, resting. They interrupted him only once to tell him the enemy had retreated to their own fort.

He stood, went to the kettles.

"How much do we have?"

The sergeant looked at him, eyes shining. Furtively he handed Christopher a purple nugget the size of a cherry.

"There is more to come, Pater, and also our own men."

"We'll not harvest our men here. How long will it take you to finish this lot?"

"An hour, Pater, no more."

"Then we leave within the hour," Christopher said, and repeated it so everyone could hear. "We march within the hour. Listen up, and let me tell you what I know.

"Cardinal Faren can revive a man eight days dead. The Vicars can hold a man so that the door does not shut on him, if they get him before those eight days. There are four Vicars within a day's ride of Kingsrock, and also the Cardinal and the Saint. It will take us a day to get from Tyring to Kingsrock, a day to summon the Vicars, and three days to preserve all the dead.

"That means we have three days to get from here to the border of the Kingdom."

He let that sink in.

"That means we leave everything. The wagons, the cannons, the ammunition. Everything. We put the dead on horses and we walk. We walk thirty miles a day. Take your rifle and five rounds of ammunition. Fill your packs with grain for the horses. Take only a single loaf of bread for yourselves. You will not starve in three days, but the horses carry our brothers, and if they fail, then we will lose them forever."

They stared at him in silence, faces shredded between disbelief and hope.

"You will bring back everyone," the sergeant said, "even the unranked, the common, the worthless? You will spend tael like water for men of no account?"

"Worthless? Who here is not worthy? What is a little tael, a little money, to the account of so many brave and true men? Tael I can replace, money I can summon from thin air, but *men* are a treasure beyond price."

Never again could he call them boys.

They prevailed upon him to take the gold and silver, also, two large sacks of rings, pendants, and amulets.

"It's as good as tael, Pater, if not so light."

They took the water bottle, of course, and the light-stones, both necessary to the march. But the fortune in equipment and supplies that Christopher had dragged out here at such effort and expense they piled in a mound and burned.

Wagons, tents, tools, paper, clothes, blankets, all up in flames. Their sole moment of levity was when his silly cot went into the fire. The cannons they packed with dynamite, dangled over the cliff, and shattered the barrels. The excess ammunition they burned in great sparkling gouts, tossing it into the fire, which consumed everything utterly.

"What the hell is that?" Christopher asked as one of the sergeants clanked by him, carrying a bundle of swords.

"Begging your pardon, Pater, but we cannot leave these behind." They were the masterwork blades and Karl's magic sword. "The men will be wanting them back."

The swords would be harder to replace than rifles, so there was no point in leaving them. But that reminded him of something, and he took off his chain-mail shirt. He tossed it onto the fire, where the heat would fuse the links into a useless mass of metal.

And then they walked out of the camp, a long line of grim men, their faces gray, their bodies brown and flecked with white and red bandages.

"Shall we burn the fort, Pater?" the sergeant asked.

That's what Nordland had wanted. In a moment of spite, Christopher answered, "No. We might want to use it again, and if the enemy occupies it, we can take it back easily enough."

What he wouldn't give to fight a simple siege, where his cannons would make everything easy. Well, once he had cannons again, that is.

<hr />

Christopher made a silent promise, to all the gods of every world, that he would never again considering hiking "fun." He stripped off his boots, massaged his swollen and aching feet. He was dizzy with hunger, exhaustion, and pain.

And this was the first day.

"We must be off again," the sergeant said.

Christopher stifled his immediate impulse to shoot the man and put his boots back on.

He had wanted to be heroic and carry the swords, but he wasn't up to it. A year of training had not erased a lifetime of easy living, nor had it made him young again. He struggled with his own sword and a backpack full of grain for Royal.

Royal carried the swords, and three corpses as well, but that wasn't as hard as it sounded, since one of them was the sack that held all that was left of Kennet. The other bodies they distributed amongst the draft and cavalry horses. Only the dead rode in this cavalcade.

They walked. And walked. And walked. Without the wagons, already knowing the way, they made good time, but the specter of death haunted their footsteps. The frozen men were tied in the saddles like the horsemen of the apocalypse, and Karl's face was a black beacon of doom. If a man paused or faltered, it took one look to make him walk again, sometimes crying from pain or loss, sometimes swearing in anger. But they walked.

After nightfall the scouts called a halt at one of their old camping places. There was still firewood stacked up—a lifesaver, since no one thought to keep even a single ax. Huddled around the small fires, they slept in exhaustion. There were so many wounded, the unhurt felt shamed.

In the morning, two men did not wake. Christopher shrugged.

"Royal can bear more," he said.

The middle of the second day, they had to shoot one of the wounded horses. Some men redistributed its load while others butchered the horse and cooked it over a fire. At least half the men had possessed enough sense to keep their bayonets, despite Christopher's extreme orders.

"Pater," a scout said, "should we not go due south?"

"Do you know the way?" Christopher asked. "Will we find camps and firewood? Will we come out in the Duke's land, to face his charges of mutiny?" The last argument seemed to be the most compelling.

"I'm sorry, soldier, I shouldn't have snapped at you." He didn't want them to stop making suggestions. But the man didn't take offense, merely nodded acceptance of his authority.

The meat was good, but then they had to walk some more. Christopher got off a second set of healing magic, but it didn't go far.

They walked from sunup to sundown again, finding relief only in the fact that their packs got lighter as the horses ate.

Infection was starting to be a problem, and several men now needed help to keep moving. The cold was harsh, and the injured men should have been resting, not walking. Crawling over the gorges and ravines was painful and slow, and it chafed Christopher's patience.

At night they walked by the light of the magic stones, pushing on until the scouts said they had made their distance. The wounded fell in ragged heaps while the others built fires and unloaded horses before collapsing beside them. Royal laid down, his burden temporarily set aside, and Christopher leaned against him, wrapping his coat as tight as he could. He had just closed his eyes, and a young man was waking him again. It was still dark.

"Time to go, Pater."

They'd lost three more in the night.

"I'm old," Christopher said. He stood up, bones creaking, then sat down again and cleared his mind, seeking meditation. It cost him an hour every morning, but he could still walk faster than the wounded, and every man he touched was a man who would not die that day.

The main army went on ahead. Christopher and his small escort caught up with them before noon.

A young man was lying in the snow. Two others stood above him, exhausted, the cold stealing their breath in white clouds.

"Get up, soldier," Christopher said. "We're almost home."

"I can't, Pater, I'm sorry," the young man whispered. His ankle was swollen and ugly, the flesh red and inflamed. Christopher was only a Pater. He could not heal infection.

"Everybody's feet hurt," Christopher said. "Get up and walk."

The man did not respond but labored to breathe, his eyes closed.

Christopher was too tired to think rationally, but he knew something had to be done. He took the rifle from the soldier standing next to him, leveled it at the prone man's chest, and pulled the trigger.

"Put him on a horse," he said.

In the echo of the blast, the men looked at him, shocked and stunned. But nobody else stopped walking.

Later, they had to shoot another horse. Now all of the horses were doubled up with the dead.

Walking south seemed easier, somehow. Their packs were empty and their goal was close.

"Just keep walking," the sergeant said, ranging up and down the line. "Keep walking." The fingers on his left hand were black.

The sun went down, and again the weather turned to their advantage. Heavy clouds hung low in the sky, and the cold abated to merely freezing instead of bitter. They stumbled by the light of their dozen torches, a parade of zombies.

Walking into the hamlet of Tyring was like walking into Heaven. Once again Christopher fell on the icy steps of a chapel, seeking refuge.

30.

DEATH BY POLITICS

The soldiers robbed the peasantry of their wagons and horses, banging on hovels, demanding blankets and food. Out of sheer pity the villagers opened their homes and their barns, bringing out cold beer and hot soup.

Christopher shivered in front of the chapel fireplace. "We'll pay for it all."

"You must rest," the town priest said, a middle-aged woman with children of various ages running around her.

"We cannot rest, my lady," the sergeant said. "Give me a fast horse that I might reach Kingsrock by morning."

"You will not make it alive in your condition," she said. "Here, Pater, write a letter, and I will send my own rider to the Cathedral." But he could not operate something as complex as pen and ink right now, so he had to dictate it to her.

"Our dead cannot rest, either," the sergeant said. "Those wagons must roll through the night."

"You are in no shape to drive," a peasant said. "We will take your corpses to Kingsrock, though we do not know the reason for your rush. The dead do not hurry."

"We will send our own with you, for they know the reason."

The sergeant bundled four of their most able men into blankets, gave them wineskins of beer and hot soup, and sat them on the wagon benches next to the drivers.

"I charge you with this task," the sergeant said. "Do not fail us now."

The guards did not respond with words. They gripped their rifles instead.

Then the wagons rolled out of town, into the dark, and the men left behind fell, one by one, into merciful sleep, some in barns, some in houses, many sprawled on the wooden floor of the chapel, its fire blazing cheerfully.

"I will pay," Christopher said, and then he fell asleep too.

He awoke with a start. His body was bruised and aching, but it was not cold. There was food, hot food. There were fresh bandages and priests. There was a Curate.

"This is more than I can handle," the Curate said. "I have saved your worst, but others will die if they are not seen soon. I have sent for wagons from the town, for oddly this village does not have any."

But Faren's carriage beat the other wagons, rolling into town before noon.

"I can't have you in this shape," the Cardinal said, and he healed Christopher on the spot, the pain and fatigue melting away like water down a drain. "Now pray, while I see to your men."

The Cardinal had a staggering amount of healing power at his command. Within the hour the army was still wounded, but not seriously. No one else would die. Christopher had renewed his spells, and he added them to the pot, but they were a sparkle next to Faren's glory.

"Recover here for three more days, then return to your camp at Kingsrock," Faren told the men. "The local priests can finish your healing. I hope you are proud of your scars, because you will bear them for the rest of your lives. This is the price of not being healed while the wound is fresh.

"You, however, are coming with me," he told Christopher.

"My men need to be resupplied," Christopher objected. "I must send a letter to Burseberry."

"You can do that from the Cathedral. On the way there, you can tell me what the Dark happened."

They got to Kingsrock well after nightfall. Christopher did not get to see much of the city from the carriage window, and then they were in a grand stable, Captain Steuben waiting for them.

"Your madness precedes you," he told Christopher. "Our Cathedral is stacked with corpses, and priests pray night and day."

"They are not going to stay corpses," Christopher said.

Steuben shook his head. "You cannot ask this of the Saint. There are too many."

"I can pay," Christopher said, but Faren cut him off.

"Hush, both of you. This is not the place."

They gave Christopher a nice room, but it still reminded him of his original cell back in Knockford.

"I'm under house arrest again, aren't I?" It wasn't really a question.

"For your own protection," Faren said. "You have no idea what trouble you've caused. Now rest. There will be time enough in the morning."

In the morning he prayed again, selecting spells for the coming days. He thought carefully about what he might need. Then he took a bath, ate breakfast, and dressed in clothes that had been cleaned during the night.

The Saint received him in a room so holy it made his beard twitch. Faren was there, and Steuben.

"Tell us your story," the Saint said. "Faren has already told us, but it is a good story, and I would like to hear it from you."

So he told them, as concisely as he could. But this time he included how Karl had died.

"I can understand reviving the Goodman," Steuben said. "But how can you hope to revive them all? What a wealth of tael that would be."

"Indeed," the Saint said, "it would be a tremendous expense. Much more than you spent raising your army in the first place. How can you afford this? I know you said you defeated many enemies, and I know in this place you cannot lie, but all the same I find myself doubtful. Forgive an old man for his weakness of faith."

Christopher didn't blame him. After all, the last time they'd met, Christopher had been begging for money. He took the purple rock, as big as a walnut, out of his pocket and set it on the table.

Faren's and Krellyan's eyes narrowed slightly, and Steuben blinked.

"Our difficulties are not over," Faren said softly. "That does not belong to Pater Christopher but to the commander of his regiment."

"Who deserted me in the field," Christopher said. "If he wants it, let him come and take it from the men who earned it."

"He describes it otherwise," Faren said, in lawyer mode. "He suggests that you committed mutiny, disobeyed a direct order, and put magic and tael at the risk of falling into the hands of the enemy."

"And if I did? How does that entitle him to this? Should he profit from my alleged crimes?"

"Your mind is sharp as ever," Faren said approvingly. "We might legally save your tael. But how shall we save your head?"

"Duke Nordland is Bright," Krellyan said. "Surely he will not demand this."

"Duke Nordland is shamed by commoners and priests," Steuben said. "And denied a huge prize. I am not so certain what he will do."

Faren looked pained. Christopher was reminded of that moment after his first duel, when the Cardinal had looked into the future and thought to see terrible things. "The Kingdom is in turmoil. Nordland has almost started one war. When he found his erstwhile allies marching home instead of marching to the battlefield, he accused them of treachery. One was Dark, so the charge was not wholly out of the question. Now the King's Peace is in danger as Bright blames Dark, and Dark blames everyone. I fear when he hears what you plan to do with his tael, he might start another war."

"And who could fault him?" Steuben asked. "What a staggering waste of tael. Consider, next year we will have two hundred more boys, but we will not have such a rock as this."

"My men will be revived first," Christopher said. "That part is not negotiable. Then my army must be resupplied. After that, I don't care if you rob me."

"You are like some kind of seed that grows disruption wherever it goes, while never taking root itself," Steuben said.

"Catalyst," Christopher said, supplying the right word, but Steuben shook his head sadly.

"To spend this tael reviving commoners will inflame passions on every side of the balance. Do not ask me why, for I do not know. I just know it will."

"Look at me not caring," Christopher said. "I can pay," he told Krellyan. "This is more than enough for your standard rate, several times over. Will you deny me this?"

"If you gave the tael to Nordland, then perhaps we could appease him." Faren explained the options. "If you claim it, as I think legally you can, then he might claim your head, as I think legally he can."

"I understood that the first time. It changes nothing."

"There will still be much left over for Nordland," Krellyan said. "Even after the King takes his tax." The King got a quarter of the tael taken out of the Wild. That was what made him King.

"Perhaps not," Christopher said. "Many of my men need regeneration. They are missing too many parts to fight. And some of my men need more than just revival. I brought one home in a sack. A small sack. If it is possible to revive him, I will, even if it costs every grain of tael in my possession.

"Is it possible?" he asked Krellyan point-blank, knowing the man could not dissemble here, not even a little.

"It is possible," Krellyan said, "but only for me. None else can do this."

"Well, then," Christopher said. "After you get done charging me for that unique service, and all of the preservation spells, and resupplying my army, Nordland can have whatever crumbs of profit are left. I'll not make a fuss."

Faren grinned, in spite of everything. "We might make a priest of you yet."

"I will revive your men," Krellyan said. "But you must understand, not all of them will return. We do not compel them, only invite them back. There are always a few that harbored secret shame or despair, and they do not return."

"They will come back," Steuben said. "For a commander like the Pater, they will return. They did not desert him in the field, they will not desert him now."

Christopher thought of his act in extremis, the young man he had shot. He could only hope for the best.

"Again you expose yourself to the world, to save those we would have abandoned," Krellyan said. "But what if we need you? Can you risk yourself so freely now?"

"You don't need me," Christopher said sadly. "Jhom can make the guns. Fae can make the powder. And Karl can lead the army."

"You underestimate yourself," Faren said. "Stop it. It's stupid and weak."

"For now, you may rest here in the Cathedral," Krellyan said. "But when the King calls you to account for your actions, as surely he will, you will go naked before him. We will save your men, but you must save yourself."

"I do not hold a grudge against Nordland," Christopher said, and surprisingly, it was true. "I will make whatever peace he allows. I just want my men back."

"This time you will kneel before rank?" Faren asked, his eyes crinkling.

"Yes," Christopher said. "I will positively grovel. I've learned my lesson."

⌘

They gave him three days before a small troop of armed men appeared at the Cathedral, bearing a warrant. It wasn't for his arrest, but only for questioning. There might be hope.

He bathed again and had his beard trimmed. He had no armor or fancy clothes, but his uniform was fresh and neat, mended by magic in the Cathedral. He would have worn it regardless of what else he owned, anyway. And of course he wore his sword, awkwardly brushing it out of the way as he climbed into the carriage.

It wasn't a very nice carriage, which was not reassuring. Still, he was a first rank, so he didn't deserve much. He still had hope, even when he entered through a side gate, for all the dark corridors and iron doors he passed, even down into the stone bowels of the great fortress of Kingsrock. He had hope right up until the black waves of the sleep spell laid him out on the floor.

When he awoke, naked and bound, gagged and blinded by tough leather, his hands confined in iron gloves, he discovered that hope had departed sometime in the night.

After an interminable period, hands lifted and carried him roughly. The echoes of their footsteps told him when they entered a larger chamber and tossed him onto a hard surface. His nose, enhanced by the deprivation of his other senses, detected foul and rank odors, the stench of blood on metal, and worse.

"Do you know why you are here?" a voice said, unpleasant and oily. "No, it is not on account of that witless coward Nordland. He hates you, yes, but in a completely ineffective and futile way. No, you are here for something far more serious.

"You have been accused of consorting with the enemy. Your fanciful tale fools only credulous priests who believe in miracles. But the men who must actually run the Kingdom are not so easily deceived. We loyal servants of the King protect his interests, even when he is not aware of the danger.

"No first rank could have come home from such overwhelming odds. No commoners could have defeated such foes. There is only one explanation. You made a deal with the enemy. They let you go to work some further wickedness."

Christopher struggled to speak but could not make any comprehensible sound through the gag. Then he realized he did not have to. They could almost certainly read his mind.

"You are clever, Pater. We can indeed. And you cannot lie to us. You will tell us everything. We are skilled at ferreting out secrets."

I am innocent, he pounded out with his brain. *You already know that, you can see that. You can see how we won. Demand demonstrations, interrogate other men.*

His thoughts were interrupted by blinding fire. They had struck him with something, perhaps a whip. Before he could frame a new thought, they struck him again and again.

"We are not interested in your innocence," the voice said, in a lull in the violence. "We want your secrets. We know you have them. You must tell us."

The pain worked against them, though. It made it easy for him to focus on something else. But that was a bad thought, because now they beat him with sticks.

In a very short amount of time they exhausted his tael, and his body felt the pain without any filter. He screamed now. He begged and pleaded with garbled ravings, demanding justice, reason, sense. But no voice answered him, and his incoherent howls merely bounced off the stony chamber before creeping into the void.

Stop it, he cried out in his mind. *I will tell you everything. How to make guns. How to make gunpowder.* Part of his mind recoiled at this surrender. He could not give in to these brutes. They were in the wrong, and sooner or later the Saint would rescue him.

"You shouldn't have thought that," the voice said, and to prove their absolute power, to demonstrate that they did not care what happened after, they drove nails through the blindfold and into his eyes.

"You see," the voice said, "or you would if you didn't have nails in your eyes, we know you have a secret. The fact that you won't tell us your secret means it is traitorous. So once you do tell us, and you will tell us, this I can assure you, then we will execute you for treason, and traitors are not revived. The only door out of here leads to a grave. We will make you crawl to that door, but we will not let you pass through it until you give us your secret."

If one does not care what one breaks permanently, and one is not worried about the victim dying, one can easily inflict an astonishing amount of pain. They did not bother with refinements like drilling teeth or bamboo shoots under the fingernails but simply smashed his legs with hammers, cracking ankles, shins, knees, and thighs as they worked up his body. Then they healed him before he bled to death, and did it again.

There was no respite while they asked questions. They never asked questions. Instead, they waited for his mind to reveal itself. But when he began to disassociate, and visions of home and family beckoned him into the deep recesses of his mind, where nothing but memory could reach him, they dismissed it as incoherent delusion. So they healed him again, brought him back to the present, and started over.

Finally they dumped him in his cell, raw and broken and bleeding. He would never walk again. His legs were fused from random healings into odd and useless shapes. His eyes itched horribly, the itch worse than the dull and pounding pain, but he was bound into immobility and could not scratch. Every time his eyelids tried to blink the nails twinged his nerves and made him scream. And the pain made his eyelids twitch.

He lay in the dark and tried to die.

Later, though time had hardly any meaning anymore, someone came into the room with him. His gag was removed.

"Stop," he sobbed, though they had not done anything yet. "I'll tell you anything."

"No, I want to tell you a secret, Pater," said a different voice, a female voice. "I don't care if you talk. I just want you to scream."

His mouth was forced open, some metal device holding it wide. With a pair of pliers she reached in and crushed one of his teeth.

"Don't drown," she said, as he shrieked and wretched on blood and shattered bone. "Not yet. I've paid too high a price for this.

"You do know who I am, yes?", Her banter was cruel mockery in the dull echoes of his tiny cell. He tried to guess what she wanted to hear. The truth no longer mattered to him, only the avoidance of pain.

"No, this is important," she said. "You have to know who I am. We have much history together, you and I. You cut me first, you know." She drew something sharp across his stomach, blood welling in its wake. "I came to relieve you of a sword you were not fit to wield. I came so many times, and each time, I offered you your life.

"I gulled the boy and cut his throat, then waited while my men went into your chapel. If you had fought less, they would have taken the blade, your Saint would have revived you, and neither of us would be here now. But you killed my men and made me flee in shame.

"I met you on the road and repaid you in kind, shooting your man. Had you given me the blade, your Saint would have revived him, and neither of us would be here now.

"I sent a sweet young woman to test her skill against you. Had you followed her to her shack and drunk her drugged wine, she would have taken the sword and spared you. True, I would have killed you anyway, out of revenge, but again, your Saint would have revived you. And we would not be here now.

"I raised an army, and allied with a lord, an act detestable to me, but you would not cooperate. True enough, *he* would not have let you live again, but by then my goodwill was exhausted.

"I scoured the land for every enemy you had made and brought all of them together to your chapel in the dead of night and opened your door to them. Against even this you prevailed. And I began to wonder.

"Bart feared you, not as a foe but as a rival. The pacifist Saint welcomed you and your sword like a brother. When Black and White both took you to their bosom, how was I not to wonder? There are Powers who live in the Deep Dark and disturb even the gods' dreams. And sometimes they walk among us as men.

"So I put my suspicion to the test. Do you know how easy it was to get your allies to turn back, to fail to meet your rendezvous? A bit of paper, a blob of wax, and around they went.

"And yet you lived. Then I understood you were more than you seemed. I spoke of my fears, and my proofs, in places where I knew those who even I fear would hear. And they, proving wise, put you to the question.

"And now here you are, caught out at last, the trap sprung by my hand. Their tests have proven your body human, which means you were only ever a mere instrument, not a Power in your own right. But that will not spare you. The Powers of Darkness do not succor failure, and the King's torturers do not succor. But even this is not enough to condemn you utterly. That, you did on your own.

"Poor thing, you don't even know how. Because it will pain you, I will tell you. Because I hate you, I will tell you only the truth.

"Your King is wroth. You took out two hundred cattle, and instead of bringing home tael, you *spent* it. What kind of harvest is that? For yes, it was the harvest, though you mooing cows comprehend it not.

"Do you see the arrangement, clever priest? The monsters give us tael. But where do they get it from? Why, from us. The nobles feed our young men into the sausage grinder and reap the bounty. The monsters' nobles, for I assume they have them too—nowhere on this wretched plane can one escape nobles and their filthy habits—the monsters' nobles do the same. They feed each other the harvest."

Her words stabbed like spears, piercing with truth.

"So no one will save you now. Your ultimate crime was surviving. Your crime was exposing the system for what it is, for making clear the unspoken but obvious, for bringing the unconscious pact with darkness into the light of day. No noble can afford to let you live, and your pathetic Church depends on the charity of the nobles."

Steuben's words came back to haunt him, the hidden balance the captain had feared disturbing now exposed.

"You will die here, in this dungeon, after long pain, and your body will turn to ash and be forgotten. But I will remember that I once bit the hand of a Power, for no better reason than I could." In laughing triumph she brought a hammer down on his groin, smashing flesh into jelly. His screams were no longer vocal.

"You ask for healing? I have none, which is a shame. I can torture you but once. Yet perhaps the guard will not tire of the disgusting pleasures I allow him. Then I will return again tomorrow, after the inquisitors have done for the day and left you broken but not dying."

"I," he mumbled around the steel gag, "can heal." He still had spells in his head, for what good they did him. Bound, he could not use them. They were not healing spells, but he could always substitute a healing if he wanted to.

"Of course," she said, "you are a priest. I will let you heal yourself, because both you and I know I will only break you again." He felt a bond loosen, and his left hand was freed. The steel in his mouth went away.

One chance to act, instead of being acted on.

He put his hand to his chest, not to the fire in his groin or the spikes in his eyes, but to his own heart, and spoke the ugly word in Celestial, harsh and clanging.

Black energy flowed from his hand, the stench of rotting meat filling the air, although in this place it was merely the smell of home. Pain again, as the organs in his chest ruptured, but the knowledge that it was the last pain he would ever feel robbed it of its power. When his mind could no longer contain words, all that was left was a face, framed in red hair, fading into darkness.

31.

REVIVAL

He lay in the impossibly white room, perfectly still. Everything was white. The walls, the floor, the ceiling, the bedsheets, the chair. Only the man standing in the doorway was not perfectly, incandescently white. But his robes were.

"It is time to go," Krellyan said, his voice urgent.

Christopher did not feel urgent. He was comfortable, or rather, he wasn't uncomfortable. More precisely, he didn't feel anything at all. He thought about that for an indeterminate amount of time.

"Is my wife here?" he asked finally.

"No," Krellyan admitted, "but the only chance you will ever see her again lies through this door."

"Okay."

Christopher got up and walked through the doorway.

32.

RETURN

He lay in the warm brown room, the wooden panels glowing with polish, light-stones flickering from the walls. A man stood beside him in white robes.

"Welcome back," Krellyan said, his voice gentle.

Christopher did not speak, his body empty and drained. Fury burned in him, but the flames were distant and cast no warmth yet.

"Do not be quick to anger," Krellyan said. "The King has been generous. His inquisitors could find no crime to charge you with. Thus your death was wrongful, and so he has released you from taxes. This alone will pay for your revival, your lost rank, and your regeneration. Your legs will be healed, your body made whole, your rank restored. The King will admit to no wrong, but he has been generous."

Christopher turned his face to the wall. Krellyan went on, with the faintest hint of desperation.

"Do not be foolish. Your enemies are legion, but you have many advantages. Unknown allies aid us; your body was left on our doorstep, when clearly our enemies meant it to burn. Nordland abides by your bargain and makes no claim. You still have at hand enough tael to gain fifth rank, with the prestige and powers it brings. You have tael and gold beyond that, to make you wealthy even by your standards. You have an army behind you, men loyal unto death and beyond. All but two have come back, an astonishing percentage under the best of times. Do not be foolish."

Christopher closed his eyes.

"What would you have of me?" Krellyan's voice choked with regret, shame, impotent anger.

Into the empty space between them, Christopher whispered, "The system is corrupt."

The men waited in silence for a while.

"Yes," Krellyan agreed, soft and sad. "The system is corrupt."

Christopher opened his eyes and stared out across the room, into the future.

"I think I know what I am supposed to do now."

ACKNOWLEDGMENTS

T his story took three months to write and ten years to tell. Special thanks to my nephews, David, Alex, Dylan, and honorary nephew, Fletcher, for their unflagging enthusiasm; to Josh, for making me rewrite the beginning; to Kristin, for making me rewrite the beginning again; to Julia, for making me look smarter than I am; to Lou, for believing in the book; and always, to Sara, for believing in me.

ABOUT THE AUTHOR

M. C. Planck is the author of *The Kassa Gambit*. After a nearly-transient childhood, he hitch-hiked across the country and ran out of money in Arizona. So he stayed there for thirty years, raising dogs, getting a degree in philosophy, and founding a scientific instrument company. Having read virtually everything by the old masters of SF&F, he decided he was ready to write. A decade later, with a little help from the Critters online critique group, he was actually ready. He was relieved to find that writing novels is easier than writing software, as a single punctuation error won't cause your audience to explode and die. When he ran out of dogs, he moved to Australia to raise his daughter with kangaroos. Visit his website at www.mcplanck.com.

Author photo by Dennis Creasy